PRAISE FOR K. I. S

THE ASSAYS OF ATA

"A gripping, well-paced first installment with a resourceful female lead." — *Kirkus Reviews (starred review)*

"*The Assays of Ata* is a thrilling exploration of identity and duty against impending doom. K. I. S. skillfully crafts a narrative that interlaces personal stakes with larger geopolitical tensions, offering a multifaceted tale that resonates well beyond its fantasy elements. The rich characterization and quick pacing provide a captivating read." — *The Book Commentary* (★★★★★)

"The pacing and suspenseful plot twists keep readers engaged, while the exploration of loyalty, love, and survival brings a much-needed emotional depth to the epic fantasy landscape. Overall, I would not hesitate to recommend *The Assays of Ata* for your next fantasy read." — *Readers' Favorite Review* (★★★★★)

"A striking introduction to a new fantasy series, this first book of *The Chronicles of Áitarbith* is an impressively elaborate and carefully crafted work of epic fantasy, with a troubled but magnetic lead character at the center." — *Self-Publishing Review* (★★★★½)

"Deftly balancing intrigue, action, and emotional heft, *THE ASSAYS OF ATA* by K.I.S. is an engrossing epic brimming with magic, machinations, and mayhem." — *IndieReader Review (★★★★.4)*

"If you like high fantasy books with headstrong heroes, political machinations, bloody battles and fantasy creatures, this book is definitely for you." — *Reedsy Discovery (★★★★)*

"As a first installment of a series, *The Assays of Ata* hits every mark for a standout start to a chronicle. Some of your favorite tropes are utilized, like rivaling kingdoms, star-crossed lovers, and an archaic prophecy. Rather than feel platitudinous though, this novel up-cycles them in a complex, engaging way... Fantasy readers in awe of great worldbuilding and immersive prose will be glad to join Ata on this adventure and whatever comes next." — *Independent Book Review*

"As the first book in the trilogy, *The Assays of Ata* attends to setting a worthy stage of political and personal interests which leads readers to appreciate Ata's delicate positions and strong intentions... All these facets make *The Assays of Ata* a top recommendation for libraries seeking series titles that move beyond kingdom-building into the milieu of women seeking to change and control their lives and influence the options of others around them." — *Diane Donovan's Bookshelf on Midwest Book Review*

THE ASSAYS OF ATA

THE CHRONICLES OF ÁITARBITH

K. I. S.

ISBN: 978-0-7961-7360-7

Cover design by Lizbe Coetzee

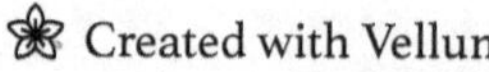 Created with Vellum

For my sisters, who wouldn't stop nagging for the next episode.

N
W
E
S
Cinnae
Harborgen
Carp
Smelir
Hurgot,
Barin River
Karppen
Smul River
Panop
Plezai Valley
Enddaien
Á
Krendai River
Pandi
Nebton
Rendian
Vrai
Debrion

Veron
Cetis
Ikondon River
ra Mountains
iterbith
Ra'aen
Isles of Eile
Scale:
0   100   200   300   400

THE ASSAYS OF ATA

CONTENTS

1

—————

A TEMPESTUOUS INTRODUCTION

I'M NOBODY! WHO ARE YOU?

ARE YOU NOBODY TOO?

EMILY DICKINSON

The fire in the oven jumped and danced wildly in tandem with the howling winds outside, the head cook swearing and sweating as he tried to save the baking delicacies from the consequences of the gales—whether by being burnt or sprinkled with ash swirling around within the massive hearth.

One would think the kitchens ideally warm and cosy, the only such place in a glass-encased palace currently being battered and bombarded by the elements—but this was sadly not the case. It was true none of the unseasonably cold breezes could rake their frozen claws past the heavy, scarred door, but the sweltering space still fell prey to wafts of sooty ash and debris barrelling down the chimney.

Ata gagged at the overwhelming smell of charred fat but had the good sense to do so behind her hand as she pretended to adjust her headdress. If the head cook caught sight of her actions, the implied disgust would be akin to sacrilege and his reaction would be uncomfortable to bear. It wouldn't be anything serious, but discomfort came in many forms for a lowly servant—think 'lavatory-related' and you'd be getting warm...

She *had* to remember: she was an obedient, hard-working servant girl. A *good* girl, who recited her prayers and catechisms according to the beads hanging from her waistband and the tomes of the Holy Sacrament of the Benevolent Order of the Gods. *At least for now*. Ata privately suppressed a smirk, maintaining her earnest, rather vacant facial expression whilst everyone scurried around in a frenzy. She continued to assiduously chop away at the parsnips, as it behoved a lowly kitchen grunt.

The persona she had assumed was that of Anita: eager to please, somewhat stupid, and easily managed. She tried to maintain a light touch with her character; it was so easy to overplay the wide-eyed ingénue or the half-witted country bumpkin and lay it on too thickly. She prided herself on her final incarnation—pretty, but vacant; eye-catching, but forgettable. In short: the perfect person to snoop under the auspices of fetching, carrying, and cleaning, whilst also being able to wheedle titbits of information from young and old with mild, if somewhat inept, flirtation. A wolf in petticoats, the perfect spy.

"You! Parsnip girl. Come here and take these capons up to the service area!" the head cook's crazed glare fell on her as he motioned imperiously. She scurried forward—slightly awkwardly but plenty enthusiastically—this was her greatest wish and pleasure: to serve the Glorious House of Hårbørgen. If she truly *believed* it, then others would too.

He muttered to himself about incompetent lackeys, disdainfully gesturing to the little browned birds artfully displayed on a shining silver plate. "Don't you dare drop them. And don't enter the dining area—be sure to hand it over to a senior server," he threatened as she haphazardly lifted the massive platter to her shoulder; only years of physical training and exertion rendered her arms and shoulders capable of taking the strain.

She didn't know how a nobody serf from the provinces, as many of the other kitchen and serving maids were, would manage the sheer weight of the plate. That said, there was sturdy stock from the countryside, so perhaps her assessment was overly pessimistic.

She heaved her load up the steep stone stairs, her momentum rushing her through the narrow servants' passages until she hurtled into the one exactly parallel with the formal dining room. The bustling back and forth of servers made the space congested, but her over-large burden ensured that she barrelled onward and everyone dodged from her path. The wood panelling and carpeted floors muffled their passing, mitigating the cold seeping in from the outdoors along with the body heat generated by the throng of servants in constant motion. Hushed murmurs and quiet footfalls seemed to be at odds with the frantic busyness abounding in the limited space of the narrow corridor.

Ata looked amongst the throng of servers for the rangy frame of her superior—the senior server whose group she had been assigned to here for the past two weeks at Hårbørgen Palace. She had been ordered to stick to her superior's side at all times till instructed otherwise, thereby being able to witness the day-to-day workings as well as receive constant instruction on pleasing the powers that be.

Famenke had gimlet eyes that missed nothing and a perpetually sour face that matched her disposition in every way. Ata liked her immensely, if for no other reason than she was abominably rude and shockingly blunt—ideal at alienating all those around her through the sheer awfulness of her personality, thereby offsetting 'Anita's' somewhat dubiously mediocre charms, rendering her significantly more likable and attractive to the others. All of this, with little to no effort expended by Ata.

However, very inconveniently at that moment, Ata could not detect the curly golden-red wisps escaping a sombre-grey head scarf (although, Hanson, the gardener's helper called it "carrot frizz") that denoted 'Mistress' Famenke's managerial presence, even with said girl's towering height. Another appreciable feature of her current mentor in the art of service was the fact that she was almost a head taller than Ata, who, due to her own notable height (at least in Cinnae) worried about standing out, but could now "hide in plain sight", avoiding notice in her overseer's shadow—even literally. Famenke had been a boon to her mission, really, if completely unwittingly.

Ata frantically looked around for any server to take her burden and enter the exclusive sanctum known as the formal dining hall, where a nobody like herself would never so much as set foot without extensive training as a server. Not that she'd actually be in service here that long, but that was beside the point.

The damned birds on her platter were cooling fast and she couldn't face the inevitable haranguing she would receive as vacantly sweet Anita should she return to the kitchens to have them reheated (or—heaven forfend—a ducal complaint be received). But none of the currently bustling servers could or would set aside their tasks and deliver the grilled geldings to the royal table and she had no time to wait for another.

Thus, without thinking too much on the possible consequences the lack of protocol of her entrance would elicit, Ata glided through the servers' door into the dining area with a straight back, sure hands, and eyes lowered deferentially.

At the massively ornate dining table, set with a forest of crystal glasses, silver candlesticks, and bouquets of multi-hued blooms, sat the Cinnaen royal family—the self-styled 'Glorious House of Hårbørgen'—and a few important officials. All were stereotypically fair, ranging from bright golds to palest whites, lacklustre straw pates to tow heads.

Even though she kept her eyes downcast, Ata knew to the smallest detail who all attended the dinner. She had, naturally, been briefed on and studied every person of significance, whether peripheral or central, to said dynastic monarchy. She therefore deduced enough about this handful of figures to identify them from a glance alone based on their appearances, mannerisms, seats at the table, or any combination of these elements.

She breathed evenly, shored up her defences, strengthening her facade of a bumbling servant girl out of her depth but trying her darnedest to pass muster. She just needed to carry the gods-heavy platter around the table while the footman (who had appeared magically at her side gripping a pair of shining silver tongs in his white-gloved fingers) deposited the birds to each individual's plate. Simple.

They approached the table together; she took her lead from the footman on whom to approach and pause next to first—a rotund, middle-aged man with a thinning hairline. *Hjarl Janssen—chief adviser to Queen Nelni.* He was holding forth on some policy or other to the table at large, not even aware of the capon deposited neatly in his plate. They moved one seat on.

Lord Svensso, general of Cinnae's eastern armies, illegitimate son of the late King Olefso, elder half-brother to the crown prince. She rolled her eyes inwardly—one would think she'd feel an affinity for one of her kind, but she didn't. Honestly, there were too many of them to feel any kind of situational kinship... His head was bent askance as he appeared to listen respectfully to Hjarl Janssen's soliloquy. He was tall, as even hunched he dwarfed his two neighbours and made the outlandishly ornate chair he sat in seem proportionate. He gave a faint nod of his head in thanks when he was served.

Their next diner was a petite female. *Princess Lenna, only daughter of King Olefso and Queen Nelni, twin sister to the crown prince.* She was only sixteen, Ata knew, and based on her posture, supremely disinterested in the entire dinner and accompanying conversation. Surprisingly, she turned her head and gave a swift smile of thanks to both her servers, although her eye contact was fleeting.

Next were two minor officials whose names Ata knew, as well as the fact that one had a serious gambling problem and the other a fondness for hunting, doting on his hounds and his horses in equal measure. Neither acknowledged their servers.

Strangely enough, it hadn't been Ata's entry into the serving class that made her take note of the lack of basic courtesy shown to the lower echelons; her childhood as a half-caste bastard had seen to that. The fact that she was of royal heritage only meant she was able to experience the full range of discrimination first hand, as well as through a lifetime of observation of "the greats" and their "lessers". Thus, it had become the standard measure by which she judged all men and women; a watershed tally. It had not steered her wrong thus far.

The next seat, immediately to the left of the head of the table, was occupied by a tall man with a sense of calm and control, his eyes constantly gauging those around him but never appearing to do so. *Lord Haaviso, Duke of Delftnör, first cousin of and chief adviser to the crown prince. Co-regent.*

His stiff gesture with long fingers indicated he declined this particular dish, so they passed him by and moved on to the head of the table, occupied by a beautiful but sullen boy of sixteen. *Prince Tensso, eldest son of King Olefso and Queen Nelni, crown prince of Cinnae and heir to the throne.* He accepted the bird onto his plate, at which he was staring moodily apparently unaware of the servers' presence, never mind acknowledging them.

To his right sat a woman whose golden loveliness did not accurately represent her age nor her character —*Queen Nelni, mother of Prince Tensso, Princess Lenna, Prince Jansso, and Prince Elsso, co-regent of Cinnae.* She was supremely unaware and uncaring of the servers as they filled her plate.

Two more lords and a lady followed, none of them of particular interest to Ata (she had their vices memorized and catalogued already); she was unsurprised when none of them expressed thanks for their dinner service. Last to be served was an interesting figure whom Ata realized with a start she had misjudged earlier. She had thought him another lord, but he was not known to her —a disconcerting experience, and one she tried to mask her face from revealing while taking in as much evidence as she could about him to dissect later.

He was a slight man with a head of silver hair styled in an elegant bowl-cut (if such a thing existed). She surmised he was not naturally of small stature but had probably been robust in his earlier life and then withered due to old age—attested to by his soft, wrinkled skin and slight jowl. His eyes, however, were a bright, jewel-blue with a crystal-like quality. And they were peering back at her with as much earnest interest as she was hiding on her part. Highly disconcerting to be viewed so minutely at close range, so she fought to maintain her slightly ditzy but well-meaning facade, half-smiling at him vacantly as he thanked her in a bygone accent with a high inflection mid-phrase and a low-toned ending. A genuine surprise, his obvious wit and intelligence brimming over in this minuscule interaction with an invisible servant.

Ata dipped a slight curtsey in response, desperately averting her eyes when they alighted upon the diner exactly opposite them... General Svensso was looking straight at her, having observed her and the old man's passing interaction with undue interest. Worse—his sharply perceptive look seemed to cleave through all her layers of subterfuge, and she sensed he could truly *see* her, for recognition appeared to flair in his gaze. She panicked, snapped her eyes downward, pretending obeisance, then beating a hasty retreat from the table of power, her covert mission potentially compromised.

Once on the other side of the wood-lined wall, she sagged against its sturdy support and breathed deeply. Even in her semi-hysterical abstraction, she considered her cover and how it would appear perfectly right for the little provincial nobody, Anita, to be completely overwhelmed emotionally and physically by the daunting act of serving Cinnaen royals. Thus, her pathetic, panting interlude against the wall would make perfect sense to the other servers in the vicinity. The entire service had lasted all of 10 minutes, if that, but Ata had lived a dozen lives in that short time.

Hopefully, she hadn't compromised her character and by extension her mission with this little fiasco. Her mind skipped back to the dining hall. The policy that had been assiduously discussed throughout their serving turn was about a new taxation law—Ata snorted silently at the stupidity. These people dined in style, in a blizzard-encased glass palace that could not truly withstand the cold nor gales, debating arcane laws related to an insignificant tax portion while the continent was quietly being overrun by armies of dark creatures... A house of cards about to crash down, the inhabitants blithely and wilfully ignorant of the imminent collapse.

"What. Did. You. *Do*?" a nasally voice whisper-hissed next to Ata, so she immediately shelved her inner turmoil to deal with its manifestation in the shape of a gangly, glaring gorgon. It seemed she had found Famenke—or more accurately, Famenke had found her. Now she was in for a monumental scolding, so she affixed a wide-eyed look of vacant consternation on her face and proceeded to breathlessly (and witlessly) defend her breach of decorum.

The footman who had wielded the tongs came in at one point, passed them, winking flirtatiously at her behind Famenke's back. She widened her eyes slightly in mock plea and he laughed soundlessly at her predicament before hurrying off. His name was Henkel, if she remembered correctly; she would keep his taunting overture in mind for future use.

Thus far, she had only half-befriended the scrawny Hanson who minded the kitchen gardens as well as cementing a love-hate relationship with Famenke (the "love" was all on her side, but she was in no doubt of the loathing with which the other woman regarded her very existence). More servant allies—or pawns—would be welcome here; ideal sources of gossip and conduits of rumour.

Everything she had gathered thus far as well as engineered had been through sheer luck and by playing the hapless, pretty thing who didn't guard her words amongst strangers. It was getting tiring not being able to launch focused assaults with direct and anticipatable paths of influence; randomly casting lures and heckles into the ether and hoping they'd eventually have the desired effect had never been Ata's way. She had always been direct and unconstrained in her actions and thoughts, knocking down childhood bullies without preamble, speaking unvarnished (and usually unpalatable) truths in public, generally making herself the clear target of courtiers at her uncle's court throughout her youth. Until Lord Danai had taken her "under his wing" as he put it, but more accurately had honed her bluntness into a sharp tool—a talon he could wield in court intrigues.

"You are too direct, Lady Atiyah," he had lectured, "It

is in nature's subtleties that life can be found. And death. A well-placed needle can wreak as much damage on a body as a hammer—with the added benefit of allowing the possibility of subterfuge by the killer, and escape. Use your skills as a needle and do not be a dull object easily wielded by others."

This said after she had beaten up three stable boys in a rage, having been manipulated by one of the older stable hands through innuendo and mockery. It had cost her weeks of banishment from her uncle's presence; a lonely existence without weekly visits with her uncle and cousin. It was during that time the king's retired adviser had come to her and offered to tutor her. Although he had always been a shadowy presence at court since she could remember, he was never at the forefront nor had her uncle, King Addai, ever shown him any particular favour in public. But there he had been, offering an opportunity to a ten-year-old royal bastard.

She had accepted with reservations she kept to herself and was initially very wary of him and his motives. She soon came to the realisation that his wiles and intrigues were his gifts, but that he was not an evil or even a bad man. He always thanked the help, she noted, and had shown kindness to the lesser citizens of the keep in a variety of small ways. And so, she had eventually learned to trust and rely on this energetic old man, his bushy iron-grey beard full of secrets and plots.

He was compassionate and witty, but he did not indulge her or allow her to feel sorry for herself.

Everything with that man was affectation—even the name he had bestowed on her, 'Atiyah', was not her real name, nor the title of 'Lady' valid, but his manipulation of others to see her as more than the unwanted, misbegotten shame of the princess. To view her as titled and respected royal offspring, wanted and valuable.

His machinations were legion and sinuous, along with his insistence that she cast off her simplistic view of right and wrong, good and bad, and wield her powers (such as they were) to play the game of politics. She was still learning, but it took effort for her to employ subterfuge—her nature was inherently direct. Still, she did enjoy the complexities and intricate planning involved, as well as the triumph of a con pulled off successfully.

As her best friend, Kaimam, had once observed: she was unscrupulously manipulative, but she was a detail-oriented monster who liked to plan everything to the nth degree and watch her chips fall as she orchestrated. She dealt with enough uncertainty as it was and therefore wanted to take charge of all she was able through subtle prediction and manoeuvring.

"A woman is a house of many rooms with a pretty façade to distract from the complexity of the structure. You are a godsdamned twisted maze covered in a blanket of gold leaf to blind the eye and dazzle the mind." She had gotten him back for his backhanded compliment-insult, but she had to acknowledge the accuracy of at least *some* of what the oaf had stated. If only he knew, she had constructed those labyrinthine passages brick by brick from a bare room—easily seen in its entirety. To change her approach to life, her very nature, into a more complex and convoluted one had taken sheer grit and will. And she still struggled with it, even as she was now ensconced in the bosom of her kingdom's greatest rivals.

For the rest of the evening, Ata's duties were exclusively in and around the ash-laden kitchens; Famenke considered this a valid shaming after Ata's imposition. She still swelled with suppressed indignation whenever her eye fell on the new addition to their ranks, but Ata just smiled at her dreamily and Famenke would stomp off to another part of the palace. When the kitchens had finally been scrubbed down to the head cook's exacting standards, Ata staggered up the stairs to her chamber. She often fantasised about assassinating the little head cook with some of the powdered poisons she was given to be used in case of emergency. She was quite sure none of the other staff would condemn her for the act; in fact, she was relatively certain most would commend her for removing the tiny tyrant from their sphere permanently.

As she dragged her aching carcass up the narrow and uneven stone stairs, she gratefully thought of her good luck in being lodged in her own room. Maybe 'room' was a bit of a stretch of the imagination—'broom closet' would have been more accurate, but the fact remained: she was hired at a time when the staff rooming situation was precarious and the shared dormitory-style chambers occupied by the other servants were at capacity. Naturally, the more senior maids were offered the broom closet first, but all declined as they were friends and enjoyed their social (not to mentioned relatively heated) sleeping chambers.

The broom closet, forming part of the outer wall of the palace, was a tiny ice box. Ata resented the cold but had trained herself over years to completely ignore physical and mental discomfort to the point that debilitating conditions merely registered as vaguely unpleasant. The privacy afforded her in the freezing cupboard space was well worth the shivering aches.

She entered the dark little room with her small candle and as much enthusiasm as a 16-hour shift completed could allow, but her training still overrode her weariness. She shut and locked the door immediately and then proceeded to carefully rifle through all her belongings—checking all the traps and ploys she had set to indicate if the space had been searched. None of them had been triggered; the individual grains of rice, salt crystals, and even eyelashes were still in the pleats of papers and dresses, and the strange folds and positions of various items remained exactly as she had left them. Her space had not been invaded nor searched during the day. It would seem she was still undiscovered—unsuspected. She heaved a sigh of relief, watching her breath fog the air before her eyes, then started bustling around to get ready for bed. She had her half day tomorrow, so she would need to write and send her weekly report to Lord Danai then. She would do so very early, as the entire process of construction and conveyance left her physically drained. Then she would be able to sleep afterwards and feign having slept in for her entire half day when Famenke predictably came looking for her before her shift started in the afternoon. She smiled ruefully at the thought of the supervisor's deep-seated dislike of pretty, mindless Anita.

Once Ata had done a brisk but basic wash using the jug of heated water she had brought up with her, she donned the ugly, heavy cotton night dress that virtuous Anita would have chosen, then added a pair of her own leggings and thick woollen socks, as well as a voluminous woollen shawl. She had brought the hot brick she regularly snuck from deep inside the kitchen hearth, wrapped it in some flannel and placed it in the bed to warm the faded and frayed linens while the tempest raged outside.

On the little cabinet upon which her jug and basin rested, she had a small, round mirror. It was warped and hazy, but still did its job admirably. She looked at herself as she started to carefully unwrap the ugly dark grey headdress she wore daily. It matched her thick woollen grey servant's dress; though she resented the ugly things and their coarse weaves, the protection they afforded her could not be overstated.

Luckily, the Cinnaens believed in head coverings for women; "a decent woman neither glories in vanity, nor her body's attractions. She keeps her hair covered for modesty's sake" the scriptures intoned, and of all the kingdoms on the continent of Áitarbith, Cinnae still kept to the old ways. Naturally, the upper classes tended to wear gauzy veils and delicate netting over their curled and styled tresses, whilst the moralising middle classes and the moralised-at working classes veered towards austere greys, browns, and blacks, with wrapped head-dresses that kept all but the veriest tendrils from the public eye.

Many of the younger generation were casting aside these constraints, but employed women were usually required to wear some form of covering, no matter how sparse, to satisfy the more conservative amongst the clergy. This was a windfall for Ata in her role as a local servant. Though her eyes were not remarkable amongst the Cinnaens who were known for their light eyes, fair skin, and pale hair, her hair she had inherited from her mother and was stereotypically Pandial. So darkly brown as to appear black, her thick mane was her one vanity (ironic, really, considering the tomes promoting female modesty and humility used hair as the symbol of feminine pride), so having to dye it for this mission would have been challenging.

As it was, she could pin the heavy lengths tightly out of the way and cover up with a very conservative head-dress. She liberally powdered the front of her hair and the nape of her neck, making the hair that did escape during her hectic workdays appear mousy brown, but light enough to avoid suspicion.

Ata completed her ablutions, only pausing to look intently at her face in the mirror again. It had become a ritual of sorts, since she could remember. When she was about three or four, she had stumbled upon a painting of a beautiful Pandial lady in the royal portrait gallery of her uncle's keep. The lady had been mesmerising, looking straight at the viewer in (what Ata now knew) was a provocative and playful manner. Her obsidian eyes laughed, her full red mouth smirked, and her thick black hair hung in flowing curtains over her bare golden shoulders.

Ata had been gripped by the beautiful woman, taking to haunting the gallery every day just to visit her lady. She did not think that anyone noticed her—both the arrogance and the nonchalance of extreme youth assume that one is always alone and unobserved in the world when you yourself are not aware of others, making no allowance for their awareness of you. But it seemed someone had been watching, because she remembered hearing the woman who sometimes acted as her caretaker loudly whisper to her uncle the night of one of his frequent visits to her nursery. As usual, she had already been abed by the time he came, but not fully asleep and therefore able to eavesdrop on the exchange.

"Has the child been well?" King Addai's husky tenor inquired.

"Yes, Your Majesty. She is healthy, if somewhat boisterous for a girl... I feel I ought to mention that the child has been going to the portrait gallery. Every day, Your Majesty. Every day. To see the portrait of Her Highness, the Princess Annaia." This was followed by silence—her uncle never felt the need to fill the empty spaces in conversations; awkward silences simply did not exist, for he was a king and all silences were therefore significant.

The woman continued: "I worry... that is, I do not think it is healthy for the child to become fixated upon the likeness of a... person... parent she will never know. One of the servants must have told her the portrait is of her mother, and I fear it will result in an unnatural obsession with the picture itself. She is already so unsocial..." the woman trailed off meaningfully. Ata's uncle had sighed wearily.

"Say no more. Do as you see fit in this case; I have enough to be contending with without my sister's byblow adding unnecessarily to my burdens." Even though his words were harsh and careless, he had entered his niece's room afterward as he had done countless times throughout her life, and proceeded to sit quietly by her bed. Just watching her. Sometimes stroking Ata's hand or hair softly, he would leave before anyone could know he spent so much of his preciously finite time with his sister's bastard he was not meant to love.

The following day, the portrait had been gone—an empty space on the wall and in her heart. But she had understood who her beautiful lady had been and had started staring at herself in her mirror at night—hair down, shoulders bare. When very young and not understanding the subtleties of her mother's pose and expression, she had tried to imitate them. To recreate it. But as she had grown older, she had been happy merely to look at herself and try to find the resemblance. Eventually, even that had faded; she had just looked at herself as she was. Acknowledging her features. Contemplating who she was. Deciding who she would be. She did this now.

She was Pandial.

She was a spy.

She would enable the fall of Cinnae.

And then the candle flickered wildly in the mirror beside her reflection before abruptly going out. Two calloused hands gripped her mouth and neck in a fierce stranglehold and hauled her back out of the chair.

2

———

THE GAME CONTINUES

Jon M. Nelson

Ata couldn't breathe, couldn't speak, couldn't move, and she had a split-second decision to make. Continue playing her role to the hilt (hopefully not literally) or break character and use her training to extract herself from the death grip enveloping her.

But she already knew she had no choice. A Pandial spy in Cinnae was one thing; a Pandial spy in the imperial palace who had served the royal family dinner was an entirely different prospect. It might be considered an act of aggression and could potentially lead to hostilities between the two nations. Their kingdoms had bad blood between them tracing back almost a thousand years, their current 'truce' an uneasy one of ignoring one another officially. Lord Danai had unequivocally told her she would be disavowed if she were discovered or exposed at the foreign court. Her path was clear—she could only hope her performance would save her now.

She fleetingly noticed the sturdy hold on her throat and mouth was not constricting her airways, only apparently attempting to subdue her potential thrashing and screams. She proceeded to flail and fight back merely half-heartedly but took great pleasure in scrabbling madly with her nails at one of the arms that was restraining her. At best, her attacker would have criss-crossing scratch marks to contend with; at the very least, he would have some spectacular bruising. She quickly worked her struggles up to a frantic crescendo and then abruptly sagged, limp as a rag doll.

There was a momentary pause as she hung floppily from her attacker's arms—her feet not even touching the floorboards—and then her assailant jiggled her experimentally, trying to elicit a reaction. It would have been comical if she weren't so worried about her situation.

"I think she fainted. You obviously squeezed her much too tightly, boy," a whisper broke the strained silence from a bit further from her—there were at least two goons, it seemed. A man's timbre, the cadence and poshly rounded vowels stirred her memory, but she could not place it at that point. She heard the tell-tale scrape and hiss of a match being struck, the blackness behind her closed eyelids bleeding into deeply warm burgundy.

"I did no such thing; I barely used any pressure ... She must just be delicate." Her assailant's hushed voice brushed over the top of her head, the same rounded, almost drawling accent used by the upper classes of Cinnae, but ever so slightly different from his confederate's. Not your run of the mill lackeys then—two nobles for sure.

"With our luck you misidentified the girl and the poor thing is just some wench from the countryside. She'll probably go off into hysterics from our heavy-handed treatment when she awakens," his deep, low tone turned slightly accusatory. The intensity of the light behind her closed lids heightened as the candle was brought nearer. She maintained her loose-limbed state as her assailant stiltedly adjusted his grip to better hold her up and her body was spun around, her head lolling back over his forearm. She was now facing toward her attacker, held against his front, and sensed she was being carefully studied. Thus, she kept her breathing even and made sure that her eyelids didn't tremble and give away her conscious state.

"Not a chance she's some innocent from the boonies, at least not in Cinnae. Look at that hair! Dark as mink and just as thick. No, my lad—this is a Pandial. Take my word for it. Or at least: she has Pandial blood in her veins." Oddly enough, delight tinged the other, creaky voice. It frightened her slightly; overt joy was not an emotion she associated with spymasters and their minions. She didn't have time to get too hung up on this fact, because her foe had suddenly changed his hold on her, sweeping her up and cradling her like a child.

As they started moving through her small room, a new panic seized her—what if they carried her to some dungeon or obscure chamber and stashed her there for questioning? She had relative faith in her abilities to withstand interrogation and torture, but if she could strategically pre-empt all of that, she might still salvage the situation.

Her furious internal calculations were sharply interrupted when she was unceremoniously released. Luckily, she had frozen in terror at the unexpected drop and thus had not uttered a sound, even when her body came to an abrupt stop on her mattress. Sadly, immediately being doused with cold water was apparently one step too far for her body's frazzled nerves, for she sat up spluttering and shrieking. Her act of playing dead had come to an unforeseen end, it would seem, as she angrily swiped at her wet eyes and cheeks, feeling the thick cotton fabric of her nightgown sloppily sticking to her skin.

Two men stood on either side of her tiny bed; both men she had last seen while serving them at the grand dining table earlier that evening. Lord Svensso towered over her on her right, the side from whence she had descended; therefore he must have been the assailant who had been restraining and carrying her.

The other, still clutching the water jug in one hand and the candle in the other, was the unknown elderly man with the bright blue gaze—which was now trained unwaveringly on her, carefully cataloguing her face in a highly disconcerting manner. Almost reverently, she thought uneasily.

She snapped back to her main goal: to convince them that they had victimised a poor, hapless lackwit. A pretty girl, who was merely in the wrong place, at the wrong time—wrongfully accused of something she couldn't truly grasp, poor thing. She maintained the strong passion that had fuelled her rage earlier, but funnelled it fully into a confused and fearful mien.

"Who are you, my lords? Why... why are you in my chamber? D...d...did I do something wrong? Is it because Mistress Famenke is angry with me for going into the dining hall when I shouldn'ta?..." and she broke into loud, wailing sobs, blubbering and babbling on and on about all kinds of nonsense. She channelled all the silliness that she deemed 'Anita' possessed and proceeded to list all the misdemeanours she could think of that maids could accrue—a fear-induced confession of sorts. Silver not polished thoroughly enough, taking a bite from the cake batter when the cook hadn't been looking, using the butler's entrance once, and many more.

She wept and wailed, wringing her hands and using Anita's breathy, slightly high-pitched accents, a regional dialectal construction thrown in here and there to complete the performance. She had finally wound down, subsiding into hiccupping sniffs, her legs crossed like a child's and her hands rubbing girlishly at her tearful eyes. Glancing pathetically up at the two males observing her, she tried to gauge the success of her routine.

The general's eyes were trained on the ceiling, a look of pained forbearance on his face. She noted he was in his mid to late twenties, with a similar facial structure to the crown prince, but with paler hair shorn close to his skull. A very handsome face, but somewhat scarred—the uneven, slim white line ran from the inside corner of his right eye, across the bridge of his nose and all the way down alongside it, finally bisecting his left upper lip. It disrupted the almost unnaturally perfect symmetry of his face, lifting his upper lip in a slight, perpetually one-sided smirk.

His compatriot, conversely, watched her avidly, dwarfed by the late king's bastard. The two men couldn't be more physically disparate—one aged, the other in his physical prime, one short and slim, the other tall and broad. It made sense that the general was the one to carry out the physical assault and do the heavy lifting, but even though Lord Svensso was the more overtly threatening of the two, she was more wary of the knowing air that surrounded the other.

"Well, aren't you a canny one, girl. And with that helpless act and those big green eyes, I'm sure you have every man within your immediate vicinity eating out of the palm of your hand or panting after your skirts. But, unfortunately for you, I am not so easily led by a pretty lass. So, I will be clear: who are you and what is your aim here in this palace?" he spoke pleasantly enough with a lightly playful tone, but Ata was not fooled. Her every sense whispered *danger*, so she decided to proceed with caution.

"Well, as to that, sir, I mean, Lord... whoever you are, or...Your Hordli-, I mean, Your Lordliness. I am Anita Bernsson and I am here to serve the Glorious House of Hårbørgen, may their reign last in perpetuity," she responded, inflecting her voice with all the trustworthy guilelessness she possessed. But he was shaking his head before she had even finished.

"I am Lord Iansso, erstwhile adviser to the former monarch, King Olefso. And you may be here to serve, but I would be mightily surprised if your service is truly to the Cinnaen crown, or that your name is what you have stated." He cocked his head to the side and narrowed his eyes. His avuncular persona put her on edge, so she looked over at the general and imploringly lifted her hands in a traditional attitude of supplication.

"Please, Your Lordliness, I do not understand what Lord Iansso means. I promise I'm a good girl. I work hard. I say my prayers..." she started listing her virtues and counting them off on her fingers, "... I can recite all the admonitions in the tomes and I have always honoured my country. That is why I am here at the palace: to serve the people by serving our leaders. And it is truly an honour to do that."

He had given her his undivided attention when she had addressed him, his expression stoic except for the involuntary curl of his lip, but she noticed his eyes—an icier blue than any she had seen before and more akin to the Vürgøn who resided in the frosty climes of the Uurgonna Mountains. Said eyes had wandered down to her chest. She had forgotten her wet state and that her clinging nightdress and the freezing room meant her body was putting on quite the show; she was not averse to exploiting men's inevitable compulsion to look at what was being displayed, even carelessly, as was now the case.

Unfortunately, the presence and careful scrutiny of Lord Iansso made even mild flirtation impossible. But she tried to balance her ditzy strategy with a coquettish one by breathing deeply so her chest expanded markedly. To his credit, Lord Svensso's eyes had immediately returned to her face when she had started speaking and had remained there, turning vaguely cynical when she plied her laughably derivative wiles.

"My apologies, Lady. But I am simply the brawn of this operation. I can be of no service to you in advancing your cause of innocence. My colleague is the brains of this investigation," he said and turned a mockingly pointed stare to his partner. It was clear he thought they had erred in accosting her—that she was exactly what she professed to be. But he would not gainsay the other.

"'Investigation', Your Lordliness?" she squeaked in feigned panic and indignation.

"I think you'll find, my dear, that it is 'Your Lordship', *not* 'Your Lordliness'," the elder commented dryly; she sensed they were both wise to her kittenish attempt to manipulate the younger. Lord Iansso stared at her intently for a few seconds, then abruptly seemed to come to a conclusion. "I need to speak to this young woman alone, I think. Would you leave us, Svens?" he had turned his head towards his compatriot and spoken politely but firmly. Momentary indecision flickered over the handsome countenance of the "brawn", then he nodded imperiously and strode out of the room. Strangely, the door shutting quietly behind his hulking retreat left Ata feeling more vulnerable. The presence of the smaller, elderly man ironically felt much more threatening to her. With good reason, she realised, eyeing him guardedly. He gave her a politely empty smile and went over to the toppled chair, dragging it over to her bedside. He also scooped up her thick shawl that had fallen in the earlier scuffle and gallantly handed it to her.

"I think you might be a bit chilly, my dear," he stated and sat down neatly in the chair she had forcibly been dragged from earlier, crossing his legs and setting his hands primly on his knee.

"I believe it would be best if we dispensed with all the theatrics of intrigue—the potential for discovery, interrogation, torture, dismemberment, death..." he waved his hand lightly back and forth to indicate the triviality of such things.

"Let us cut directly to a point where *you* will know, categorically, that you can trust *me*. And *I* can know, beyond a doubt, that I can trust *you*. If both of us are not satisfied... Well, we can address that eventuality once we've crossed this first bridge."

His engaging smile and forthright manner did not soothe her one whit, for she realised the "eventuality" probably referred to unpleasant consequences for her. Of the permanent variety. "Would you be amenable to that?" he asked, courteous to a fault. She nodded warily, keeping her face relatively blank, her cards firmly up her sleeve in case she needed to revert to her hapless Anita mask.

"Wonderful!" he leaned forward slightly and

lowered his voice conspiratorially. "If I were to say to you: 'Assayed in gold and onyx, wrought in shade and light', then you would respond...?" Her breath left her in an audible whoosh and more than surprise, she felt lightheaded with relief.

"I would answer: 'Of gold and onyx, only the former can be assayed through fire'," Ata said promptly; Lord Iansso sighed and sat back casually. She realised he must have been tense before, for if she had thought him charming and kind earlier (if distressingly so, under the circumstances), then his current ebullience could only be described as dazzling.

"There now, my girl. All that unnecessary cloak and dagger 'is he, isn't he' nonsense has been dealt with, and about time, I would say. But youth's stubbornness, I suppose," and he lifted his shoulders and gave her a satirically accusing smile, "I assume you are the infamous Ata of Danai's?" his voice had gone so soft, she had to lean closer to catch it all.

"Yes. I am Ata. But how do you know my Lord Danai?" she could not shake off almost a decade of training and so she still held back any commitment to information that he did not already possess. The fact he knew her name meant defending its secrecy was a moot point, but she would not give him things easily— even if he did use the code Lord Danai had assured her, unequivocally, meant the person who knew it could be trusted implicitly. Lord Iansso seemed to sense her recalcitrant reticence, but smiled at her fondly.

"Ah. As to that, if *he* did not tell you, then I will maintain an old spy's tricks and keep my cards close to my chest, young thing. But suffice it to say: I do know Danai, and have done for more decades than I care to count at this point. Moreover, I also know about your little mission here in the Hårbørgen palace...

"But I confess, Danai has been rather vague—which is not unusual for the old rogue, let me tell you—uh, vague, yes. He has been rather *unforthcoming* about the ultimate goal of your small foray into our midst. Would you be able to elucidate for me, my dear?" and he cocked his head to the side as before, bright blue eyes trained on Ata expectantly.

"I cannot tell you, I'm afraid," Ata said as she got up from the narrow bed and started rifling through the trunk beneath for a tunic to replace her sodden night-gown. She didn't really care if she was being rude. Now that she knew she wasn't going to be suspended from her thumbs in the dungeon, her comfort became her priority. Her leggings had also somehow suffered in the drenching, so she needed to swap them for another pair as well.

In fact, she was becoming increasingly annoyed with the entire situation—for all the unnecessary fright she had suffered, the physical manhandling and above all: sitting wet in a freezing broom closet whilst being questioned by two men who had imposed on her small but private sanctum. Two men, moreover, who had, that very night, eaten a leisurely dinner that *she* had served them and would be returning to more opulent chambers than this to possibly a warm bath and definitely a luxurious bed. She was, actually, fuming. "In fact," she continued, mangling her dry clothing in her hands, "even if I *could* tell you, I would not."

Rather than becoming annoyed or even angry at her obvious disrespect, Lord Iansso chuckled in the face of her attempt to antagonise him.

"I see you are put out with our treatment of you, but pray: how would you have proceeded to investigate an obvious spy in your midst? And may I remind you..." when she had started to answer furiously, "that I had no guarantees that you were Danai's pet. One cannot simply approach a potential spy—or even assassin—and provide them with the first half of a most secret and well-guarded failsafe. Even the fact that Danai chose to share it with *you* at this point in your career is miraculous. But then, being who you are, exceptions must be made, I suppose..." Her brow had furrowed at being referred to as a pet, but she was more curious about the reference to who she was.

"What do you mean 'who I am qualifies me for exceptions'?" she paraphrased, but he only grinned at her and tapped the side of his nose in an archaic gesture of 'I know something you don't'. Her inherent temper burned brighter, despite all the years of exercising rigid self-control. *Infuriating man. Little hobgoblin. Gnome!* The fact that he seemed aware of her internal name-calling, yet smiled indulgently as though pandering to a child in the throes of a tantrum, made her see red. She needed to do something, to keep busy, or she would thump him. So she strangled her rage and stomped over to change behind the tattered screen next to the door. Anything to cool off mentally. *Physically she was plenty cool, thanks to the pair of them!*

"May I know what gave me away as a spy?" she called belligerently from her shielded position as she yanked at the obstinate garments that clung to her and would not disengage. She had noticed Lord Iansso had deliberately turned his head toward the corner furthest from where she was currently being strangled by her own clothing. He seemed to be intently studying her charcoal sketches that she had pinned to the horrible, frayed wallpaper, but obligingly responded.

"It wasn't any one thing in particular. But one does tend to develop a nose for deception after as many years as I have been in the business... And I must commend you as well as Danai, whenever I get the chance, on your skill. Only a truly seasoned spy or spymaster would have spotted you, rest assured. However, dare I say it? Your vanity could lead to potential problems..."

"What do you mean?" she barked, offended. She was *not* vain at all, considering, objectively, what she looked like. She knew she was beautiful now, but she had not always been, so she had immediately noticed the increase in male and some female attention in her mid-teens.

She had also definitely noted the increase in negative looks, comments, and behaviour towards her. All because of the fact that she *did* eventually resemble her mother somewhat, as she had so ardently wished, but with even more striking colouring—almost all Pandial were categorically black-haired, golden-skinned, and dark-eyed.

She often resented her looks because they were a bitch to disguise, making it difficult to play unobtrusive characters when you drew the eye. But she thought she had succeeded and had been proud of her skill in downplaying her looks or even rendering them cheap and tawdry. Now, faced with this comment by Lord Iansso, it seemed she had not been as competent as she thought.

"Why, the fact that you did not simply dye your hair, girl," she could hear his surprise that she did not immediately gather his meaning.

"I wear a headdress and am extremely careful. In the weeks I have been here, no-one has seen my hair."

"Except for me and young Svens, two lords of the kingdom—one a spymaster and the other a general of Cinnae. Not very circumspect, is it?" She had finally managed to disentangle herself from the wretched nightgown, which dropped with a wet *plop* onto the floor. *On to the leggings...*

"Well, how was I supposed to know you'd come barging into my room when I was undressing?" she returned indignantly, trying not to lose her balance with her one leg held prisoner by the garment at the ankle as she attempted to force it off by stepping on the fabric with one foot, anchoring it, then lifting her other leg off the floor. *She should have removed her socks before the leggings.*

"You should always expect anything and everything in this line of work," for the first time since she had met him, he sounded miffed, "if the wrong person finds you the way we did tonight, with a glaringly obvious physical indication that you don't belong, your life would be forfeit. Do you understand me?"

"Yes. So... I should dye my hair then, you mean?" *One foot free! Only one more to go.*

"It is better to be prepared for unpredictable exposure, so yes. I did not take you for a vain creature, I must say." He sounded perplexed.

"I'm not, at all. It's just... I..." she breathed deeply, "it reminds me of someone, and I'd like to keep the reminder, if at all possible." The silence that followed seemed heavy; she had ceased struggling with her clothing just as her second foot had emerged from the heap on the floor. She clutched the dry tunic, ignoring the goosebumps all over her body as her entire focus awaited his response.

"I see. Well." He cleared his throat awkwardly, "I underst-"

What he understood, she would never learn, because at that moment, the door flew open and Lord Svensso stormed in, his expression clearly showing his impatience and his determination to lecture Lord Iansso on making him wait outside the chamber that long. Instead, he staggered to a halt in front of Ata, expression shocked as she stood there, flabbergasted, in the altogether.

After a stunned, seconds-long delay, she hurriedly, fumblingly lifted the scrunched tunic in her hands to cover herself as she hunched over and turned away from him. Without a word, she surmised from the retreating footfalls and the sound of the door closing that the general had turned and left the room. A hoarsely humorous chuff sounded from the other side of the chamber.

"That'll teach the boy to knock before storming in. Gotten much too forceful in recent years," Lord Iansso chortled, clearly not considering her feelings on the incident. She stuffed those feelings down and proceeded to carefully but efficiently don the rest of her clothing. A sudden thought occurred.

"He also suspected me. Besides you, I mean."

"Who suspected you," his tone was calm, yet she felt

a quiver of fear at the coldly calculating edge that had crept into his voice. She came out from behind the screen and approached the bed again, sitting on it as the only chair was occupied by her "guest". Luckily the bedding had only been showered with a few drops—she had been on the receiving end of the lion's share.

"Lord Svensso. He... he *looked* at me when I was serving this evening. Like he knew me, knew me for what I was." Ata was obviously tired, because she sounded fanciful even to herself.

"Did he now?" the old man threw a calculating look her way and smirked shrewdly, "And was his look one you had seen on men's faces before, or are you still a bit naïve in that department? I wouldn't have thought so with the implicitly salacious little manipulation you tried this evening." He was referring to her abortive attempt at flirting with the general. She felt annoyance rise again.

"Of course not. He wasn't looking at me with any kind of *carnal interest*. He suspected me... Or rather, it felt like he had recognised me. Maybe he has been to Pandi, to Enddaian Castle, and saw me there at some point?" she was almost hopeful that was the case, because otherwise it meant there was something about her that elicited suspicion, making her mission here virtually impossible.

"No. He has met General Erdai at previous peace negotiations, but on the border only. I can say with absolute certainty that he has never laid eyes on you before you came here. Maybe you should just ask the man yourself?" again the sly innuendo crept into his voice, "I can easily call him back in now you're fully clothed, so his delicate sensibilities won't be sullied unduly." Plenty of sarcasm, but at least now the little gnome was mocking Lord Svensso, not her.

"I will ask him at a later date, I think. If I get the chance... I am actually exhausted and need to rest before I face the battle axe known as Mistress Famenke. I did not lie in my earlier confession—my silver polishing skills are up to maggots, which she knows. No rest for the wicked, as they say," she gave him a reserved smile.

Ever the gentleman (except when attacking servant girls in their rooms), Lord Iansso rose and gave her a distinctly low courtly bow that made her feel flustered. Even at the Pandial royal court she was not used to receiving obeisance; if she was not mistaken, she had just been on the receiving end of the Cinnaen version of a bow reserved for a princess royal. Rather than address this, she chose to pretend ignorance and curtseyed prettily in return (in the Cinnaen style to prove she could).

"Sleep well, *Anita.* Your service is much appreciated, my dear." And he strode towards the door, where he paused and then turned back with his hand on the doorknob. "You look more like your mother than you realise. Your hair is not your only inheritance, so you should not eschew changing it, if that will potentially save your life." And then he swept from the room.

THE NEXT DAY, Ata's half day, saw her encode her missive to Lord Danai. Though tricky, she managed to imbue her annoyance at being in the dark regarding Lord Iansso. She then proceeded to carefully lock her door and then to map out the runes and powerlines for construction and conveyance on the floor.

It only took her about an hour now, due to assiduous practice over many years. Usually, the readying of a space for Commanding took hours. Ata dusted off her hands with satisfaction as she surveyed her handiwork; the chalk marks in repetitive patterns, integrated with numbers and symbols, looked like a complex artwork rather than a working to Command.

Their ancestors had called it 'magic', but over the centuries, academics became authorities on the arcane arts, rendering them transparent and scientific—useful to all. 'Magic' became 'Commanding', 'spells' became 'workings', 'incantations' became 'casting of scripts', and the clear, standardised formats meant accessibility and safety that had not been possible previously.

Although only individuals who manifested the ability to Command could power the workings, anyone who studied the lore and texts was able to ready or set up a space for Commanding. Those with the ability to Command were called the Abled, whilst those without the ability, but learned in the construction of Commanding, were known as the Knowledgeable.

The act of Commanding itself did drain one's energy, but theoretically, if the Knowledgeable prepared multiple spaces for Commanding, then a single Abled could Command between ten and twenty workings a day. Ata was Abled, but her capacity to Command was average at best. All considered, however, it was a definite skill in her espionage arsenal.

She carefully checked her markings; a single disruption of a working once the Commanding started could be deadly, both to the individuals in the immediate vicinity of the Commanding and to any others tied to it, irrespective of geographic distance. In this case, Ata and Lord Danai were the most at risk.

She cautiously stood in her designated position amongst the swirls and letters, the coded dispatch exactly in its correct place, then started her script. She felt the draw of energy from herself, its gathering power in the invisible conduit constructed through the workings, waiting to be released and funnelled to its eventual destination.

As the power reached its zenith and she approached the trickiest part of the script which would push the energy into the "between", a key rattled in the lock of her door, and to her horror, the panel swung open.

3

———

THE ENEMY OF MY ENEMY

LET THOSE WHO WILL OF FRIENDSHIP SING,
AND TO ITS GUERDON GRATEFUL BE,
BUT I A LYRIC GARLAND BRING
TO CROWN THEE, O, MINE ENEMY!

LUCY MAUD MONTGOMERY

All the carefully edited, moderated, and curated texts on Commanding categorically stated the same thing: clear, pedantic preparation was key to success and any interruption of a casting of a script was unequivocally disastrous. And disaster was surely about to be unleashed not only upon Ata, but on whoever was coming into her room unexpectedly, Lord Danai who was linked to her working, as well as any hapless souls within range of the casting.

Not only that, but should the first and most pressing crisis of the interrupted casting be averted, there was still the consequence of discovery to contend with. For no maid would have even the vaguest idea of how Commanding worked, never mind the training nor skill to actually attempt it on her own. Her cover was as good as blown.

In desperation, as she saw the door reach the apsis of its arc, she dramatically slowed her speaking, dragging out the script without actually interrupting the reading. In a split second, she perceived the boiling point of energy caught precariously in the space isolated by the complex power lines marked out on the floor.

She haplessly "grasped" with her conviction at the roiling mass of energy and shoved it downwards, into the stone floor, shaping her intent wordlessly and praying she didn't bring the entire storey crashing down. Her nonverbal aim was to erase all trace of her working, including the encoded missive to Lord Danai—a severance of his investment in this casting, thereby separating him from any consequences the interruption might elicit.

She had no real hope of succeeding, but still shut her eyes and focused madly, letting her voice fade to a breathy whisper, then silently mouthing the last of the script as the door banged against the wall.

The force of the energy dissipating into the floor made Ata's ears pop as her eyes flew open, the sensation

in the room similar to how one would think the immediate aftermath of an earthquake might feel. Strangely
silent, but a doubtless implication that something significantly momentous had occurred.

Famenke, who had stepped into the room at the
same time, staggered to a stop and looked around in
shocked incomprehension. She had evidently perceived
the strange atmosphere, but now all was normal—birds
chirping, sun shining palely through the small window,
with silence in the room—so she was probably questioning her split-second experience. She looked over at
Ata, her face immediately scrunching into a furious
scowl.

"Based on previous experience with your half day, I
brought the skeleton key. I don't have time to stand
knocking away at a lazy girl's bedroom door while she
sleeps away the daylight hours." She glanced critically
around the room as Ata looked too—dreading the harridan's reaction to the chalk markings on the floor.

It had all disappeared, just as she had so implicitly
willed. Not a speck of dust remained, nor a scuff. The
paper with her encoded message had evaporated
without a trace.

"One would think that you would apply the kind of
assiduous cleanliness in your duties as you have clearly
done here."

Even a compliment from Famenke was couched in
criticism, though now that both the dooming crises

were averted, Ata felt her anger at the woman's intrusion spike. She had almost caused so much damage through her breach of Ata's privacy!

"Might I ask why you have come to my room now? It's my half day and I am only due to start my shift this afternoon," she stood absolutely still, struggling to maintain her usual Anita-like silliness.

Famenke looked at her sharply, clearly picking up on the unusual barb in the customarily placid maid's rejoinder, but Ata must have managed to pull off a fittingly vapid expression, for Famenke dismissed her with a shrug and turned toward Ata's 'observation' wall —covered in what appeared to be her artistic endeavours in charcoal, but was actually a minute documentation of the palace layout and features, as well as its inhabitants.

She glanced back at Ata, surprise and a hint of something else—could it be admiration?—in her gaze.

"These are *very* good... You drew them?"

"Yes. But I still need a lot of practice. Do you think the crown prince or queen would care for a portrait?" it was the silliest thing she could come up with under the circumstances; she was so unused to anything approaching a compliment from this salty woman. Famenke gave her the usual look that questioned her intellect and did not deign to answer, instead choosing to progress to her reason for coming.

"Lord Iansso has requested that you clean his rooms.

Usually, such requests are not necessarily honoured, but as Lord Iansso has always been highly circumspect in his behaviour towards the servants, and he is... advanced beyond an age where he might be driven to... impose, Mistress Mella has agreed."

Ata tried not to make a face; the housekeeper, Mistress Mella, was a sour-faced old trout who was obsessed with gaining the attention of the upper classes whilst bullying those of lesser consequence to herself.

She was sure the considerations Famenke mentioned were Famenke's alone, for although her disposition was just as sour and miserable as the house-keeper's, it hid a genuine care for others. She might despise you, but she would still try to protect you from harm nevertheless. Which was why even her unpleasant, alienating personality didn't put Ata off too much.

"Should I go now?" she asked and started towards the door with enthusiasm.

"No, brainless girl! You are not fully dressed! Only your headdress is on... and one sock. Honestly, it's a wonder you manage anything..." Ata spent a pleasurable half hour pretending idiocy while getting ready, constantly being berated by Famenke. She was grinding her teeth by the end, finally screeching at a retreating 'Anita' to "get out of her sight". Ata left with a wide grin on her face.

She muddled her way to Lord Iansso's rooms, spreading her reputation of uselessness and earnest incompetence by asking for directions over and over and then doing the exact opposite, leaving a trail of tutting and head shaking amongst servants in her wake.

When she finally arrived, nothing could have prepared her for the bedlam that abounded. The rooms themselves were humble in all senses of the word—size-wise, style-wise, position-wise. These were not the apartments of a particularly influential member of court. But she was not fooled.

Furthermore, it looked as though an explosion had taken place within the walls, the debris left behind being hundreds of books and papers haphazardly spread on the floors, tables, and chairs. Also: plants of every variety—potted, drying, artificial—stood in the corners, hung from the ceilings, and were pinned to the walls.

She had never in her life seen so much chaos contained in such a limited space. In the middle of it all sat her quarry, glasses perched on the end of his nose as he peered at the roots of an ordinary-looking specimen. Ata could have sworn it was just a regular weed, but what did she know.

"Ah! Come in, come in, my dear! Welcome to my humble abode," he jumped up from the table and hurried over to her, ushering her into the rooms as though she were an honoured guest rather than the help he had requested to tame this monstrosity.

He must have noticed her chagrined expression and

her eyes wandering upward in horror upon spying some more weeds dangling from the small chandelier above them.

"Not to worry, my girl. Not to worry! Requesting you come and clean here was merely a pretext for getting my hooks into you. I would never dream of letting you get your grubby little hands on any of my treasures in here. Rest assured: I would never ask you to mess up this perfection."

She eyed him dubiously, unsure if he was being sarcastic or truly valued the revolting clutter that surrounded them. As his eyes always twinkled merrily, his tone always sounding earnest—whether meant or not—she could not come to a conclusion.

"What can I do for you, Your Lordliness?" she wittered, playing 'Anita' fully, for she did not know how secure his rooms were, nor if anyone else lurked out of sight. He smiled warmly at her, eyes crinkling.

"Why don't we go for a little walk, you and I? There are some storage rooms that need sorting and cleaning. That is the task I have set aside for you today."

They moved toward the door, which he opened for her, murmuring quietly: "You will forgive me if I don't offer my arm, I'm sure." She had not expected him to, as she was, for all intents and purposes, a servant, and no lord, no matter how eccentrically gallant, would accompany a maid as though she were a lady.

She shook her head and smiled as she preceded him

out the door, absolving him from any guilt, but a pained expression flashed across his countenance before he quickly shut the door, locked it, then walked ahead of her down the corridor.

They took a convoluted path through the palace to a part she had not yet been to. After her head became thoroughly turned about, despite all her best efforts to keep track of their route, they came to an abrupt halt in a somewhat threadbare hallway, in front of a rather shabby door.

Once they had entered another set of modest rooms —this time scrupulously clean, if slightly old-fashioned in terms of furnishings—Lord Iansso knelt at the compact fireplace, lit a small fire, and eventually settled into the comfortable chair in front of it.

"Please, take a seat Lady Atiyah," he motioned graciously. Ata started at his use of the honorific assigned to her exclusively by Lord Danai, then narrowed her eyes. Lord Iansso was plainly showing off his intimate knowledge of her life in Pandi.

She very purposely cast aside her Anita-veil, striding brusquely forward and dropping into the seat without preamble—her usual gait and air of assurance clear.

"You're very good, I must say. You keep your little servant character *just* on the right side of ridiculous. I find it rather entertaining just watching your inter-actions."

She merely lifted her brow challengingly.

"I see you want to know why I facilitated this little *tête-à-tête* so soon after our conversation last night..." and he proceeded to discuss the various intrigues in the Cinnaen courts, giving her plenty of information and tips on whom to keep tabs on and whom to avoid.

"Now that I have laid my cards on the table for your perusal, so to speak, I would like you to tell me a bit about our little Gruxhoon problem..." At her carefully blank look, he showed the first hint of impatience at her apparent unwillingness to share information.

"Come now! I am only asking for information that would expand my understanding of the problem facing us—the sharing of which can, in no way, endanger or undermine Pandial interests. Are you not a believer in *quid pro quo*, Ata?" After carefully considering his words, she unbent slightly and nodded slowly.

"I reserve the right to hold back information I believe would be detrimental to the Pandial cause. But I will say as much to you—it only seems fair, seeing as you have not clapped me in irons and *appear* to have a working relationship with Lord Danai..."

"Handsomely said; that suits me down to the ground. Now then—what is the situation regarding the Gruxhoon?" He leant forward, invested. She might have experienced some surprise that he immediately cut to the very heart of her reason for being here, but realised he was much better informed than the rest of the Cinnaen court.

"Well, there have been several minor skirmishes with small groups of Gruxhoon in the south-western provinces. We are unsure where they have come from, but suspect they are somehow landing on our shores via the Debrion Strait."

"But where do they *come* from?" he pushed. She hesitated momentarily, but proceeded.

"Lord Danai believes they originate in the Debrion wastelands and are crossing the strait in small vessels, clearly geared towards avoiding detection."

"And their ultimate aim? Have any been captured and questioned?"

"No. Any attempts at capturing surviving Gruxhoon warriors have been foiled by their traditional practice of 'Enexha'," she frowned worriedly, thinking of this custom of committing suicide before experiencing the "dishonour" of captivity, "the fact that they are so diligent in their practice of this apparently obscure ritual concerns Lord Danai greatly. We have been unable to gather any true intelligence regarding their motives because of that." Lord Iansso grimaced.

"Well, it definitely is concerning... According to historic documents—which have been 'mythologised' in recent years, I should add, the practice of Enexha amongst the Gruxhoon had fallen completely out of favour more than a thousand years ago, well before their expulsion from Áitarbith. Thus, their use of it now, rather than risking capture, indicates a potentially larger plan that needs protecting through secrecy—even unto death."

"That is what Lord Danai has argued, but the Pandial council disregard this by denying the practicality of the Gruxhoon and merely blaming their 'backwards, superstitious and barbaric natures' for this reoccurrence. One of my close friends has fought the Gruxhoon and he says their military prowess is unequalled. Pretty impressive for 'uncivilized louts'... But the council is more concerned about spreading panic and the resulting economic consequences should it prove to be a false alarm..."

"What do they think of the Gruxhoon's incursions? Surely the fact that they are invading Pandi so secretly concerns them?"

"They are, for all intents and purposes, unconcerned by these small groups of warriors. Nor do they see any serious ramifications in the Gruxhoon's mere presence. They are convinced not enough of them exist to ever truly invade the continent, but one or two on the council agree with Lord Danai that it is alarming.

"The Gruxhoon have not been particularly violent thus far, contrary to their historic *modus operandi* of raiding, raping, and pillaging—they only resort to fighting when challenged by our soldiers. The Pandial council feels this proves their point that the Gruxhoon are not a true threat. But I am apprehensive that they are purposely withholding from raiding to avoid drawing attention; this entire endeavour smacks of scouting expeditions. Though for what, I can't fathom."

"Possibly to gauge the current political climate on the continent? To ascertain our readiness to mobilise should we be invaded?" Lord Iansso leant back, looking deep in thought as well as disconcerted.

"So, you think they will invade properly if they find circumstances to their liking? Like the largest kingdoms being at odds—essentially ignoring each other to an extreme degree, retaining archaic discriminatory views of each other to such an extent that they refuse any kind of cooperation? Or the smaller kingdoms being almost exclusively concerned with building their economies, so that they have no military structures in place?" Ata had described the current situation of Àtarbith continent exactly.

"A worryingly accurate summation, my dear, but yes. We would appear ripe for the picking through our lack of cohesion or even basic ability to work together."

"And the Cinnaen stance that the Gruxhoon no longer exist is beyond detrimental to opposing these scouting expeditions—to pre-emptively nipping them in the bud," Ata said bitterly, referring to the belief that was actively bandied about as "official" fact: that the Gruxhoon had been driven into the Debrion wastelands almost a thousand years before, after the last large-scale, multi-nation war where the creatures were finally expelled from the continent for good.

The official line was that they had become extinct in the wastelands, as not even traders who sailed the shores of the Debrion continent (for the precious dye-making snails that lived there) had seen hide nor hair of them in five centuries.

Gruxhoon had passed into obscurity and then mythology in that time, becoming creatures that mothers threatened their children with to force compliance, but didn't believe for one second still existed. The bogeyman under the bed. However, the bogeyman was still very much alive and crawling out of its hidey hole while everyone was essentially denying its existence.

"Well... Sadly, most people won't believe something unless they see it with their own eyes—and sometimes not even then. Now, what is your purpose here at this time? I assume it relates to the Gruxhoon situation?" Ata blinked slowly.

"I cannot tell you that, I'm afraid." Ata kept her tone polite, but final. She waited to see how the spymaster would react to this.

"Hmm, we'll circle back to that in a minute. Is the current Cinnaen minister to Pandi Lord Delsso?" Ata pulled a face, nodding. "Has he been apprised of the Gruxhoon situation?" Ata debated how much to share, finally deciding to proceed with caution.

"As to that, I am unsure of the extent of the information imparted to him, for the Pandial council poo-pooed the suggestion that we inform the Cinnaens. I am aware, however, that Lord Delsso was informed via... indirect means, with the express aim that he communicate this to his superiors here in Cinnae. Lord Danai's enquiries to that effect have suggested Lord Delsso refrained from doing so," Ata cocked her head and lifted her eyebrows questioningly.

"Yes—Danai did contact me; and no, none of the information regarding the Gruxhoon was received through the official channels at this end."

"Only unofficial ones?" she asked tartly, to which he just responded by chuckling.

"Back to my previous question regarding your immediate role here—how about I ask some more specific questions based on concerns I have about your presence, which you can either answer or not, as you prefer?" Ata thought for a moment, then nodded in acquiescence. "Grand! Are you here to somehow undermine the royal family's rule?"

"No, my role is purely observational."

"Observing what, precisely?" he shot back.

"General behaviours and trends..." she saw his sceptical expression and decided to continue, "...It *is* my first assignment, so I suspect it is more a training exercise for me. For surely Lord Danai has more well-placed and established informants here at court already—as do you in the Pandial court." He narrowed his eyes as he weighed the credibility of her statement.

"Perhaps... But I suspect your role might be a bit

more specific than that, if I know Danai's machinations at all. Very well—I am satisfied with this information for now. You may get back to enjoying your half day. My apologies for imposing on your morning off," Lord Iansso smiled at her graciously, rising to his feet and accompanying her to the door.

"You only need to take a right, then two lefts, and straight onwards after that to reach the foyer. Forgive me for my little obfuscation with our convoluted path earlier—I have so few diversions in my old age," he shut the door with a chortle.

Upon turning around, Ata was shocked to find herself face-to-face with Lord Svensso, who leaned almost indolently against the threadbare wallpaper of the opposite corridor wall, studying her impassively. He had clearly been observing her and Lord Iansso's interaction at the door silently. *The sneak.*

She bristled at his perusal whilst simultaneously feeling embarrassed for thinking about their previous interaction. *She should have moved the screen slightly. She should have locked the door. She should have disintegrated on the spot.* In Pandi, nudity was not something particularly shameful or taboo, but in more conservative Cinnae, this was not the case. Also, having been paler than other Pandial and naturally shy because of the intense discrimination shown towards her, Ata was much more body-conscious than her country women.

Lord Svensso's obvious embarrassment during the

whole fiasco made it that much more horrifying to her. She waited for him to address her, but as he continued to study her like an insect under a glass, she felt her temper rising. Straightening her spine, she lifted her chin and opened her mouth to ask him what he was about.

"You... girl!" Ata's head snapped to the side, noting Mistress Mella, the royal housekeeper, bustling towards her imperiously. She had clearly not yet caught sight of the general due to the angle of the corridor, but Ata had immediately transitioned to Anita upon perceiving her presence. Ata turned back to him and addressed him in shrilly ringing tones.

"I'm so sorry... y-your... Your Holiness. I mean, Your Lordliness! I am lost and I don't know where I am... Who is Lord Iansso? I do not know him... and I do not know if I know him, so I don't know if I have seen him— or if I could have seen him. Not knowing what he looks like. Or who he is..."

She babbled breathily, bobbing multiple curtseys and wringing her hands—ostensibly overcome by the grandness of the person in front of her. The conde-scending woman had reached them, reacting in shock at finding Lord Svensso there. She sank into a fawning curtsey—much too low for their respective social posi-tions. *The toadying snipe!*

"My lord, how may I be of service?" she simpered, however, before the infuriating man could respond and give away Ata's almost bizarre about-face, she interjected.

"His lordliness, he asked... he said... he, he was looking for someone called 'Lord Idsso', but I don't know who that is. And I got lost here anyway, so I don't know how to get to the kitchens—Mistress Famenke will be so angry with me..." she bleated, letting piteous tears gather in her eyes as she stared forlornly at the sycophantic housekeeper.

"Silly girl! What is your name? There is no Lord Idsso at court!"

"I think she misunderstood me, Mistress Mella. I merely commented that I was meeting Lord Iansso and could not tarry to give her directions," Lord Svensso interjected; Mistress Mella's eyes snapped to "Anita" and she began to swell indignantly like a bullfrog.

"Do you mean to tell me, that this *impudent* girl had the temerity to ask a *general of Cinnae* for directions to the kitchens," her wrathful tones filled the space, "a servant, who should be undetectable and provide impeccable service, was imposing on a member of the royal court?" Ata felt distinctly annoyed that he had phrased it in such a way as to make her seem even more idiotic than she was aiming to appear.

"Please, Mistress, do not be too harsh on the girl. She looks a good sort, once she's learnt her duty and avoided too much drama. She seems to have the unfortunate tendency to get into situations she isn't particularly able to extricate herself from without assistance," his poker face needed to be punched *hard*, Ata decided. And with that, the horrible man took a perfunctory leave of them, abandoning her to be lambasted by her superior for an unpleasantly long time.

AFTER THAT, Ata settled into her role as palace maid a bit more successfully. Anita somehow managed to befriend quite a few of the other maids through subtle manipulation on Ata's part—chatter, deceits, and small fripperies as gifts (or implicit bribery).

The footmen and male staff were easier to get on side—she either provided them with titbits purloined from the palace kitchens, or else flirted shamelessly. If women were easily 'bought' with gossip and gifts, she thought cynically, then the way to men's hearts was definitely through their stomachs—or slightly lower in their anatomy.

The wall in Ata's room became completely covered by charcoal sketches of her observations, until she was gifted with a set of artist's pencils by none other than Prince Jansso, whom she had surprisingly made an impression on one evening when she had helped the palace nursemaids out of a tight spot.

Being treated to an evening off as a reward by the head cook for doing an excellent job and finishing early with the pastries that were her assigned task (*wonders never did cease, it would seem*), Ata had been looking forward to washing her clothes and spending a quiet night reading.

Alas, disaster struck—one of the junior nursemaids found her on the stairs and practically begged her to take her shift in the royal nursery, as she had made a muddle of her own schedule and had an appointment she could not miss in town. Ata had agreed sweetly as Anita, but swore inwardly as Ata at this inconvenience. All said, it had been a very enjoyable evening, though.

There was another nursemaid, Jansken, who was middle-aged and benevolently firm with the two little princes who romped around their extensive rooms. When Ata had been inexorably drawn into their games of make believe and chase, Jansken had merely smiled as she set out the princes' supper things, waving them off and encouraging them to keep playing.

Six-year-old Jansso, tow headed and stocky, was the intrepid leader of the duo (being the elder), while three-year-old Elsso, white-blond and still baby-plump, was his adoring shadow. They were delightful, appearing to take a shine to their temporary nursemaid. When Ata finally fell into her bed exhausted that evening, she had felt a squeezing sensation in her chest. She thought of her uncle and her cousin, Mindaia, back in Pandi, dreaming of her childhood that night.

In many ways, Ata was content at the palace. Her

assumed identity was so unremarkable, the lack of notoriety so different from what she was used to at the
Pandial court, that she gloried in the relative anonymity
she enjoyed at the Cinnaen court. Here, she was not the
bastard daughter of the dead princess; here she was not
the jumped-up little half breed. True, she wasn't *actually*
herself and sometimes chafed at the limitations playing
such an insipid character placed on her, but all considered, she was truly happy.

A large part of this joy, surprisingly, was derived
from the frequent interactions she had with Lord Iansso,
who insisted she call him Ians when they were by themselves. In many ways, he reminded her so forcefully of
Lord Danai—even physically—that by the end of the
first week she was convinced the two of them were
somehow related to one another.

In other ways, he differed significantly from her
Pandial mentor: Ians was so ebullient and witty, he
almost sparked with life and liveliness while Lord Danai
was staid, with a dry wit and dark sense of humour. He
also always retained a strictly formal relationship and
form of address with Ata, whereas Ians was unconstrained by social restrictions, yet always acted with
perfect manners and respect.

She could almost liken their relationship to that of
an uncle and niece, whereas her relationship with Lord
Danai was categorically that of a respected teacher and
his favoured student. Ians had even assisted her in fixing

her hair, which she attempted to dye by herself and had bungled *badly* shortly after their initial meeting.

A significant length needed to be cut off, but he had smilingly rolled up his sleeves and gone to work. Now, her hair was multihued, appearing naturally light brown with sun streaks throughout, and she no longer lived in fear of a headdress malfunction exposing her as a Pandial spy.

A last and very satisfying positive for Ata in recent weeks was the apparent upper hand she had gained in her (admittedly limited) interactions with Lord Svensso. Following the incident in the corridor which led to a string of punishments for the hapless Anita (and by default, Ata) at the hands of Mistress Mella, Ata could not stand the man.

Unfortunately, he and Ians clearly had a close relationship (similar to her and Lord Danai's mentorship, she supposed), thus she inevitably crossed paths with him from time to time. He also seemed to hold her in some contempt, but acted like an automaton—all rigid and expressionless, with mechanical politeness and all the warmth of an icicle.

Shortly after the dreaded corridor-incident, Anita had been assisting Famenke in serving refreshments at the Cinnaen council meeting, the human ice sculpture being present. When she had noticed his beady eye on her, looking at her with so much intensity—and clearly no positive thoughts—she inevitably wanted to crack his stoic façade. So, she very deliberately crossed her eyes.

The momentary expression of shock on his face had been priceless and well worth the risk of being caught pulling faces in a room full of elevated personages. To add insult to injury, she cheekily winked at him before turning, blank-faced, to Famenke to continue pouring the beverages. She hadn't looked directly at him again after that.

Since that incident, whenever she was in his presence and caught him looking at her, she would respond with some outlandish facial expression—the extent depending on how many others might see it too. She always ensured others were also in attendance, making it impossible for him to address her impertinence. He, in turn, didn't seem to know what to do with this and therefore steadfastly ignored her. Except when she caught him looking again.

Thus, life at the Cinnaen palace went on as it always had—bustling and bursting at the seams with social-climbing opportunists, salaciously scandalous courtiers, the constantly-fawned over royals, and the staff that kept them all fed, washed, and clothed. Despite the constancy of these carryings on, Ata had an odd sense— a pulling at her mind, a disconcerting franticness in her dreams—that something would happen soon to upend this normalcy.

4

BUTTERFLY ON A WHEEL

One mouse, two mice
Three mice, four,
Stealing through their tunnel,
Creeping through the door.

Softly! Softly!
Don't make a sound.
Don't let your little feet,
Patter on the ground,

There on the hearthrug,
Sleek and fat,
Soundly sleeping,
Lies Old Tom Cat.

If he should hear you,

There'd be no more,

Of one mouse, two mice

Three mice, four.

Clive Sansom

The sign Ata had been waiting for had finally arrived. A footprint. Or a paw print, depending on how you defined Gruxhoon and their appendages. As sentient beings with a human-like intelligence, the argument could go one way; however, with their beastly, fanged snouts, tails, and claws, the opposing case could be made as well.

Ata didn't really care about the terminology so much as the fact that a smudged, almost undetectable print had been left in some soft mud in the woods near the palace. It was also complete happenstance that she came across it—being a palace maid meant very little actual time in the outdoor areas surrounding the palace. However, on that morning almost six weeks since her arrival at her temporary abode, Ata had been sent to help Hanson collect recently sprouted mushrooms; she had been "nominated" to assist in collecting (i.e., drawn the shortest straw—literally).

Hence, she had been up before dawn and accompanied the gardener's assistant into the damp and misty woods, muttering internally while Hanson taught her some choice local descriptions of the early morning—

"the arse crack of dawn" and "at sparrow's fart" featured prominently.

She had found a goodly patch of a non-poisonous variety—Hanson had lectured her interminably, which she supposed was fair, considering the consequences should she get it wrong—then wedged herself securely against a massive tree root to pull them up a bit more comfortably (hunching or crouching that early in the morning in the damp was intolerable).

There in the lee she had spotted it; to any other, it would have looked like a smeared animal print, but Ata immediately recognised it and *knew*. The Gruxhoon had been sheltering here, in these woods, not a stone's throw from where the entire Cinnaen royal family slept peacefully. They had tried to erase any signs of their presence, to what end, she wasn't completely certain, but she could hazard an accurate guess. As her role was strictly observational on this mission, she could only wait to see what unfolded—and make her own preparations.

Consequently, Ata took to carrying various 'necessities' on her person at all times, most ensconced in numerous pockets she had haphazardly sewn into the inner lining of her servant's garb at the outset of her assignment. She had been quite proud of her ingenuity, as the pockets possessed concealed openings and were scattered all throughout her voluminous skirts in unexpected places.

Additionally, she began wearing thick leggings and

durable boots beneath her dresses while working and explained away her odd attire (if anyone noticed and commented) by claiming she needed the extra warmth and support because of the recent spate of cold weather, which was even more bitter because of the fact the palace was almost entirely constructed of glass.

With any, more logical questions like: "But why don't you just wear thicker, winter underwear?" she would stare at the questioner with a vacuously quizzical expression until they took themselves off, muttering about nitwits.

She also watched a lot more carefully and tirelessly listened in on others' conversations for any hint of the Gruxhoon's presence—especially those of the gardeners and groundskeepers when they found themselves in the kitchens or anywhere else in her vicinity.

An incomparable source of information in this regard was Hanson, who had befriended her first when she had come here "from the country", and whose freckled face always wore an expression of mischievous glee. Should she ask him about or even hint at something, he would happily expound on all and sundry.

The lad was always eager to win her approval. Based on the signs and her personal experience, Ata suspected he'd had a very unhappy childhood, as he had been taken in by the head gardener—Blenkens—and his wife, away from his own parents who lived a few miles away. From his enthusiasm and apparent hunger for friendship, Ata suspected neglect and isolation in his previous home life as well as some loneliness in his current one.

As their friendship grew, she gifted him her favourite charm from her Enstroi chain—a chain on which all Pandials collected charms representative of their life's wishes, achievements, and disappointments. It was a record of sorts, initially used in a religious capacity for the gods to tally at the end of their lives, but in more recent years had fallen into a cultural practice adhered to by most—even the non-believers like Ata.

Of course, she hadn't explained the keepsake's cultural significance or that it had been wrought in silver for her by her best friend, Kai; she had only described it as the star of Hancin, the guiding star for travellers in Áitarbith. Hanson had been inordinately pleased with the lucky charm and the pun involved.

She liked the jackanapes, for even though he craved camaraderie, he liked to play pranks and had a mocking tongue full of witticisms aimed at those he disliked— Famenke being one of the many. For all that the two resembled each other in terms of colouring, they were constantly at each other's throats like cats and dogs. It was very amusing to witness, but once drawn in, extricating oneself became virtually impossible.

Even though she thought she had concealed her increased alertness well, Ians picked up on it and pointedly asked her during one of their regular consultations in his 'spy parlour', as she had dubbed his secret rooms. Casually and charmingly, as was his way to set his prey at ease, he spoke.

"What has happened that you are so energised, my girl? You're positively buzzing with unspent vim…" he eyed her speculatively. "Could it be that some swain has caught your eye?" Her mind immediately bypassed all the 'reconnoitring flirtations' she was maintaining with the various members of staff and jumped to Lord Svensso and her habit of pulling faces at him. *Ludicrous.* She frowned at Ians.

"Why is it when a woman seems animated or happy, people always assume she must have a love interest?" she asked cynically; Ians leaned forward conspiratorially.

"Because women are by their nature nurturing and constructive compared to men's selfishness and ego, my dear. Thus, whether romantic, familial, or friendly, love is inherently the reason for a woman's happiness."

"I think, *Your Lordliness*, you assign too much inherent goodness to women," Ata responded dryly, thinking about what she was withholding from the old rapscallion. She experienced a brief pang of guilt, followed by worry for his fate should the Gruxhoon's presence prove calamitous. But she shook it off, in the secrecy of her own mind proving her point.

"By assigning superhuman decency to us females, you negate our humanity. Elevating us and putting us on a pedestal removes women from the level of being human, with human faults and human flaws. And by overestimating our morality, you underestimate our potential menace." Instead of looking cowed, Ians looked triumphant.

"Well said, Ata!" he only used her true name when he was feeling very much in charity with her, "I was wondering whether you'd preen in my estimation of women's superiority, agree with me on the face of it while leaving me to my delusions to be exploited in the future, or point out the flaws in my thinking. I see you've gone with the latter option," he smiled warmly, not realising she had also chosen the second option unbeknownst to him.

"Do you think the Cinnaen and Pandial kingdoms would ever be able to reach an accord? That they might somehow work together?" she asked without truly considering her question. She worried Ians's quick mind would ferret out her reason for asking—her concern over and hope for a future alliance between the two nations. He looked slightly pained, yet considered her question before answering.

"I believe the right motivations would allow for some kind of accord. However, under current circumstances, there is too much power and pride on both sides for them to compromise—and that is what a true partnership requires. Compromise with the aim of benefitting all equally. Sadly, that is not a possibility for our two kingdoms, nor has it been in many centuries."

Ians shook his head, but seemed to move on to the next topic, leaning towards her. "Now, would you mind telling me..." and then the door opened creakily to admit that infuriating icicle, the austere automaton, Lord Svensso.

DESPITE ALL ATA'S additional attentiveness, the next few days passed without incident (besides Anita pissing off Famenke with her poor polishing skills) or further signs of the Gruxhoon in the vicinity. Thus, when Ata received a request from Jansken, the younger princes' nursemaid whom she had befriended and become quite close to (or as close as 'Anita' could get to anyone), she readily accepted.

The poor woman had been suffering from a migraine for two days straight and had entreated Ata to cover her shift with the two boys for the evening. Ata happily accepted and wound her way up to the fourth-floor nursery, carrying a tray of warm milk and biscuits as well as a book secreted in one of her numerous pockets for when the boys were asleep.

The ill woman departed for her bed and after some last games, milk and biscuits, and a bedtime story, the two little boys were tucked in and fast asleep. Ata also nodded off in the rocking chair near the fire, cosy and replete.

She was awoken by the sharp sound of breaking glass, followed immediately by hysterical screaming and loud shouts. Ata jumped up and rushed to the large windows which overlooked the stable yard and, further along, the barracks which could be seen in the distance. Usually dark with only a few pinpoints of light for those who had nightly sentry duty or work, the entire world outside seemed to be ablaze.

The stables were burning and the whinnying screams of the horses shrieked across the valley. She couldn't make out the barracks through the smoke, yet the cacophony of shouts from beyond the smoky haze rose up as well, proving that they were also aflame. But it was the presence of figures on the cobblestones below that apprised her of the fact that this was no mere accident.

All the men still standing were fighting huge, hulking Gruxhoon. There were numerous bodies lying around too. As she watched, multiple figures fell before the onslaught of the creatures that then proceeded towards the palace—entering below and moving beyond her view. *They were in the palace.* And they weren't the first ones, considering the sounds that had awoken her; the shouts and screams still echoing through the corridors from further in the building.

The very thing Lord Danai had predicted had

happened: the Gruxhoon had launched a surprise offensive, choosing the most strategic place and group to attack. Even with the substantial number of soldiers a stone's throw from the palace in the barracks, they were woefully unprepared for the might of Gruxhoon warriors. Even a nominal number of raiding groups would be devastating. It would be a massacre, with the entire royal family of one of the oldest Áitarbithian lines falling in one night. Enough of a blow for the Cinnaens to finally set aside their pride and join the Pandial kingdom in an alliance.

Lord Danai had sent Ata to monitor the situation and to bear witness when the inevitable stroke finally fell. It seemed she would witness the fall of a dynasty this night. Her heart quaked at the thought of all the people she had come to know; knowing she couldn't save them from their own, self-imposed ignorance.

"What's happening? Why is there so much noise?" a muffled, high voice asked behind her; she turned to find Jansso sleepily sitting up, his hair sticking in all different directions. Elsso had also awakened, his lip quivering and eyes enormous and tear-filled.

The shouts and cries had become louder, thumps and roars reverberating through the dainty palace. Ata looked at the two children and realised her brief required her to walk out the door and find a safe spot from whence to survey the unfolding events. She must leave them to their fate—it was no choice, really.

"The castle is being attacked and bad people are in the palace. We need to leave the nursery and go and find a place to hide," she whispered urgently as she ran to their closets to grab some warm clothes in case they needed to find shelter out of doors.

"We're not s'posed to leave here. Svens says, no matter what happens, we must always stay and wait for help to come! He will always come. He promised!" Jansso stubbornly said while Elsso had started to wail in fear. Ata hurried to their beds, tunics, leggings and cloaks clutched in her arms. She dumped them on Elsso's bed, scooped up the bawling boy and hugged him to her, trying to quiet his hysterics.

"Jansso—listen to me," she crouched down beside the obstinate prince, purposely omitting his title, looking him directly in the eyes—willing him to listen. "There are creatures in this palace that are like animals. The soldiers cannot fight them properly, and they're coming to try and hurt you.

"I don't want to frighten you, but you must understand: they are coming to kill you. And they won't care that you're small, or that you are children. They only care that you are Hårbørgen heirs. We must leave *now*. We will go and hide somewhere else in the palace; I promise I will take you back to Svens when it is safe. I *swear* it to you."

Indecision warred on the tiny face, but between his fear of the chaos clearly rampaging through the palace and his trust in her, she won out. He nodded and quickly started dressing in his warm clothes while Ata wrestled the frightened Elsso into his things. She prayed she was worthy of Jansso's hard-won trust.

Once done, she approached the door, carrying a quietly crying Elsso and holding Jansso's hand tightly. When they reached it, she spoke softly and with conviction.

"Boys—it's very important that you listen to everything I tell you. You must stay quiet, *no matter what*. I don't care how scared or sad you are. It doesn't matter what you see when we leave this room. And you must listen to my instructions at all times. If I tell you to run, you run. If I tell you to hide, you do it. If something happens to me, I want you to find the closest, smallest, deepest place you can fit into and crawl in there to hide. Try to find somewhere no-one can reach you. Closets or even a lavatory, if you have to. Do you both understand me?"

Her tone and the sounds of the fighting assailing them must have been serious enough, because both princes nodded fervently.

"Good. Now remember: be quiet. We only talk when absolutely necessary." She then shifted their positions so Elsso was straddling her piggyback and extricated a long-bladed knife from its sheath beneath her skirts. Jansso eyed it warily, but dutifully took the hand she offered him in a tight grip and followed her out the door.

The corridor was dark and appeared empty. She supposed the fact that the nursery was so high up meant it was taking the invaders longer to reach it than other parts of the palace. Creeping along the passageways, Ata inwardly lamented the lack of any furniture to provide cover.

They immediately entered the nearest access to the servants' passages, as Ata suspected their narrowness and apparent unimportance would dissuade the Grux-hoon from traversing them. This appeared true until they stumbled over the corpse of servant girl on the landing between the third and second floor. Her throat had been shredded with so much force she had almost been decapitated.

"Don't look, boys. *Don't look*," she whispered force-fully, trying to follow her own advice. She recognised the girl as one of the housemaids who liked to gossip about boys and stole an extra helping of dessert after dinner some nights. She tried to avoid looking at her vacant eyes and slack face.

At one point, they had to return to the main corri-dors, as the servant passageways didn't run parallel to all, meaning servants were required to traverse the public spaces to reach the next set of concealed passages. She gently pushed the panel aside, peering through the narrow slit to the large, luxurious corridor beyond. It was poorly lit.

She listened carefully, but could only hear the sounds of devastation further away. *Not here.* Hastily pushing through the panel, she tried to rush quietly to the next hatch to a set of servants' stairs.

This hallway was a wide one—a main thoroughfare of the palace—and it was littered with bodies. Ata warned the boys not to look, trying to do the same herself whilst simultaneously attempting to determine whether there were any Gruxhoon bodies. She noted a few, but the overwhelming majority were soldiers with some servants or courtiers here and there.

As they moved down the silent corridor, she heard a rhythmic thumping sound, accompanied by small squeaks, getting progressively nearer. They quietly and warily approached what in the dark appeared to be a pile of bodies moving back and forth. It turned out to be something even more sickening. Ata recognised the red-gold curls, even in the gloom, Famenke's headdress cast aside somewhere unseen and the girl completely dwarfed by the large Gruxhoon body on top of her.

Ata felt horror and rage in equal measure, her own trauma from so long ago roaring back across the years. She let go of Jansso's hand and disengaged Elsso from her back, handing him to his brother, tightly pressing them against the opposite wall and indicating they needed to be quiet. She then purposefully turned their faces to the wallpaper, away from the atrocity being committed a few feet away.

Approaching surreptitiously, she quieted her footfalls. She needn't have bothered—the beast was blind and deaf to everything except its own monstrous gratification. She couldn't reach the thing's throat, as it was so tall she would have had to climb up its torso to reach the neck.

Thus, she made sure she struck with lightning speed and precision, aiming for its kidneys and then for the rest of the torso. She didn't even pay attention to how many times she plunged her knife into it, but when it had stopped writhing and slumped over, she flourishingly slit the thing's throat for good measure.

Shoving it off the prone figure beneath, her gaze met Famenke's wide eyes in her tear streaked, bloody face. The woman lay and stared at her, apparently stupefied so Ata bent over, pulled her dress back down over her legs, and grasped her hands, hauling her into a sitting position.

"I know this is difficult, but you need to get up and come with us. It's not safe here and I have others depending on me, so I can't stay with you. We can deal with what has happened later. Now—we must survive," she whispered urgently, hoping the indefatigable senior servant was still in there somewhere and would heed her words. Famenke's eyes blinked multiple times, then she heaved herself to her shaking legs.

Ata promptly grabbed the two boys, Elsso taking his position on her back once more while she instructed Jansso to hold firmly onto one of her inverted pockets. Then, supporting the limping Famenke, they made their way towards the entrance of the servants' stairs. When they reached the hidden panel, Ata ushered Famenke through, but just as Jansso entered, a spinechilling bellow sounded a few feet away. Ata swung around, throwing Elsso through the doorway as she watched a Gruxhoon storming towards them.

It was bloodcurdling, having a seven-foot Gruxhoon charging you on its haunched, beastly long legs, its claws fully extended to shred, to decimate. From one beat to the next, Ata's training kicked in. She froze. Waiting until the last possible moment, when the Gruxhoon had committed to its final assault motion, she dove downward and sideways—its outstretched claws missing her by a hair's breadth.

She immediately spun around, now a few feet behind the creature as it crashed into the portal—too large to pass through without some manoeuvring and with too much momentum to halt its breakneck progress. Ata didn't hesitate; she ran full tilt towards the massive back, half-climbed it and at the apex of her flight, stabbed down into its flesh with all her might. Then she let gravity have its way, using the knife as a support and dragging it down with her full weight.

Her momentum was enough to force the blade

through sinew and flesh before it caught on something and halted with a meaty jolt. By the time the creature had grasped the damage she had wrought—a fatally deep furrow running down from its shoulder to its mid-back—she had realised she couldn't dislodge her weapon from its flesh and released it.

The wounded warrior turned, but Ata was already waiting with a short sword scavenged from one of the fallen soldiers on the floor. It bellowed at her in rage and attacked, using its long limbs to try and grab her rather than charging as before, ready to rip her apart with its superior strength. Ata used all her survival instincts and combat skills, slashing at its claws and arms, dancing one way, then the other.

She realised that the Gruxhoon relied heavily on its immense strength and deathly claws but did not know the finer nuances of sparring on an equal footing. Its wound rendering it less able to use its immense strength, as well as inhibiting its long reach meant Ata's understanding of duelling gave her the upper hand.

Every opening in its defences she exploited; within a few seconds, she had carved its torso so effectively that ribs were visible through the dripping gashes. The substantial wound in the Gruxhoon's back must have finally resulted in its inevitable conclusion, merely delayed by the creature's adrenaline, its movements slowing.

Ata struck viciously, stretching and slashing

upwards, splitting its neck precisely and ending the fight. The corpse dropped heavily to the plush rug carpeting the hallway, twitching slightly a last few times. The entire encounter had only taken about two or three minutes, but she felt as though she had been fighting for hours.

This had been the first Gruxhoon she had killed in combat (not counting the despoiler she cut down earlier). She looked down at herself; she was drenched in the stinking reddish-black blood of the Gruxhoon and in the darkened hallway it looked like she had been covered in tar. A stain. Impossible to clean off.

Almost in a trance, she grasped the handle of her knife—the knife her uncle had gifted her so long ago—and wrenched it out of the carcass with a wet suctioning noise. Her head snapping up, she glanced down the corridor alertly before rushing to the access of the servants' entranceway.

Famenke waited there, the boys huddled in a dark corner off to the side, heads bowed and clutching each other desperately.

"Let's go." And they proceeded as they did before, traversing corridors of corpses and rooms full of ruin. When they heard fighting or sounds of movement, they found an alternative route. Ata would not risk it, even if it meant avoiding other survivors. They finally made it to their destination—the kitchens.

The floors were a bloody mess, scattered with body

parts and internal organs. Elsso tucked his tear-wet face tightly into Ata's neck and Jansso did the same in her skirts. Their feet squelched through the meaty pulp till they reached the larder at the far end of the kitchens, still locked as per the dictates of the head cook.

"Famenke. Can you stay with the boys for a moment and comfort them? I'll be back in a second." Ata kept her voice calm, worried by Famenke's dead-eyed stare and lack of response. To her relief, the woman started doing as told, taking Jansso's hand from Ata's skirts. Little Elsso just huddled next to a tin of peaches and cried quietly as Famenke patted his back in a semblance of comfort.

Ata then went back out to the darkened kitchen; she had spotted the remains of the head cook, who kept the key to the larder on chatelaine at his waist. It took some searching; the jumble on the kitchen floor was various people, but Ata eventually found the set of keys amongst some entrails.

She took a few candles, lighting one from the last remaining coals in the fire before returning to the larder. Unlocking the sturdy door, she ushered them all inside and locked them in. They then proceeded to settle in, with some sacks of wheat repurposed as a sort of bed for the boys to sit and lie on. Elsso had fallen into a troubled sleep, twitching and whining at intervals, but Jansso just sat and stared stoically ahead of him in a sort of trance.

Ata let them be, starting to undress quietly and efficiently. Her headdress had been lost during one of the skirmishes, so she shed her torn servant's dress, noting that it was covered in the blackened blood she had been soaked in when she had slaughtered the two Gruxhoon. Beneath she wore her thick leggings and sturdy boots. From within the many pockets of the crumpled dress, she withdrew a dark tunic and donned it, touching her Enstroi chain that she had taken to wearing around her waist beneath her clothes.

Lastly, she removed all the bits and pieces from the rest of her pockets, placing them in a light bag beside the two boys. As she tied her hair back, Ata crouched where Famenke had collapsed next to a shelf of dried goods.

"Famenke. Do you need any kind of medical care? Have you been injured?" the servant turned blank eyes to her, shut them firmly and shook her head. Her hands were clenched tightly into fists. "I am really sorry to do this, but I need to go out and find Lord Svensso, or whoever else can take the princes to safety. We are not really safe here; it is only a temporary hideout. If the palace falls fully—and I don't doubt it will—a few sturdy Gruxhoon could break down the larder door within seconds."

"Gruxhoon." It was the first word Famenke had said since they had found her that evening, surprising Ata.

"Was that what those... *things*... were? Fairy tale monsters?" she seemed incensed, almost unbelieving.

"Yes. But they are as real as you and I are, as their presence here proves. But we don't have time to discuss this—I need to leave you here so I can find help. We need to think of the boys," Ata let the urgency she felt enter her tone.

"Are you capable? I realise... you are not... that you might not be fully able right now, after what happened. And I am *truly* sorry. There will be time for sympathy and recovery later, *but only if we survive this*." Famenke had started shaking her head vehemently. Ata sighed inwardly at having to now convince her, but was completely dumbfounded by Famenke's reply.

"I'll go. You must stay with the princes."

"What? That's insane! You can barely speak—you've been attacked and are in shock. No. I am much more capable right now and should go. You'll stay and protect the boys, and—"

"Don't you understand? Yes, you're more capable than I am right now; I can't protect them or make decisions that will benefit them. The way you fought that thing..." her eyes snapped back to Ata's face, her usual incisive gaze back.

"You are no housemaid from the provinces—you have military training. And the way you speak and carry yourself isn't at all like the Anita I have known..." She kept looking at Ata with those same sharply perceptive eyes with which she had critically watched 'Anita'. Then she heaved a sigh, the deadened look returning.

"Who or what you are makes no difference right now. Our survival depends on working together; in that, at least, we can trust each other. As you say: the rest can wait till after. So, you—whoever you really are—who can actually physically defend these children and make lucid decisions must remain. I will go and find help. Sneaking is well within my current abilities... if I don't return, then you'll at least be able to continue with a chance at surviving."

Consequently, Famenke left the larder on silent feet and Ata settled in beside the boys to wait. Once she joined them, she lifted Elsso's head onto her lap and Jansso cuddled up to her, apparently falling into a light slumber. Thus, she waited.

It was in this position, some time later, that a deliberate and repetitive scratching noise at the larder door drew her attention. Her immediate alertness must have registered with the two princes, because both instantly sat up, their movements sharply furtive—reminiscent of hunted woodland creatures. Ata took her knife and purloined short sword, approached the door, and quietly placed her ear against the aged wood.

5

HERE BE MONSTERS

IN THIS SHORT LIFE THAT ONLY LASTS AN HOUR
HOW MUCH—HOW LITTLE—IS WITHIN OUR POWER

EMILY DICKINSON

The scratching continued, a repetitive pattern to it, and Ata decided to risk trying something she had never done before. Once, when she had been bored and the weather had been horrible, she had browsed through abstruse texts in the Pandial Royal Library and Archives.

Kai and Mindaia had just declared their feelings for each other, necessitating sixteen-year-old Ata to act as their alibi, accompanying them to hidden, unpeopled locations and then having to somehow give them their privacy for courting. Therefore, she was huddled amongst the tomes on obscure Commanding lore for hours at a time.

Most of it was dry as dust and very boring, but she soldiered on, trying to avoid listening to the giggles and whispers from a few rows along. *She loved them both, but they were a pain in her arse.* There, she came across an interesting premise, written in the margins of a pompous academic's overview of Commanding history.

The writer suggested that Commanding had always been done without any extensive preparations; no rooms, chalked graphs, nor symbols were used. Instead, the Abled had been so skilled and controlled in their casting that they could shape their intent within their minds and Command a script thus—off the cuff.

Ata had never entertained the notion that she would even consider trying it, but in this moment, where certainty of what was on the other side of the door was a matter of life and death for them all, she took the plunge.

Loosely raising as much Commanding energy as she could, she contained it with her concentration on what she wanted to do. She started chanting the instructions (a simple script she put together in her mind) on what she wanted the energy to allow her to access: a view of what was outside the door. And, just like that, she "saw" the outside of the larder door as though she were standing in the kitchens.

It was the merest glimpse before all the energy had

been drained in a flash—this type of casting clearly took much more energy than the prepared kind—but it was enough for her to know what to do.

Unlocking the door swiftly but quietly, she opened it and hastily tugged the boy hunched at her feet through the portal, shutting and locking it again just as quickly. Hanson looked worse for wear, his hair matted with blood and singed close to his scalp on one side. Soot smudged his face and hands while his clothes were covered in ash. Yet it was his expression that was the most changed.

Gone was the sneaky smile and humorous twinkle. He looked as though he had aged years, the eyes staring from his face those of an old man, hobbled by life's brutality. His nose sat askew on his face, badly broken, the blood pouring down his chin and onto his tunic.

Ata didn't think, she just reacted. She pulled him into an encompassing hug, holding onto him tightly even as he thrashed and wriggled to throw her off. Slowly, his fighting ceased, only to be replaced by full-body shivers, the sounds of his sobs muffled against her chest, but still clearly audible in the confined interior of the larder. She saw Jansso and Elsso remain on the flour sacks, but they were watching the exchange between her and Hanson closely.

Finally, Hanson's sobs and shaking subsided, his body hanging limply from her embrace. She loosened her grip and looked down into his face. He still looked as he did before, but some of the soot had been washed away in rivulets by his tears.

"I'll need to set your nose, Hans," she stated matter-of-factly; before the boy could even voice a response, whether agreement or argument, she had seized his nose between her fingers and tugged it forward *hard*. Immediately smothering his cries against her torso once more, she stroked his head tenderly as he regained control. Again, once he was quiet, she allowed him to step back from her.

"Do you have any other injuries?" at his dubious, half-accusing stare (he had clearly not forgiven her for fixing his nose yet) she whispered sternly: "You need to tell me if you're hurt! We can do our best to fix you up before Mistress Famenke returns. She's gone to fetch help so we can all find a way to get to safety. But if you're injured, you might slow us down, which would endanger us all. Be brave—don't risk someone else's life because you want to avoid a little pain now."

He gave her a rueful look, then slowly nodded, lifting his soot-covered hands so she could see them properly in the light of the single candle. Ata drew in her breath sharply.

"I burned them trying to help a mare. She was trapped in the stables when they were burning, so I let some of the horses out. It was too hot, and I couldn't get to the others... This mare... she was on fire, but her legs were all broken and she was burning to death. I tried to put out the fire on her. I burned my hands doing it," Hanson lifted his raw hands with their gaping and blackened wounds that Ata had taken for soot before.

"She just lay there and screamed... Her skin was all burned away—black and s-sticky. And it quivered. She shook. She sh-shook s-so much, but I couldn't help her!" his voice rose in a wail, necessitating Ata to shove her hand over his mouth and grip his head tightly while trying to avoid his minor wounds.

"You need to be quiet, Hans," Ata whispered urgently, "I know... I know you've seen things tonight. Terrible, horrible, dreadful things. Things you would never have been able to imagine. But we'll get through this and the things will eventually go away. Now, I'm going to let you go so I can clean your hands. Do you understand?" His eyes glistened hugely above his smashed nose and her own hand, but he nodded none-theless. She bade the princes scooch over and seated Hanson on a bag of flour. Finding some wine used for cooking, she made him soak his hands in it. Big tears rolled down his cheeks, but he didn't make a peep. She nudged him in solidarity and spoke softly to him to try and distract him from the pain as she also proceeded to clean the cuts and burns on his head and neck.

"What happened to you? How did you know to come here, to the larder?" she asked him. He proceeded to tell her how he had awoken in Master Blenkens's cottage (where he stayed) on the outskirts of the grounds, to the sounds of the attack. At first they thought it was an accidental fire, but when they had rushed to the stables to try and help fight the flames, the Gruxhoon had been there, killing all the people they could lay their claws on. Hanson spoke with a deadened voice, describing the chaos and mutilation.

"They... they looked like things from the hells. I didn't know things like that existed. Like demons. They killed Master Blenkens. Tore him into pieces. He yelled at me to run and hide when he saw them. So I did. In the stables that weren't on fire. But the fire got to them too..." he sniffled and almost wiped his face with his wine-soaked hand, but was stopped in time by Ata. "They killed all the people. Scratched and ripped them apart. Even the soldiers that came. They died so quickly. It was so ugly."

He went quiet for a while, then seemed to shake himself. "I told you about the horses. I *had* to help. The monsters killed all the people, but they left the horses to burn to death. All of them had gone by the time I freed the horses. Then my hands were burnt... I was really scared. I didn't want them to find me. I saw them kill some of the cadets who came to help—just boys like me. They didn't care."

"I'm really sorry you had to see all of that, Hans," Ata spoke quietly as she gently smeared plenty of honey onto his hands, "What happened then?" She needed to encourage his talking to keep him present.

"I hid in the kitchen garden. In the small tool shed built against the wall. It's so small, but I fit inside. I... I heard when they attacked the kitchens. I couldn't move. I couldn't help," he looked at her hopelessly and whispered shamefully, "I didn't *want* to help. I was so frightened."

"You couldn't have done anything to help the people in the kitchens, or at the stables, Hans. As you said: the Gruxhoon are monsters. They are killing machines and you are only a boy. You did the best thing by hiding. Because now, you're alive to help us," and she made meaningful eye contact with Jansso, who had been eavesdropping shamelessly.

Ata had tried to shoo them to the side and speak softly enough with Hanson that they wouldn't be exposed to anymore horrors. But it was impossible—she gave it up for a lost cause. The two boys had seen too much already; she couldn't protect them from that any more than she could from Hanson's words. Luckily, Elsso had passed out again, huddled against his brother. Jansso, to give him credit, realised what she meant and nodded enthusiastically.

"How can I help you?" Hanson asked belligerently, some of his old spark coming back in his recalcitrant response.

"You already have by bringing us information. Otherwise, we would be sitting here, not knowing what happened. We only heard things—we didn't see anything. And it's really important to know as much as possible. So, you are being immensely helpful," Ata tenderly wrapped his hands in torn shreds from her discarded petticoats. They were good, solid cotton, and the cleanest part of her ensemble after their arduous journey through the massacred palace. Hanson accepted her reasoning, nodding slowly. "How did you come to find us? Were you just taking a chance, or did you know we were in here?"

"I came out of the shed when I heard whispering in the kitchen. I was scared, so I took a long time. I found Mistress Famenke at the kitchen door leading back to the palace. I begged her to stay with me, but she said she couldn't. She told me to come here—that you would let me in. I was... *so, so* happy when she said that you were alive," the boy hiccupped pathetically with this acknowledgment and Ata's heart squeezed.

"I promise, I will stay with you, Hans. You will come with us when we leave the larder. I will look after you," and she hugged him tightly. He was as clean and as cared for as she could manage under the circumstances, so she rocked him back and forth for a while, which he childishly and shamelessly took comfort in until his breathing deepened and he seemed to nod off. She put him down and Jansso, with a maturity far beyond his age, manoeuvred so he and his little brother lay snugly beside Hanson. Two princes and a garden boy all cosied up together. Before she could withdraw completely, Hanson eyed her sleepily.

"You're different from usual... cleverer. Sharp. It's a bit scary," he mumbled with a slow blink.

"I'm still me," she whispered back, "just a bit more competent. And we are definitely still friends; that hasn't changed." To which he nodded faintly, accepting her words at face value.

"Okay." He drifted off between one breath and the next; Ata withdrew closer to the door.

And so she waited for Famenke to return.

As time passed, she heard a whispered exchange between the young gardener's assistant and the little prince.

"She's your friend?" Prince Jansso sounded quite impressed, if somewhat doubtful.

"She gave me this..." Hanson had clearly indicated in the affirmative and was showing the prince something small tied around his neck. The charm she had gifted him weeks before. Some more time passed without a sound.

"I'm so scared," the younger acknowledged in a low whisper.

"Me too. But, if you want..." a long pause, then Hanson continued, "you can borrow my charm. It brings good luck. It's Hancin, the night star that guides all travellers."

"Are you *sure*?" Jansso sounded awed by this temporary guardianship that had been bestowed upon him. Only silence came after, followed after some time by the deep breathing of sleeping boys.

Another hour passed (Ata had started counting and making knots in a pilfered drawstring from a storage bag to keep track of the time) and she began to worry about their precarious situation.

If her calculations were correct, Famenke had left them over two hours ago. It should not have taken that long to bring help, which left only a few likely scenarios: a) the castle had fallen, and/or b) Famenke had been killed. Either or both of these hypothetical situations meant that no help was coming and that she and her charges were essentially sitting ducks. Fish in a barrel, with no opening besides one to escape from and that option was becoming less likely by the minute.

Thus, she came to the conclusion that they needed to flee the palace altogether. Hopefully, the kitchens would be overlooked by the Gruxhoon who had captured the palace, and as most of the Gruxhoon would be inside the building, they might be able to slip through their ranks on the palace grounds. A plan began to take shape, so she wakened Hanson (which, in turn, roused both princes).

"Hans, could you find your way from the kitchen gardens, through the orchards, into the woods? Without any light, that is?" she whispered urgently. Hanson frowned in consternation, clearly not liking the path her thoughts were taking. "Maybe... but, we mustn't leave here! Mistress Famenke said she'd bring help. And she *always* does what she threatens," the last part dryly. Ata shook her head.

"It's getting later, which means it's early morning. The sun will be rising soon, and then we won't have the cover of darkness to facilitate our escape. I would rather we make a run for it and be able to return, should the palace be under Cinnaen control, than sit and assume it will be, only to be stuck here with the Gruxhoon breaking down the door, which, incidentally, is the only way out of this larder..." she watched as the boy came to realise she was right, the sag of his shoulders her sign of his acquiescence.

"In the beginning, I'll go first, Hans. Elsso will be on my back and Jansso will hold onto my belt. You must bring up the rear and watch our backs. Once we leave the kitchen gardens behind, you'll take the lead and I'll hold onto your shoulder. You'll watch the front while I watch our backs," and after a momentary pause, she handed him her prized knife, keeping the filched short sword for herself. Hanson's eyes were large, his expression dubious as he eyed the long-bladed knife.

"It's my favourite weapon and has saved my life many times. It was a gift from my uncle after somthing very bad happened to me, allowing me to always be able to defend myself afterwards," she encouraged him. He looked at her, nodded, then took the knife gingerly. She quickly showed him how to hold it.

"Avoid a confrontation if you can; just warn us and we'll try to escape them. They are fast, but so are we. Physically, we are no match for them. But if you are up against one, remember: you are small and agile compared to them. They are large and strong, but their swiftness and dexterity are hampered by their size. Dodge and dive, if you must," Hanson didn't look convinced, which was when Jansso decided to add his two cents.

"She knows how to fight them. She killed two of the Gr—, the uh, G—... the things," his earnest little voice piped up. The awed look on Hanson's face when he turned his attention to her once more made her feel awkward. The ability to decimate and destroy, to take a life brutally, should not elicit such looks of admiration.

"Let's go. Here, Jansso, take our bag of tricks and carry it over your shoulder. And remember: always be quiet. Even when warning about a threat you see—just tug on me." All three little heads bobbed emphatically, making her feel briefly overwhelmed by the sheer responsibility she had—that of preserving three young lives. Then she shook it off and they exited the larder.

The kitchen was just as they had left it: poorly lit, messy and mucky with the remains of the kitchen staff. She didn't pause to give the boys a chance to dwell on it, making their way to the door that led to the kitchen garden. It was very dark outside—no sign of the dawn yet, thank the gods.

Eerily silent, it made the hairs on Ata's neck and arms rise. The unnatural quiet was disconcerting. The kitchen garden, though compact compared to other parts of the palace gardens, was still big enough that she couldn't see its entirety under the current lighting conditions.

They proceeded cautiously and quietly, Ata's senses on hyper alert for any slight sound or movement. When they reached the edge of the thick, creeper-covered wall, they halted, ensconced in the hanging vines blackened by the shadows.

She peered around the wall's edge, letting her eyes scan the open ground they had to cross before reaching the somewhat dubious "cover" provided by the orchard trees' shadows. Here, the moonlight was not impeded by the tall palace's shade; it shone silvery bright—potentially starkly exposing.

Ata huffed in annoyance and looked toward the edges of her range of vision. Dark, murky, and mysterious. She thought to try and use Commanding in a similar way as before, but immediately realised she both lacked the energy to fuel and the strength of will to contain the working. They just had to risk it.

Moving forward, once they were exposed in the open area, she rushed noiselessly across the space until they reached the inadequate shadows cast by the fruit trees in the orchard. Just as she allowed a momentary sense of relief, she saw the moving shadows at the tree line of the woods on the far periphery to their right. Her eyes widened in horror as she realised the sheer number of Gruxhoon that had been noiselessly and (almost) motionlessly waiting. And they must have spotted them, for they were moving swiftly in their direction.

"Run!" she hissed as quietly and urgently as possible; she shot off down the lane of fruit trees, dragging Jansso behind her. She still tried to remain as quiet as possible, but it was no use, really. They were being charged by an overwhelming number of Gruxhoon, so unless they found the perfect hiding place, they would be slaughtered. There was no outrunning these beasts.

She sensed Hanson a few feet behind her but could not afford to look back. Glancing to the sides, she was relieved to note there were no creatures parallel with them—they were ahead of the charge. *For now*. Then her eye strayed upward, to the limbs of the fruit trees, when an idea struck her.

She looked at the trees in the woods that ran alongside the orchard, the left in particular—*they were so close*. The branches of those trees were sturdy, the canopies dark and sheltering, virtually impossible to penetrate, especially in this darkness. She slowed slightly, just enough to grab Hanson's hand and drag him sideways, towards the woods, bringing them to a screeching halt before a thick trunk.

"Up!" she wheezed, slinging little Elsso as high into the boughs as she could, then grabbing Jansso and doing the same. Last was Hanson (a bit more difficult) and once he had a grip and could climb higher himself, she scrambled up as well. "Higher!" she frantically hissed, dragging the two princes with her, completely disregarding any damage she was causing them in the brutal ascent. Broken bones could mend; a corpse stayed dead. "Stop!" she snarled breathlessly, as she sensed more than heard the encroaching approach of the Gruxhoon.

The boys went completely still, Jansso awkwardly half-balanced with a toe on a branch whilst clutching another much higher up, arrested mid-heave. Ata soundlessly wedged her shoulder under the boy's bottom, acting as a perch. She held her breath, watching and listening. Then she saw them. Gruxhoon. Groups, multiples, more than she had ever seen together streamed past the tree, below them. After a few seconds, the stream slowed, the Gruxhoon no longer running but appearing to be looking around, hunting their prey that had been *just* out of their reach a few seconds ago.

The four of them hung there, not daring to breath. Not daring to think. The Gruxhoon milled beneath them, grunting and garbling at each other in their language, clearly mystified and looking for their quarry that had magically vanished. Ata's heart lurched when one of the Gruxhoon lifted its snout high and sniffed loudly, clearly trying to scent them. Her lack of energy be damned, she shut her eyes and constructed a Commanding script with all her will to escape and her need to survive; a casting, the main aim of which was 'secrecy', 'hiding', 'camouflage'.

With the energy draining from her dangerously fast, a momentary light-headedness assailed her. But as she watched, the Gruxhoon looked up, right into her eyes. Elsso stiffened next to her, clearly seeing exactly what she was. But the Gruxhoon's eyes, reflecting an animal-istic gold in the sparse moonlight within the woods, moved listlessly from side to side. It still appeared to be looking for them. Grunting in apparent annoyance, it turned to its pack and snorted and growled some more, clearly conveying their lack of success. Then they slowly moved away, out from beneath them and further into the woods to try and track them.

Releasing her Commanding, Ata felt herself grow cold as though all her blood had been drained from her suddenly. She struggled to hold onto her perch while her vision went bright at the edges and then abruptly completely white as her ears filled with an overwhelm-ing, thundering roar. She sensed, as though from far away, small hands tugging and clasping at her extremities.

When she came to, the whooshing sound in her ears

abating and her vision returning, she saw she had been kept in the tree by her three charges—Elsso and Jansso clinging to her arms and Hanson clutching at her leg while she dangled precariously like a sack of potatoes from her limbs. The children had saved her.

Ata stiffly and awkwardly clambered deeper into the tree, finally settling on the thickest branch high up, joined on the adjoining, slightly slimmer limb, by the two princes. Hanson wedged himself in a hollow in the tree trunk to her right. She pulled a length of rope from the bag she had carried.

With some manoeuvring, they all managed to tie themselves either to their branch or the trunk. Signing to them that they would not speak, Ata then indicated with simple gestures that they should rest in the tree till later. All of them nodded and did just that.

Ata was completely exhausted from her run and the two impromptu Commandings she had performed, the last of which had apparently shielded them from the Gruxhoon's senses. So effectively did it work that they had been rendered invisible though they were mere feet above the Gruxhoon's heads and their commander had been looking straight at them... She dozed off as well.

Suddenly jolting awake, Ata felt as though something was *very* wrong. She had momentarily forgotten where she was, but in a split-second recalled all that had happened. She heard the birds chirping in the woods which, with the slight rise in temperature, told her that sunrise wasn't far off, although the woods were still dark as the night around her. She looked sharply around, seeing both Elsso and Jansso asleep next to her on their branches, sagging slightly and being held up by their rope belts. When she looked sideways towards Hanson, her heartrate doubled. He wasn't there. Jerking her entire body so she could look downward, she saw him climb nimbly down the tree—now at the lowest branches.

"Hans!" she whisper-shouted, noting the two princes started awake at her words, "Don't climb down! Come back!" Hans couldn't have truly heard her, but he must have also sensed them, because he looked up—his face full of scrapes and cuts, some that she had doctored and some new from their hasty ascent. Making a face at her, he tried to convey something meaningful. She shook her head frantically, showing she didn't understand, and started untying herself so she could go after him and stop his foolishness.

He made an exasperated waving off motion with his bandaged hands, then jumped down to the ground. He bent down and rifled around in the grass and leaves there, moving further from the trunk till he was almost at the edge of the wide tree's cover. Rising abruptly, he triumphantly held her long-bladed knife aloft in victory. He had clearly dropped it at some point, either during their flight or while they slept in the night, and had gone down to retrieve it. *Risking his life, the foolish child!*

He gave her a wide, ebullient smile; the same kind he had worn before this horrible night. Suddenly, he was seized from behind and hauled into the arms of two Gruxhoon.

Ata stuffed her fist into her mouth to keep from shrieking, feeling the two boys next to her whimper slightly, the surprise attack catching them all unawares. Luckily the birdsong covered their whines. Hanson, to his credit, didn't make a sound, even when they snatched him. Ata watched in horror, frozen by indecision. Immediately after Hanson was grabbed, about twenty Gruxhoon came into view beneath them, all focused exclusively on their prisoner.

She couldn't do anything—she would give away their position and though clumsy and ungainly, Gruxhoon could definitely climb a tree to extract their victims. Failing that, they would chop it down with as little trouble. She couldn't risk the two princes being discovered, for there was no way her interference with what was happening below could save Hanson. She was completely helpless.

One of the Gruxhoon who had been holding Hanson let go while the other got a better grip on him, holding him in such a way that his body dangled while he was only supported by his shoulders. The one who had released him now placed its clawed paw around the boy's neck and then it began to speak.

"Human... where... are... where... are... the heirs...?"

though badly articulated with snorts and grunts in between, it was clearly speaking. Ata was dumbfounded. Never, in all the centuries of human-Gruxhoon interactions, had Gruxhoon been able to communicate with humans using *language*. They were clearly intelligent life forms, with complex social and cultural structures, but they were so other compared to humans, so monstrous in their slaughter of people, that no-one had ever thought to bridge the communication gap. Until now, it would seem. The Gruxhoon had overcome the disparity and were using it to ferret out children to kill.

"If... you... tell... tell... us... you... will... you... live..." the thing continued. Ata caught her breath, heart careening wildly. A part of her willed him to give in to save himself. Even if it meant her and the princes' discovery and death. She didn't want him harmed.

Hanson remained silent, his face so pale and his eyes so big, he seemed to be in a state of shock and physically unable to speak. However, when the commander turned to the side to grunt-speak to one of its fellow creatures, Hanson's eyes rose to their position high in the tree and locked onto Ata's, the bleakness in them too much for her to bear. There was so much in his eyes, her friend who was staring at her as he faced death... or sacrificed their lives for his.

6

A TANGLED WEB WOVEN

"WILL YOU WALK INTO MY PARLOUR?" SAID
    THE SPIDER TO THE FLY,
"'TIS THE PRETTIEST LITTLE PARLOUR THAT
    EVER YOU DID SPY;
THE WAY INTO MY PARLOUR IS UP A
    WINDING STAIR,
AND I HAVE MANY CURIOUS THINGS TO
    SHEW WHEN YOU ARE THERE."
"OH NO, NO," SAID THE LITTLE FLY, "TO ASK
    ME IS IN VAIN,
FOR WHO GOES UP YOUR WINDING STAIR
    CAN NE'ER COME DOWN AGAIN."

"SWEET CREATURE!" SAID THE SPIDER,
    "YOU'RE WITTY AND YOU'RE WISE,

How handsome are your gauzy wings,
    how brilliant are your eyes!
I've a little looking-glass upon my
    parlour shelf,
If you'll step in one moment, dear, you
    shall behold yourself."
"I thank you, gentle sir," she said, "for
    what you're pleased to say,
And bidding you good morning now,
    I'll call another day."

Alas, alas! how very soon this silly
    little Fly,
Hearing his wily, flattering words,
    came slowly flitting by;
With buzzing wings she hung aloft,
    then near and nearer drew,
Thinking only of her brilliant eyes,
    and green and purple hue—
Thinking only of her crested head—
    poor foolish thing! At last,
Up jumped the cunning Spider, and
    fiercely held her fast.
He dragged her up his winding stair,
    into his dismal den,
Within his little parlour—but she
    ne'er came out again!

AND NOW DEAR LITTLE CHILDREN, WHO

MAY THIS STORY READ,

TO IDLE, SILLY FLATTERING WORDS, I PRAY

YOU NE'ER GIVE HEED:

UNTO AN EVIL COUNSELLOR, CLOSE HEART

AND EAR AND EYE,

AND TAKE A LESSON FROM THIS TALE, OF

THE SPIDER AND THE FLY.

MARY HOWITT

That woman was here again. The Pandial spy. And Ians had just taken up with the little bitch over the past fortnight as though they had known each other all their lives! Thick as thieves, they were. No, worse than that. *Opaque as spies.* Whispering in corners, sharing meaningful looks. Having meetings, like the one he had just inadvertently interrupted.

No-one else would have noted anything amiss between the apparent trainee palace maid and the "retired" royal adviser who now pottered around with his plants and his books. But Svens was attuned to intrigue in all its shapes and forms; he needed to be if he wanted to protect his father's legacy, to guard his siblings and the very kingdom itself. Threats were everywhere, within and without, and he had to be on his guard. Had to anticipate their moves. *Had* to be infallible. Thus he noticed the interloper's slow but sure envelopment into the secret fold of palace life.

When he entered Ians's private parlour, Svens had stopped short on finding a grey-clad palace maid snugly situated in his usual armchair in front of the tiny fireplace, Ians in the one opposite, leaning toward her in a conspiratorial fashion.

The "former adviser" (i.e., current spymaster) kept a set of very modest rooms in the Hårbørgen palace, highly appropriate for his cover of retired non-player on the contemporary political stage. They were always untidily busy. Books, potted plants, and various knick-knacks seemed to sprout up everywhere your eye fell. No surface was uncluttered, no wall uncovered. So very odd when one considered the painstakingly neat figure Lord Iansso presented to the world at large. Svens had no clue how Ians knew where anything was in that mess.

But those rooms were for his tinkering, the façade he showed the world—a doddering eccentric's haven. *These* rooms were his covert ones: just a parlour and a bedroom, comparable in size to the ones occupied by senior servants and just as obscurely situated within the palace's warren-like space. Only a select few even knew these chambers existed, fewer still what they were for.

The two figures had glanced up upon his entry,

making him feel oddly awkward under their scrutiny—
blue eyes and green piercingly perceptive, taking in
every little detail about his appearance without seeming
to do so. *Fucking spies.* Svens eyed them stoically and
said in his most colourless tone:

"My apologies. I'll wait outside till you're done." The
Pandial's look was carefully blank as she turned her face
to the fire, dismissing him as though he were of no interest. A flash of her expression when he had barged in on
her on the first night they had met came back to him; a
momentary smugness flared (she had not been so blasé
toward him then) before he suppressed it soundly. *Not a
fair thought; that aberration should be forgotten. For both
their sakes.* Predictably, Iansso oozed charm and immediately set about remedying the slightly uncomfortable
moment.

"No, my boy. Don't go. Pull up a chair and join us.
Anita here has a pressing question she has been wanting
to ask you."

"I do?" the spy responded in consternation, her
expression quizzical. Svens tried not to notice her voice,
as for some reason it affected him strangely. Since he
had heard its low, husky rhythms, the merest hint of a
southern, clipped quality to it, he had avoided listening
to her if it could be helped.

Luckily, in all her interactions outside these rooms,
she adopted the breathy, higher-pitched tones of a

Cinnaen country girl, as that was the character she was playing. But he had overheard her speaking shortly to Ians on a previous occasion, unguardedly, and he had been shocked and dismayed at his reaction to her true voice.

"Yes. You mentioned it the night we all officially met..." Ians's utterance held some kind of emphasis Svens couldn't gauge.

"Oh!" she looked uncomfortable for a second, then turned her eyes to Svens, the sharp intellect and almost challenging gleam in them disconcerting. He was so used to seeing them dreamily vacant on the very few occasions their paths crossed in the palace generally. "I wanted to ask you, but haven't had the opportunity over the past few weeks: how did you know I wasn't Cinnaen that first night? At the dinner?"

She meant when he had first noticed her when she had served at the intimate royal dinner he had attended. She thought he had somehow deduced she was a spy, or at least a foreigner, when he had looked at her. But it was both more and less complex than that. Less complex in that he *hadn't* suspected she was a spy or even an outsider. The fact of the matter was she had drawn his attention, but in a more complicated way than mere prurient interest. It had felt like he knew her when he first clapped eyes on her, or more accurately, it had felt like he recognised her from somewhere.

Only after the dinner had he and Ians met in the old

man's parlour and eventually decided to sniff out the possible spy; Ians because he sensed she was not authentic, but Svens more because he hoped questioning her would trigger his recognition. His hopes had not come to fruition, even when he had gotten a *most* thorough view of her. Identification had still eluded him and it continued to. Svens had wanted to utilise their agents in Pandial to find out who she was, but Ians's lack of support or interest scuppered that initiative, and, frankly, stirred Svens's suspicions and enmity toward her.

"It wasn't anything overt that I noticed... I must admit, it was more Ians's obvious interest in you that piqued mine. Nothing more, I'm afraid," he lied smoothly. He wouldn't acknowledge the strange thrill that had passed through him that first time he had clapped eyes on her. She was already a potential danger without realising she had some kind of hold over him. And even worse, she clearly didn't respect him or his position, going by her ridiculous, childish practice of pulling faces to undermine him. For some reason it left him flustered and awkward; most unlike his usual, controlled self.

"Oh. Well, then I needn't have worried all this time," she said, pointedly addressing Ians. "That, at least, is a relief. Thank you for putting my mind at rest." This aimed at Svens, who didn't deign to respond. There was a long pause where no-one spoke;

Svens knew he was behaving boorishly but he was hoping his subtle refusal to be drawn into a discussion would indicate to the woman that she should depart. He was always punctiliously polite in all situations, but when it came to his mentor, Ians, the usual protocols that had constrained him his entire life just slipped away.

Their easy comfort with each other—the only such relationship he had ever had—had been a lifelong life-line and anchor to him, the bastard prince who was no prince and never could be. Not that he had ever desired titles and prestige, but fully belonging would have been a nice addition to a childhood and adolescence of rigid control, endless tutoring, as well as the expectation of dedicating his entire, illegitimate existence to his father's dynasty.

"Well. I think I should be going. The kitchen cabinets won't scrub themselves..." she stated into the silence, rising energetically from the chair and striding past Svens, who turned to open the door for her. As she passed him, she turned her head slightly and, *the cheeky baggage*, pulled a wry, clownish face at him.

He made to speak, but she transformed before his eyes as she passed through the door. Her gait became languid, her entire manner airy and whimsical. A distinct blankness smoothed over her features while her sharply sparkling eyes became abstracted as she passed out of sight. This was her servant-persona, the character she played; playing them all for fools. He resented being made a fool of.

"Now, that was very unlike you, my boy. So sullen and unsociable! You are sometimes a bit brooding, I grant you, but never in the presence of others... Your protector's façade is too entrenched for that. But look at you now! All but telling the girl to take her leave," though Ians's words were accusatory, his tone was light and insinuating. "I wonder *what* could have gotten into you?"

"I don't trust the woman, despite your assurances—which, by the by, are not much in the way of assurances, seeing as all you have given me is 'I can vouch for the girl'. Nothing more. No other information regarding who she is and what her business here is! What I do know is that she is Pandial and playing a role to insert herself into the very fabric of my and my family's lives. She could be an assassin, for the gods' sake!" Svens usually tried to contain his stronger emotions, but gave vent to them now to the one person with whom he felt he could.

"You overstate the situation, Svens. I understand you are driven to keep your family safe and to maintain control over the security of the state; this is my endeavour as well. And believe me when I say: this girl is no threat to us."

"But—"

"No. It is simple. If you trust me, then you can trust

what I tell you: Ata is no danger to you, the House of Hårbørgen, or the Cinnaen state. Unequivocally I tell you this," a steely note had entered his mentor's voice; though the assurances somewhat appeased Svens, Ians' slip brought him up short.

"'Ata'? That's her name?" The brief, pained expression on Ians' face showed he had not meant to divulge that piece of information. There and gone in a second; the manipulative scoundrel could just be playing games with Svens, who couldn't be sure his chagrin wasn't a charade.

"Yes. But I'd thank you to keep that information to yourself. She would not be happy to know I had disclosed that to you."

"Is that a typical Pandial name? I have never heard it before..."

"Nor will you. It is unheard of, at least in the last few hundred years. As far as I have been able to find out, it is an archaic word from one of the many minority languages that were subsumed into the Pandial kingdom over the years. Depending on the dialect, it can either mean 'gift' or 'ancestor'; but the records are old and poorly kept, so I am speaking under correction."

"You've put a lot of thought and research into a mere name of a minor player, if your previous assurances are to be believed," Svens let a mildly accusing note enter his voice. Ians just gave him a roguish wink, tapping the side of his nose.

"Be that as it may, and as fascinating as I find discussing the lovely Ata—as you clearly do too," Svens frowned in annoyance at Ians's teasing, "I think we should move on to your briefing on the current state of our military affairs?"

So, they discussed the Cinnaen military training programmes, current structures, and the subtle shifts of power and authority within the upper ranks. Lord Bransso, the general of the western armies of Cinnae and Svensso's military mentor, had recently been pushing for the entire Cinnaen army to go on prolonged manoeuvres in the Uurgonna Mountains to the east of Cinnae. Svens had insisted on retaining a battalion of soldiers at the barracks positioned between the Cinnaen capital, Canø, and the Hårbørgen palace.

"I feel disloyal for standing so firmly on this... Lord Bransso has supported me throughout my military career. He even took the shameful business of my promotion to general with aplomb, when for all intents and purposes, the king had made a nepotistic appointment in me," Svens looked at his loosely clutched fingers. King Olefso had been such a contradiction, never giving any attention nor affection, yet openly and proudly acknowledging his paternity. Never interacting directly as a parent with Svens during his childhood and adolescence, but constantly promoting him throughout his military career.

Even Svens' army career had not been of Svens'

choosing (although he had flourished and valued it); the king had ordained his entry into the military academy, irrespective of Svens's wishes. He had long ago known and accepted that he was a piece on his father's chess board. A rook or a knight; there merely to facilitate the protection of King Olefso's legitimate family and their reign. Even though he knew his rise through the army's ranks was inevitable due to the king's interference, Svens still worked himself to the bone to be worthy of those positions of power.

When he had been appointed as a general (much too soon, considering he was merely twenty-two at the time) Svens had been mortified. Thus, he had requested a meeting with the then-general, Lord Bransso, laying his cards on the table and openly admitting he was underqualified but that the position had been forced on them all (as all the commanders understood). However, he stated that he would place himself under the auspices of Lord Bransso to learn and to train—to eventually be competent in and worthy of the post.

Lord Bransso had accepted. Hence, it was determined that he would command the eastern armies whilst Lord Bransso would retain command of the western armies. Almost five years on, he liked to believe he had risen to the occasion, developing his skills in command and military strategy. Now, though, with his and Lord Bransso's first marked difference of opinions, Svens felt a little at sea.

"He is an honourable and reasonable man, most of the time. He will respect your differing from him if based on solid reasoning. It is always better to be prudent, to have enough troops to foil a coup or a sneak invasion. It's necessary. You did well, Svens," Ians nodded.

"You believe the Pandial might initiate a sneak invasion?" Svens enquired sharply, but seeing Ians's meaningful expression, snorted derisively. "Oh, I see. You're referring to that ludicrous fairy tale we've been fed by one, lone voice in your intelligence network... Even our own ambassador to Pandi disregards the claims because *their own council* does!

"No, I'm sorry, my friend, but here is where I still differ from you. Bring me proof, bring me evidence I can see and I will personally apologise to you. But until then, do not bring me legends and myths, whispered about amongst spies and cutthroats." He tried to ignore the disappointed look in his mentor's eyes; he could not be expected to prepare for an attack by creatures that no longer existed and perhaps never did, as far as they had probably been enhanced by poetically exaggerated re-tellings.

"I am sorry you feel that way and pray to the gods you will not come to regret this stance you have taken, my boy."

"I can only deal with so many potential threats; some I have to disregard due to their improbability...

Unfortunately, I must leave you now, on this low note. I need to meet with my commanders, after which I have an appointment with the queen," Svens tried to keep any emotion from the last part of his statement. A meeting with the queen rated *very* low on his list of favourite things to do. But needs must when the devil drives...

"Then I wish you good luck and a pleasant day further. Until we meet again," Ians stuck out his hand to clasp Svens's in the traditional 'working man's' or 'soldier's clasp'. No bows or pomp between them, just camaraderie based in equality.

SVENS SPENT a pleasurable lunch with his comrades in arms and closest friends—Hjarl Ransso Helmsson, a lieutenant colonel, Lord Blÿnsso Erksson, a captain, and Samsso Blensson, a lieutenant. He had grown up with these boys (all nobles except for Sams), attending the military academy alongside them. Together, they had endured countless hours of drills on the training grounds and hazing in the barracks. They had fought ambitious pirates on the northern coasts in the same squad and now navigated their careers in which, essentially, they were on different rungs of the 'chain of command' ladder.

Svens had ordered Rans's battalion be the one to

stay behind from the large-scale manoeuvres Lord Bransso had decreed, which in turn ensured that Blÿns's company remained, under which Sams's platoon fell. They discussed the incidents amongst their troops and the movements of the majority of Cinnae's army, as well as each other's personal lives.

"So, tell us, oh reticent one! Any lady loves on the horizon for our great general?" Blÿns, the joker and lothario of the group, was deep into his cups as it was his day off, while the rest of them drank well-watered wine sparingly. Svens's propensity for playing his cards close to his chest, especially when it came to his romantic relationships, irked Blÿns in particular, so he often light-heartedly mocked and tried to embarrass Svens.

His mind immediately flitted to the Pandial spy. *Ata.* But he summarily set aside the thought of her in any other capacity than the one she currently held, and not even that. She was a dangerously lovely reptile, a snake, like the bright little venomous serpent that wriggled beneath the muddy surface of the riverbed, disguising its deathly beauty to entrap some of its prey, then slowly revealing its iridescent scales to mesmerise and feed on the remaining victims.

He seemed to fall in the latter group, knowing what she was and *still* falling under her spell. Yet he would not fall, because he could not—would not—relinquish the burden placed on him by his father. And thus, he had to stoically resist this outlandish fascination with *that woman*. Svens chose to go with his usual, bland response to his friend's question.

"No-one I would tell you cretins about. Especially you. I like her too well to introduce her to such a reprobate, for you will only try and steal her away and embarrass us all with your efforts."

"Oh! You cut me to the core, friend! I would never try to undermine you with your girl..." and Blÿns twitched his eyebrows villainously. They all laughed heartily at his playacting, listening to his long-winded and well-wined rendition of his newest romantic interest who had sent him packing in a comical series of ridiculous events. Svens smiled at his friends' antics, feeling a deep sense of appreciation for their light-heartedness amidst all the pressure he experienced in the rest of his life. As they were leaving, Rans, his closest friend, walked next to him.

"I know we were messing around before, but I am curious: how's Lord Bransso treating you after your objection to his plan for the entire army to go on manoeuvres?"

"He's unreadable as always, in his effusively blustering way, but he agreed to my suggestion without any objections of his own, so I would assume he has accepted my reasoning. I... don't trust the calm we're experiencing right now. Even the pirates on our northern shores haven't been raiding along the coastlines. I hate to say it, but something's got to give…" Svens made a face.

"And where do you think the threat will come from?" Rans asked seriously. Svens pondered for a moment, but already knew the answer.

"Pandi, without a doubt. I hesitate to say it, but their military is the most expansive on the continent right now. Based on the numbers and descriptions of their armed forces we've received in reports from our ambassadors and spies, the Pandial are more than equipped to fight a war. Maybe even launch an offensive, who knows? Which is why I completely agree with Lord Brasso's initiative to send our army on manoeuvres. But we need to do more; we need to swell our ranks, make it more attractive for non-aristocrats to join."

"I know. Just look at Sams's situation; he is the best of us all—the hardest worker. Yet, because he has no birth, he can't progress beyond a lieutenant's rank. Not that lieutenant is anything to sneer at, but if you have no possibility of advancement for the rest of your career, it makes you re-evaluate your career choices… And other, non-aristocrats will no doubt consider this, should we start canvassing for more troops," Rans wasn't particularly vocal; he was similar to Svens in that they tended to be observers rather than talkers. But he clearly felt very strongly about this issue. Svens sighed.

"I will work on a proposal to put before the military council; we must somehow make the Cinnaen armed forces more merit-oriented... The Pandial armies do not differentiate between baseborn and aristos *at all*, for the gods' sake!"

"Yes, but they have some very strange traditions and practices in general. I wouldn't lead with that fact when you do the pitch to the council," Rans nudged Svens's shoulder jokingly. Just then, Blÿns and Sams joined them, the former loud and obnoxious due to over-imbibing at the tavern they had eaten at. Winding their way through the streets, they finally arrived at the barracks.

"I must say goodbye here. I have a meeting with the queen and a few council members," Svens said, clasping each of their forearms in farewell.

"Give my love to her. She is a sight to behold but a termagant of the first waters," Blÿns hiccupped.

"Have some respect. She is the mother of the crown prince and the co-regent," Sams intoned stiffly, to which Blÿns made a negligible motion of apology before stumbling off to find a bunk to sleep of his drunk. "His mouth will get him into some serious trouble yet," Sams observed, shaking his head.

"Not if his other parts get him there first—did he tell you when he had an affair with a blacksmith's wife and then tried to make up to the self-same blacksmith's sister?" Rans responded.

"I honestly prefer not to know what he gets up to. It means I can claim ignorance should I need to bail him out of a jail cell," Svens said, pinching the bridge of his nose in mock-exasperation. He then left, waving to his friends, dreading the meeting to come with his father's widow.

"You cannot be serious!" the queen lambasted Svens's latest proposal. "What would that *cost*? Expand the army, you say? I cannot fathom the reason for such a thing..." she turned to Lord Haaviso, her co-regent, in appeal. "Lord Haaviso, what is your opinion here? Surely you do not think this is a necessary objective for Cinnae at this time?" Svens felt his irritation surge but maintained an impassive expression. He was ice; nothing could get his blood up. Especially not anything that this harpy could say. Lord Haaviso seemed to consider his stance, then said:

"I would like to hear Prince Tensso's thoughts on the matter before I give mine," and he waited expectantly on the teenager's response. Svens actually thought his cousin's approach was a sound one; Tensso would have to rule soon—five years would go by in a flash, so the boy needed to practice his statecraft and decision-making before then. This real-world challenge was an ideal one for him to exercise his logic.

Looking at his half-brother, Svens tried to view him objectively. The boy was tall for his age, golden-blond, and fit. He had trained part-time at the military academy since he was ten years old and was a fair hand with a sword. Svens knew this because he personally sparred with the prince twice a week; the boy had a lot of potential. Though currently inconsistent as most teens were, Tensso had good work ethic. Unfortunately, his academic studies did not progress apace with his physical training. The young future king struggled to concentrate for long periods at a time, detesting reading and writing. For these reasons, his tutors despaired of him and his academic skills were severely limited for someone in his position.

Svens knew Tensso felt the immense pressure of being the heir to the Cinnaen throne, as his half-brother had, once before, expressed a lack of desire to be king to Svens in confidence. Of course, that could just be adolescent contrariness. Svens realised he was unable to view Tensso impartially; he was too emotionally invested in his half-brother's life, having watched him grow up and even having had a hand in his training. Theirs was a good relationship, the boy being eager for his older, illegitimate brother's affection and respect despite his mother's animosity toward the king's eldest offspring, whom she despised. Now, he looked slightly alarmed at being required to voice an opinion.

"I... well, isn't it always better to have a stronger military presence? It is there to protect us in case of danger," he hesitantly put forward.

"And what danger, pray tell, could threaten Cinnae, the greatest kingdom on the continent of Áitarbith?" Queen Nelni snapped at her son in irritation. The boy withdrew into his shell. Svens felt indignant and attempted to support his brother who had been trying to support him.

"The very nature of unforeseen dangers is that they cannot be foreseen. A true strategist plans a system that could address multiple scenarios, however unlikely. It is anticipatory." Svens tried to keep his voice mild and respectful, but the queen's nostrils flared and her eyes snapped fire.

"You would beggar the state coffers for *maybes* and *what ifs*? Your point of view is clearly that of a simple soldier's, not a state leader's. But then, your training and role have never been those of a leader's. Lord Haaviso?" her voice was a blade that pierced the room, demanding the duke's response. Lord Haaviso paused.

"Though I commend Lord Svensso for his suggestion, as well as his reasoning, unfortunately the royal treasury cannot finance such an expansion of the army at this time. I would also point out that the element of meritorious advancement through ranks, though morally admirable, would require a major overhaul of current norms and precedents that have stood for centuries. Not a minor task in the least. I would suggest that we shelve the expansion of the Cinnaen armed forces till the next fiscal year, when we can revisit its feasibility..."

Svens crushed his disappointment and frustration mercilessly within himself, nodding dutifully to King Olefso's ducal nephew. He respected Lord Haaviso, but also found him to be a typical politician—overly-cautious and unprepared to dip into state funds to pay for necessary structures and social upliftment.

"Well said, Cousin," Queen Nelni stated triumphantly, snapping the cover shut on the brief outlining Svens's proposal. "Thus, I close this meeting. Have you taken all the minutes?" she turned to her secretary, a nervous little man with fussy moustaches who had been scribbling furiously throughout. At his nod, she rose grandly and swept from the room with a brusque farewell to them all, only pausing to patronisingly call her son to join her on her evening promenade through the palace gardens. The boy slouched in her wake unenthusiastically as she quit the meeting room.

Svens bowed respectfully to Lord Haaviso, Hjarl Janssen, and the two other lords in attendance, before leaving the room as well. He needed to retire early, as he had a long ride the next day to report the result of this meeting to Lord Bransso where he was camped halfway to the Uurgonna Mountains. Svens could have sent a missive via a courier, or even commissioned one of the Abled to send word to the general, but he felt honour bound to relay the information himself. He therefore made his way to the barracks about a mile from the palace, where he always preferred to sleep.

Much later, Svens was rudely roused from his slumber, in the early hours, by choking clouds of black smoke and the hysterical shouts announcing they were under attack.

7

A BAT OUT OF HELL

Death, be not proud, though some
    have called thee
Mighty and dreadful, for thou art
    not so;
For those whom thou think'st thou
    dost overthrow
Die not, poor Death, nor yet canst
    thou kill me.

John Donne

Humble pie was not something Svens enjoyed eating, but in this case, he would happily sit down and dine with relish in Ians's presence. *If only it meant they survived this night.* Svens seriously questioned their ability to survive; most of the palace inhabitants wouldn't. He knew this for certain when he caught his first glimpse of their attackers.

Gruxhoon. Mythical beasts that had apparently been driven from the Áitarbith continent centuries before and that no-one believed still existed. *Except for a handful of Pandial and your mentor.* Facing this overwhelming attack now, within their own palace, Svens was tempted to chastise himself but resisted. There would be time for that—maybe—after this, but now it would be ineffective and indulgent. Not useful to survival. His first priority should be his siblings. He hadn't even bothered dressing properly, only halting briefly to grab his longsword and a baldric with short sword and a few daggers attached.

In the corridor of the officers' quarters, he bumped into a bleary-eyed Blÿns and a tightly-strung Sams, the former wearing only leggings and clutching his short sword, while the latter was dressed in stringently correct uniform.

"Who's attacking?" Blÿns had hissed, hair sticking in all directions and red-rimmed eyes darting all over as they hurried along the corridor.

"Gruxhoon!" Sams snarled, his usual cool slipping under these tense circumstances.

"What? That's impossible!" Blÿns snapped.

"I saw it with my own two eyes through the

windows. The palace stables are on fire, the barracks are burning too, and there are beastly creatures all around, slaughtering everyone in their wake!" Sams shouted, the sounds of fire and screaming becoming louder as they ran down the stairs toward the front door of the officers' barracks. "Believe me, I couldn't believe it at first, but I have read the stories like everyone else; these *things* that are attacking us look just like the descriptions in the histories!" Before Blÿns could respond, Svens grabbed both by their forearms, blocking their path and halting their headlong progress just inside the door.

"I believe you, Sams. You should too, Blÿns—it'll make for less of a shock when you step outside. That said: we need a plan..." his two subordinates straightened, their gazes sharpening. "We need to split up. Rans was at a meeting with the city council last night and slept at an inn there, so he's not here to help deal with this.

"You two: go through all of the barracks and organise the soldiers into their squads. Send the cadets to safety —the woods, the city, I don't care, just out of the way. As each squad of soldiers is ready, mobilise them; send them to the various points in the area, some to quench the stable fires, others around these barracks to secure the area. But most importantly: send some squads to the palace *as soon as possible*! We need to protect the royal family!" Both nodded emphatically, saluted, then split off into different directions once they exited the building.

Svens made his way to the palace, trusting his friends to acquit themselves well of their tasks. He was running across the training grounds in nothing but a tunic and leggings—no shoes or armour—when he encountered his first Gruxhoon. There were three of them perched on a pile of dismembered cadets, by the look of things, waiting outside the doorway of the training quarters for the rest to come running into their expectant claws.

Svens could make out some boys cowering inside the door, but the fact that the roof above their heads was on fire meant that they had a choice: wait and have the burning building collapse on them or exit and meet the three monsters lurking with talons and fangs at the ready. Their compatriots' corpses beneath the beasts' feet gave a good indication of what fate awaited the lads. Svens didn't even pause in his run, changing direction slightly and storming the creatures at full speed, exploiting the fact that their attention was locked on their hapless prey inside the billet.

Taking a running jump at the one nearest, he raised his longsword overhead, and as he reached the zenith of his leap, brought the sword down with all his strength, decapitating the thing. The creature remained standing, its body momentarily unaware it had been dealt a death blow; Svens's forward momentum and descent meant he just missed crashing into the corpse, but still managed to get his leg obstructed by its collapse. He lifted the sword again, raising it sufficiently to skewer the next Gruxhoon through the torso, although the sudden loss of impetus jarred his arms and the weapon stuck into the beast's torso like some grotesque kebab. Svens immediately relinquished his hold on the hilt, grabbing his short sword from its sheath and stepping back quickly.

By this point, the two remaining Gruxhoon were aware of his presence; although the second was mortally wounded, it still had the wherewithal to fight Svens, along with its completely unharmed partner. He immediately slashed sideways at the unwounded beast, hoping to wing it so he could even the playing field. It parried his attempts with its razor-sharp claws, springing forward in its own assault.

Svens retreated speedily, grabbing a dagger from his belt in his left hand and using both weapons to block the Gruxhoon's two paws mid-swipe; he then smashed the creature in its snout with his head, shoving forward with all the strength in his frame. It stumbled backwards into its partner that then fell over, pinning itself into the dirt with the tip of the sword protruding from its back. The unbalanced, unharmed Gruxhoon brought its body forward on its legs, as well as bringing its arms forward that had been spread to try and regain its balance, but Svens had already lunged with his own weapons at the ready.

The sword entered the Gruxhoon's right side, piercing between the ribs, sideways and in an upward trajectory vivisecting its organs; the dagger plunged deeply into its neck. Svens whipped it out immediately to unleash the plume of arterial blood from the well he had created as he stepped back out of its reach. The creature stood briefly then slammed into the earth next to its headless compatriot, black blood pooling outward fast and drenching the soil. The remaining Gruxhoon was wriggling half-heartedly where it was pinned to the sod, looking macabrely comical.

Svens dispatched it quickly with the longsword he retrieved from the corpse of his first victim, the so-called 'bastard sword' having been his favourite since he could wield it in his late teens. He felt a deep kinship with the weapon and used to call it his "brother in arms", an epithet his friends had found amusing. Once again it had not let him down. About ten cadets were standing behind him, staring at the bodies spread out in front of them—those of their classmates and the Gruxhoon.

"Cadets! You need to retreat into the woods immediately," Svens ordered as he picked up, wiped, and re-sheathed his weapons. "You do not try and engage the enemy. These creatures are more than capable of killing you. As you can see." He swung his arm to encapsulate their peers' remains.

"Go, now. Use the shadows and break into smaller groups to draw less attention to yourselves. Dismissed!" the boys' training kicked in, superseding the horror and awe of their experiences thus far; they saluted before jogging off in twos and threes towards the woods. Svens continued toward the palace, eyes constantly scanning for any more Gruxhoon.

HE HUSTLED SOUNDLESSLY down the corridor on the way to his brother's and sister's rooms on the second floor. Not much time had passed since he had killed the three Gruxhoon, but he had not taken the most direct route to the palace. Much as it pained him to sneak and avoid the hotspots of fighting, his first priority was to extract the royal family from the palace to remove them from danger. Once he accomplished that, he would return and fight these destructive invaders, these creatures of the night.

He had used a secret entrance to the palace via the drains, an unpleasant but effective route. His siblings would all have locked themselves in their rooms as per his standing orders. Hopefully the sheer number of rooms and, unfortunately, the large number of courtiers and staff in the palace would keep the creatures busy and make it easier for the princes and princess to escape particular notice. It was their only chance for survival until he could get to them... He noticed sounds of movement further down the corridor between Lenna's and Tensso's rooms. A potential risk should he try and find his brother; he would first check on Lenna, then proceed from there.

Finally, he reached Lenna's apartments and, once he'd confirmed the dark hallway was free from any Gruxhoon, knocked rapidly on her door, using the coded rhythm he had made the children memorise since they were young. Seconds passed; they felt like years. Then the door opened a crack and a narrowed eye peered at him suspiciously before the portal was thrown open fully. Lenna slammed into him as he quickly manoeuvred them into the room, shutting and locking the door immediately. He pried Lenna off of him and held her at arm's length.

"Where have you *been*?" she keened, her face red and splotchy from crying.

"I had to make my way from the army barracks. I came as fast as I could," he soothed in a low voice, looking around her. "Why are you alone? Where are your ladies? Your maid?"

"All my ladies were at a social evening when the attack happened. I chose not to attend, but told them to go... When the shouting and smashing started, I sent Henda, my maid, to find out what was happening. She didn't come back..." it looked like the waterworks were about to start again, so Svens tried to forestall it with more practical considerations.

"Is your brother in his rooms?" she looked uncomfortable, then shrugged.

"I don't know... I think so? He might have gone to a soiree with that awful Lord Ernso."

"Alright. I will go to Tens's apartments now; you must stay here till I return. Once I have you both, I'll stash you in a safe room and go and fetch Jansso and Elsso... If Tens isn't in his rooms, then I will come and get you and we'll first go and get the two boys, then hide you all in the safe room. I will go on to find Tens from there." Although she seemed to disagree with his proposed plan, she wisely kept it to herself.

He made sure to shut her inside her closets before departing down the corridor to her brother's abode. The commotion he had detected earlier at the landing of the main staircase had subsided, but he carefully slid along the furthest wall and kept his passage as noiseless as possible. The same coded knock at his brother's door was met with no response, so Svens forced the door open as surreptitiously as he was able and stepped into the darkened chambers.

It looked as though a whirlwind had passed through them: furniture was upended and thrown into corners, the heavy drapes had been torn from the railings here and there, and the floors were squelchy and sticky. A sour smell permeated the air, as well as the oppressive stench of smoke. Svens shook his head. Although the room appeared to have suffered in the attack, he had seen enough rooms after a debauch to know the sights and smells. There had clearly been some kind of mindless drinking party here earlier, but apparently none of the participants remained.

At that very moment, a subtle sound near his head alerted him to the movement it accompanied and he ducked just in time to avoid the swinging bottle. The attacker didn't have much control over his limbs, so when the bottle reached the furthest point his arms could reach and he didn't release the makeshift weapon, it pulled Prince Tensso off his feet and into a sprawl of limbs on the wine-soaked carpet. He didn't even have the wherewithal to untangle himself and lay cursing and grunting at Svens's feet. *What a mess.* Svens leaned down and lifted his half-brother off the floor, holding him upright by the scruff of his neck. Tens's eyes were bleary, his complexion pale, and his hair a sweaty mess.

"What the fuck are you doing, sneaking in here! I'll have your neck for this!" he bellowed, then finally managed to look up into Svens's face, a silly grin immediately breaking across his drunken countenance. "Svensh- I mean, Svens! Why are you here?" he genuinely seemed puzzled by Svens's presence.

"The castle is under attack, Your Highness. I am here to extract you and your siblings and take you to a place of safety," Svens's words were stiff and formal; he tried not to be disgusted by his half-brother's state of intoxication (or tried not to show his disgust, at least).

"What? No... it, it can't be that bad? I'm sure it's just a falsh, um, *false* alarm?" Tensso looked aghast and very young suddenly, despite his inebriated state.

"Believe it. We don't have time to discuss this—the longer we take, the worse your and your siblings' chances of survival... Please come with me, Your Highness," and Svens took his arm and drew him to the doors of the ruined rooms.

"Is it really that bad... Brother?" Tensso asked tentatively, but Svens ignored the informal address and nodded peremptorily. "Is Len okay?" Tensso continued as Svens stuck his head out of the door to ascertain if the coast was clear. He didn't deign to respond, just took the prince by the shoulder and dragged him along to go and find his sister.

As they approached the previously precarious area, the staircase landing, Svens turned to the prince and signed that they needed to be completely silent. The drunken fool nodded earnestly and then proceeded to trip loudly over his own feet at the most indefensible point—landing with a loud *whoof* on the floor.

Instantly, reverberations of scrambling from the level below rang up the staircase. Svens snatched the boy up by his collar and swung them both into the doorway of the nearest set of rooms, praying the ridiculously wide door casing would conceal them sufficiently.

He shoved his hand over the sod's mouth, effectively silencing his gasps, then also quieting his own heavy breathing. The sound of large bodies rushing up the stairs was thunderous, but the stifling silence once the strides halted on the landing was a thousand times worse. Warning the prince with a murderously stern look, Svens released his face and placed his hand on the hilt of his short sword, ready to draw and slash should their poor hiding place be exposed.

The grunting snapping sounds of the Gruxhoon's communication amongst themselves went on for a while, Tensso's eyes going comically wide at hearing the beastly noises, his first "interaction" with the monsters. The creatures seemed to come to some kind of conclusion, then slowly retreated down the stairs. Svens was not fooled, shaking his head at Tensso to show they would not be leaving their hideout yet. So they waited... and waited.

After what felt like an age, Svens finally indicated to the prince that he would check that the coast was clear. Speedily sticking his head around the panel, he saw the landing was devoid of any large shapes. So was the staircase as far as his view permitted. Shoving the boy ahead of him, he kept a tight hold on the clumsy fool and sped toward Lenna's apartments.

When they got to her room, the door hung ajar, the hinges broken out of the wall; Svens already sensed she was no longer inside. He burst into the space, but a quick search proved his initial suspicions correct: Lenna was gone.

"Where is she?" Tensso asked dazedly, staring at the dark and empty chambers.

"I don't know," Svens grunted, trying to control his own rising worry over their sister. She had just been there a short while before. He shouldn't have spent so much time coddling a drunken Tensso.

"What do you mean 'you don't know'!" the prince's voice rose hysterically; Svens grabbed him and yanked him roughly closer.

"I. Don't. Know. And if I hadn't been off chasing your sodden arse, having to mollycoddle you in your rooms because you are fall-down drunk when the palace is under siege, then perhaps I would have her safely with me!" his voice rose in a scathing whisper, the first time he had ever spoken to his pampered brother with anything except patience and respect. The boy's eyes widened.

"Do you think they got her? Is she dead?" Tensso whispered, horrified. Svens released him from his grip.

"I don't know." Svens took a few calming, deep breaths, then levelled stanch eyes at his brother, "But I will find her. I swear it." For some reason, his dire, almost threatening words brought a look of relief to Tensso's face. And reverential trust. "Let's get you to the safe room, Your Highness."

SVENS crept along the fourth-floor corridor towards the nursery, from whence loud grunts and snorts were emanating, as well as the sound of large bodies moving around and furniture being bashed about. *The boys.* The Gruxhoon had clearly found the nursery and had attacked.

Svens went cold—he had taken too long in getting Tensso situated in the safe room he had created on the ground floor, behind a secret panel in the secondary dining room. He had taken too long losing Lenna. He had not been here for Jansso and Elsso... His chest felt tight, but he pushed down the overwhelming grief that assailed him and progressed to the doorway. He would slaughter these fiends who had taken his baby brothers.

Quietly entering the nursery door, he gripped the short sword tightly in one hand and a dagger in the other—there wasn't enough room inside to swing his bastard sword effectively. The beasts stood with their backs to him, their four large and ungainly bodies rendering the spacious nursery cramped. *Perfect for stabbing at random.*

The light of dawn speared through the large glass windows, illuminating the creatures in their brutish ugliness. As he approached their backs quietly, but with purpose, a *treik* trumpeted outside, drawing their attention to the windows. They crowded towards the panes to get a look at what was happening outside.

Svens didn't hesitate. He struck down two before they even realised they were under attack; he stormed the remaining two closest to the large windows and smashed into them, causing a knock-on effect. The one at the back lost its balance and crashed through the window, the sound of the substantial splat of its landing delayed mere moments by the fall. Svens didn't think, he just attacked in a frenzy, finally coming to himself when he had been hacking at the bloody, carved carcass of what used to be a Gruxhoon but was now unrecognizable except as 'meat'.

Swiping carelessly at his blood-drenched face, Svens approached the windows and looked down, disregarding the remains of the Gruxhoon so recently plummeted to its death. Large numbers of Cinnaen soldiers were streaming into the palace from the direction of the garrison, their arrival heralded by trumpets. He spotted Blÿns directing the squads; clearly they had retaken the palace. He turned back to the room unwillingly and searched for the remains of his little brothers. It only took a short time to come to the conclusion that they weren't there, at which point he raced from the room to launch a search of the palace.

The last pockets of fighting finally fell before the superior number of the Cinnaen army by mid-morning, although it appeared most of the Gruxhoon had retreated into the woods. The Cinnaen numbers were not so great as to follow the Gruxhoon's retreat. Rather, they remained and sought to retake the palace properly. Many of the Cinnaen court and servants had died during the attack—more than two-thirds of the palace inhabitants. Fortunately, Queen Nelni had survived by hiding in another secret safe room near her own chambers, as well as Lord Haaviso and Hjarl Janssen.

Unfortunately, Ians seemed to have perished in the slaughter, but because many of the victims were not whole and scattered about, it had thus far been impossible to confirm an accurate death toll. Some escapees were still finding their way back while others were coming out of hiding *inside* the palace.

Svens had searched high and low for Lenna, Jansso and Elsso, finally hearing that one of the servants had at least seen the two princes alive at some point during the evening. He had her brought to him immediately and was confronted by a hollow-eyed redhead whom he recognised as one of the servers at royal dinners. She bowed in deference, which he waved aside.

"You know something about my... about the young princes, Mistress?" he asked, too tired and beleaguered to bother with niceties. She nodded jadedly.

"Yes, my lord. They were hiding in the larder in the kitche— they're not there anymore!" when he had started towards the door. "They were with... a s-servant girl. She took them away, I think. At least, that's what we agreed she would do if I didn't return, and I couldn't..." she seemed haunted. "There were too many Gruxhoon so I hid inside a laundry chute when a group of ten came close. I would not have survived otherwise." Even though he sympathised with her trauma, his need to know about the boys was more important.

"Which servant girl? And who gave you the authority to 'agree' on any plan regarding the young princes' safety?" he asked belligerently. She eyed him somewhat sardonically, considering her tattered state and the disparity in their ranks.

"Seeing as most of our colleagues were scraps of meat on the floors, we didn't really think we needed permission to save their lives," her voice was devoid of inflection, but her words were audacious. He conceded she had a point.

"And the servant?" he prompted. She hesitated, then answered.

"Anita Bernsson, the new maid in training."
He should have known.

It was shortly thereafter, when an emergency council meeting had been called, the queen venting her spleen over their lack of military preparedness, that a cadet barged into the inner-library, their temporary meeting room.

"How dare you," she started to berate the boy, "enter here without the express permission of your superi—"

"They're attacking again! The G-Gruxhoon! They're attacking, and their numbers are more than before!" the boy yelled in a quavering treble. "Lord Blÿnsso bade me inform you, to say we do not have the manpower to hold them off for long. Also, we have received distress calls from all our coastal cities… Thousands of Gruxhoon have landed up and down our western shores. They are attacking and burning all before them!" Rans had stood up, having joined the war council after riding like a madman from town in the wee hours to participate in the last quellings.

"How long can the remaining forces guarantee our position here, did he say?" Rans asked, prioritising their own situation over the others' distress calls for the present.

"He says an hour, two at most. But there's no guarantee some couldn't get through our lines… the palace isn't fortified or defensible," the boy seemed almost faint at having to criticise the royal palace in the presence of the queen and crown prince.

"Thank you. Wait outside the door until we call you back to relay our response to Lord Blÿnsso," Rans said. Then he turned to the council: "What shall we do? The entire army is three days' march—probably closer to four days—from here. We have a nominal force that cannot hold the palace for even a few hours." His summary conveyed the direness of their situation.

"We will stay and fight these... things! This is the Cinnaen palace, a bastion of our line and a symbol of our power. We will not cede it so easily," Queen Nelni snarled. A heavy silence fell.

"No. We must retreat. Flee now, so we can fight another day and win back what is taken," Svens didn't look at the queen, for he knew she was staring daggers at him.

"And where, pray tell, will you have us flee? With the deluge coming from all sides, the creatures will catch us on the run. It will be a slaughter!" she hissed.

"The only option... our only chance of survival, to be in a position where we can fight back, would be to approach the Pandial king and—"

"I will not listen to this, this... *insanity*! Go crawling to that uncivilised nation for succour? I'd rather die a queen than live a beggar!" and she threw herself into her chair, staring venomously at Svens. Lord Haaviso raised tired eyes from the table.

"We need to decide. As co-regent, I will place my trust in the decision of His Highness, Prince Tensso, thus making it a majority vote." The queen scoffed at this but kept her peace.

Svens ignored her hysterics, turning to the prince who had been listening in pale silence to the discussions.

"Your Highness. There are some within the Pandial council who warned of this very thing months ago, when we in our arrogance and conceit dismissed it out of hand as impossible. Well. I fought said 'mythological' creatures, and they are *very* real. And deadly—to our nation. To underestimate them, to act in arrogance, will lead to our demise." The boy was silent for a beat, then shared his decision.

"We have been shamed by our unpreparedness. We danced and drank, and because we approached these warnings with frivolity and carelessness, those in our charge have died horrible deaths. Furthermore, we stand on the edge of being conquered—in one, fell swoop—by a species we considered subhuman, even non-existent... I will not be disgraced by my carelessness again," he was looking straight at Svens, who held his gaze.

"We will retreat from here with as many civilians as we are able to save, both from the palace and from the city. We will send word to Lord Bransso and the army to meet us at Pansø, close to our southern border, where we will set up camp. In the meantime, we will send emissaries to King Addai of Pandi, asking him to join us in the fight against these invaders. We will hope and pray they are amenable to an alliance." The silence at the table was deafening.

"Well," Lord Haaviso coughed, "there you have it."

"And the coastal cities' distress calls? Will we leave

them to their own devices?" the queen's sarcastic voice rose. Svens shook his head regretfully.

"For now, we must look to our own survival. At best, we can send word via fast messengers to inform them of our own dire situation and our inability to help them at present. Once we have reunited with the full Cinnaen army, we can send them the necessary reinforcements. Until then, we are as helpless as they—even more so, for they have fortifications at most of their positions..." Lord Haaviso was nodding as Svens was speaking, as were all the other participants in this emergency council.

"Very well. Then, let us do as much as we can..." Lord Haaviso said with finality, everyone springing into action, the queen's unhappy refrain in the background ignored.

As Svens walked towards the door, he felt a hand on his shoulder; turning, he was surprised to find Prince Tensso there.

"Will you be leading our retreat, Brother?" his use of the familial soubriquet, the second this day, surprised Svens, especially after his earlier impatience with his future sovereign. He studied his brother who would be king... Tensso's usually sullen face was set in serious lines; it wasn't every day you lost an entire kingdom within mere hours.

"I am sorry, Your Highness, but I cannot."

"Why not?" he demanded, frowning in confusion.

"Because I swore an oath and I plan to see it through."

"And how will you do that?"

"I will find them, even if it means scouting around the palace or further afield, so I cannot leave with the rest of the court at this time..."

"I see," and Tensso smiled for the first time that day.

8

AND THEN THERE WERE THREE

SHADOWS, SHADOWS,

HUG ME ROUND,

SO THAT I SHALL NOT BE FOUND

BY SORROW:

SHE PURSUES ME

EVERYWHERE,

I CAN'T LOSE HER ANYWHERE.

FOLD ME IN YOUR BLACK ABYSS,

SHE WILL NEVER LOOK IN THIS,—

SHADOWS, SHADOWS,

HUG ME ROUND

IN YOUR SOLITUDE

PROFOUND.

GEORGIA DOUGLAS JOHNSON

Hanson's face would haunt Ata for the rest of her life. Hanson laughing when she made an "accidental" dirty joke as Anita. Hanson pulling a mocking face behind Famenke's back. Hanson lighting up as though from within when gifted her Hancin charm. Hanson's innocently sleeping countenance next to Jansso's in their larder hideout. Hanson's face now, staring starkly at her as he was held by the Gruxhoon threatening to maim and murder him in cold blood if he didn't give them up. Such a small thing... all he needed to do was point upwards. Not even that; he could just stare at them pronouncedly and the game would be up.

But all the little boy did was look into her eyes for a moment, then he screwed his eyes shut and shook his head resolutely. The Gruxhoon commander continued to threaten him in measured, brokenly-grunted Bithian, the *lingua franca* of the Áitarbith continent, but he continued to deny them, obstinate though terrified. Jansso and Elsso had somehow managed to soundlessly move closer to her, clinging to her arms in fear of being exposed. In fear of what would happen to the boy who had been their companion in the darkest hours of their short lives.

The entire cluster of Gruxhoon began moving further and further from the tree, dragging Hanson's small person with them—out into the orchard where

Ata could no longer see what was happening from their perch up high in the tree. She started frantically contemplating sneaking down from their refuge and somehow overpowering them through surprise—all twenty-seven she had counted beneath the tree earlier—when Hanson's pained shrieks startled her into immediate mindless action. She was halfway down the tree when his screams suddenly cut out. Only ghostly silence for a few moments—no birdsong even as dawn broke. Then the grunting laughter of the Gruxhoon echoed through the trees.

Before Ata could completely lose her head and proceed on her downward trajectory to somehow "save" Hanson, Jansso's grip on her hand brought her back to reality. She couldn't leave these two boys now. Twenty-seven Gruxhoon, no matter how surprised by her attack, could not be overcome by one woman. So she huddled on the branch she was on, turned her face to the trunk and pressing it against the rough bark *hard*, she cried silent tears for her first Cinnaen friend.

When a significant amount of time had passed since any sounds of Gruxhoon were heard, Ata decided it would be best to make a run for it. If they were somehow surrounded by the Gruxhoon in the next few hours, they would be stuck in the tree without water or food. The longer they remained, the weaker and more vulnerable they'd become. They needed to have freedom of movement to escape to a different area; then they could contact the Cinnaen court (whatever remained of it) and return the boys... It was the best—if somewhat vague—plan she could come up with after the night they had just had.

She looked up to find the two princes still tied to their perches, leaning against each other in a doze. She tugged at Jansso's toes; his eyes immediately snapped open and homed in on her—a disconcerting ferocity and focus on such a young face. She indicated they needed to descend, to which he responded by shaking his head emphatically. Elsso, who had awoken as well, clung more tightly to the trunk as though it were his only lifeline. Ata realised no reasoning would move the two boys, only actions. So she slowly started climbing down the tree. Clearly, they didn't want to lose her presence, for when she glanced up under the pretext of checking the sky, both princes had untied themselves and were clambering down as well.

Upon reaching the lowest branches that still sheltered them from general view, she waited for the boys to catch up, taking Elsso into her arms when he reached her. He clung to her like a little monkey. She leant in, right by Jannso's ear, whispering instructions.

"We have to be very careful now. I haven't heard any Gruxhoon for a while. We must try and get far away from here, so we know we are safe. You must do exactly as I say..." Jansso's serious, dirt-smudged face nodded. She noted his eye was blackening—perhaps he had been struck in the face by a branch in their harried ascent? Or maybe she had smacked him in the face during their breakneck run through the orchard...

"If anything starts chasing us and we need to run, I can't drag you by the arm again. It slowed us down too much last time. When I say 'run', from now on, you jump on my back and hold on using your arms and your legs while I run. Stay as close to my body as possible." When Jansso frowned, but nodded, she sighed. Then she proceeded to use the ropes that had kept them in the tree to tie Elsso to her front the way she had seen peasant mothers tie their babies to themselves during harvest time. Thus, even if she let go of him or he lost his grip, he'd still be anchored to her.

"Let's go!" she murmured, carefully dropping to the leaf-carpeted ground and immediately placing her hand on her sword hilt in case something stormed her. Nothing moved. The birds still sang. She reached up to help Jansso down, noticing he still carried the sack she had repurposed in the larder, containing all the bits and bobs she had stashed on her person in expectation of this very situation. *Well, not exactly like this.*

As she turned to walk on, she heard a soft gasp from Jansso and whirled around, her short sword raised, ready. There was no threat, just Jansso staring down at his feet. Then the boy bent and picked up Ata's long-bladed knife—the one Hanson had died trying to retrieve. He must have dropped it when they grabbed him, and they hadn't noticed it amongst the leaves.

Jansso looked up at her with huge eyes, holding the weapon out to her. She hurriedly took it and placed it in its empty sheath at her thigh. A weapon was a weapon—and they needed to survive. Jansso's hand on her belt was the sign, so she started to walk briskly but furtively through the trees.

At first, she just tried to move deeper into the woods, for she reasoned the Gruxhoon would stay close to the palace. She was quickly disabused of this notion by the afternoon, when they started hearing the grunting and snorting sounds of the Gruxhoon echoing amongst the trees.

They had stopped at a small stream to drink and wash a bit, but when the first sounds reached them, both boys rushed to Ata, who quickly tied Elsso to her followed by Jansso hopping onto her back and clinging like a barnacle. Though they were small and she was tall and fit, carrying both boys simultaneously was a significant burden and would undoubtedly hamper her should she need to run. For now, at least, they just needed to stick closely together while she navigated the safest route to avoid the creatures making those noises.

She walked like this for hours; the rest of the day passed with her constantly redirecting their steps in the opposite direction of the Gruxhoon's noises. By early evening, Ata was exhausted, yet she needed a better idea of Gruxhoon numbers and movements in the woods.

So, Ata and the boys climbed another tree where she tied them to the highest branches they could safely rest on. Then she went scouting. Both boys had been vehemently opposed to being left alone; even though her heart bled for them, it was a necessary abandonment.

"I swear I'll come back for you, Jansso," she whispered urgently at his truculent expression.

"You promised Hanson he could come with us... that you'd keep him safe," he whispered angrily. Ata felt as though she had been punched, winded and sore, and fought the deluge of grief that threatened to engulf her completely. She had not thought of Hanson all day, had not *permitted* herself to think of him. All that existed were the boys and her responsibility to get them out of there safely.

"I will come back," she reiterated once she could breathe under the oppressive weight of her anguish. Climbing down from the tree, she made sure to take note of where it was and what it looked like, then scurried quietly into the dark woods. What her foray revealed was overwhelmingly frightening. They were essentially surrounded by hundreds, if not thousands, of Gruxhoon camped out in smaller and larger groups with fires burning to helpfully pinpoint their locations.

The question of why they were in the woods bothered her greatly. Why didn't they set up camp at the palace and its surrounding area? Why were they in the woods? They weren't hiding, as their open fires exposed them easily to the naked eye. Worse: she had started moving southward, apparently having subconsciously decided to try and get as close to the Pandial border as possible. But it seemed their southern journey was being blocked precisely by this vast force of monsters.

They would need to first pass through this army, *somehow*—possibly to the east—and then wind their way to the south at some point. Ata's geographic knowledge was quite good (Lord Danai had drilled her on it incessantly) but there was a significant difference between being able to navigate an area with a map you know back to front and navigating it *without a map*, from memory. She just had to, though. Plus, she had a plan. She hurried back and woke the princes hastily.

"Boys. The entire forest is crawling with Gruxhoon; there's a whole army in here. But, if we leave now, their firelight tells us where they are, so we can try to slip through their ranks. If we can do that before sunrise, then we will be able to move faster and escape immediate danger..."

Elsso had clearly gone beyond the point of understanding what was happening, but Ata was surprised Jansso was still following along doggedly. He had always been a highly intelligent boy—an old soul, his recent experiences compounding those qualities. He nodded tiredly, so they climbed down and she tied Elsso to her.

Jansso clung to her belt, having noted the droop of her shoulders and correctly deducing her extreme exhaustion. She would not be able to keep going without rest soon. They just needed to make it through this night...

Carefully traversing the potential minefield that was the royal woods, Ata kept her eyes peeled, so when a golden light seemed to tinge their environment, they moved in the opposite direction. At one point, this technique stopped working and only had them pinballing back and forth between encampments, so she adapted. They approached the light, then skirted around the edges of the camp, thereby being able to find the sweet spot between camps.

This increased the risk of discovery as well, for the Gruxhoon had sentries guarding their sleeping comrades, their eyes superior to hers in the dark (as she surmised from the inhuman golden sheen of their pupils). It was exhausting, but she started to become hopeful that they would succeed, when a sudden hair-raising commotion swept through the woods. All the Gruxhoon in all the camps came to life, streaming between tree trunks in a north-westerly direction. Back to the palace.

Ata panicked; they were between these camps and not particularly well-concealed. It would be piss-poor irony should they be discovered by a Gruxhoon tripping over them! Hurriedly lurking towards another tree, she surreptitiously tried to shove the boys into its branches. Just then, she heard the approach of multiple creatures, so she dove into some shrubs a few feet from the tree the boys were dangling from—from its lowest branches.

She watched frantically from her position low on the ground, having wriggled herself further into the damp, muddy pulp of leaves and other debris to make up for the sparse cover of the brush. Jansso seemed to be struggling to push Elsso further out of view of the tall Gruxhoon who were streaming through, between her own hideout and the boys in the tree. *Don't look up...Don't look up... Don't look up.* Suddenly, a surge of Gruxhoon in the ranks caused a few to trample through the brush to the side, nearly squashing Ata. *Don't look down... Don't look down.*

It felt like an eternity, watching the high-hocked paws of the Gruxhoon thunder by, praying to gods she didn't believe in that the creatures looked neither up nor down. Finally, the numbers dwindled, then ceased altogether. Ata stayed frozen in the muck, eyes darting all over to ascertain if the exodus was truly over... She counted until ten minutes had passed, then slowly lifted herself out of the quagmire beneath the meagre bushes, leopard crawling towards the tree.

Raising herself slowly against the trunk behind which the Gruxhoon had all passed, she looked up and noted that Jansso had managed to squish Elsso against the trunk using his own body to hold him there, anchoring them with his arms and legs gripping the bark desperately.

She hissed up at them, gaining their attention. Their little figures sagged in relief and they basically dropped down bodily into her waiting arms. She wasted no time in tying Elsso to her, Jansso hopping onto her back, and then jogging in the opposite direction from whence all the Gruxhoon had come, essentially. Whatever disaster was about to befall the palace, it had made their own escape more achievable, and she was grateful.

When the sun began to rise, Ata could go no further, halting their desperate escape hike. The boys wilted when they disembarked from her sorry frame, all three struggling mightily to climb another tree. Ata had insisted, even though the boys seemed ready to mutiny.

"Just this once more... the trees are here and they add another level of safety. One more time, boys..." and they had acquiesced. They slept uncomfortably. They slept poorly. But they *slept*.

"I's *so* HUNGWY!" Elsso volunteered later that same day as the late-afternoon sun warmed them on their trek. He had become a lot more vocal once they left the denser woods behind and were trailing through a sparsely-wooded, well-sunned landscape.

"I know, little man..." the boy seemed to get a real

kick out of the nickname, she had noticed over the past few hours. "I don't have a bow or any arrows. If I did, we'd hunt some rabbit for supper." He smiled shyly up at her at that. Now he wasn't frightened out of his mind, he was an absolute cutie pie. Jansso, on the other hand, had been quiet and withdrawn; so unlike the precocious boy she had gotten to know in the palace nursery. He held onto her belt as always, but for all the interactions he participated in, he might as well have been wandering far afield.

"I tell you what. Let's stay in one area from now on... We'll stop for the evening. I have some wire in my bag, so we can set a few snares to try and catch some food?" Elsso probably didn't understand everything she had said, but he understood that food would be the result and therefore nodded eagerly. *Such a sweetheart.*

Thus, she called a halt when they came to a spring—they were all almost mindless with thirst at that point—and she went about setting a few traps. Finding a sheltered area between some rocks and bushes, she created a small bed for the boys using her torn servant's dress and petticoats (shoved into the makeshift bag for possible further use). They had a nap there, enjoying the warmth of the sun on the stones behind them although Ata couldn't sleep, finally giving up and dozing seated against the stones: a half-sentry.

When the boys awoke, she showed them how to make a fire, then went to check the traps. Luckily, two yielded a squirrel and a small rabbit. *She'd take it.* She then proceeded to take down their traps, skinned and disembowelled the animals (insisting the boys participate), as well as brewing some tea for herself with the coveted Pandial Liata—a poisonous flower that, when taken correctly, acted as an amazing pick-me-up.

They cooked the meat as well as they could without any salt or other ingredients, but luckily Ata had a small tin in the bag to catch the drippings from the cooking meat. Once cooked, Ata put out the fire, much to his royal highness Prince Jansso's disapproval, and they ate their miniscule portions with relish. Ata gave the lion's share to the boys, but forced down a few mouthfuls—she needed to have enough fuel to carry them, if needed...

Jansso sulked throughout because he had wanted a warm fire in the evening, until she explained the fire in the darkness was a beacon to their position. He was still such a small boy, she realised, for all his maturity. Again, the boys slept in their nest; though Ata joined them to add her body heat for their comfort, she remained awake and alert to any sounds that might indicate a threat. When the sun had risen sufficiently to provide them with light, she woke the boys and they set off once more.

The next two days fell into a similar pattern with Ata not getting much food or sleep, but instead drinking as much tea made from the dried Liata petals as she could safely take. All of them became more unkempt despite their best efforts to wash with cold water in streams. There were no settlements in these woods, or at least none that they came across. When they finally left the woodland behind, the boys openly rejoiced. Ata only felt the exposure as an almost visceral sensation of being naked and vulnerable.

They trekked across open grasslands. Eventually, towards the end of this, the third day after their escape from the palace, they walked along ploughed and planted fields toward a farmhouse on the hill. The boys were ecstatic, jabbering about what they would eat, the beds they would sleep in, and constantly talking about how 'Svens' would come and fetch them soon.

Lord Svensso featured extensively in all their child-like narratives—clearly, he enjoyed the unchallengeable position of godlike protector in the boys' minds. It seemed he made the time to spend with his little half-brothers, teaching them useful and meaningful skills along the way. He sounded like a good man, to hear them speak of him, without whose influence they would undoubtedly have been monstrously spoilt.

They also spoke about their other siblings, 'Tens' and 'Len', with a lot more familial irreverence. Though they loved their older twin siblings, they did not hold them in the same esteem as Lord Svensso. Of their mother, the queen, they didn't speak at all.

"Will you stay with us here, at the farm, until Svens

comes to get us, Ata?" Jansso asked, suspicion colouring his tone.

"I will stay with you until your family takes you from me. I promised, remember?" half-challenging, half-reassuring. "But remember, we might not be able to stay at this house the whole time. We will just ask and hope to stay tonight. If everything seems fine and the people are willing, then we can ask for further help..." the princes nodded in the affirmative. Although Jansso still sometimes challenged her, they clearly trusted her judgment implicitly, minding her admonitions and instructions to the letter.

They couldn't have dreamt up a more welcoming reception than the one they received once they reached the farmhouse. The farmer, Belson, and his wife Hilde, were middle aged, their children all gone off to apprentice or farm on adjacent farms. They hadn't heard of the attack on the palace, sharing concerned looks with each other, but happily housed the three bedraggled escapees in their humble home. As Elsso predicted, they had their three wishes that each had listed on the road granted.

First the boys and then Ata bathed in a large, copper tub in the kitchen, with hot water (the greatest of luxuries). They were given sturdy, if somewhat worn, tunics and leggings that had belonged to the farmer's children. Then, they had sat at a rough-hewn, scarred farm table and eaten a hearty meal of bread, stew, and apple pie.

Lastly, they were given proper beds to sleep in, Ata in the lean-to next to the house where Belson and Hilde's eldest son used to bed down, and the boys in the loft of the thatched farmhouse. All their dearest wishes granted, the boys dropped off to sleep without a further care. Ata, on the other hand, asked for provisions and a map just in case they (or she) needed to move on unexpectedly within the next few days.

"You don't need those things!" Hilde had fussed while still handing over salt, bread, and an empty waterskin. "You will stay with us until word can be sent... Can you imagine! Royal princes and their nurse in our house? This'll be something to tell the grandchildren!" then she bustled off, leaving Ata to make her way to her own bed. She immediately fell into a dreamless sleep. Dark and deep.

THE SOUND of waves crashing on the shore brought Ata to wakefulness. That, and the acrid, pungently suffocating smoke. Her eyes snapped open in the gloom of the lean-to as she frantically tried to orient herself. *Fire!* The sound, the smoke, the orange radiance all around—there was a massive fire somewhere.

Rolling off her low cot, she stuffed her feet into her own boots, still damp from being cleaned earlier. When she swung open the door, the sheer magnitude of the sight that met her eyes staggered her to a halt. Everything. *Everything* was on fire. As far as the eye could see —the fields, the woods in the distance...

Limned in all of this chaos and destruction stood thousands of tall, beastly silhouettes in the flaming glow. *Gruxhoon.* An entire army destroying the valley they were in. She stumbled back inside, grabbed her weapons and bag, then charged out the door. Looking up at the farmhouse, she was relieved to see it hadn't been set alight—yet. But the hysterical screams and animalistic bellows coming from inside were not a good sign.

Peering through the window, she saw six Gruxhoon in the house. Belson was pinned to the boards beneath two creatures' paws, his intestines trailing on the floor beside him, though he was still weakly trying to crawl out from under them towards his wife. She was being held down by two on the kitchen table they had eaten at earlier, skewered through her arms with their claws while another was mounting her. The sixth Gruxhoon was slurping bestially from a bottle of homebrew Belson kept, gurgling in laughter at the antics of its brethren.

As horrified as Ata was, she couldn't take on six Gruxhoon—even with the element of surprise, which she wouldn't have in these circumstances, and... *The boys.* She looked up toward the loft and saw Jansso's terrified little face looking down at the scene on the ground floor. Luckily, the Gruxhoon hadn't bothered to climb the ladder to the loft, possibly because of the ungainly shape of their lower paws, nor had they looked up.

Ata moved away from the window and peered higher; the walls of the house were wattle and daub, whitewashed brightly, the roof thatched. She could climb the wall and through the roof; take the boys out that way. Then run. *Leaving their hosts to their fate.*

She shook the guilt off, to be suffered later. Using her trusty knife, Ata efficiently dug foot and handholds and climbed upward, finally reaching the thatched overhang. Sweating profusely, her muscles screaming, she grasped the reeds and heaved herself onto the slope from below. She gained a steady, anchored perch, then hacked through the thatch with her short sword, knowing any sounds would be drowned out by the din of the blaze and the attack below.

Once she had created a sizeable hole and peered through, she looked straight into the frightened faces of her boys. Wordlessly sticking her arm through the gap, Jansso lifted Elsso slightly higher so she could grasp his arms and pull him through. Then she snagged Jansso the same way.

Dangling them as far as possible over the edge of the farmhouse roof, she dropped them onto the roof of the lean-to which was not particularly sturdy. Jansso's fall took him straight through it, his downward trajectory fully halted by the bed. Elsso followed, then Ata clambered down the wall haphazardly, falling the last few feet gracelessly.

"Let's go!" she grabbed Elsso, but Jansso snatched his arm away.

"What about Mistress Hilde and Master Belson?" he yelled, tears streaming down his face.

"We cannot save them, Jansso. We will die if we try and enter there!" she snarled, her own helplessness and his accusation burning her with shame.

"What if you don't go in? What if you just shot them? Through the window?" Jansso persisted doggedly, his anger turning into pleading.

"With *what*, Jansso? Wishes? I don't have a bow and arrows!"

"There's a bow in here, somewhere. Master Benson was saying he would find it tomorrow and take us hunting. He said it's here!" Jansso was bawling at this point, setting Elsso off in her arms. She hesitated temporarily.

"Okay—look quickly. If all three of us can't find it in sixty seconds, then we're leaving," she warned, going down on her knees and feeling around beneath the cot as she counted aloud. The boys scurried into the corners and started throwing things out of their way in their search. When she reached thirty-four, Elsso squealed triumphantly.

"I gots it!" He only had the unstrung bow, the string dangling from the one end, but where there was a bow...

"I have the arrows!" Jansso cried, shoving them into her hands.

"Okay. Boys, go to the back of the house and follow the path down to the river. Hide if you hear anyone coming! You know Master Belson told us about the small jetty he built in the shallows? Go there and wait for me. If I don't come, go into the water and hide under the jetty till someone comes... Do you understand me?" Both nodded, then were gone.

Ata rushed to the window, stringing the bow as she reached it. In the time it had taken her to rescue the princes, Hilde had been badly used. She was bloody; clawed in her face and torso. One of the beasts had just climbed onto her, the others who had finished scratching and rooting through Hilde's belongings carelessly. The couple's life, built up together over years, trashed in minutes.

Ata felt her hatred soar, so she took aim and let loose. Kai had always said her knife fighting was deplorable, her grappling above average, her swordplay passable, but her archery skills were first class. Now she was motivated to strike true, she felled three of them before the others became aware of the attack.

Unfortunately, two were too far away and at awkward angles in the room where her arrows couldn't find them. The third, still on top of Hilde, got an arrow in its spine, immediately paralysing it from the wound down. The shock made it lose its grip on Hilde and the table, and it slid to a heap on the floor. Luckily, its snarling compatriots came rushing to its aid, perfectly in range of her bow. So she let loose once more.

All were lying on the floor when she jumped through the window; those still twitching or just winged she slew with a few slashes of her short sword. Rushing to Belson's broken body, she found his spirit had already fled, his last sight the destruction of all he loved. When she went to the table, Hilde had already bled out a lot. Too much. She was still present, though, so Ata took her grasping hand and made sure Hilde could see her, could talk to her if she wanted to. Words seemed beyond the poor woman, but her eyes lighted with recognition and she squeezed Ata's hand. Before she too left, she managed a few words.

"Beside... Bel..." Ata suspected she knew what Hilde's dying wish was, and so—once the light of life had flown from Hilde—she pulled what the Gruxhoon had left of the poor woman off of the table where she had raised her family and dragged her next to the remains of her husband, Belson. Then she left that house of sorrows behind her.

Quietly making her way to the riverbank, Ata had to duck and dodge incessantly due to the increasing number of Gruxhoon running around. When she made it to the jetty, she found the two princes hanging onto the wooden stilts beneath; no boats left for them to use. She would have to make do.

"Come on, boys. We're going for a swim down the river," she whispered with feigned enthusiasm.

"Els can't swim at all, and I'm not so good at it..."

"Just hold onto me; we'll float amongst the reeds together."

"You promise you won't let us go?"

"I promise."

9

DEAD TO THE WORLD

Sleep, sleep, beauty bright,
  Dreaming in the joys of night;
  Sleep, sleep; in thy sleep
  Little sorrows sit and weep.

Sweet babe, in thy face
  Soft desires I can trace,
  Secret joys and secret smiles,
  Little pretty infant wiles.

As thy softest limbs I feel
  Smiles as of the morning steal
  O'er thy cheek, and o'er thy breast
  Where thy little heart doth rest.

O the cunning wiles that creep

The chaos of the temporary Cinnaen refuge (or military encampment, since the army's arrival) resembled a battle in and of itself. The ground was churned mud, the noise overwhelming, and the sheer number of people scurrying back and forth frenetic.

Lenna both hated it and was thrilled by the life exuded. In her limited experience, life, *true* life, did not exist outside of the maelstrom of pandemonium. Not in the staid, controlled existence she had suffered for most of hers—every second accounted for and managed by her mother, her governesses, her ladies-in-waiting, every word weighed and judged for content suitability and taste, every breath and action stifled for fear of overexerting her fragile frame. As tragic as the fall of Hårbørgen Palace was, it had broken through the pomp and protocol encasing her, shattering courtly control over her very being for now.

In the nine days since that fateful night, Cinnae had been turned on its head; most of the coastal strongholds had fallen within days of the large-scale invasion, with only two still holding against the Gruxhoon hordes buffeting their defences. Further inland, civilians were suffering a full-scale extermination by 'mythological' monsters with an appetite and talent for destruction.

"Do you think we will be expected to stay *here*?" the affected, fussy tones of Lady Ansi rose, followed by concerned murmurs from the other noblewomen present in the tent. Spaciously sumptuous compared to the other shelters in the encampment, one of the command marquees had been repurposed for the use of the courtiers, specifically the ladies. At least, those who had survived the 'Night of Terror', as the attack on the Cinnaen palace had been dubbed.

There weren't enough chairs to be had, so the ever-beleaguered servants (again, those who had survived the horrors of that night) had cobbled together floor seating by covering most of the area with thick rugs, carpets, and cushions donated by aristocrats who were able to flee their mansions and chateaux with some household items. The ladies now lounged around their makeshift salon, bemoaning their current circumstances and eating fiddly snacks, somehow procured despite extensive rationing imposed by command (someone's servant needed a raise for making something lavish out of the barest essentials).

Lenna had absconded to the periphery of this group of privileged moaners, leaning against the tent's stabilising poles and gazing out at the hustle and bustle of the encampment, the sides of the structure had been rolled up to form an open-air pavilion, the interior easily becoming stuffy due to its upholstered contents.

Thinking of Lord Iansso, her father's trusted, retired advisor, Len hoped he was alright, wherever he was... She owed him so much, having spirited her away from the palace and depositing her here safely. They had travelled in dangerous circumstances for days, the lovely old gentleman taking great pains to see to her comfort and survival. He was unfailingly kind and intimidatingly competent.

Sighing deeply, Lenna took note of a commotion further down one of the makeshift tent-alleyways. *Just out of her sight.* Craning her neck, she shielded her eyes from the sun's glare (so much stronger now they were so far south) to try and see what the hubbub was about. Then she shrieked and dashed forward, leaving the ladies behind her squawking and spluttering in a high dudgeon over her mannerless departure.

"Svens! Svens! *Svens!*" she shrieked, hopping up and down and waving her arms like a hoiden, trying to get his attention amidst all the servants, lackeys, and commanders swarming him as he strode in the direction of the command tent. He must have just arrived, for the parts of him she could make out were dusty and travel-worn. He handed over the reins of his horse to his manservant, Perkki, whose stocky, compact figure trotted off with the steed in his wake.

Finally, he caught sight of her. Face stoically unreadable as always, he jerked his head sideways. *She should follow him.* Lenna nodded and proceeded to trail him and his helter-skelter entourage to a standard military tent. Svens entered, leaving his followers behind at the door flap, but then waited patiently for her to go in before dropping the flap and tying it shut.

Turning, he gripped her upper arms hard and stared at her in silence for a few moments. His throat bobbed, and despite his placid expression, she sensed he was experiencing a maelstrom of strong emotions.

"You can't even begin to imagine how happy I am to find you here, Len!" his voice shook with suppressed emotion, "I have spent the past nine days and nights searching for you... I barely slept, barely ate. Coming back here, I had forced myself to accept... I thought you were d—... gone." He seemed completely overcome; Lenna was truly touched by his dedication, and his apparent emotional investment.

Always having been the sibling he had interacted with the least, there just seemed to be a divide between them. Not animosity, precisely... More an awkwardness borne of the disparity in their statuses, ages, and sexes. She was a princess, loved and cosseted since the moment she drew breath; he was a bastard soldier a decade her senior who had been surrounded by men and military pursuits his entire life. They had not met often during their lives, and then only in the presence of others. She didn't know how to interact with him, how to get to know him. But he clearly still cared for her—a true brother, albeit an illegitimate one.

"Are Jansso and Elsso here too?" he asked, eyes alight with hope. Hating to crush it, she shook her head slowly. His eyes shuttered, face appearing to age by a decade in front of her. "They must be somewhere... with *that woman*," he muttered in frustration. "They *must* have survived." Even to her ears, his tone sounded desperately hopeful rather than confidently certain.

"What woman?" she asked, but he just pinched the bridge of his nose and shook his head. He was absolutely filthy, with a full flaxen-gold beard coming in on his face—so unlike his usual cleanshaven, pristine appearance.

"Nevermind. I'll find out, if it kills me. But for now: how did you come to be here? How did you escape the palace before I returned to your room that night?" He moved to a small table next to his cot, an ewer and dish with soap waiting. "You don't mind if I start washing up while you tell me? The general and his staff are waiting to brief me, but I need to hear this before anything else happens." Nodding, she took a seat on the cot to free up some space in the cramped tent for his ablutions.

"You know Lord Iansso?" at his jerk and shocked expression, she continued quickly, "He found me in the closet shortly after you left. He said there were Grux-hoon further up the corridor, opposite from where you were going to Tens's rooms. They... they came into the room. Two of them." She shuddered at the memory of the creatures. She had never been so frightened in her life before. Sadly, that had not been the case subsequently.

"Lord Iansso had already shoved me halfway out the window by the time they broke the lock and came in. He then followed and we climbed up the drainpipe that runs beside my windows. I don't know what we would have done if it had been any of the other rooms! Those... *things* tried to follow us, but they were too clumsy and heavy to manage. They even tried to rip the pipe off the wall with us still hanging onto it, but it's made of metal, so they weren't able to. We succeeded in shimmying down the pipe once they had run back inside to try and head us off upstairs.

"After that, we avoided all the Gruxhoon on the grounds and made our way to the woods where we found a horse that hadn't been killed. We escaped on it, at first going west, but then the invasion came from the coast, so we turned southward. Some farmers in a town or two put us up; they gave us horses, but most of them were also packing and fleeing in advance. They told us about this encampment, so Lord Iansso brought me here..."

"Where can I find him? We might need to include him in future councils, as he foresaw this and would be a vital source of information," Svens asked as he noisily washed his face and neck. Len bit her lip in concern.

"I don't know." Svens continued drying his face.

"Well, I'll just asked Perkki to track him down. The old man should be around here somewhere close by. He's always sticking his nose where it shouldn't— "

"You don't understand, Svens. No-one knows where he is." This got his undivided attention. "At least, no-one that I have spoken to—probably no-one in this camp... He left the day after he brought me here. Without a word to anyone about where he was going."

"But that's... *why*? We need his expertise. He has been banging on about the bloody Gruxhoon for months! What the hells could be more important than helping us now? What do the commanders, the general, think about his absconding?" Svens was clearly flabbergasted—and angry. However, he was keeping his ire tightly leashed. Her eldest half-brother had always seemed such a cold fish to her, yet up close and under these circumstances, Lenna realised he just exercised an extreme level of control over his emotions, which were just as strong as any other person's might be.

"From what I can tell, nobody has really noticed his absence; I have tried to be circumspect in my enquiries because I don't want to draw too much attention to it. It would seem suspicious... and he clearly knows more about the Gruxhoon than any innocently uninvolved person should. The way he knew to avoid them these past days, their habits and practices..." Lenna grew quiet, the pieces clicking into place. She looked sharply at Svens: "Lord Iansso isn't retired, is he? Nor is he only an advisor?" Svens's uncommunicative, straight face was enough—no answer was, in itself, an answer.

Lenna continued: "He's a spy of some kind. But I would bet every last one of my jewels that he is on Cinnae's side. He wouldn't have risked his life saving me if he is undermining the Cinnaen cause. And you said he warned you for months about a possible Gruxhoon attack?" at this, a slightly uncomfortable expression passed over Svens's face; Lenna recognised it as shame before it disappeared.

"Yes. I can categorically vouch for his motives and loyalties... But his absence and wealth of Gruxhoon knowledge would appear suspicious to others in our camp, Lord Bransso in particular," he admitted as rubbed his shorn head frustratedly.

"Yes. From what I have deduced from the other courtiers, the general has already been trumpeting about 'enemies within' and poking around, looking for spies who feed the Gruxhoon information. They seem to evade our forces constantly, but find and attack them when they don't expect it and are at their most vulnerable... He is convinced this cannot be coincidence, or, heavens forbid, superior military abilities on the Gruxhoon's part..." Her half-brother ignored her faint tone of irreverent mockery.

"It might be best if we don't bring too much attention to Ians's absence, though why he decided to go missing at this time is beyond me," frustration bled into Svens's voice before he sighed. "Well, I am pleased you're safe, Len. You don't know how pleased... But I need to wash more thoroughly and change my clothes, so it's time for you to go, I'm afraid." He smiled to soften the expulsion, and she went away with a lot to consider.

THAT NIGHT, Lenna shared a small, intimate dinner with her brothers, a crown prince and a general, in Tens's tent. Her mother would have pitched a fit if she had known they were dining with Svens, but ever since Queen Nelni had come to the realisation that her two youngest sons were missing, most likely dead, she had been in a state of mourning—keeping to her tent and constantly waited on by her lady's maid. Lenna went to see her every day but could only stomach so much of her mother's pendular extreme rages and pitiful laments before excusing herself from the queen's presence.

Her mother's personality had ever been thus; intense highs and severe lows, the woman herself mostly vain and self-centred but loving her children inasmuch as they were extensions of herself. Lenna had always had a fraught relationship with her mother, for neither could understand the other. They were alien in all senses of soul and nature.

Ever since Lenna's arrival at the army camp, Tens

had been annoyingly affectionate, constantly wanting to spend time with her, talk to her, and get her opinion about *everything*. She had found it exceedingly odd, seeing as they had been at loggerheads before the palace attack. When she had confronted him about his odd turnabout, he'd confessed feeling extreme guilt over his treatment of her when he thought she had died and wanting to make it up to her, to be a better brother. *As if.*

"What is it like, further north?" Tens barely touched his food, eagerly questioning Svens about what he had seen while searching for her and the boys these past days. Svens mostly gave noncommittal, vague responses, eating ravenously of the decadent fare. Lenna once again noted the upper-class servants' uncanny ability to procure superior rations for the 'haves' as opposed to the 'have nots'. Even in a war the social disparities were maintained.

"You seemed much more invested in the discussions with the commanders today, Your Highness," Svens offered, maintaining his respectful formal address in the presence of the servants waiting on them.

"He is eager to make up for his previous neglect... for constantly carousing with that *awful* Lord Ernso and not being in a fit state for anything when the 'Night of Terror' took place," Lenna said flippantly, then noted the sudden absence of silverware clinking on their plates and found both her brothers frowning at her.

Svens's was accusatory, Tens's tinged with a deep blush of embarrassment.

After that, the conversation became stilted, with Tens becoming more and more withdrawn and making Lenna feel both defiant and guilty for shaming him in front of Svens whom he had hero-worshiped since she could remember. Soon after, she excused herself for the evening and Svens rose to accompany her to her tent, both of them taking their leave from a silently introspective Tens.

"That was really poorly done of you, Len," Svens bit off in hushed tones as they walked through the twilit camp, its hustle and bustle ongoing. "Why were you so cruel to your brother?" her hand resting on his arm felt how rigid his entire posture had gone. Lenna sighed.

"Tens and I had a falling out... about something I wasn't supposed to know about. But I felt very strongly about it, so I told him my opinion," she whispered as they wound their way to her own tent.

"What! Are you serious? Do you think this is some garden party, Len? You've both survived—against enormous odds, I might add—the invasion of your home by Gruxhoon! You've always had a good relationship, now because of some childish tiff, you're holding a grudge during these times of life-or-death?" his harsh assessment, though somewhat accurate, was not based on the full picture.

"Tens had a m- mistress." She was shocked at her

own audacity in saying this. Svens scoffed, doubt emanating from his entire manner.

"Since when? I never heard of it!" Suddenly annoyed by Svens's lack of perception, she rolled her eyes at this.

"He's not a boy anymore; we're both almost seventeen! And it's not as though men are treated the same as women... Especially not nobles. Tens is a crown prince and heir to the throne! Just because you're always busy with military manoeuvres and playfighting doesn't mean the court stops spinning its intrigues." The last part she said bitterly. How was it that her illegitimate brother could escape them, but she was condemned to suffer the restrictive court games for the rest of her life?

"Just as well I was busy with all those 'military manoeuvres and playfighting', or we would have been in quite the pickle with this invasion, wouldn't we, Sister," he snapped, so unusual for Svens and his iron self-control, and halting her abruptly. "I'm sorry, Len. I didn't mean to snap at y—" Lenna flung her arms around him there in the velvety darkness of early evening.

"You called me 'sister'... I didn't think you thought of me like that!" she whispered fiercely, apparently leaving him temporarily dumbstruck.

"How else would I think of you?" he muttered in confusion. Stepping back out of her embrace, he made an effort to get their discussion back on track.

"Who was Tens's mistress, Len?" he asked, patting her awkwardly on the shoulder.

"Countess Brelan," she responded, surprising him. Countess Brelan was the widowed wife of a noble from Karppen, a small principality on the south-west coast of Cinnae (and neighbour of Pandi too). She had joined the Cinnaen court a few years before on the arm of her previous lover, a Cinnaen diplomat who had spent time in Karppen.

Young and beautiful, the fact that she had caught the prince's eye was not surprising, however, she was not of particular importance in the Cinnaen court, so the prince even being aware of her, never mind taking her as his mistress, was quite surprising. Not to mention the fact that their mother, the Queen, would not tolerate her son's attentions being bestowed on so 'lowly' a candidate... Svens shook his head in bewilderment.

"You're sure?" he hazarded.

"Of course! No-one knows I know, but that horrible Lord Ernso introduced them secretly and Tens was head-over-heels for her after that. I tried to warn him against it, which is why he didn't speak to me. He cut me off, ignoring me for *weeks*..." she became maudlin. "He refused to see me and vulgar Lord Ernso got this pleased, condescending expression on his face every time we met. It was truly *horrible!*"

Lenna took Svens's arm and kept walking. "Now, because he feels guilty after thinking I was dead for a few days, Tens is being so attentive. But I can't seem to forget his choosing his feckless friend and temporary bed partner over me, his twin sister. Nor forgive it," she looked at him earnestly. "I know this is a failing on my part; that the tomes of the Holy Sacrament require us to forgive and to forget trespasses against us, but my heart cannot do that right now. I think I need time." Svens was quiet for a while, pensive.

"Perhaps try to refrain from being cruel to him, at least..." he ventured, "You don't need to forgive him, necessarily, but just withhold any barbs." Nodding, she felt guilty about humbling her brother for no reason other than malice. Upon reaching their tent, they said goodnight and Len retired. Before getting into bed, she performed the ritual invocations according to her string of prayer beads, adding a final entreaty to the gods to return her baby brothers to their family. Her last thoughts before the welcome oblivion of sleep were of them, and to wonder who "that woman" was.

IT WAS pure luck and happenstance (should you ask an unbeliever) or an absolute miracle (should the faithful be asked) that Lenna was on the outskirts of the encampment when her entreaty to the gods was answered, in prime position to witness it.

Accompanied by her tall, temporary ladies' maid with red-gold hair, she had been walking through the camp, trying to provide assistance where she could—

unsuccessfully. There were few things so truly useless as a pretty face and a flawless lineage when it came to practical problems of everyday suffering and hardship. Thus, when shouts rang out from the guards on duty a few feet away from her and her maid, she happily turned to the distraction from her own utter worthlessness as an *aide* to the layperson.

It seemed a hunched, malformed figure had appeared from the open fields to the north-east and was staggering towards the camp almost drunkenly.

Though larger than an average man and bipedal, it was too small to be a Gruxhoon, nor was it agile enough. It was very oddly shaped, shuffling awkwardly forward at a slow jog, the weight under which it staggered distributed unevenly and top-heavy.

As it neared, a part of its malformation moved, a small head with hair sticking everywhere popping up over its shoulder. *A boy.* The person was carrying a boy. As Lenna started moving towards the approaching figure without thought, a second head became visible— a child clutched to the person's chest. At that point, Lenna began to run forward, for she had recognised the heads, even at this distance. She would know her brothers *anywhere.*

The figure carrying the princes reached the guards at the same time Lenna did; Lenna screamed the guards down from their defensive stances, swords pointing directly toward the approaching "threat" as they shouted at it. Then the form collapsed, the two boys yelling and crying in unison. The tangled heap was a woman, lying on her side, clutching Elsso to her chest while Jansso clung to her back.

They were all revoltingly dirty—all brown, with even the pale hair of the boys obscured by the muck. The woman also had brown-golden hair, but it was covered with the same brown mulch, as were their clothes. And they stank to high heavens; a strange earthy, decaying smell. Lenna didn't stop, immediately lunging forward to grab her brothers.

"Elsso! Jansso! You're alive!" she didn't even know what she was saying, there was so much noise and chaos around them with the guards shouting for support and sending word to their superiors. She tried to pry Elsso from the woman's chest, only to realise he had been lashed to it with rope.

Jansso had dismounted from the woman's back, but he did not come to Lenna. Instead, he crouched down next to the woman and was yanking and pushing at her urgently, shouting at her to get up. Through the cacophony, his high voice cut to Lenna.

"Ata! Ata! You need to get up. We can't lie down. We can't stop! Ata! You can't stop now!" he yelled over and over, his voice hoarse and hysterical, tears pouring down his face. Lenna focused on the woman. *Ata*. More than the filth, one thing radiated from her. *Exhaustion*. The kind that spoke of ceasing to live, ceasing to breathe, it was so intense. Her eyes were sunken in, her cheek-bones prominently stark in her pale face, lips cracked and bleeding.

She looked ancient; Lenna thought that this was what death's face must look like. This Ata looked like she had not slept for many ages. Yet, her eyes were open and trained on Jansso as he pulled at her arm, her shoulder—never leaving his face and intently watching him.

To Len's amazement, the beaten woman managed to roll onto her knees, then made the herculean effort of heaving herself upright. She staggered, righting herself on shaking legs, Jansso immediately grasping her hand and looking up at her with an almost desperate adulation. Lenna had seen similar looks on the faces of supplicants at the feet of their deities. Turning her face to the guards, the woman's eyes caught on Len, who was closest.

"I... h- have... br- brought... th-the... the... prin-princes." Voice creaky, cracking on every other vowel. This *Ata* was completely broken, a shadow of a person utterly drained. But her eyes were compelling, and Lenna felt compelled.

"Thank you, Ata," she said carefully, taking an unwilling Jansso's hand and instructing her maid to take Elsso once one of the guards had cut the ties that bound him to his guardian. Els was sobbing in distress by the time he had been separated from Ata. When the woman's eyes rolled up into her skull, exposing the whites grotesquely, Len yelled at the guards to catch and support her, which they did immediately.

"Your Highness... I know this woman. She... she was a servant in the Hårbørgen Palace. She was on duty in the nursery when the attack happened and made her way downstairs to hide the princes in the larder. I think she saved them and brought them all the way from there..." her temporary maid, Mistress Famenke, she was called, urgently whispered to Lenna, who had picked up her pungent brother and was rocking him as he cried plaintively. She could still hear Ata's name amongst his wails.

"You mean they came all that way together—and on foot for the most part, by the looks of it... But could one walk that far in ten days? It's almost 500 miles!" Lenna asked, eyeing Ata, who was being propped up by two young guards. She hadn't passed out but seemed dazed and half-delirious.

"I think, if I may be so bold, Your Highness, that questions can be asked later... If the commanders—the council—are made aware of her and the role she played in rescuing the princes, they will want to question her immediately. From what I see here, she will not survive long without rest. Proper rest. Can we trust them to care? She seems a few heartbeats away from dying right in front of our eyes," Mistress Famenke's words jolted Lenna. Her own eyes proved the truth of this observation and she could not allow the woman to whom she owed her brothers' lives to be essentially tortured merely for the sake of edifying the council. Thus, Len made a choice.

"Bring this woman with us to my tent. She and the princes need care and rest, which they will receive there without interference." She used her most imperious voice and haughty manner; despite much muttering and attempted disagreement, she quickly managed to browbeat the young soldiers into bending to her will. Lenna breathed a sigh of relief when she finally had the three survivors installed in her tent with Famenke acting like a whirlwind of efficiency in washing and caring for them. Soon, they were all bundled into a bed made in the corner in the same way the courtiers' marques had been created, with rugs and cushions. The three lay snugly together, wrapped in blankets. *Dead to the world.*

It wasn't long before the dreaded summons came in the form of Svens at her tent entrance, insisting she relinquish them all.

"I am very sorry, my lord, but I cannot," Lenna had not even permitted the tent flap to be opened by so much as a crack, speaking to him and his cronies outside through the fabric, sensing his anger and frustration with her. "I will only allow my mother, the Queen, and our personal physician to enter. And then, only to see my brothers. No-one else is permitted entry until my charges have received the necessary care and rest. I absolutely forbid it on my authority as princess royal."

Quaking at her own audacity, Len was not even sure she had the requisite authority to do this. She was quite certain she did not, but stuck to her conviction that this was how it should be... She might not be any use to anyone else in this entire encampment—not even her older brothers or mother—but she was inherently necessary to those she protected inside her tent now.

"Your Highness! You do not have the authority to withhold access to a potential spy!" this from Lord Bransso, who sounded absolutely livid. He would run roughshod over her, easily.

"I apologise for my tardiness," Tens's voice rang through the flimsy walls of their little refuge, "do I understand correctly that Her Highness, Princess Lenna, is refusing to relinquish the woman who brought Prince Jansso and Prince Elsso safely to the encampment? That she is insisting on ensuring the woman is in good health before allowing the council access to her?" Tens's voice sounded strong and clear; Lenna lowered her head in anticipatory defeat. After her set-down last night, her brother would still be angry with her.

"Yes! Upon her 'authority as princess royal'," Lord Bransso spat with sarcastic venom.

"Well, it is very simple, then. I will add my authority to hers, seeing as you seem to find it lacking, my lord. No-one will enter *my sister's* private tent, nor in any way approach the woman, Ata, whom she nurses there, until Her Highness, Princess Lenna, sees fit for them to do so. Per *my* authority as crown prince and supported by my regent, Lord Haaviso," Tens's voice had not lost its pleasant tone throughout and was followed by the murmured agreement of the Cinnaen duke. It appeared her brother was very much on her side.

"After all," she heard the regent placate, "What difference does a slight delay in questioning make? She is not going anywhere in the shape she's in, based on the reports of the guards." It always fascinated her how the man managed to diplomatically soothe even the most ruffled of feathers.

Also, Lenna felt all her residual ire resulting from her brother's previous, callous disregard for her melt away, for who could but forgive someone who backed you when you yourself were backed into a corner?

10

PAYING THE PIPER

To borrow trouble (North American expression)—take needless action that may have detrimental effects.

Google Dictionary Box

Neither a borrower nor a lender be;
For loan oft loses both itself and
friend,
And borrowing dulls the edge of
husbandry.
This above all: to thine own self be
true,
And it must follow, as the night
the day,

THOU CANST NOT THEN BE FALSE TO

ANY MAN.

WILLIAM SHAKESPEARE, HAMLET

J ans hurt all over. His head, his eyes, his arm, his legs, his... *"If it hurts, that's good. It means you're still alive and your body is working well enough to tell you it's sore."* Ata. His eyes shot open, then shut tightly before opening more carefully. Looking straight up. The light was too much; it wasn't enough. Jans huffed. Everything was bright, pale shades: whites, creams, greys. *He was in a tent.*

Suddenly the loud sounds from outside made sense; the creak of wagon wheels, people's feet clomping through suctioning mud, shouts and chatter as people moved past. He was basically outside too, just a thin canvas between him and the rest of the world.

Surreptitiously, Jans let his eyes rove around, careful not to move at all and give away his wakefulness. The sound of murmuring voices was closer than the rest of the outdoor sounds. *Someone was in the shelter with him.* He saw the tent ceiling rise narrowly upward as he lay on the floor, feeling his brother's butt sticking into his side. Els *always* curled up like that—folded in half, with his backside jutting out and pushing whoever slept next to him further and further till they fell off the bed.

Which always happened to be Jans... He could make out Ata's deep breathing—she must be on Elsso's other side. Jans immediately relaxed knowing they were all here. *All safe.* Just like she had promised him over and over. Closing his eyes, he drifted off again.

"I insist that they be moved to a more appropriate place!" Jans jerked awake at the shrill sound of the queen's voice.

"I am sorry, Mother, but that is not possible... They are exhausted beyond anything I've ever seen. Even Lord Vensen is shocked at their condition. They clearly haven't been getting enough food or rest... They were encrusted with dirt, their bodies covered in cuts and bruises. Elsso has a black eye and Jansso's arm seems to have been dislocated. It looks like they managed to pop it back into its socket at some point, but Lord Vensen has bandaged it tightly to avoid further jostling and damage."

Len's hushed tones were much more soothing; Jans kept his eyes closed, listening. *He wouldn't leave! Even if the royal physician said they could!*

"Why are they in such a state? Does that... *physician* have any idea?" Queen Nelni responded.

"Well... we haven't been able to speak to any of them yet; they've been sleeping for twenty-five hours straight... We *have* managed to get them to drink water and broth, but they were basically delirious—mindless with exhaustion, so—"

"I don't need to know all that. What does anyone know about what happened to them? Why were they so neglected by this woman... and who is she? She's not one of the nursemaids, that much I know." The queen's usual impatience was on full display.

"She was a new maid at the palace; Mistress Famenke says she befriended one of the nursemaids and that, as far as she could make out, they had swapped shifts so she was with the children when the palace was attacked... But we're not sure, as all the nursemaids were sl— ... died during the attack," Jans felt that now-familiar twist of his stomach. *Poor Jansken! And everybody else who died...* he stopped his mind from going to the things he had seen when they were trying to escape the Gruxhoon inside the palace that night.

He saw them enough in his nightmares already. His hand moved of its own volition, searching... When it found Ata's arm, it crawled down to her hand and grasped it tightly. The pinching feeling of nausea in Jans's belly subsided. *He was safe. They were all together.*

"Well, that kind of lax approach to minding the boys will not be tolerated in future..." the queen snapped. "To have the princes of Cinnae in the charge of just anyone? Not seemly *at all.*"

"She saved them, though," Len's quiet voice, "against tremendous odds... Lord Vensen believes they covered the entire distance from the palace on foot. It appears she carried them for most of it." Her voice became more hushed. "I saw for myself that she had tied Els to her body. I suspect she couldn't carry him in her arms anymore, so she resorted to that." There was a shuffling nearby, one of the quilts lifting at their feet. "See? I've never seen feet look like this..." a gulping, gagging sound followed.

"That is revolting! Cover those immediately or I will be ill!" the queen's voice rose, disgusted.

"I just wanted to show you that this woman—her name's Ata—didn't just neglect the boys gratuitously. I'm sure she took care of them to the best of her abilities under the circumstances. They didn't want to leave her when we tried to take them. Covering over five hundred miles to get to us... She could have easily left them on the way and gone directly over the border to Pandi by herself, without the burden of two children."

"Why would she go to Pandi?" the suspicion in the queen's voice was obvious to Jans. A short silence.

"Because, according to Svens's information, she is Pandial."

"What!" the squawk was abrasively loud, but Els and Ata slept on. "Do you mean to tell me a *filthy*, back-woods Pandial had two sons of the House of Hårbørgen in her power? For ten whole days!" no effort was now made to contain the volume. The queen was livid.

"Calm yourself, Mother! They need to rest!" urgently, "And to be completely frank, I don't care if she was Gruxhoon! She brought my brothers through occupied territory, at great risk to herself, saving their lives on multiple occasions. For that reason alone, I will give her all my care and respect. Whatever her politics or affiliations."

"That is perfidious! The Pandial want to subjugate us, to gain the upper hand and—"

"I think the Gruxhoon should be our primary concern right now. There are even those amongst the commanders who are saying we should form an alliance with Pandi to—"

"That will never happen as long as I have any say in it! This is the opportunity those lowland peasants have been *waiting* for to overrun Cinnae and—"

"Yes, Mother. We all know your stance. But yours is not the only opinion that will stand under current circumstances and pressures," another half-squawk half-shriek of disdain from the queen. "I think, for all of our sakes, that you should go and rest, Your Highness... They will still be sleeping for quite some time, but I will send word when they have woken up," Lenna tried to use a soothing voice to keep the peace, which seemed to work, as Queen Nelni departed shortly afterward.

"You can stop pretending to sleep now, Jans," Len said softly once the space had quieted again. He slowly opened his eyes and considered her. She still looked the same as always, except her hair covering and dress were much simpler than usual. Her face was also a bit pale.

He felt a lightening of his spirit, a happiness. *At least <u>she</u> was alive.*

"How did you know?" Jans's voice was low and hoarse. "Can I have some water?" she immediately brought a glass and jug, refilling it twice before he stopped drinking.

"I've always been able to tell when you're faking... How're you feeling?" she asked, wiping his hair off his forehead where it had been plastered. She was always touching and hugging them. It was how she showed she loved them.

"M'okay," Jans mumbled, trying to dodge her ministrations. She took the hint and went to prepare some food for him. *He was starving!* As he ate the thick soup awkwardly with his left hand, Len tried to make conversation.

"Do you want to tell me what happened? How you got here?" he stopped his slurping and frowned, shaking his head vigorously.

"Can you at least tell me how your shoulder got dislocated?" she asked softly, trying to catch his eye while he was assiduously avoiding hers. He muttered something and took a large bite of food. "I'm sorry—I couldn't hear you..."

"Tree."

"Tree? And? Did you fall out?" her puzzled expression suddenly enraged him. *Why was she so stupid? Thank the gods they hadn't been stuck with her—they would have been dead before they'd left the palace.* Sudden guilt. *It wasn't her fault she didn't understand...*

"No. She... they were chasing us. Needed to hide quickly, but I was too slow. Ata saved me... grabbed my arm and dragged me up. Up into the tree. They almost grabbed me—my leg. *So scared!* But she saved us." His words wouldn't come properly; his breath wouldn't come properly. *So stupid!* He realised his face was wet and he was sobbing, spilling the last of the soup over himself.

"It's alright, Jans. You're safe now. I'm sorry. You don't have to talk if you don't want to," and she took him in her arms and cradled him on her lap like a baby. He fell asleep again.

OVER THE NEXT DAY, all Jans did was sleep and eat. Eat and sleep. He was so tired. When Elsso started having regular nightmares, twitching and whining, the maid with the bright hair that curled out of her headdress would hold him and he'd stop. She wasn't very pretty, but her face got nice when she was holding Elsso. Jans noticed.

He quietly watched everything and everyone. He didn't want to talk to anyone. It made the queen, his *mother*, angry when she came. She shouted. He didn't care. Ata was still sleeping, which worried him. He also saw her feet that had made the queen so uncomfortable. They made him uncomfortable too.

Len and the maid were showing the healer, Lord Vensen, and cleaned them while he gave instructions. Ata's feet didn't look like feet. They looked like the uncooked meat he'd seen in the kitchens sometimes. Or the floor of the kitchen that night, all bloody and raw... *No! Don't think about that.* She must have been in so much pain when they were running.

Jans also had times where he went somewhere else —somewhere nowhere. He'd 'wake up', but he hadn't been sleeping, just staring. It was confusing. Then, the bad thoughts also came... What if Ata never woke up? Would she be dead? No, she promised she wouldn't leave them. But she'd also promised Hanson...

"I'm cold! And my feet hurt!" Jans hated her. She kept making them walk.

"I know, Jans. Just a little bit further, then I'll find us a nice place out of the wind to rest," her voice was all one level, her feet dragging, but she kept going. They had been in and out of the river for two days and nights. This was the first time in ages they hadn't been hiding from Gruxhoon in the water. Still damp, though they had left the river behind many hours ago.

They hadn't eaten anything except roots and nuts that Ata found along the riverbank. She had tried to make them eat a raw fish she caught the first night, but Els had cried so loudly she had stopped. She ate it, though. Gagging all the while. It was disgusting.

"I'm not going anymore!" Jans snapped, stopping and crossing his arms. Ata halted a few paces ahead, lifted her face to the sky and sighed deeply. Elsso was huddled against her chest, eyes open and staring while he sucked his thumb. Their nursemaids would've shouted. But they weren't here. No-one was. Except Ata.

"Jans... please keep going. We need to keep going. We need to stay together. Otherwise the Gruxhoon will get us." Ata knelt beside him, grasping his shoulder to force him to look into her eyes. He had listened and obeyed, even though he didn't want to.

That night, they lay under a tree, between its coarse roots. Ata had insisted, in case they needed to climb it in a hurry because of the Gruxhoon. Jans absolutely refused to sleep in another tree again, so they had compromised.

She had shot some squirrels, meaning his belly had at least something in it for a change. But as tired as he was, his brain wouldn't stop thinking. About things. Things he didn't want to think about. Like Hanson. Like if his brother and sister now looked like the dead servant they had seen on the stairs in the palace. Or like the people they had seen in the dark corridors, lying all around.

"Ata?" Els snored softly. Ata didn't bother untying him from her body anymore except when he needed to go do his business. (Ata called it that, and they all preferred it to their nursemaids' "go potty")

"Yes?" Jans knew she didn't sleep, even when her eyes were closed. She held her bow with an arrow half-nocked at all times, even when they were resting.

"Do you think Hanson hates us?" A long pause.

"Why do you ask that?"

"Because we're alive and he isn't... because we didn't save him?" More silence, the insects and night sounds jarringly loud.

"No, Jans. Hans doesn't hate us. He knew he was going to die, and he still chose to let us live. That's what he did: he sacrificed himself so we could live. Someone who loves you does that, not someone who hates you." Jans was confused.

"How could Hans love me? We didn't even know each other before."

"You get different kinds of love. The most obvious one is the love for your family, but sometimes, love isn't just for someone you know very well... Although, he and I were very good friends, so we had friendship—which is a kind of love. But the love he had for you and Elsso was the love for another person, someone who is just another person like you. A person that you like and respect, even though you don't actually know them that well. And also: a love for the right thing, to do the right thing. Does that make sense?" Jans didn't understand, exactly, but he would think about it some more.

"Like a hero? Who cares about people he doesn't know?"

"Exactly like that... Hans was a hero," her voice was hoarse.

"Do you think they will give him a hero's funeral, like in the army? With a salute and a poem?" Jans had always been excited by the idea of war heroes, mostly because that's how he saw his big half-brother, Svens. When he heard stories about heroes from the stories, they looked like Svens in his head.

"I... I'm not sure. I don't think so. There will be too many people to find and bury—if the Gruxhoon don't take over the palace for a while," Ata sounded really sad.

"So, no-one will care when he's buried? Nobody will say what he did—that he's a hero?" this felt really wrong to Jans. Hanson had saved them; he should be buried to show that.

"We could have our own ceremony, if you want? We don't have his body to bury, but the body isn't really him because his spirit has left it, so that's not such a big issue..." Ata suggested.

"I still have his charm—the one he gave me for good luck... We could bury that?" Jans suggested; Ata was quiet for a long time again, then agreed.

They had held a small 'ceremony' under the big, old tree that had protected them. They buried the pretty silver star Hanson had lent Jans, everyone said 'thank you' to Hans, and Ata had cried a lot. Jans hoped she would miss him as much if he also died.

"Ata?"

"Yes, Jans."

"I love you." She smiled sadly at him.

"I love you too, Jans."

"And Els?"

"And Els."

"Like family, right? Not just because... just for the right thing?" She had looked at him very seriously. Then she nodded.

"Like family, Jans."

She had picked up Els, taken Jans's hand, and they kept going.

When Ata finally moved, finally woke up, Jans moved close to her immediately. He knelt down, trying to keep his balance with his right arm tied to his body. She groaned, then opened her eyes. They snapped sharply into focus, fixing on him; her face didn't change but her expression softened. Then she closed her eyes and tears ran down the sides of her face.

"We made it." Her voice didn't sound like hers; it rasped like an old woman's. Jans didn't even think, just lunged at her, clinging tightly as she softly patted his back. He was crying again. *Ata.* At some point, Elsso also found his way to them and was wriggling into their shared hug. His wails were half-hearted, but continuous.

It took a while for them to calm down, at which point the maid helped prop Ata upright and gave her water and soup. She couldn't lift her arm after she'd eaten half, so Len came and fed her the rest. Jans could tell she wanted to talk again.

"I'm Lenna, Ata," Jans could see amusement on Ata's

face. He had become very familiar with it and every other expression she had.

"I know, Your Highness. Thank you for the soup... and the care." Ata's gaze flicked over the interior of their shelter. "I thought I'd be kept on bread and water in some kind of prisoner's confinement... I assume I should be thanking you for these accommodations and the protection you've clearly provided?" Len flicked her hand dismissively.

"It's nothing, considering what you've done for my brothers. I owe you a great deal—the House of Hårbørgen owes you a great deal for restoring its heirs—"

"I didn't shred my feet and risk my life for the *heirs* of the House of Hårbørgen, nor for any favours owed. I chose to do it for myself and for Jans and Els. Forgive me, but I don't need your gratitude," Ata was blunt, then smiled commiseratingly. "Even if I am making extensive use of your hospitality at the moment. For which I am grateful, but would rather not view as some sort of exchange for something I have given freely." Lenna didn't look insulted or annoyed; she looked riveted. Then her expression hardened.

"Nothing is for nothing, *Ata*. That has been instilled in me since the cradle and my subsequent life experience has not changed my opinion on it. You, like everyone else at court, seem to play games with words.

Let us have plain speaking between us, if you please?"
Ata nodded, face indecipherable.

"Who are you? The general, Lord Svensso, says that you are Pandial. I can only assume a spy, even though he did not say so, because you entered Hårbørgen Palace as a servant, purposely imitating a provincial Cinnaen when it's clear you are well-educated. Maybe even nobility, from the way you carry yourself and speak to me, a princess, as though we are equals... Then, too, you have some kind of military training, for both Mistress Famenke and Elsso let slip that you've singlehandedly slain a few Gruxhoon in the course of your escape. No mean feat, even for seasoned warriors... Though I am not entirely sure of the accurate number of your body count, to be fair."

Len smiled almost apologetically but Jans knew she wasn't sorry. She had the same expression when she beat him at parlour games. She was a sneaky one. But Ata didn't seem worried.

"Your Highness is very observant, for which I commend you. Unfortunately, I can neither confirm nor deny any of your statements as I am not bound by any oath of allegiance or law of subjugation to you, nor the House of Hårbørgen. You may make of that what you will. However, although I respectfully decline answering any questions regarding myself and my reason for being at the palace, I am more than willing to share the details of my time with the princes," she looked at Jans and smiled warmly.

"Very well, I accept these terms. However, I should warn you that the Royal Council, including the military commanders of Cinnae, will not. Once you are handed over to them—which is an inevitability, as I can only keep you from them for so long—they will ask the same and more detailed questions. A refusal to answer them would not go well for you, irrespective of what you have done to aid my brothers," Len was being her earnest self, the person she saved for her family. Jans had never seen her speak so openly to someone outside their family, never mind a stranger.

"Do not worry about me. Though, I appreciate your concern, I will manage whatever lies ahead." Jans hoped she would, because he refused to think that anything bad could happen to her. *They were here. They were together. They were safe. Just like she'd promised.*

"You're not in trouble, Your Highness," fat Hjarl Janssen said with a kind smile on his face. Jans wasn't fooled. He didn't like him. Didn't like his face. The hjarl wouldn't tell him where Ata was; he had been there when they took Ata away from them. Jans and Els still stayed with Len but Ata had been taken somewhere else. She had needed a stick to lean on to be able to walk out of their tent because her feet were still ugly and hurt. The men who took her didn't care.

Jansso *hated* them. More than he had ever hated anyone before, even Ata when they were running away from the Gruxhoon.

"I want to see Ata!" Jans repeated stubbornly. "I don't want to tell you anything without her here. I *demand* you bring her to me!" Jans had never used that word before but had heard his mother and other courtiers use it often enough. If he was a prince, then they had to listen to him. He glared at the faces around the table.

They were in a big tent with all the important soldiers (including Svens) all around. Jans was angry with Svens. He was supposed to be a hero, to help people who needed help, but here he was asking stupid questions and working with the people who had taken Ata away from them. She was hurt and she needed them. When they had needed her, she had done everything for them. Now she needed them and these awful people wouldn't let them see her or even tell them where she was. He hated Svens now. Svens wasn't a hero. He was a bad guy. Like the Gruxhoon.

"Prince Jansso, please, just tell us what happened when you left the palace that night—where did you go? Whom did you see? We need your help, Your Highness," Svens had leaned closer, using his 'serious face' to make Jans listen. He wouldn't.

"I want Ata," crossing his arms, Jans stared at Svens hard. The general sighed and rubbed his scar and nose hard. Then he turned to the other men and, in low voices, they discussed something. Jans didn't care. He wanted Ata. Someone left the tent and some time later, a slow, uneven stride came through door-opening. *Ata.* Jans didn't even think; he was on his feet, hugging her within seconds. She rubbed and patted his back, making soothing sounds. *They were together.* Elsso, who had been seated with the redheaded maid started squirming and making a fuss.

"Ata! I wants Ata!" he squeaked, finally managing to wriggle free and join Jans in gripping Ata's legs, holding on for dear life.

"I hope you haven't been making a fuss, Your Highness..." Ata said clearly, yet her grip on Jans's shoulder told him she had missed him too. She was glad they were together; he had done that. His heart swelled with pride. *They were together again.*

"Now that we have you all here together—as per Your Highness's insistence," said Lord Bransso, the scary, big general with all the medals and loud voice, "Could we proceed with the questioning?" Ata hobbled to the chair Jans had been in before, and once seated, both boys clambered onto her enthusiastically. Jans had missed being close to her; he hadn't been able to sleep without her familiar presence there. This was right. The men were all looking at each other with serious expressions, some surprised. Then, they started answering questions for a very long time...

They explained everything that happened during their escape—the palace, the larder, the tree and Hanson, the farm, the river, the constant running from the Gruxhoon. Ata had carried them and run most of the way. That was why her feet looked the way they did. But the important council people didn't seem to appreciate that. They just pulled faces and tried to catch Ata out in a lie; to find out where she came from and why she helped them.

Ata never said it was because she loved them, that they were family, so Jans didn't say it either. *But he knew.* When they started to take Ata away again, he and Elsso shouted at them but it didn't make a difference; they were carried kicking and screaming back to Len's tent. Then Svens was there, trying to talk to them, but they wouldn't listen.

"Jans, this is unacceptable conduct. You and your brother need to start behaving *right now*! You *will* eat, and you *will* sleep when told. You don't need this 'Ata' with you—she isn't anything to you. Yes, she helped you, but she isn't your mother or sister; she's a stranger. She will *not* be involved in your lives moving forward."

Svens had dropped their titles and had his strict face on. "Do you understand me?" forcefully; Jans didn't say anything. They would see who outlasted whom.

Finally, Svens left, shaking his head and muttering

about "undue influence". The day passed with Len begging them to eat something, then nagging; finally she tucked them into the bed on the floor. Els managed to doze off but Jans just couldn't sleep—which was just as well, because as he lay and stared at the canvas wall of the tent, subtle movement outside drew his attention. Before he could become frightened, Ata's voice whispered.

"Jans?"

"Ata!" he started to sit up.

"Shh! Don't draw attention to me... Just lie down and listen carefully." He lay back down.

"Did they let you go?" he whispered, eyeing Lenna and the maid who were sitting near the tent entrance, talking quietly and intently.

"Pffft, no. I... found my way out of their custody. Listen..." she paused, "I have to leave for a whil—"

"No, you can't! You said—you *promised*—we would stay together!" Jans tried to keep his voice down. Luckily, some soldiers were singing loudly outside and it drowned out their whispered argument.

"Jans! You need to listen to me... We did stay together and I brought you to your family safely. Now, I must go to my family. They need me," Jans felt tears leaking out of his eyes; he tried to force them to stop by squeezing his eyes shut.

"But we're family, you said. You said you loved us like family. You don't leave your family!" he quietly whined.

"I'm not leaving you, Jans, and I'll always love you and Els," she paused shortly, then continued, "I keep my promises, right?"

"Yes…" he didn't mention Hanson, because he knew how much she had wanted to keep that promise and it hadn't been her fault she couldn't.

"Well, I swear to you, we will be together again. I will make it so. But for now, my brother, my uncle, and my cousin need me. They need my help against the Grux-hoon. If I go now, I can help everyone—even your brothers and sister. Everyone in this camp. But I *must* leave now. Understand?" He did, but he didn't want to.

"Ata… Are you a spy like they keep saying?" he asked to try and keep her there a bit longer, and because he had been wondering. She was quiet for a bit.

"Yes, Jans. I am. But you mustn't say anything to anyone. Not even your brother, Svens. You understand? I'm trusting you with an important secret." He did understand, plus he wasn't going to tell Svens anything. He was still mad at him. Then a worrying thought occurred to him.

"Do you love being a spy?" Ata gave a muffled chuckle.

"Sometimes. Not now, obviously."

"More than you love us?" he didn't mean to sound so sad, but he couldn't help it.

"No, Jans. I don't love it that much," she said, her usual tone telling him she wasn't lying.

"And you promise you'll come back? You won't leave us forever?" he whispered, swallowing audibly.

"You have my word, Jans. We will see each other again. And I will keep loving you, even when we're not together anymore." There was silence between them while the song the soldiers sang reached its crescendo. "Do we have an agreement, Your Highness?"

"Yes," his voice wavered.

"And will you tell Els goodbye from me—tell him I promise we'll be together again?"

"Yes; I'll tell him all the time, so he won't forget. Don't forget!" he felt anxious. "And don't die." He felt silly saying it, but did anyway. He heard her smile.

"I'll try my very best, Jans... But I must go now."

"Ata?"

"Yes, Jans?"

"No-one ever told me they loved me before you." Silence.

"I know, Jans."

She didn't say anything else, so Jans assumed she had left and fell into a deep sleep—something he hadn't been able to do since she'd been taken away. Everyone was awoken a few hours later by the camp alarm being sounded. Shortly after all the noise broke out, Svens shouted at their tent entrance. The maid (Menke, she said they could call her) stumbled to the flap and opened it; Svens stormed in and came directly to Jans and Els. He crouched and grasped Jans's shoulders firmly.

"Jans! You need to be honest with me! Did *that woman*, Ata, come to you this evening? Did she tell you where she was going?" his face was harsh in the half-light of the tent, his manner urgent. He looked *very* angry.

Jans just smiled at his brother.

11

CASTLES IN THE AIR

Oh, but now old friends they're acting
  strange
And they shake their heads they tell
  me that I've changed
Well something's lost, but something's gained
In living every day

I've looked at life from both sides now
From win and lose and still somehow
It's life's illusions I recall
I really don't know life at all

Joni Mitchell

Enddaian Keep was everything Hårbørgen Palace wasn't. Neither picturesque nor breathtaking, it did not speak to the artist's soul and it most definitely did not elicit flights of fancy in the viewer. What it was, was secure beyond anything imaginable—a fortress of rock and elements that could withstand a millennium of attacks to its black-ore walls, its ramparts unassailable. The only beauty to be found in its stark precipices and unbreachable battlements was the loveliness of absolute unassailability. A guarantee of survival within its sanctum.

Ata looked up at the high vaulting of the city gateway, the cloud break drenching her face beneath the dark cowl as she rode along the winding path through Enddaian Town, up the embankment towards the castle. Not wanting to draw attention to herself, she made her way to the back of the keep, to the servants' gate; there would still be plenty of eyes watching—she had spotted at least three agents who noted her arrival in town. These being the ones known to her, she had no doubt there were just as many unknown to her reporting to their masters. Care on her part could only go so far in keeping her presence a secret.

At the gate she smiled at the guards, both of whom had been on manoeuvres with her at some point over the past three years, and she was waved through with only a nominal word of welcome. Her nag, whom she had dubbed 'Svensecond' because of its stubborn nature and subtle spite, was left in the stables following a thorough brushing and feeding. The gelding wasn't worth much compared to the blooded destriers in her uncle's stables, but it had carried her many miles from the Cinnaen camp and was all she had. *A stolen, ancient hack your only valuable possession. Pathetic.*

She made it to the corridor of her room before her demons caught up with her, the first one being Lord Danai, standing rigidly at her chamber door. He straightened even more (if that were possible) at the sight of her, his expression barely changing. But she noticed the release of tension around his eyes and knew he was pleased by her safe return.

"Well met, Lady Atiyah," he intoned, bluntly striking his chest with his fist. Ata blinked. Only a few months away and even their most prosaic practices suddenly seemed quite foreign. She had become used to effeminate bows and curtseys, or at most the working class clasping of forearms amongst Cinnaen men. Now, she would have to reacclimate to the traditional fist-to-chest salute between current and former military combatants (whether male or female) and the jerky nods between everyone else.

Pandial culture was less flowery than Cinnaens' but just as entrenched in historic protocol and commonly accepted practice. Unlike Cinnae, Pandi was largely meritocratic—titles of career and achievement superseded those of birth, and though the aristocracy had immense power, socioeconomic mobility was high with middle and even working-class citizens being able to work themselves upward in society. The main (if not only) respected means of such self-promotion was via the military, although advantageous marriage still provided another, less salubrious mode of hierarchical leapfrog.

Historically a warlike nation, the Pandial were very practical and systematic as well as committed to enhancing and empowering their kingdom through self-sacrifice. Kings fought alongside subjects, princes trained with commoners, and *everyone* was required to undergo military training in their youth, then to contribute their service to their country intermittently throughout their lives. The most significant deviation from the Cinnaen approach? These mandates included women.

Viewed as barbaric and uncivilized by the other kingdoms, nevertheless, the largescale promotion of this system by Feldai the Great three-hundred odd years before had rendered Pandi *the* continental military power. Cinnae was their main rival to that title, however, having seen their army up close, Ata noted that their antiquated approaches—archaisms hearkening back to their glory days—had weakened them significantly. More than anyone on the continent was truly aware of, apparently. She had been shocked by what she perceived as the overall weakness of the Cinnaen army compared to what she knew of the Pandial military. Yet none of the current governments seemed aware of the starkness of this disparity.

"Well met, Lord Danai," she smiled, thumping her chest over her heart with her right hand. The salute had initially been the same for all, the fist over the heart being the symbolic element, however, over the preceding century it had deviated slightly, changing so that one now used their dominant hand to thump the opposite side of their chest. For most, it remained over the heart, but for the minority whose main sword arm was their left, this was not the case. Like Lord Danai, who was left-handed due to necessity.

He had been injured as a young man, rendering his right arm almost useless due to most of the muscle being cut away after a wound went septic. He never spoke of it, so Ata had ferreted out the information from Verana, the ancient local midwife. The old woman also made herbal remedies and supplied Lord Danai with a tincture for his health. The fact that the spymaster of Pandi trusted her not to poison him spoke to her inherent status as a local bastion, as well as her categorical incorruptibility.

"Thank you for meeting me at my very door to offer welcome, my lord," Ata added mockingly, unlocking it with the key she had temporarily suspended from her Enstroi chain. It had survived her cross-country flight with the princes as well as her more recent escape from the Cinnaen refugee camp and subsequent travel to Enddaian. She entered first, seeing everything as she had left it—Min, her cousin, had the only other key and had clearly ensured it was cleaned and dusted in Ata's absence.

The smell of fresh beeswax permeated the compact space. Ata felt a familiar ache of gratitude beneath her sternum. When finally able to arrange an audience with Princess Mindaia, she would find some subtle way to thank her for this act of service.

"Have a seat, my lord," Ata indicated the wooden stool, dropping her saddlebags on the floor and lowering herself gingerly onto the end of the bed. It seemed her lot in life to only have tiny, sparsely furnished rooms belong to her, irrespective of buildings.

"Thank you. I trust you will forgive my running you to ground immediately upon your arrival, but I require accurate information from the horse's mouth, as it were..." his sharp, obsidian eyes, ageless in his aged face, cleaved through artifice. She had forgotten their razor quality. "Is it true the Cinnaen stronghold has fallen to the Gruxhoon invasion?" Ata sighed heavily and rubbed her itchy eyes; her failure to return timeously had basically negated her usefulness as informant. All her time at Hårbørgen essentially wasted.

"I should think any information I am able to provide would be sadly outdated by now... Your other agents will have already apprised you of the Gruxhoon invasion; they are probably better informed than I, at this point."

"What detained you?" dispassionately, but Ata wasn't fooled. She arched her brow.

"Do I really need to tell you? There's no way you do not already know—one of your many sources would have flown to tell you of why I was delayed."

"Yes, I am aware," dryly, "but I would like to hear from your own lips why you felt the need to compromise not only your own mission, but potentially involve Pandi in an international incident because of your interference?" The last part was clipped; he was clearly working hard to control his significant temper. She remained defiantly silent.

"How would it look to have a Pandial spy inside the Cinnaen royal family's home? And then: your knowledge of the Gruxhoon would've exposed you to suspicions of aiding and abetting their invasion. Not just you, once again, but the Pandial government too!" even in a towering rage, he never raised his voice. It curdled one's blood, the level of cool control this man exercised over himself (and others). Silence. "Those were not rhetorical questions, Ata!" he snapped. She was in deep shit if he used her given name and not the faux honorific that was particular to him.

"They were only children..." she stated, not looking away from him. "Would *you* have been able to leave them to such a fate?"

"It is not a question of what I would have done, but what you *did not* do! 'Observe and report' only! Your meddling could have undone all of our plans," he raged in his tightly controlled way. "Two fewer heirs of Hårbørgen would've cemented their desperation, and consequently their amenability to form an alliance with Pandi," he added as an afterthought, enraging Ata.

"My conscience would never permit me to allow such a thing. I could not—would not—stand by and do nothing."

"We, as tools and servants of the greater good do not get to have a conscience, never mind letting it dictate our actions!"

"But I have a conscience and soul, and will compromise neither!" he glowered at her.

"Not even for the greater good? Thousands of lives saved, potentially, just by allowing two to be lost?" he hedged, coldly logical.

"Not even then."

"It is dangerous to be so uncompromising, Ata. *Deadly*, in the game of politics."

"I don't play games, nor would I want to if it meant I would be a party to something so monstrous as leaving two children to be slaughtered. You don't face the reality of it when you receive your orders... They're almost nebulous—abstract, maybe. But facing the reality is very different."

"In the writing of history then, if you object to my previous game analogy?"

"Again: *not even then.*"

"We must agree to disagree, then."

"So be it." They were both silent for a long while, the seconds ticking by as they glared at each other.

"You are a very stubborn woman, Lady Atiyah," he stated wryly, an olive branch from this unyielding man.

"I wouldn't want to make life too easy for you, my lord," she smiled ruefully at him. "Speaking of... Why did you not inform me about Lord Iansso?" His face had not so much as twitched at the mention of the Cinnaen.

"What of him?" *Annoying, devious man!*

"The fact that he is a close confident of yours; he knew everything about the Gruxhoon situation... He even knew I would be at the palace, my *name*, but not my ultimate role," she left the implication dangling there. A baited hook.

"Suffice it to say I interact quite closely with Lord Iansso. We have much in common—"

"But not your loyalties."

"Some—the most important ones—we do have in common. We just manifest our support of our loyalties in disparate ways." Nodding, she thought of her and Kai's similarities and differences. Lord Danai's description aptly described their relationship as well.

For the rest of the hour, Ata explained in minute detail all that had befallen her. However, she tended to gloss over her interactions with Lord Svensso for reasons she did not care to acknowledge, even to herself. All she knew was that she did not want Lord Danai's not-insignificant attentions shifting to such a competent and apparent threat to Pandial interests in Cinnae's vulnerable state. She would rather keep him in ignorance for as long as possible.

JUST AS SHE EXPECTED, Kai found her by that evening. As had always been the practice at Enddaian, all were welcome to attend collective dinners in the great hall of the keep. Long trestle tables ran lengthwise through the large space; seating tended to be set out based somewhat on rank and somewhat on personal preference. Thus, the upper echelons sat closest to the dais where the royal table stood perpendicular to all the other tables, giving the royal family and their particular guests for a meal an unencumbered view of the entire gathering.

Though she was genetically part of the royal family, Ata had never been placed at the main table (whether by order or invitation). Her last name, Denada, the patronymic assignation for the illegitimate child of an unknown male, meant she sat at the lowest end of the tables. Only servants were lower on the totem than she and her ilk, but they ate in their own dining hall below stairs.

Although Lord Danai shared the unknown-illegitimacy patronymic, he had distinguished himself in his youth through combat and diplomatic services to the kingdom, thereby being elevated to the peerage. Thus, he was generally seated at the higher tables with the other lords and ladies. Sometimes he was invited to the head table, though not often; he preferred to maintain a low-key presence, avoiding any sign of familiarity with the king.

"Look what the cat dragged in! Your hair looks... interesting," a deep voice mocked behind her seat on the bench. *Her second demon.* She didn't deign to turn from her half-eaten meal.

"Even if I shaved my head completely, I'd still look better than you do, you pillock." An exuberant burst of laughter erupted.

"Fair comment... I cede the point," and the bench shuddered as his large self settled next to her. She gave him serious side-eye. He still looked the same as when she left: shaggy, thick black hair that curled slightly, ever-present shit-eating grin. No wonder he had so many girls after him—just as well dimples had never been to Ata's particular taste. "What? No hugs and cuddles?" Arms hammily thrown wide in invitation. *The ridiculous, theatrical idiot.* She flattened her mouth, unimpressed.

"In no iteration of the known world would I stoop to hugging you in public. I've been pranked once too often, you clown."

"But you would in private, eh?" he smirked at her then dropped his arms and gazed at her ruefully with calf-like adoration. All for show. "Didn't you miss me even a little, lovely?" the bashful boy act was in full swing and Ata sensed many eyes on them, most of them female. Such was always the case when hanging out with Kai... that and jealous jibes, spiteful gossip, and malicious collusions. Women's vicious territorial disputes put any brash, simplistic male posturing to shame.

"Like a hole in the head, buffoon," Finishing her meal, she rose to leave. Falling in beside her, he strutted in his particular manner. Once in an empty corridor, he halted her with a hand to the shoulder, then clutched her tightly to his chest. The hug continued interminably. "You can let me go now." Her voice was muffled against his chest.

"I really did miss you, you know," he murmured, giving her a last, rib-cracking squeeze before releasing her. She grinned up into his beloved face.

"I know, *Brother*." He cast a dubious look up and down the corridor.

"Don't be calling me that in public, I beg you. Otherwise people will have some serious questions about our familial proclivities," his eyebrows hitched up and down meaningfully. She rolled her eyes.

"I suffer assumptions about our 'romance' for your and Min's sakes only," she whispered, "but I'm not going to constantly play into it to the detriment of expressing my real feelings... Life is short, and I want to be able to say most of the important things that need saying in my life, Kai." His joking mien transformed into a serious one.

"I'm sorry, Ata... I'm just messing about. But I can tell you're not in the mood. Do you want me to leave?"

"No. I don't want you to go; I'm sorry I'm being difficult. I really *am* pleased to see you, Kai." His face broke into a heart stopping smile.

"Me too, *dearest Sister.*" So they retired to her room for conversation while she sketched him for the umpteenth time in their long history. She noted the new nicks and scars, the same expressions of her best and closest friend. She added the drawing to her collage on the wall; all the familiar faces from her life—some at different stages of their own journey. A disarrayed time-line of sorts.

They spent the whole night talking about his promotion and her horrifying escape, uncaring that this "proved" their purported romantic relationship further to those who paid attention to such things.

"WELL, well, well... if it isn't the missing by-blow, returned to the fold at last!" malice permeated the male voice, and chuckles accompanied the witticism. Ata didn't pause her sparring; Kai would exploit it, even if he despised the rat, Lord Fordai, now tormenting her. 'Take no prisoners', and all that. Ignoring Fordai's taunts was never a good idea, but there was no help for it.

"Where did you disappear to for all these weeks, bastard brat?" the voice continued. He would never use such language if any of the superior officers were present—only when it was lowly grunts like them. Kai didn't count, although he had attained the rank of lieutenant in her absence—quite the achievement, and one for which she was so proud of him.

They were all contemporaries, having trained together since their adolescence; and for some reason, *Lord* Fordai (to Ata, per his insistence) could not stand the sight of the two of them. The simplest explanation for his hatred was that they were both half-bloods, but Ata didn't think that was it. For someone who seemed to despise them so thoroughly, his sister, Lady Kenttai, couldn't seem to cease chasing after Kai. It was almost embarrassing the lengths to which she went to gain his attention... Ata might have felt a measure of sympathy for her, had she not been a raging bitch towards Ata, whom she considered her main rival for his affections. *If only she knew!*

"I didn't realise you're transferring to our squad, *Lord*

Fordai," she observed casually once her bout with Kai had finished. Of course that arse had beaten her like a dirty rug. *She'd be all shades of bruised tomorrow.* The other boy's lip curled derisively.

"I'm not, thank the gods! I have been promoted to War Council's Secretary Adjunct and therefore no longer train with this company," arrogance oozed from his every word and action. It irked Ata, despite her best efforts; she would never admit out loud that he was an excellent fighter whose skills would be missed in their field drills.

"How fortuitous you were promoted... Nepotism seems to be standing you in great stead. Isn't your father, the duke, on that council? Perhaps it also ensured he wasn't sent on the scouting expedition four months ago?" she'd turned to Kai who had insouciantly been drinking from the water ladle, for the last comment. He snorting with suppressed laughter. She should have kept her mouth shut; Fordai did not take any form of belittlement well. And he was as vicious in his retaliations as the rodent she associated him with, never coming at you head-on, but always sideways. Dark eyes narrowed as a flush stained his tan skin. He might have been considered good-looking if his gods-awful personality hadn't warped him so.

"That's rich, seeing as you seem to be kept safe and sound while that stupid lummox behind you is forever being sent on scouting expeditions... Probably lined up some protection through that old, bearded goat you're constantly following about. You must be really good on your knees—like mother, like daughter," even his supporters deemed this a tad too far. It was one thing to insult Ata, but an entirely different prospect to malign a princess of the blood.

Snarling, Kai advanced with intent, but she grabbed his arm to stop him. Some of her earliest memories were of hissed vulgarities related to her mother; courtiers, servants, soldiers—anyone who thought her weak and unprotected—trying to impose their authority on a hapless, helpless child. But she wasn't a child anymore, and she controlled this narrative. They wouldn't see her bleed, even metaphorically.

One of their superiors, a captain, approached, she noted out of the corner of her eye. He would join their little huddle shortly. Fordai stood with his back to him, unaware of the imminent, looming presence of authority. And she smiled pointedly into his triumphant face.

"Aw, a lady never tells... You must be quite exceptional on your knees yourself, considering the plum positions you've managed to attain through the years." He lunged at her, apoplectic—his ego had always been greater than his sense. Luckily, his followers had noted the arrival of the captain and weren't completely mindless; they held him back with all their might. The consequences for unsanctioned fights amongst soldiers were harsh.

"Although," she fastened her baldric, "I'll give you a friendly warning: do not malign the king's sister within the hearing of anyone who would carry such tales to him... He might not have much fondness for *me*, but it is a well-known fact he adored his little sister." With that parting shot, she and Kai moved on to the archery butts.

"He is a real piece of shit," Kai groused as they once again took their positions in front of the targets. Ata didn't respond; such an obvious fact needed no confirmation. Plus, Kai was just trying to distract her. She nocked her arrow; Kai followed suit. "A dung-head..." he expanded, "...a turd-cake..." She ignored him, drawing. He did too. "...a stool sample..." She aimed carefully, bowstring on kiss button. "... the fetid faecal freak..." Exhale. *Release!*

She turned to Kai; he had shot at the same time as she. Face darkening with annoyance, he swore as he glared at the targets.

"'Fetid faecal freak'? Really?" she quirked her head. He huffed ruefully.

"It was alliterative—and worth a try... Gods! Don't you ever miss, Woman?" they moved to collect their arrows. "There goes another shooting session..." Completing their various training exercises, they finally left, sweaty and achy, with Kai still sulking over their running archery tournament outcome.

"How about I buy a round at the 'Drink-in Hole'?

Would that help restore your recently punctured ego to previous, overinflated proportions?"

"I don't need a pity-drink from you, thank you very much," sourly.

"Fine… How many times have you lost at the butts, again?" she teased. He really was ridiculously, childishly competitive.

"Shut up!"

SINCE HER RETURN, Ata had been arguing tirelessly for a formal alliance with the Cinnaens, now that they were so vulnerable, if only to Lord Danai. A week passed before Ata was summoned to attend King Addai at his breakfast—not to be confused with attending the breakfast as a guest of His Majesty and thus dining with him. Her role was to *attend* the monarch, i.e., serve him as he entertained the invitees to his breakfast table.

She dressed circumspectly, as expected. Even though Pandial women could, theoretically, do all tasks historically reserved for men as well as wear the accompanying attire, for such formal, honoured occasions, a traditional dress was considered customary. Ata owned the sum total of two dresses, as opposed to her numerous pairs of leggings and tunics; she had one pair of slippers, yet multiple pairs of sensible boots. Sadly, all of her 'formal wear' was frayed and faded. She was a practical stepping stone in her uncle's court, not a glittering jewel on display whose only worth lay in her presentation, and her wardrobe was a stark reminder of this fact.

Keeping her head down upon entering her uncle's private chambers, she made her obeisance where he sat in his breakfast room, then took a stance against the wall behind his left shoulder. He hadn't shown any particular interest at her entry or greeting, continuing to read the stack of reports arrayed alongside his silverware and crockery.

There was one other courtier in attendance; a small man with a weaselly face, misleading in appearance, for Ata knew him to be trustworthy and intelligent. He acted as advisor, agent, and representative to the king whenever the need arose; thus far he had acquitted himself well of these tasks. They proceeded to await the arrival of His Majesty's guests.

Finally, the door opened softly, Her Highness, Princess Mindaia entering and accompanied by her aged companion, Mistress Dreka. Another difference between the Cinnaen and Pandial princesses; the former was constantly accompanied by a gaggle of perfumed and powdered ladies-in-waiting, twittering like a flock of frivolous finches.

The latter, conversely, was never seen out of the company of a silent, owlish matron who had been her childhood nursemaid. Stolidly implacable and loyal to a fault, Dreka was a stalwart servant of the royal family. Mindaia did not look towards the back wall where the two attendants stood, but turned to her nurse and nodded emphatically, after which the woman left the room to await her return summons.

"Well met, Father," the princess performed the fist-thump salute, reciprocated by her father. They had both completed their training as behoved the monarchs of Pandi, King Addai probably much more adept in his military career compared to kindly Mindaia, but neither shirked their respective duties to their realm.

"Well met, Daughter. Have a seat," and they began to make desultory conversation as servants brought platters of eggs with pastries, bowls of fruits and grains, and plates of cheese. They laid out the fare and left; it was common practice here for people to serve themselves from communal plates, even at formal dinners.

"Lord Uldai, would you return these various reports to their compilers?" King Addai's voice instructed. The young lord scurried forward and collected the pile of papers.

"It might take...some time, Your Majesty. I would have to find the various authors. I regret I do not foresee returning in fewer than... three hours?" The king waved his hand in a 'let it be so' motion, hastening the man on his way. Once he had left, Mindaia looked directly at Ata.

"Please join us, Cousin. You have been missed," her

deep brown eyes—doe eyes—shone with sheer contentment. The king did not turn nor support her statement, but neither did he gainsay her, so Ata sank into the third seat. "How are you, Ata? We heard you were injured while away?" Min's heartfelt concern was comforting.

"Yes, I was, but nothing too serious... Just my feet that were in poor shape, but I managed to... find a ride for the entire journey afterwards, so they healed fast." Also: she had managed to utilise Commanding in a way that she had not known was possible. For some reason, she had kept this a closely guarded secret, neither telling Lord Danai nor Kai. She felt unnerved by the extent one could *'ad lib'* when casting, shaping the power with focused intent rather than words, and didn't want to share it with anyone. Not quite yet, anyway.

"I am so pleased to hear that! Can you tell us anything of your travels? Anything at all?" though politely neutral, Ata sensed the burning curiosity beneath the placid words and tone. Although she had never said so, Min envied Ata her more extensive freedom. She did not resent Ata, exactly, nor did she try to change her role and circumstances, for she understood that purely by being who she was she would be denied many things as well as be entitled to many others.

It was the trap of being who they were; they could accept it and do the best they were able to within their respective frameworks, yet still reserve a small corner of their hearts to nurture resentment over their lot in life.

In deference to Min's somewhat caged existence (*weren't they all in cages of one type or another?*), Ata shared the most innocuous parts of her time in Cinnae without actually divulging where she went and why. Eventually, they had eaten their fill, but her uncle hadn't said anything—only listened.

"I will say good day to you both. Your Majesty," Min performed her salute to her father, who returned it, "Cousin." A smile and salute. Then Ata and her uncle were alone. It felt strangely awkward; she could not remember the last time she had been alone with King Addai. Was it when she was a child and he would sit by her bedside? A man she knew and yet didn't, fully. He now leaned back in his chair, contemplating her almost absentmindedly.

"Am I dismissed, Your Majesty?" Ata enquired politely, bringing him out of his brown study. He frowned.

"You have made your report to Lord Danai, correct?" She nodded sharply; he mirrored her nods, abstracted. He appeared to be waiting for her to say more.

"He and I had... somewhat of a difference of opinions, you could say," the king quirked his eyebrow in question. She decided to be forthright, even if the king did consequently think her a fool (though hopefully not a traitor). "I couldn't stand by and watch the youngest Hårbørgen heirs fall to the Gruxhoon during the palace invasion. You see, they're not just 'heirs'; they are more than that. And less. Just two little boys who didn't deserve to die for being who they were."

As always, the king's expression was indecipherable. "Lord Danai all but called me simple, too moral, and said I will fail miserably at the game of politics. But I cannot be sorry for the lives I saved. Even at the cost of potentially exposing Pandial..." She paused; she might as well state her main aim in returning now—this was why she had left Jans and Elsso, after all. "And, what's more, I am strongly convinced we should offer Cinnae an alliance, irrespective of whether they initiate such discussions or not." Holding her breath, she awaited his reaction.

"Strong words, but we shall gauge their wisdom in the times to come... Sometimes, it is better to refrain from any actions and observe how things unfold. I will take you recommendation under advisement regarding an agreement with Cinnae. Now, I have much to be getting on with. You are dismissed, Sergeant." Well, there was her answer, then. After all her frantic manoeuvring, a lukewarm dismissal... Rising, she saluted and made her way to the door.

"Ata?" she spun in surprise at the tentative utterance. He *never* used her name.

"Yes, Your Majesty?"

"You're sure you are...well? You weren't harmed at all, on this mission?" She had never seen him uncertain before either. His current concern surprised and touched her.

"No, Your Majesty. I am well."

"Good." Awkward silence. "Well enough to be sent on a military reconnaissance mission? A potentially dangerous one?" She nodded.

"Alright, then."

12

———

THE SCALES FALL AWAY

Truth also is the pursuit of it:
Like happiness, and it will not stand.

Even the verse begins to eat away
In the acid. Pursuit, pursuit;

A wind moves a little,
Moving in a circle, very cold.

How shall we say?
In ordinary discourse—

We must talk now. I am no longer sure
of the words.
The clockwork of the world. What is
inexplicable

Is the 'preponderance of objects.' The
     sky lights
Daily with that predominance

And we have become the present.

We must talk now. Fear
Is fear. But we abandon one another.

GEORGE OPPEN

Tensso's clinging exhaustion seemed to drop from his shoulders like a cloak when the Pandial delegation came into view, riding towards them in rigid formation. Their dark, nondescript shades of clothing, including the leather jerkins and armour, contrasted starkly with the shining, engraved metal breastplates and helmets of the Cinnaen armed forces as well as the bright colours denoting different regiments that they wore underneath. Tens himself wore the blue and silver of the House of Hårbørgen, crisply pressed by his manservant, Bernt.

"Your Highness, the Pandial delegation approaches. We shall remain here until Lord Svensso has spoken with them and confirmed all is well, then we will proceed by having them attend you here," Hjarl Janssen murmured to him, and Tens felt a swell of annoyance. As always, Svens would be at the forefront of everything and Tens would be cosseted and held back with the women and the children. *Insupportable!*

"I'm quite sure a handful of Pandial cannot best my private guard; I shall ride out and meet them." Urging his mount forward, his personal protection of four premier soldiers separated from the crowd of courtiers and guards in their section of the column to join him.

"Your Highness, I must protest! To allow even a single Pandial within striking distance of our future king would be folly! It takes only one well-aimed blade to wound fatally... We cannot be sure of the Pandial's willingness to parlay!" Lord Bransso, the senior general of all Cinnaen armed forces rumbled urgently—and bombastically, as was his way. Tens had never liked him and couldn't wait to finally be crowned, if only to summarily replace the old windbag with his half-brother, Svens, whom he considered the superior strategist and warrior, as well as the better man.

"Correct me if I'm wrong, Lord Bransso, but are we not currently on the border of Cinnae and Pandi, with a veritable horde of Gruxhoon at our backs, and thus asking the Pandial nation for succour?" He spoke seriously, without letting his open disdain and sarcasm show. He was less successful than Svens (against whom he measured himself in most ways) at drawing a veil over his true feelings, but he felt pleased with his improvement in that area. His brother's basilisk stare was his ultimate goal in playing the game of politics.

"Yes, Your Highness, but—"

"So, essentially, Pandi need not even exert the effort to be rid of us Cinnaens. They could just sit back and watch the Gruxhoon annihilate us..." Tens let his final words hang over the small assembly of advisors. "All things considered, I reckon we're safer with the Pandial than by ourselves, waiting for the Gruxhoon," he concluded with finality and continued forward to join Svens's party in approaching the Pandial group. Showing no outward surprise at being joined by Tens and his guard, Svens merely acknowledged the prince with a respectful nod.

"His Majesty, King Addai, welcomes you, Prince Tensso, and your court and citizens, as guests of the Pandial nation," the man who spoke was not clearly differentiated by his clothing from the rest of his compatriots—neither rank nor regiment seemed to be indicated in the random assortment of vestments—yet his entire persona conveyed authority. He wore his power like a mantle for all to see, his grizzled and scarred appearance both frightening and fascinating. "I am General Erdai and these are my staff. We speak on behalf of His Majesty, King Addai, and our people."

"It is an honour to meet you, Lord Erdai. I thank His Majesty, King Addai, and your people for taking us in under these circumstances." Tens hoped he sounded regal enough—he felt like a puppy posturing before a battle-honed wolf. With a lupine grin, the general's scarred face twisted into a grimace of humour.

"It's 'General Erdai', Your Highness. I am no lord." There was a momentary silence, shocked on the Cinnaens' part, yet merely watchful on that of the Pandial. Tens could not remember ever being gainsaid nor corrected on his mode of address by anyone up until this point of his life. It must be an indicator of the uncompromisingly proud stance the Pandial took with regard to their cultural practices. Tens was unsure how to respond to this utterance, so merely nodded in what he hoped was regal acquiescence.

"For entrance into Pandial domain, my men will distribute themselves along your columns and accompany you over our border. We have set up camp in an area nearby that will accommodate your numbers and where we can negotiate the terms of our cooperation and aid," the general continued, muttering from the Cinnaen ranks indicating their dislike for the authoritative and somewhat brisk manner of these arrangements. Tens did not much care for the "glory" of his dynasty, nor the required deference others seemed to expect it should elicit, but he did bristle at being spoken to like a boy without agency.

"I shall require your word of honour that all these Cinnaens will not be harmed in any way should we cross the border prior to a treaty agreement," he heard himself state; the older man didn't react, but a black-bearded man behind him suppressed an almost approving smirk, ducking his helmeted head before Tens could analyse his features properly.

"Naturally, Your Highness. My word that on my life no harm shall come to them through direct action by the Pandial army. However, I cannot meet your all-encompassing demand of categorical safety, irrespective of the circumstances. You understand?" Such a reasonable statement could only be assented to.

Further along the column, Tens spotted two familiar faces and purposely turned his gaze away. Lord Ernso and Countess Brelan had been quite unabashed in their hounding of him over the past weeks since their evacuation from the palace. He had diligently avoided their company and their presence in that time, for he had come to the realisation that he became a version of himself with them that, though amusing, was not much of a leader. Or a responsible brother, for that matter.

Where before he had dismissed Len's cautioning words and warnings regarding his group of friends, subsequent to his embarrassing state during the Grux-hoon attack, Tens had reassessed his entire history of interactions with those in his 'inner circle', and found them to be both profoundly hedonistic and lacking in any merit. Hence his self-imposed estrangement from them. It was difficult, and he often felt guilt when he caught their subtly accusing stares, but his mind had been made up, and sadly, their friendship was a necessary sacrifice on the altar of the Cinnaens' future survival. Tens could not afford frivolous distractions during these troubled times.

The black-bearded man remained as Tens's guide, accompanying him and his guard over the border whilst all the other Pandial warriors dispersed (each accompanied by one of Svens's men) to guide the columns of Cinnaens. Five thousand civilians and soldiers, with tens of thousands more on the way over the next few weeks. The entire surviving Cinnaen court. Tens hoped he had made the right decision in trusting a Pandial-Cinnaen treaty would save them from the Gruxhoon.

His guide turned out to be intelligent and tentatively welcoming, knowledgeable in the fauna, flora and geographic details of the much more arid landscape they now traversed. He shared this information in a gruff but friendly way, displaying a quick wit and lack of deference for Tens that immediately appealed to the youth. He was neither a boy to be dominated nor a prince to be fawned over. He was merely a man who knew less about something than another and so was being educated as an equal.

"This is the Liata flower—very deceitful. It was originally named for the venomous serpent of the same name, for it is poisonous to humans in almost all states," 'Blackbeard' (as Tens had dubbed his guide, having forgotten the man's foreign-sounding name) explained. "However, one of our greatest historic Commanders also dabbled in alchemy, and he discovered the secret of this beauty... Her heart, when taken in minute doses, helps build up an immunity against the rest of her, finally overcoming the deadly consequences of her defences.

"Once a person's system has acclimatized to the heart of the flower, its petals and leaves pose no threat and are in fact very beneficial to whomever drinks a tea made from them. It can keep you awake for longer periods of time and allows you to exert more energy for longer. However, take too much of it for too long, and your body will collapse under the strain of its effects."

Blackbeard looked at Tens and smiled slyly, "Many Pandial men take it on their wedding nights." To which Svens, who was riding with them, snorted in good-natured humour. Tens liked Blackbeard, with his seemingly endless knowledge and preparedness to share it with, essentially, an interloper in his country; one whose kingdom had historically looked down on the Pandial and denigrated their culture.

"THOSE ARE UNACCEPTABLE TERMS, MY LORD!"

"It's 'Colonel', actually."

"Bloody hells! How is one supposed to keep track of all your godsdamned ranks?" Lord Bransso snarled and pounded the table. The blustering oaf had reached breaking point with the Pandial delegation, shown by his final rant about their lack of hereditary titles.

"We tend to expect the ability to keep track of individual ranks, being in the Pandial *Army*," came the dry response, enraging the Cinnaen general even further. Svens sat, deadpan as usual, while all the other lords scratched and fidgeted in frustration. Tens sighed.

"I suggest we move on from this particular point and circle back to it once cooler heads prevail," Lord Haaviso, the only Cinnaen besides Svens not huffing and puffing in disgust, stated matter-of-factly. Tens sighed again—*this was going to be a long day...*

By the end of the meeting, they had come to somewhat equitable agreements. Surprisingly, 'Blackbeard', Tens's guide since entering Pandi, had played a significant role in bringing that about. Tens had found him companionable, with a good sense of humour, but he clearly spoke with as much authority as General Erdai based on the part he played in the negotiations.

Future trade agreements were settled upon, with Tens having cemented the deal by committing thousands of acres of private Hårbørgen land to the exchange. Although the Cinnaen generals and ministers grumbled and argued, they knew that some concessions would need to be made. All considered, the absent King Addai's requirements to ensure Cinnae's survival were not particularly egregious. Tens would have expected more greed and vindictiveness, but found only logic and open dealings.

It was just as well the queen had not been present for the negotiations; it was deemed 'preferable' by all involved (besides her and her minions) that she not be given the opportunity to permanently estrange the nations with her acid tongue. Tens was pleased.

Though he suffered Queen Nelni's presence and attentions—he was the favoured heir of her making, after all—he looked forward to the time when he would be able to cast aside her cloying presence. Retire her from court to a nice country manor, perhaps. She had never been a mother to him or his brothers and sister, and he frankly resented her longstanding mistreatment of Svens. She was a cruel and selfish woman; power-hungry yet lacking in strength of character. He had never been blind to those facts, despite trying to make excuses for them when he'd been younger. For now, she just had to be appeased; a tall order considering all she held dear had essentially been stripped from her over the past month.

"Thank you all for the time and energy dedicated to forming this alliance. We will celebrate it properly once we arrive at Enddaian Keep, but for the time being, let us rest for the night so our journey may commence as soon as possible," General Erdai stated, then he and his staff proceeded to beat their chests in the Pandial military salute to those who served in the

Cinnaen army, and nodded jerkily to those who did not.

Tens found their customs fascinating, as well as the underlying menace—an ever-present readiness—that seemed to permeate every Pandial's actions. One sensed their military prowess in their mere presence. He had always felt the same way about Svens, who evinced a constant preparedness to do battle, but had thought his brother the exception. Here, amongst the Pandial, it appeared to be the norm, and led Tens to suspect they would not be so easily overthrown by the Gruxhoon as Cinnae had been.

"So, my young friend. What do you think of Enddaian?" Blackbeard boomed good-humoredly as they approached the capital of Pandi.

"It is very... secure," Tens responded carefully, hoping he did not insult his new, ebullient friend. He need not have worried.

"Yes—it is that. Completely unassailable since it was built more than seven centuries ago," the Pandial preened proudly on his mount. The gelding had to be one of the best examples of destrier Tens had ever seen, and he wondered once again at Blackbeard's status.

Though he now knew the man's name and title (or lack thereof), he still preferred to use his nickname, which Blackbeard had winkled out of him during one night of heavy drinking on the road. The man had roared his mirth when Tens had slipped up and used the moniker, vigorously slapping him on the back in camaraderie. Subsequently, the warrior had insisted Tens keep using it. "It makes me sound quite fierce and warlike, doesn't it," he had joked.

As they started the ascent out of the valley, up the steep slope to the town and castle, Tens considered their week-long sojourn in Pandi. In many ways, the lifestyle was simple, primitive even, with bare basics considered the norm, even amongst nobles. Humble food, sturdy weaponry, practical utensils.

The fripperies of Cinnaen culture, though beautiful and artistic, seemed out of place in their current predicament and so the austere, stolid nature of Pandi appealed strongly to Tens. Simple, honest practices; simple, honest dealings. The homes they passed, once through the gates of the town, were not particularly different from the peasant dwellings in Cinnae, however, the affluent styles and architecture in Cinnaen towns and cities diverged significantly from those here.

A refugee settlement had been created at the foot of the hill, in the valley below Enddaian. Tens and the most senior members of the Cinnaen court would be housed, at least temporarily, at Enddaian Castle, whilst the rest of the court and Cinnaens would be accommodated in the settlement named 'Cinnaian Landing'.

They had ridden through it, and though meagerly built up and consisting largely of tents for the time being, it was still an improvement on their interim tent city in Panø back in Cinnae.

The Pandial seemed to be meeting the criteria of the agreement to the letter. Now, faced with the wide black walls of the aged castle (impregnable by all accounts) Tens felt a measure of relief and safety that he had not felt in the thirty-three days since the Gruxhoon attacked the palace.

He caught a glimpse of Queen Nelni behind him, to his right, as well as Len being accompanied by a young, female Pandial soldier. It was much easier to identify the Cinnaen women amongst the Pandial ones, their pale veils and headdresses distinguishing them from the varying dark shades of the Pandial's hair. Making their way to the stables inside the keep, to the left of the cobblestoned yard, they all dismounted in varying degrees of stiffness. Svens wandered over to them, not showing any signs of discomfort. *Of course not—his half-brother was superhuman.*

"You will rest now, my young friend, and join all of us for dinner in the dining hall," Blackbeard said, quietly and kindly, "You have had a long and wearyi—"

"Your Majesty has returned," an eager female voice called across the yard, the words echoing off the stone surfaces. A young brunette in heavy velvets, followed by an elderly attendant, hurried gracefully towards them.

She was very pretty, with big brown eyes and warm, honey-toned skin.

Though her eyes alighted on him and Svens first with interest, she returned her attention to Blackbeard and thumped her chest in what Tens now knew was the salute between those who currently served (or had previously served) in the Pandial army. This girl was in the army? She didn't look particularly warrior-like.

"Welcome back, Your Majesty. I hope your journey was successful," she smiled at Tens and Svens. "Judging from the size of the party that has arrived, as well as your missives, it was. Welcome to Enddaian Keep, Your Highness. I am Princess Mindaia." The one positive aspect of being completely flummoxed was Svens's accompanying look of sheer confusion (one he had never worn before in Tens's presence). Tens looked at his Pandial friend in perplexity; Blackbeard wore a wry expression—not guilty, exactly, but more in the vein of an indulged child caught in a prank.

"You will forgive my subterfuge, Your Highness?" said the man Tens now understood to be the Pandial king. "It was done without malice, I assure you... When one is a king, one can only gain a true picture of another's character by not being oneself." It was not an apology, but impenitent self-justification. "I hoped to share the information gently upon our arrival here, but Her Highness, the princess, seems to have forestalled me..." and he turned his droll expression on his now-blushing daughter. Despite their exclusive use of titles, there was an obvious warmth of feeling and a closeness between the two members of the Pandial royal family. Tens looked at Svens for guidance, but as per usual, the general maintained a noncommittal façade.

"I honestly don't know what to say, Your Majesty... I know I should be, if not angry, at least morally outraged, but I fear I am too tired to feel much of anything." Tens frowned in confused exhaustion.

"Please, Your Highness. Come inside so you may be taken to your chambers to rest!" Princess Mindaia exclaimed, ushering Tens and his entourage through the castle doors.

The rest afforded Tens in his spacious, if sparsely furnished, chambers restored him to a semblance of normalcy. Luckily, his servant, Bernt, had been permitted to accompany him (most of the personal servants of those who were now housed in the castle had remained in Cinnaian Landing), and was able to guide him and various other courtiers to the communal dining hall.

As with everything else, the spacious room was warm and inviting, but not particularly ornamental. Tens, Len, Queen Nelni, and Svens were ushered to the main table which overlooked all the others perpendic-ular to it. King Addai and Princess Mindaia were already seated, as well as Lord Haaviso and a Pandial lord whom Tens had not yet met.

Dinner seemed a relatively informal affair, with hundreds of people coming and going as they wished, and platters of all the food on offer placed on the tables —diners were expected to serve themselves from them according to their own preference. Of course, Queen Nelni had kept up a vitriolic, whispered monologue throughout, but Lord Haaviso was seated next to her and had to suffer her thoughts on the Pandial court. She did not speak too loudly, as the king was on her other side and had apparently managed (through sheer force of personality) what no-one in the Cinnaen court had: to be spared her every thought.

As the night progressed, Tens noticed Svens, who was seated next to the Pandial lord—a duke named Bendai—had gone ramrod straight in his seat, an icy expression on his face. The duke continued to speak, appearing unconcerned that his dinner partner seemed, in his very controlled way, about to punch him. Tens only knew his half-brother was suppressing an urge to do violence because he had been acquainted with the sphinxlike man since he could remember. And he could tell: Svens was absolutely livid.

Upon glancing up and catching Tens's eye across the length of the table, the Cinnaen general lifted an imperious brow and thinned his lips even more. As Tens opened his mouth to comment, a hubbub at the entrance of the hall drew the attention of everyone at the main table as well as the other diners. Approximately one thousand heads turned to witness a company of Pandial soldiers enter.

Garbed in their dark, mismatched leathers, the group was altogether about ten strong, and all looked rather worse for wear. Covered in scrapes and bruises, a few sporting split lips and black eyes, while two were swathed in bloodied bandages, the company seemingly pulsed with restrained energy.

The two at the forefront inexorably drew one's attention. Both tall, the man and the woman; both pale-skinned, with dark hair. They moved with a lethal kind of grace, neither gliding nor stomping, but in sync to an alarming degree and carrying large hessian sacks over their shoulders. Heads high, shoulders thrown back, their features displayed clear-cut and distinctive even from a distance. *Eye-catching.*

Reaching the small open floorspace in front of the royal table, they were laughingly cheered on by their comrades who seemed to be overflowing with high spirits, a sense of victory emanating from them. Almost perfectly mirrored, they thumped their chests in salute to the high table, bowing their heads simultaneously.

When they looked up, Tens felt as though he'd been punched in the stomach; bludgeoned over the head. Pierced through the heart. The woman was the most beautiful he had ever seen. Arrestingly so. Even with dark circles beneath her bright green eyes and covered in the muck of travel and combat. He was so overcome by the ephemeral epiphany of her existence that her compatriot's words only registered after some time.

"... proof of what has been the highly-debated question of whether the Gruxhoon have infiltrated Pandi, as they have already done in Cinnae." Len's horror-stricken gasp was followed by the buzzing of a thousand observers' mutterings and whispers: both the man and woman had opened the sacks they carried, emptying the gruesome contents onto the pristinely scrubbed floor tiles.

Decapitated heads. Gruxhoon heads. Easily fifteen skulls landed and rolled here and there, the rictus of death stamped over every countenance and crusted with blackened Gruxhoon blood. The sound of someone retching off to the side punctuated the horrified semi-silence.

"This was a party that raided along the Vrendai river. Unlike previous groups of Gruxhoon, these ones weren't merely content to scout; they had destroyed twenty farms along the riverbank and were in the process of decimating the small village of Vrend's Jetty when we came upon them."

The stunning woman was speaking; though her voice was low and tingle-inducingly husky, her tone was aggressive and accusatory. The more Tens watched her, the more he realised that, though she was undoubtedly attractive, she was not necessarily the embodiment of beauty he had first thought... Rather, there was a compelling *something* about her that attracted you the moment you noticed her. This undefinable quality rendered her significant, somehow, and made you unable to look away or disregard her.

It was quite clear she held most of the people in the room in contempt. A dangerous attitude to display so clearly amongst the most powerful in the land. He felt a sense of dread on her behalf.

"If we had waited on the council's say-so, hundreds more would have died horrifically. Despite our reports over the past nine months clearly stating the potential danger, which the council saw fit to disregard!" the clipped, pristine vowels of her Pandi Bithian accent making her pronouncement even more abrasive in its cutting clarity.

As a last, very clear message, the woman turned to a Cinnaen at one of the lower tables and deliberately curtsied in an exaggeratedly Cinnaen style; however, disdain dripped from every line of movement.

"Who is that man?" Tens asked Princess Mindaia, who was seated beside him. She coughed delicately.

"Lord Delsso, the Cinnaen minister to Pandi." Tens didn't understand the young woman's gesture, but it was clear most present did, for a rumble of amusement echoed in the hall. The Cinnaen lord looked livid, a dark blush washing over his countenance.

Tens turned to see what the Pandial king, the head of the vilified council, would say in response. In Cinnae, the consequences of a lowly soldier speaking to the ruling class in such a manner would be dire.

"Thank you for your service, soldiers," the king nodded curtly to the group still waiting on the edge of the floor, "and yours, Lieutenant Kaimam and Sergeant Ata. For providing this irrefutable proof, along with your eyewitness accounts and those of your squad, of the Gruxhoon's violent attacks on Pandial soil. It would seem, we are now at war in Pandial too, not merely due to our recent alliance with Cinnae."

Now, the king's eyes moved to the people in the hall —encompassed them all in a glance—and he raised his voice. "We, the kingdom of Pandi, have been invaded and violently attacked by the Gruxhoon, creatures of darkness. What say you, the people of Pandi? Do we go to war?" As one man, all the Pandial in the hall rose and bellowed in the affirmative, stomping their feet once. "Do we drive these creatures from our mother land?" he bellowed.

"Yes!" the crowd boomed, stomping once.

"And do we drive them from Áitarbith's sacred soil?" he had himself risen, looming large over the royal table.

"YES!" the Pandial court thundered, stamping their feet rhythmically. In the chaos that followed, (everyone moving around, everyone talking at once) Tens gazed at the woman. *Ata.* But her eyes were fixed to his far left, an aggressive frown marring her lightly-freckled alabaster skin. Tens swung his gaze there and found the Pandial duke, Lord Bendai, sneering condescendingly at her. Next to him, Svens glared at her just as ferociously—the most emotion Tens had ever seen on his face.

Then the penny dropped. Ata! The woman who had saved his baby brothers and carried them five hundred miles. Jans and Els hadn't yet stopped talking about her. Every time he saw them, it was "Ata this" and "Ata that". Svens and most of the military council still got all het up about her so-called "miraculous escape" from the Cinnaen encampment some weeks before.

It still grated that both guards (who were older and beyond dependable, in Svens's own words) had fallen into a deep sleep without any apparent interference, thereby missing an injured woman hobbling from the tent she was being kept in. Add to that: she managed to disappear without a trace with a smugly reticent Jans's foreknowledge, and Tens understood Svens's dented pride. He looked back at her, but she was highly invested in her discussion with her partner, Lieutenant Kaimam.

Their physical closeness and the familiarity with which he playfully pinched her arm implied they were more than just comrades. Tens felt a flare of annoyance; an odd possessiveness that made no sense, considering he had never even spoken to the woman.

Objectively speaking, the two suited each other. They made an astonishingly handsome couple with their clear-cut features—straight noses, high cheek-bones and flawless visages—as well as their robust, lithe figures. A gods-arranged match, as the expression went. And Tens hated how well they matched. They seemed to reach a conclusion in their intense conversation, after which they saluted the king and moved out of sight.

Tens noticed a bearded, elderly man who sat close to the front at one of the tables make meaningful eye contact with Sergeant Ata as she moved past, and she responded with a slight, almost negligible hand motion. Clearly they knew each other and had some way to communicate with each other. If what Svens (and the Cinnaen council, for that matter) believed was true, this Ata had acted as a spy in the Hårbørgen Palace in the months preceding the Gruxhoon invasion.

It was probably true, considering her military skills shown in her lethality towards the Gruxhoon (displayed this evening as well as during the 'Night of Terror' at the palace, according to Jans and Els's accounts). The fact that she had saved his brothers negated any potential ill-feeling or suspicions Tens might have harboured towards her otherwise, although he knew Svens was not of the same opinion. Tens did wonder what her stake in the entire scheme was, but tended to believe she was, on the balance, trustworthy when it came to his family's lives.

As the diners at the royal table arose to retire for the evening, Lord Bendai walked next to Tens.

"It seems Your Majesty has been impressed by the

royal bastard of Pandial," he murmured with a sly glance. "She is quite *something* to behold, isn't she?" Tens felt a crawling disgust at the lascivious insinuation in the man's voice. He was old enough to be her father.

The nobleman continued: "She is the illegitimate get of my late cousin, Princess Annaia. The father is unknown, hence the unpredictability of the offspring. But she has always shown the same libidinous proclivities as her mother," Lord Bendai shrugged indolently, moving in the opposite direction to Tens once they'd exited the dining hall. "Recently, at least it seems she has finally limited her slutty habits to only pumping the half-breed lieutenant," and with that shockingly crude pronouncement, the Pandial king's ducal cousin disappeared amongst the throng of courtiers.

"That... *man*.... is a disgusting maggot," Svens voice growled in Tens's ear, making him jump. He hadn't realised Svens had overheard the duke's information on Ata. Though Tens felt disinclined to believe what the Pandial had said, how well did they truly know the woman?

"Why would he use such... strong language and descriptions, though distasteful, with strangers if they weren't accurate?" Tens asked unwillingly. It felt disloyal to the woman who had saved his brothers. And what did he care if she was infamously promiscuous here at court? It should not matter at all, considering the service she had rendered his family. *But it did matter to him.*

"All I know is, he had plenty to say about illegitimate children in general—just as strongly worded and without any consideration for their value as people and individuals. He also had much to say about women and the impoverished, but not anything I would care to hear nor repeat. The man is a lech and a bigot. Though I have no particular love for Lady Ata, to allow his description of anyone a place within your frame of reference would be a grave mistake. He is not to be trusted, that man," Svens paused after his unusually virulent tirade.

"What do you think of her, then?" Tens asked as they reached the door of his chambers. Despite Tens's personal guard being constantly present, Svens had insisted on staying in Tens's rooms with him. Lenna's chambers were right next door and Jans and Els were in her keeping, so Svens could keep an eye on them all. Luckily Len had retired early and had not been present for the discussion of Lady Ata's character.

"I don't know what to think, honestly... On the one hand, she saved Jans and Els, which is something that can never be repaid—the scale can never be balanced out. For that, I am immeasurably grateful.

"But when it comes to trusting her with anything in the future? The fact that she is an unknown and unknowable quantity compels me to say I distrust her, and probably always will. Her loyalties are too confusing and saving the boys might have just been a ploy or a command from her handler." The general rubbed his scar and nose roughly.

"But the blatancy of her presence here... Does the Pandial king not owe us some apology or recompense for clearly sending a spy into our household?" Tens asked dubiously. To his relief, Svens shook his head.

"No. It would be best to let sleeping dogs lie, in this case. We are the dependent party, and how would such a chest-beating exercise go over? 'Excuse me, Your Majesty, but how dare you send your niece to spy on us... oh, and by the by, thank you once again for assisting us in this war'? No. The Lady Ata has escaped us in this instance, but we must keep our wits about us with her. 'Once bitten, twice shy', as they say..." Svens became lost in thought, then snapped back to the conversation. "I think we've had an eventful few days, so I will say 'goodnight', Your Highness."

Just as Svens was about to lie down upon the odd chaise in the corner, a muffled shriek from next door could be heard through the wall.

"That's Len's voice!" Tens exclaimed; Svens was rushing to the door when they heard a clear cry.

"NO!"

13

AN ITCH…

ITCH (N.)—AN UNEASY IRRITATING SENSATION… USUALLY HELD TO RESULT FROM MILD STIMULATION OF PAIN RECEPTORS; A RESTLESS OR STRONG DESIRE TO DO SOMETHING.

MERRIAM WEBSTER ONLINE DICTIONARY; GOOGLE DICTIONARY BOX

Ata was hot under the collar. She was sweaty and out of breath, thoroughly exhausted and thoroughly annoyed.

"Hi, Ata! See, Jans—it's Ata!" a northern drawl cried, the sound carrying across the training yard and gaining the attention of all the soldiers currently drilling there. Ata bent down and pretended to check her leg braces to avoid acknowledging Princess Lenna, who had also dragged Jansso and Elsso to the military practice grounds today. The princess's hero-worship, although flattering, was starting to wear on Ata, who had never been one to suffer the attention of others nor their imposition on her private life.

Already on the first night of the Cinnaen court's arrival at Enddaian, the princess had gotten Ata into hot water with none other than General Svensso. Princess Lenna had insisted on inviting Ata to her rooms for a warm beverage, to which Ata had only agreed so she could check in on Jans and Els. Sadly, both had been asleep by that point. The princess, insisting on a verbal rendition of Ata's "thrilling adventures" in the army, had become so enthusiastic when Ata described their engagement with the Gruxhoon hunting party they had defeated, that her exclamations of shock and horror during the re-telling were taken for cries of distress, resulting in the door being smashed in by the Cinnaen general-*cum*-royal-bodyguard. Ata was questioned extensively on her presence in the room, resulting in the Pandial king lightly berating her for her thoughtlessness.

"You could have handled that a bit more circumspectly," King Addai shook his head. It was after two in the morning and their first private audience since her return—since the scene in the dining hall. She had let her temper get the better of her there and awaited his censure for that as well. It had not been a good evening for her disciplinary track record...

"You should apologise to Prince Tensso and General

Svensso for the incident. We've only just gotten our own people on side to commit to a war on our own behalves; it wouldn't do for the Cinnaens to develop a grievance over some triviality," he must have noted her look of surprise and chuckled tiredly. "You thought I was unhappy about your little tirade against us—the Pandial Council? On the contrary... it was the ideal opportunity to incite the greater Pandial nation to action." He leaned forward as though imparting a secret.

"There are few things that the Pandial on the street hates more than ineffectiveness and lack of action. Our failure to do anything until now, and the resulting violence visited upon the Pandial, has goaded them to join the cause. Ideal, really, considering general consensus before your impassioned display was that the Cinnaens should deal with their own problems, by themselves. Many questioned our envisioned involvement through a treaty with Cinnae..."

The king leaned back in his chair, sighing and rubbing at his eyes. "Though I should take you to task for making such a scene, the results have very much been in our favour." It wasn't a direct compliment, nor a 'thank you', but it was the closest her uncle could come to it. His eyes snapped open and focused on her shrewdly.

"You will therefore swallow your pride and apologise to the Cinnaens," her expression must have shown her rebellion, because signs of humour spread over his face. "If nothing else, consider it penance and in lieu of an apology owed for losing *your temper in the dining hall." Her uncle, for all his quietly subtle observation, was a manipulative bastard. Like most of the men in her life, really...*

Hence, she had proceeded to offer a wooden and lacklustre apology to Prince Tensso, General Svensso, and their entourage the following day. But she had resented the hells out of it. What could have been laughed off as a tiny misunderstanding had turned into an overblown incident with Ata chastised as though *she* were in the wrong. The arrogant Cinnaen fool had swanned about ever since with a superior air. Or rather, more of a superior air than usual. It drove her insane. No, *he* drove her insane.

And worse? It wasn't all hatred, because she definitely did not hate the way he smelled when they sometimes passed close enough for her to notice, nor did she dislike his transparently blue eyes, or his scar-quirked lip, or his pale-gold skin. Far from it. Even his hair, which he had clearly not shorn since the invasion of the Gruxhoon and was growing out thickly golden exerted an almost mesmerizing power over her. Ata constantly fantasized about running her fingers through it. She *despised* that she didn't hate everything about him. Little did she know that the worst was yet to come...

The previous night, she had had her first dream about him—and not a chastely platonic dream either. Waking sweaty and frustrated, she had made her way to the dining hall that morning and found the architect of her suffering sitting at the royal table, eating breakfast with his insufferably smug non-expression. She wanted to punch him for unsettling her so much. Never had she faced such a debilitating issue that she could not overcome through sheer dint of will nor hard work.

The only saving grace of the entire situation was the fact that he was oblivious to her unbridled, unwanted infatuation with him. *With his body*, she corrected. Moreover, he clearly did not feel the same way about her and even appeared to hold her in some contempt. The fact that he had not started to wink at her or slyly brush up against her as most of the Cinnaen courtiers and soldiers-in-residence had begun to do was a huge relief to her burdened ego. Clearly, Lord Bendai and his offspring, Lord Fordai and Lady Kenttai (as well as others of their ilk) had been spreading the much-abused rumour of her "loose" reputation amongst the Cinnaens. A completely unfounded fallacy created in her teen years by the malicious collusions of Lady Kenttai and her following.

These tales had made little to no impression on the much more permissive Pandial community, as sexual intercourse was not the shameful secret it was in Cinnae, to be whispered and hypothesised about in dark corners by unmarried maidens, or suffered through by married matrons in fortitude in their marriage beds whilst their husbands frequented brothels to meet their physical needs the rest of the time.

In Pandi, sex was not necessarily openly discussed nor exhibited in particularly public ways, however, what people got up to in their bedrooms was not judged in an overly harsh light by society. Women had much more agency than in Cinnae when it came to their chastity (or lack thereof) and Pandial laws were rigorous in having fathers contribute to the raising of their children, irrespective of marriage. Where questions of paternity and inheritance were at stake, though, illegitimacy was still viewed with disdain and condescension.

However, the Cinnaens' arrival at the Pandial court meant their frigid and superficially judgmental views on people's love lives came with them. The resurgence of her 'reputation' meant Ata increased her public displays of affection with Kai. It was slightly awkward for the two of them, but it also strengthened his 'alibi' to cover for his relationship with Min. Complicated, yet working to benefit all involved. Once her faux romance with Kai was reinforced strongly enough, the suggestively vulgar offers from the Cinnaen newcomers dwindled significantly.

"Ata!" Despite her best efforts, Ata couldn't ignore the pull Jans's voice exerted over her. It was almost as though she were physically connected to him with a string, and when he called her, the string was wrenched hard. She had no choice but to follow it to its anchoring point.

"Your Highness," she gave the respectful Pandial nod to non-combatants. Elsso, whom she only noticed then, shyly turned his face into Princess Lenna's leg, avoiding Ata.

"Not 'Your Highness', Ata. *Jans* and *Els*. Like before, when we were running away from the Gruxhoon," the forceful tone of Jans's voice surprised a laugh from her. In all their recent interactions, she had tried for a more formal mode of address, but the boys would have none of it. She found that she couldn't gainsay them, nor could she politely take a step back in their relationship. They were a necessary part of her daily life—irrevocably her family.

"No, you're right. But I'll tell you what," crouching down as she had done during their cross-country escape, she made direct eye contact with her boys, "when in public, my—... the king of Pandi and the princess always address each other formally, to show the respect they expect from others. But when they are at ease—alone, or in an informal environment—they use each other's names or more personal titles... Wouldn't that be a good compromise, *Your Highness*?"

Jans considered for a few seconds, then nodded gravely. "Good!" and she smiled brightly at him. He moved suddenly as though to hug her, which she swiftly blocked. "I'm really filthy, Your Highness, and it's very public here. How about we agree to meet after I have completed my training today, like the other times? We can have a private lunch where we can hug and be as informal as we like?" she whispered the last part, the boys nodding eagerly.

"That sounds like a wonderful idea," Princess Lenna smiled keenly. Ata worked to maintain her smile without faltering. Although she would always be grateful to the Cinnaen princess for caring for her after their arrival at the refugee camp so many weeks ago, she found the girl's cloying earnestness wearying. At least she could manage the princess's adulation somewhat, unlike—

"Good day, Sister... Brothers... and Lady Ata," another eager voice interrupted her thoughts. *His Highness, Prince Tensso.* Who, for some inexplicable reason, had been overtly infatuated with her since their first evening at the castle.

"Your Highness," she thumped her chest and avoided eye contact; not in deference, but to elude his (by now customary) look of adoration. Her attention fell to his companion. *Of course,* it would be General Svensso. A flush crept up her neck. She was blushing. *Blushing!* Just because he was in her presence. No moment could have been more fortuitous for the ground to open up and swallow her completely. Her body was betraying her at every turn. If only she had General Svensso's glacial facial talents; and yet, though his features betrayed no readable emotion, she got the distinct impression her presence irritated him.

"Are you finished with your training session?" the prince asked, "I was hoping to be able to see you spar..." he seemed downright crestfallen to have missed her mediocre talents. As she made to answer, Kai moved up beside her and swung his sweaty, muscular arm across her shoulders.

"Now, now, Sergeant Ata! You can't be slacking off and setting such a poor example to our troops. Come back so I can show these good Cinnaens how a rug is beaten," the last part he had growled in her ear, pretending as though he were whispering some endearment to her, sweet nothings instead of an insolent challenge.

She itched to elbow him in the breadbasket, but pulled her face into what she hoped was not a pained smile. Prince Tensso was scowling, General Svensso looked coldly disapproving, and Princess Lenna and the little princes seemed eager to see her go up against Kai.

Just then, four Cinnaen officers joined them. *Ah.* These were General Svensso's subordinates and childhood friends, from what she had learnt about him so many weeks ago in preparation for her Cinnaen mission. *Lieutenant Ransso, Captain Blÿnsso, and Lieutenant Samsso.* The hermit, the flirt, and the workhorse, she had nicknamed them as a mnemonic technique.

One quietly dependable, one charmingly audacious, and one ambitiously strict.

"Your Highnesses," they intoned and bowed; she felt Kai's sharpening interest behind her where she was still clasped to his side, his stance overtly possessive.

"Welcome, my lords," Kai crowed, good-naturedly, drawing the attention of most of the Pandial soldiers drilling near them. "Would you like to join our sparring session?" he paused significantly, "or... no, I see you are all dressed up and probably wouldn't want to dirty your pristine uniforms. My compliments, by the way—so neatly pressed!" *Oh no*. The idiot wanted to taunt them into a competition. And he'd probably have everyone wagering on the outcome; his favourite play to make some ready cash.

She noted the stiffening postures of the Cinnaens, of whom there were now more than twenty, the three commanders having been followed by some of their troops. This needling was an inevitability, really. Soldiers were abrasive and territorial at the best of times, with an excess of youth, energy, and arrogance; the Cinnaen and Pandial, with their pre-existing prejudices simmering below the surface while being forced into close proximity, had been circling each other for weeks now. Eager for any little provocation to justify a bust-up.

"Hey, Ren! Come and see how nicely they've ironed their bright, spiffy uniforms!" Kai called to one of his favourite drinking buddies—an inveterate troublemaker at the best of times, was Renam. Wolf whistles immediately arose from the Pandial soldiers, accompanied by some derisive chuckles and snorts.

"As you can see, we take pride in our appearance... An army should look like an organised unit, not some piratic rabble that got dressed in the dark off of a brothel floor," Lieutenant Samsso responded coldly, his stockier frame radiating rigid self-control. The latter part he had murmured so that the princess and young princes couldn't hear, only those closest to him. Kai exhaled a light-hearted guffaw but the increased rigidity in his arm told Ata he was not necessarily so sanguine.

"I mean, looks are all well and good, but an army should actually be able to fight, no?" Kai teased, "Though, we understand if you'd rather not spar with us. You need to keep yourselves looking as neat as possible for your return to your homeland." Ata tried to surreptitiously pinch Kai out of sight and managed to get his hip, but he shifted slightly out of her finger-pincers' reach. The tension in the air had increased dramatically. Even the young princes were quietly hanging on the words of these "big men".

"Provoking us won't make us more likely to accept your challenge," Lieutenant Ransso responded evenly, a slow, almost-friendly smile taunting them. "Another key aspect of a successful soldier is complete and utter discipline." The Cinnaens seemed to emanate self-congratulatory haughtiness, and with that, they believed the exchange concluded, for they began to move away in neat rows. But of course, Kai would have the last laugh. Or punch—whichever got him what he was angling for.

"Well, we might not know much about your swordplay or archery skills, but we sure as hells know you can run really well..." the momentary lull before a storm, then the twit drove in the final nail. "You managed to cover over five hundred miles in record time, perhaps the most successfully speedy retreat in all of Áitarbith's history. Now *that's* a skill we have very little familiarity with, I can tell you!"

Two of the younger Cinnaen soldiers had swung around and started running toward them, the rest not far behind. They hadn't drawn their weapons, just seemed intent on having an all-out brawl, starting with pummelling Ata's stupid friend who was currently still holding onto her. The Pandial soldiers at their back didn't wait for an invitation, the two opposing groups throwing themselves at each other with verve, the meaty sounds of fists meeting flesh filling the air.

Ata had just ducked the wild swing of a Cinnaen soldier when a loud shriek halted the tumultuous chaos. General Svensso stood with a Cinnaen *treik* in hand; the brass, tubular instrument that emitted a sharp, high tone was used to gain the attention of large groups, and therefore a staple in the military. Both the Cinnaen and Pandial armies had, independently, developed a basic code of long-distance communication using the instrument.

"This exhibition is beneath us all. Desist *immediately!*" he ordered, his involuntarily snarling face *almost* expressionless, except that his eyes snapped. "If you are all so eager to measure yourselves against each other, then by all means: let us all participate in your various drills, Lieutenant Kaimam." Kai, standing to her right, grinned ebulliently, the smarmy bastard. "Make no mistake: I will report this uncivilised breach of discipline to your superior officer."

Suppressing his grin, Kai nodded in a cowed fashion, but Ata wasn't fooled. He would take the resulting punishment without complaint, having gotten the result he had aimed for from the outset. The more senior Pandial officers had finally joined the group, and between them and the Cinnaen officers, a rota of close combat events was put together. The sense of anticipation was now almost tangible, with a crowd of civilians gathering on the edges of the grounds and many of the more affluent ones managing to find a seat on the pavilion reserved for when the nobility wished to view military drills.

"This is going to be so much fun, Ata, my girl," Kai enthused beside her. She doubted this, but was herself caught up in the competitive spirit of it. Noticing her friend's eye blackening, she snorted derisively.

"Does your eye hurt?" she wheedled. He pulled a face designed to elicit sympathy.

"Terribly!"

"Good," she snapped, "You deserve it!" then turned back to proceedings.

Those involved in the brawl appeared to be the only ones who would be 'competing' against each other, so they divided into their respective 'best events'. Unsurprisingly, Ata was assigned to archery along with three other Pandial, one of them female. Sanam was a petite, dark girl in her late-teens who had the most amazing archery skills. She came from the Pandial midlands which were thickly forested, and her borough, specifically, was known for its highly proficient archers due to their main trade, hunting.

She and Ata did not know each other particularly well personally, but they worked exceptionally well in paired drills. Quirking her eyebrow at the girl, Ata was met with a half-nervous, half-enthusiastic grin. Upon noting Captain Blÿnsso's attention fixed pointedly on the small woman, Ata stared severely at him till he noticed and hurriedly deflected his gaze from San, who was blithely unaware of the exchange as she strung her bow.

Kai was, of course, in the group assigned to swordplay. He winked at her when he saw her looking, then smouldered ridiculously, playing to the crowd. *The buffoon.* She slowly shook her head at him in exasperation. Min would be so annoyed when she found out he had risked disciplinary action for mere, boyish competitiveness. And, per usual, she wouldn't nag *him* about his laddish behaviour, but would corner Ata and quietly remonstrate until she extracted a promise from a harassed Ata to try and reign him in. A lost cause, in her expert opinion.

"He needs someone to hold him back—restrain him—from his every whim, Cousin!" Min had intoned in a low voice, a few days after their return and the Cinnaens' arrival. They were in the grand gallery of the castle, a long room that was well lit and cosily wood-panelled, built by their great-grandfather as a wedding gift for his young bride. Not a happy union, considering she was a mere child of fifteen and he a twice-widowed fifty-year-old, but she had managed what his prior wives had not, producing the one heir needed and subsequently spending her twilight years cossetted in peace in this lovely gallery, her husband having predeceased her by a half century.

"Min, you know I try, but it is impossible. <u>He</u> is impossible," but a dreamily charmed expression had flitted over Mindaia's face at these words. Ata gave it up for a lost cause. Min worshipped the ground Kai traversed; Ata was constantly surprised no-one had thus far twigged onto this great secret over the years, not even Lord Danai. Although, the fact that Ata had actively been shielding them with all her hard-earned deviousness probably helped.

She and Kai were approaching their twenty-first birth-

days—not that the Pandial set much store in nor celebrated birthdays—making it five years that he and Min had been together. In court years, that was a ridiculously long-kept secret, considering the heir to the kingdom was involved. But then, Min had always managed things her way; she was a managing little thing, in her quietly unswerving manner. The very fact of her relationship with Kai was a testament to that, for she had been in love with the newly-promoted lieutenant all her life.

Ata had known the moment she had introduced her slightly-younger cousin to her best friend when they were seven and she barely six. A spark of fascination had kindled in the limpid eyes of the only child of the king of Pandai. Kai, the dynamic lout, had never seemed to think of her in any other capacity than that of the princess royal, and after that as Ata's cousin. Sweet and nice, but not really anything more. But to Min, he was everything—always had been, and always would be. A tragedy, for there was no way the half-Cinnaen silversmith's son would ever be considered a match for the future queen of Pandi. Social stratification might be more flexible in Pandial culture, but not to such an extreme degree that the heir to the throne could marry so far beneath her station.

"Why do I even bother," Ata had muttered, drawing a soft smile from her gentle cousin.

"I'm sorry, Ata. You have all your days dealing with the two of us... and with everyone else's expectations to boot. My father's, Lord Danai's, your commander's..." At that moment, *they were met by Queen Nelni of Cinnae, as well as Lord Haaviso and a few of their entourage.*

"Oh, good day, Your Majesty," Min smiled and dipped her head; Ata noted the tightening of the woman's mouth at the perceived slight in being greeted with the Pandial courtesy as opposed to the Cinnaen one. "My lord," another head-bob.

They acknowledged Min, if somewhat unenthusiastically, then turned their attention to Ata. She saw recognition flair in Lord Haaviso's expression, his eyes leaping first to Ata, then back to Min, noting the unmistakeable familial resemblance. The fact that she had dyed her hair dark again, as well as cutting it in a sharp line just below her chin seemed to render her unrecognisable to the queen, who looked down her nose condescendingly and awaited an introduction.

"This is Sergeant Ata," Min smiled congenially, though Ata knew it grieved her not to claim Ata as family. She had admitted as much privately a few years prior, but maintained the status quo instituted by her father regarding Ata's role in the royal family (i.e., no official role or public acknowledgment at all).

Thus, Ata had the sparsest of claims to them: attributed by birth to the deceased Princess Annaia and raised at court, but no further status, wealth, or property assigned her. She nodded smartly at the two Cinnaens and their sycophantic following.

"It is a pleasure to meet you, Your Majesty. My lord," she tried to keep her voice well-modulated and her countenance unmemorable.

"Is 'Ata' a common Pandial name?" the queen enquired sharply, "only, we had a Pandial agent secreted at Hårbørgen Palace, and she—"

"Ata!" she'd notice that little voice anywhere. "Ata! It's Ata, Els! ATA!" and then she was struck hard in the legs by two small bodies. Looking down at their golden heads—one somewhat paler than the other—and felt a lump in her throat stifle any words she might want to set loose. They were safe, and once again near her.

While on their most recent mission to find the Gruxhoon, she had bothered Danai constantly with Commanded missives inquiring about news of the princes, which she knew he would have received from his various agents. Like a spider at the centre of his web, pulling on his woven threads. But news relayed via multiple points was not the same as seeing them, of holding them. Her boys. Looking up, her vision snagged on their nursemaid (none other than Mistress Famenke) who stared back with a somewhat annoyed expression. Well, 'hello' to you too.

"You're <u>her</u>! The snake within our midst!" the queen screeched, the connection finally made once the princes had confirmed Ata's identity beyond a doubt. "An officer in the Pandial army, no less!" she turned urgently to Lord Haaviso, continuing, "I insist we be permitted to take her into our custody and question her regarding her role in the invasion of Cinnae!" There was an awkward silence, the princes' rising protests subdued summarily by the look from Lord Haaviso and Ata's grip on their shoulders.

"I am sorry, Your Majesty, but that will not be possible," Min pleasantly interceded in this fraught scenario. *"Sergeant Ata is a member of the Pandial armed forces, her role and actions over the past three years exclusively determined by her superior officers. As per our agreement with Cinnae— indeed, your very presence as guests of the Pandial people— you are precluded from making such demands regarding our citizens."* Without raising her voice, or letting any animosity bleed through, Princess Mindaia put paid to the notion.

The subsequent discomfiting silence was broken by whispers of the hangers-on and the venomous hissing harangue Queen Nelni poured into the ear of Lord Haaviso. The other Pandial courtiers in the gallery had also drawn nearer to witness the uncomfortable scene playing out. Upon the approach of two royal ministers to smooth over what could be a spoke in the wheel of Pandial-Cinnaen relations, Ata extricated herself subtly, whispering a promise to the princes of future meetings, then made herself scarce.

Of course, the entire affair had been bandied about, becoming the main topic of discussion that evening in the dining hall. Frustratingly, Ata's role in rescuing the Cinnaen princes had spread like wildfire, creating huge division amongst the Pandial. Most seemed to perceive her intercession as sentimental weakness and lacking in strategy, while a minority thought it a wonderful display of mercy as well as an ingenious move in securing goodwill from the Cinnaens, and thereby facilitating the recent treaty.

She had caught General Erdai's beady eye on her

multiple times at dinner; she made it a point <u>never</u> to be noticed by him, as he was a frighteningly single-minded specimen of military prowess. It did not do to be within his sphere of notice... From his expression when they made eye-contact, he was in the former group of Pandial who considered her a soft-hearted liability.

The Cinnaens also seemed to be divided in their opinions of (and resulting approaches to) her. Some seemed to unbend more towards her, a tentative trust established by her rescue of their youngest royals. However, there were plenty who were even more suspicious of her than they had appeared to be before. They questioned her motives and thought her a devious manipulator. No doubt they had also lent out their ears to the Pandial singing her praises for neatly manipulating the Cinnaens with her "ploy". There was no winning with some people...

Speaking of which, she could easily guess which group General Svensso and his colleague, General Bransso, fell into, for their manner toward her had been stiffly formal on the very few occasions they interacted, suspicion tingeing their every expression and behaviour.

"Do you think their commanders are any good, or are they just nepotistic figureheads?" Ren, Kai's scallywag friend, asked loudly. To be fair: it was well-known that the Cinnaen army did not promote commoners beyond the rank of lieutenant, reserving the higher ranks for their aristocracy. To a Pandial, it was unthinkable to promote someone in the military based on birth instead of ability—a rankly untenable tenet.

"We shall soon see, I suppose," Ata responded quellingly, as the last arrangements were finalised. She hoped none of the aforementioned officers had heard his putdown, but of course, Captain Blÿnsso's snarling smile nearby indicated otherwise.

"As agreed, we will complete a few combat drills together—the Cinnaen and Pandial troops present," Colonel Derkam, the most senior Pandial officer on the practice field, announced. Their audience began to clap, but Colonel Derkam continued, "The drills we will run are grappling, swordplay, knife-fighting, archery, and freeform, commencing with the archery and knife-fighting first, then grappling and swordplay, followed by freeform, where any close-range weapon may be utilised by combatants. As always, the weapons are blunted, and none of the combatants will be aiming or executing killing blows," the last was an ominous warning. *Transgress at your own peril.*

Ata noted Lord Fordai and his cronies amongst the spectators. Next to him, whispering excitedly into his ear, was Lady Kenttai, decked out in eye-catching finery, the jewel tones making her stand out like a bird of paradise amongst the more muted plumage of her peers.

Ata peripherally noticed Prince Tensso's comical double-take upon seeing Lady Kenttai, then the quick back-and-forth glances, measuring her similarity to Ata. Between her, Min's, and their cousin Kenttai's looks, their great-grandmother's notable facial structure clearly marked them as relatives.

When Kenttai noted the prince's apparent interest, she fluttered her eyelashes coquettishly at him, his half-shocked recoil and studious refocusing of attention on the combatants conveying a decided lack of interest in her flirtation. The arrogant woman seemed to take the Cinnaen prince's reaction in stride, her eager gaze passing over the soldiers on the field till they found her usual quarry: Kai. *Typical.* Ata rolled her eyes. *How trite.*

Then the other woman's eyes jumped further on, a new, more fervent interest sparking. Bemused, Ata followed her line of sight and stiffened involuntarily. *General Svensso.* Ignoring the swooping sensation of intense misgiving in her belly, Ata forced her attention back to the commander. What did she care if the voracious Lady Kenttai was interested in the Cinnaen general. She didn't. *Not at all.*

"Ensure your bows are strung, and check your stock of arrows," their overseeing commander instructed, and Ata noticed the combatants participating in the knife-fighting had paired into their respective rings.

"Go forth, and don't embarrass us, young Ata," Kai intoned near her, his infectious grin belying his words. She caught General Svensso's blank countenance in the same group, studying her dispassionately. So, he was also in the swordplay grouping. *Interesting.* If he was matched with Kai, she'd ask her friend to give him a smack or two from her, both for his condescending attitude and the inner turmoil he was causing her.

"Archers, take your positions at the butts!"

14

... YOU CAN'T SCRATCH

There was a girl with an itch on her
    nose,
so she scratched her toes.
The same girl had an itch on her
    thigh,
so she scratched her eye.
It was a little confusing,
this itching and scratching.
We couldn't tell if she was missing or
    catching,
this itch moving all the time.

Kent Annan

His attention was riveted on her; she seemed to have that effect on most people. Particularly powerful men, he thought sourly. The knife-fighting was forgotten, all attention fixed on the two women dominating the archery component of the informal contest between the Pandial and Cinnaen troops. Though Svens resented the manner in which they had been baited into participating, it was admittedly proving an effective distraction from the hours of strategic council meetings (both exclusively Cinnaen ones and collaborative ones with the Pandial council).

He had not been out and about in the last two weeks, so when he had agreed to accompany Tens to the Pandial military training grounds, he thought it would be a pleasant opportunity to stretch his legs—nothing too strenuous. Until he noticed *her* conversing with Len and the boys.

Whenever possible, he avoided the lovely serpent that had somehow slithered into the Cinnaen royal family's hearts and minds. Len could not stop chattering about all her many accomplishments (which mostly boiled down to thumbing her nose at authority, as far as Svens could tell), and Jans and Els were completely in the woman's pocket, like two little lapdogs eagerly awaiting her every word and gesture. The most worrying, if slightly more subtle, was his brother Tens's crush, despite never truly having conversed with her.

She even elicited very strong emotions in Queen Nelni, though of a completely opposing nature to those of her children. Svens was convinced he was now, for the first time in his life, second on the queen's list of most hated adversaries, Ata having taken top position.

The diminutive figure of the other female archer loosed her last arrow in that bout, the targets placed at a distance of sixty yards. The white target stood out starkly, the small black spot at the centre—what each archer was aiming at—looking miniscule from that distance while the different-coloured fletching of the four archers remaining in the 'competition' peppered the straw target. Even from a distance, the disparity was glaring.

The Cinnaen light and dark blue were spaced around the outer part of the large white circle, the bright yellow of the small Pandial woman closer to the black centre, with the last one having *just* made it onto the black dot. But unequivocally, three red-fletched arrows were grouped so close together as to appear to be a single arrow from afar—right at the centre of the innermost black circle. Ata was the clear winner of the final round.

She turned to her competitors, a wide, joyful smile spread across her face. He didn't think he'd ever seen her so uninhibitedly happy. The petite woman smilingly saluted to acknowledge the winner while the two

Cinnaen soldiers bowed diffidently to her. Svens was impressed, if somewhat unwillingly.

"She is *good*, I suppose... But with that face and figure, why would she be messing about with arrows and targets with her free time? She could be doing plenty else..." Blÿns murmured to him, having been knocked out of the archery competition the round before. Svens wondered if *he* could knock him out before being exposed to anymore such drivel.

"But wait, the archery component is not yet complete!" a voice rang out from amongst the observing soldiers. *That loudmouthed braggart.* Svens found his annoyance increase rapidly. "Our Ata can shoot with the same accuracy at a ninety-yard distance," Lieutenant Kaimam continued, "why don't you show them, Sergeant?" <u>Our</u> *Ata*. Ata's look of surprise and then poorly concealed annoyance implied her response would not be favourable, but the windbag continued—and she let him. "Why not make it interesting? Let's make it a respectable one hundred yards?" She just maintained her strained smile. Some cadets rushed in and re-set the target, much further out.

Svens couldn't (wouldn't) explain why he had disliked the Pandial lieutenant so much almost from the moment he had become aware of his existence. But the fact remained: he *loathed* the dark-haired man who now grinned and cajoled everyone into a better mood. *A charmer and a boaster*. Far be it from Svens to question Lady Ata's taste in men, but...

"Ten silver says she hits the eye," the bothersome gnat bellowed, followed by multiple challenges and acceptances. Ata's mouth and eyes narrowed at him, her displeasure at being bet on unmistakeable.

"Ten silver on all three arrows hitting the eye, or just one?" a voice shouted from the crowd. The knife-fights had concluded, Sams the clear victor. He didn't bask in the glory, but made his way to Svens to observe the final trick of the archery division.

"Either... Let's say one," Lieutenant Kaimam responded off-handedly, but was met with a scoff of derision from the heckler—a well-dressed young Pandial lord standing next to an ostentatiously accoutred woman bearing a striking resemblance to Ata. Svens had immediately noticed her, but a brief study revealed her to be his nemesis's lesser both in appearance and manner. Though her features were less finely wrought than the archer currently waiting to shoot, Svens surmised not-Ata was undoubtedly quite vain, enjoying the attention her finery and status brought her. Her tittering, flighty persona was as unlike the business-like, irreverent Ata as it was possible to be. Despite constantly being at odds with that woman, he infinitely preferred the latter.

"Two gold! On the sergeant *not* hitting the target thrice," another voice joined the haggling. A collective gasp from the spectators at the exorbitance of the bet—that braying ass, Kaimam momentarily silenced. Two gold was more than the income of a working-class family for a twelvemonth. The speaker, Svens noted, was Lord Bendai, the man he had taken such a dislike to on their first night in Enddaian. Unsurprising, that he was betting against the woman whom he had smeared so thoroughly to the newly-arrived Cinnaens. Clearly, Ata had powerful enemies at court, one of them her ducal second cousin.

Svens felt an unwelcome squeeze of sympathy in his chest. He didn't want feelings of solidarity to take root, but they inevitably had when he had learnt that Ata's heritage and circumstances were very similar to his—a royal bastard, undoubtedly used for the benefit of the dynasty, irrespective of her own wishes or needs.

"Very well. Two gold," Lieutenant Kaimam finally responded, much less flamboyantly. He was risking a fortune on someone else's skill, highly dependent on unforeseen circumstances and chance.

"Do you even *have* two gold pieces to risk, Officer?" Lord Bendai mocked. The light-hearted lieutenant's slight pause said it all—he didn't. Svens sensed the arrogant satisfaction of the group on the side-lines, so he purposely made eye-contact with the now-seething, helpless Kaimam, nodding meaningfully and tapping his belt where a coin pouch would usually be. He would spot the money should the bet be lost. The man's eyes widened in fleeting surprise, then a viciously triumphant smile broke across his face. Before he could help himself, Svens responded with a conspiratorial grin, such was the boyish liveliness he beheld.

"I do have that very amount available to me, as a matter of fact, Lord Bendai," the lieutenant crowed, never breaking eye-contact with Svens. "I will take you up on that bet; two whole gold pieces on Sergeant Ata landing three of her arrows smack dab in the centre of the target!" Shocked cheers followed, soon hushed in anticipation of the outcome of this outrageous gamble.

Ata took her stance, a dead quiet descending over the watchers. The target was so far away, Svens could *just* make out the black circle inside the large white one. She paused for a moment, squinting back at Kaimam reproachfully when her attention snagged on Svens.

It was the oddest sensation that assailed him in that moment, similar to an electric current suffusing his entire being, anchoring him to the earth beneath his feet. *Gods-touched.* That was the closest description he could find to define the feeling. Then she glanced away and it was over, like it had never happened. Yet he felt changed, somehow.

Ata expertly drew the bowstring back, arrow cocked, so it touched her pursed lips. A long pause. Then she loosed the first. Smoothly, she continued to fire the second and third arrows in quick succession without pausing or taking time to focus again. There was a stunned silence after the three-second volley, the crowd unable to see the placement of the arrows clearly at that distance.

Two cadets raced to the target and dragged it closer with frantic enthusiasm. A neat grouping of red-fletched arrows clustered inside the black dot, barely a hands-breadth separating them all from each other. Blÿns whistled in the brief, awed silence amongst the combatants who were closest.

"I've never seen such accuracy before at that distance. *Never*," he muttered, eyeing Ata speculatively. Svens suppressed the urge to thump the idiot for his brazenness. Colonel Derkam, who had made his way over to assess the result, cleared his throat, pride at Ata's feat and by extension, Pandial's, pervading his entire manner.

"It is a clear bull's eye; all three arrows are inside the centre!" he yelled, the crowd shrieking in disbelief and elation. Svens spared a quick glance for the party that had wagered so heavily against the sergeant who was now being clapped on the back enthusiastically. They wore almost identical sour expressions; unsurprising, considering the audacious Kaimam had sauntered over and was relieving them of the two gold pieces they owed him with a shit-eating grin. Upon his return, when he tried to hug Ata in congratulations, she punched him in the stomach, hard. Svens felt a vindictive thrill suffuse him.

"What? I knew you'd do it, Sweetheart," the man choked, curdling Svens' stomach. But Ata was having none of it.

"I can't *believe* you bet that much! I was beside myself with nerves, you egotistical, selfish, showboating piece of sh—"

"We will continue with the next drills," Colonel Derkam stated loudly. Svens noticed Ata's hand that still clutched the bow was shaking so badly the entire weapon shuddered. *So she wasn't so cool and infallible.* Noting his attention on her hand, she quickly steadied its shaking against her leg, avoided eye contact, and blushed. Despite all his self-chastisement and control, Svens was charmed by this rare display of uncertainty. *She was so lovely...* What was he thinking! She was a spy and untrustworthy; her blushes pure serpentine wiles and manipulation, he reminded himself.

"It appears thanks are in order," the loudmouth had sidled up to Svens as they made their way to the rings where they would be assigned their swordplay opponents.

"No thanks necessary. Although, technically, I should be entitled to some of the winnings from *our* bet, no?" Svens didn't really care about the money, but he relished a chance to needle the man whose buffoonery irked him. *Only* the buffoonery, of course. Nothing else.

"The best I can offer you is one of the coins," Lieutenant Kaimam offered easily, "But that's the most—the other must go to Ata, you see." With such finality, Svens's curiosity was piqued.

"She is in need of funds?" She was a royal. A bastard royal, to be sure, but they were still usually supported in luxury.

"No, she doesn't *need* it *per se*, but it's her due. The rest you can have, but at least half should go to her, seeing as it was her skill that earned it in the first place."

"You will get nothing out of the whole thing, in that case..." Svens stated as they reached the sword fighting arena right in front of the pavilion. The other man shrugged his shoulders nonchalantly, then grinned wickedly.

"The looks on the Bendai clan's faces were my reward, I can assure you," he rubbed his hands together in an exaggerated fashion. *Ah.* He disliked the duke and his followers as much as Svens did. Against his better judgement, he found himself liking this jokester; he and Blÿns were cut from the same cloth; a showy piece undoubtedly, but sturdy and dependable nonetheless.

All attention fell to Colonel Derkam, who partnered them up with other soldiers for the first round of sword-play. Svens' relief at escaping the fool's witticisms was short-lived, for it seemed the man could handle a sword with aplomb. To such a degree, that the two of them faced each other in the final round.

"We meet again, General," Kaimam's face was streaked with sweat and dirt as he bowed, mockingly imitating a more traditional Cinnaen courtesy for a person of very high status. Svens ignored his attempt to rile him. He had watched the lieutenant's last bout, having finished his before.

The man's technique was not the most amazing he'd seen, but he had a flair for exploiting his environment as well as unanticipated distractions. Lieutenant Kaimam wasn't a pristine, gentlemanly artist with a sword—he was a brawler that took every gap he saw and constantly pushed at his opponent's defences till one erred and he had an in. A dangerous opponent here, and deadly in a real combat situation.

"So it seems... And please, feel free to call me Svens. In here, we are equal, are we not?" Svens gave a slight smile. He never understood why, but his smiles never seemed to engage and warm people to him. Instead, others had informed him there seemed to be a threat inherent in them. Perhaps it was the consequence of his scar? Reasons aside, he had learnt to utilise it in such situations where subtle intimidation worked in under-mining an opponent's confidence. Apparently not *this* opponent, who smiled back broadly.

"In that case, you may call me Kai; seeing as we are on such *equal footing* here," and then the bastard struck without warning.

"You know, you could concede..." Kaimam's black hair (much too long for a soldier, in Svens's opinion) was plastered to his scalp with sweat, his chest expanding rapidly as he wheezed.

"After you—I insist," Svens responded, not in much better shape himself. They had been at it for over two hours, with short periods of rest throughout. The crowd had mostly dispersed, only the most dedicated still spectating. The other 'events' had concluded since, with just the two of them remaining (and their collective stubbornness, of course). Svens felt as though his legs were made of lead and his arm ready to drop off.

"Just finish it, for the heavens' sake!" a familiar voice called irritably from the side lines. The fact that Ata hadn't left like most of the others chagrined Svens no end. For some reason, it seemed to compound the strangeness of this entire bout—the thought of not winning against Kaimam, with her in attendance, brought a rush of discomfiting determination to him.

The heat of the day was upon them, a much more onerous experience here in southern Pandial than in northern Cinnae. Svens had noted, peripherally, that Princess Mindaia had joined the remaining crowd and stood next to Ata, a look of politely placid interest showcasing the inherently different natures of the two cousins, for Ata's face was drawn into a cantankerous scowl.

As they engaged again, Svens felt a brief frisson of

panic; Kai's increased power in his strikes, his suddenly nimble footwork, indicated a surge of new-found energy that Svens couldn't match. Then he spotted the minute opening in the man's defenses, no doubt the result of exhaustion and the effort to overwhelm his opponent with his attack. Within seconds, he had managed to land a 'killing' blow to the lieutenant's neck. Kai's head bowed as he leaned on his weapon in exhaustion, Svens's blunted sword resting threateningly against his jugular.

"I yield, oh great general," he grinned tiredly yet still mischievously, "but I'll never surrender." The audience applauded, good-natured jibes exchanged by men who had, mere hours before, been at each other's throats. The Pandial had scraped a victory, gaining three wins to Cinnaens' two, Svens's tenuous triumph keeping the Pandial from an ignominiously disparate loss overall.

"Fair enough," Svens grunted, secretly wondering and worrying how he'd be able to leave the small arena without hobbling. If his current discomfort were any indication, his muscles would be unpleasantly stiff on the morrow. Without thinking, he offered his hand to the lieutenant, who looked at it in puzzlement, clearly never having seen the 'working-man's clasp' amongst the Cinnaen nobles currently residing in Enddaian.

Before Svens could explain the convention or drop his hand for a more traditional bow, a warm, slightly smaller hand slapped against his arm and clasped it firmly. A tingle of awareness zinged through him and he knew who it must be even before he looked.

"Like this," Ata's tone of forced patience, along with her attention, was directed at the Pandial lieutenant standing next to her as she instructed him, but her arm lingered in Svens's grasp.

"Ah, I see," Kaimam intoned with interest, "I've never seen this salute before—my apologies. I did not mean to slight you, general."

"It's not usually used by Cinnaen nobles," Ata responded, sounding as though she were lecturing a class of students. "The working classes tend to use it, though sometimes soldiers do too, to show respect or camaraderie."

Svens's attention had wandered down to her hand on his arm. The colour of their skin was almost the same (tanned) but his had a slightly pinker undertone compared to hers. Her nails were short and her hand supplely sinewy—not particularly feminine, and definitely not soft as Cinnaen noblewomen's hands were. He could feel the slight scrape of callouses. *She was right-handed.*

The palpable silence finally dawned on him, Ata inspecting him with a puzzled quirk to her mouth. His momentary confusion gave way to chagrin; he let go and dropped his hand immediately. The lieutenant glanced between them with calculation, the potentially uncomfortable silence building until Princess Mindaia skilfully joined them.

"Congratulations, General Svensso, on your victory. It was thrilling to watch," she smiled kindly.

"We Pandial won the overall event," Lieutenant Kaimam loudly added, verging on abrasive, then tacked on a remembered "Your Highness" with shamefaced alacrity. The formerly easy-going jokester had become uncharacteristically serious and seemed almost jealous of any perceived praise given to Svens and the Cinnaens. Very odd, considering Ata had been present throughout the morning and afternoon and thus her presence couldn't be the reason for this flare of apparent ego.

They made polite small talk until one of the Pandial commanders came and cleared the training grounds for the next shift of soldiers. Svens gratefully made his way to Tens's chambers, his jolly mood somewhat under-mined upon spying Ata and Kai wandering off together, her berating him without pause as he playfully responded.

After washing, Svens decided to forego remaining in Tens's rooms for a nap—the prince had returned and was mooning over his newfound muse, Ata. Svens couldn't face having to listen to another man, even his own brother, sing that woman's praises. Thus, he took himself off to spend some time with his youngest half-siblings, having shamefully neglected them in light of the Cinnaen exodus and constant subsequent negotiations with Pandi.

"Welcome, my lord," Len's lady's maid and the boys' temporary nursemaid intoned as he entered their rooms, which adjoined both Len's and Tens's.

In the few short weeks they had been here, the tall servant, Mistress Famenke, he recalled, had taken to the Pandial practice of keeping her hair uncovered—as had quite a few other Cinnaen women (though many, including Len, had chosen to retain this cultural and religious link to Cinnae). The vivid shade of the servant's hair was eye-catching, especially amongst the dark shades of the Pandial, eliciting significant male attention from various sources, according to Perkki, his valet. The maid's dour manner and biting sarcasm proved highly effective in dissuading any attentions from progressing too far, Perkki had also informed Svens.

The man was an inveterate gossip, sharing all manner of titbits while shaving and dressing him. Though Svens preferred to dress himself, Perkki had been particularly insistent that *he* perform this office whilst they were in Pandi. A point of Cinnaen pride, he called it. And Svens knew better than to argue with the man. Luckily, he tended to leave Svens be when in the field.

"Svens! You came! You were brilliant today!" Jans shouted, rushing forward alongside Els to half-hug, half-salute him. What followed was an overexcited babble of congratulations and descriptions of the fights, as well as imitations of the moves employed, invisible weapons at the ready. The boys were virtually frenzied in their attempts to show and tell simultaneously. Svens laughed, settling on the divan and putting his feet up. Their antics were wholesome and entertaining; a balm to his incongruously depressed spirits. Mistress Famenke sniffed in disapproval as she placed some refreshments on a small table for that purpose.

"And Ata was *amazing*... We told you she was a perfect shot with a bow? Didn't we? She killed all the Gruxhoon at Belson's farm with it," Jans flung himself down next to Svens, breathless from his exertions.

"She's 'mazin'," Els echoed, laid out on the carpet at their feet, arms and legs spread like a starfish.

"We should give her a charm, like an arrow, for her chain!" Jans continued excitedly, Els nodding along.

"Charm? Chain?" Svens was intrigued—the boys had never volunteered any concrete personal information about Ata without prompting. They either sang her praises reverentially or answered questions that were put to them during interrogations about their flight from the palace, never adding extraneous details. Jans and Els had gone suddenly quiet, eyeing each other conspiratorially. Jans looked at Svens, all speculation, then appeared to make a decision in his serious, little-boy way.

"A charm for her Enstroi chain. To commerate, uh, comrate... come- commem—"

"'Commemorate'," Svens offered.

"Yes, to... com—... that word—her victory today," Jans finished proudly.

"But first we needs to give back Hanson," Els volunteered, a serious expression on his little face. Jans looked pained.

"Not Hanson, Els, *the* Hancin charm. And, yes—Len said she comm—, commishen— ordered one already. We just have to wait for it to be finished so we can give it to Ata." Svens was no more enlightened than before.

"Perhaps explain from the beginning... What is an Enstroi chain?" His confusion must have been evident, because Jans heaved an exaggerated sigh of annoyance that clearly questioned Svens's mental acuity.

"Ata wears an Enstroi chain... she says most Pandial have them. It's what a Pandial hands to the guardian at the gates of whichever of the heavens they end up at when they die so they can show what their life was about. So, they put charms on the chain for the important things that they do in their life..."

Svens recalled the various examples he had seen of such chains on the Pandial he had encountered throughout his life. Not all were visible, but he had definitely spied charms dangling from a variety of different chains. Some had been worn looped or pinned to chests, others around necks, still others draped across shoulders and torsos. There were lavish gold ones, austere steel ones, and glowing copper ones. How had he never thought to ask about their significance before?

"And peoples too!" Els volunteered, face sticky from where he had waded into the sweets on Famenke's tray.

"And *people* that are important in their lives," Jans corrected. "Ata gave Hanson, the boy that escaped with us from the palace, one of her charms from the chain. And he gave it to me to hold for him."

"The garden boy?" Both boys nodded.

"And she gave him the Hancin charm?"

"Yes—it's the guiding star," Jans offered helpfully, his attention temporarily focused on selecting a treat from the tray before his brother decimated them all.

"I know," Svens responded drily. When his brothers seemed unmotivated to continue, he prompted, "Why do you need to give the charm back? Did you somehow lose it in your escape?" Both boys looked suddenly tormented, their snacks forgotten.

"No... Hanson, the boy, was caught. By the monsters," Jans had paled, Els gripped his arm tightly, and Svens regretted pushing the subject. "We couldn't bury him, because we had to run away. Ata was *so* sad later. So we buried the charm. His charm. Instead of him."

"Like a hero!" Els piped up tremulously.

"Ata said Hanson was a hero. That he loved us, because he died to save us," Jans continued, a bit belligerently as though he expected Svens to disagree with this title. A sharp sound startled them from the conversation; Mistress Famenke had dropped some glassware next to the rug, shattering a few pieces. Svens went to help her gather the mess without thinking, but she waved him away almost imperiously, though not before he saw her wet face and trembling mouth. Also noting the proud lift of her chin, he affected ignorance and returned to the boys.

"This Hanson definitely sounds like a hero to me," he said seriously, looking into both boys' eyes in turn. They appeared relieved by this assessment; almost as though his opinion on this subject was one of indescribable importance and he had somehow passed a critical test. Perhaps he had. "And you want to replace the charm for Ata?" he prompted further. Both nodded in unison.

"To remind her of Hanson—because when she dies, her Enstroi chain should have something for him on it. Because he was *our* hero." Here Jans hesitated, then hastened on, "I want to add him to my Enstroi chain too, when I get one." Svens tried to keep the surprise from his face.

"That's something you would like? An Enstroi chain?" he hazarded. Jans nodded.

"Me too!" Els enthused happily, putting his hand up as though he was being selected from a crowd for some kind of fun activity.

"We already asked Len, but she said she'd first have to think about it because we're Cinnaen and an Enstroi chain is Pandial," Jans added.

"Well. We'll see what we can do..." Svens offered, not sure how he felt about this Pandial tradition that two Hårbørgen heirs wanted to actively pursue. Their adherence to a foreign practice could have far-reaching consequences.

After this, the afternoon progressed with laughter and lightness—the boys, as always, were little whirlwinds that could bring humour to even the dullest of topics. Svens felt emotionally rejuvenated as he was leaving, only to have the surly nursemaid draw his notice as she ushered him out the door. Her slight hesitation when she had his undivided attention quickly dissipated, though.

"If... Their Highnesses wish to carry Enstroi chains, then surely they might be permitted to do so?" he was floored by her audacity in addressing this, but she continued, "to have a— a means to be more aware of important things in one's life could only benefit someone? Make them more self-aware and conscientious?" her eyes flashed fiercely then.

"The boy who died, Hanson, deserves to be remembered. And if not in a tangible way by the very people whose lives he saved, then who?" She didn't wait for a response, merely curtseying promptly and shutting the door on Svens's nonplussed self. Really, if it wasn't *that* mystifying woman, then another stepped forth to confuse him.

COME EVENING, the dreaded muscle stiffness had not set in as expected, allowing Svens to nimbly ascend the low dais to the royal table. The fact that a ferocious thunderstorm had descended, thunder and lightning and extremely low temperatures in tow, meant his muscles and bones might have ached that much more.

Luckily, Lord Bendai was not in attendance—perhaps his humiliating loss of the bet on Ata had temporarily cowed him. One could only hope. However, General Erdai had taken pride of place, and seated next to Svens, he was surprisingly engaging. Even more so: he was forthcoming about the next steps to be taken to garner the support of other nations in Áitarbith. Although thoroughly discussed in collective meetings, the details of the most sensitive of these negotiations (that of attaining the military support of the Vürgøn) had not yet been decided upon. Til now, it seemed.

"We will send a small diplomatic party to put our suggestion to the tribes, although, the fact that they are distinct groupings without a central body of authority does complicate the situation," the general drank deeply from his wine goblet. He grimace-grinned at Svens, making him wonder if that was what his own scarred smile looked like... *No wonder it didn't warm people to him.*

"Personally, I don't know whether inviting the Vürgøn to join the fray is a move of genius or stupidity... Only time will tell. But I do know that they are notoriously impossible to pin down in agreements."

What Svens ascertained during dinner was that a mostly Pandial delegation would leave for the Uurgonna Mountains the following day, with one or two senior Cinnaen officers. General Erdai heavily hinted he would prefer Svens to be one of them, to which Svens tentatively responded in the affirmative pending confirmation from Lord Bransso and the rest of the Cinnaen Council. He felt a thrill of excitement at discovering new regions he had never traversed before; he had also never met any Vürgøn, so this would be a journey of many firsts for him.

The storm had intensified by the end of the meal, flashes of lightning intermittently blazing through the narrow castle windows, the pounding rain and thunder drowning out almost all sound except those closest to a person. As he rounded the corner on the way back to the Cinnaen royal siblings' chambers, he was distracted by movement in the shadows of an alcove, strategically placed so those passing by couldn't see properly within with normal lighting (or lack thereof in this castle). However, Svens's stealth training had conditioned him to always scan for peripheral movement, aided and abetted by the flashes of tempest-driven illumination.

He focused sharply, slowing his steps, but not enough to draw attention. A dark-haired woman was straddling a man's lap, facing towards him and away from the corridor. Despite the shadows and low light, it was clear the couple were in a very intimate embrace and mistakenly under the impression they were not visible to those passing in the corridor.

Both were passionately distracted, and just as Svens reached the end of the corridor and a clear line of sight, lightning illuminated the man's face and the woman's profile starkly. Recognition sent shock coursing through Svens.

15

UNDER ONE'S SKIN

You can try
To get under my skin
While he's on mine
Yeah, all on my skin
I wish you knew that even you
Can't get under my skin
If I don't let you in

SABRINA CARPENTER

Hunger gnawed at Ata's belly, feeling as though it were burrowing through to her spine. She couldn't remember when she had last eaten a proper meal; the mission—surviving—took precedence over any personal comforts like a full stomach or a good night's rest. The sun beat down on her head where she was hunkered amongst the roadside brush, the camouflaging mud caked on her face and hair smelling earthy and working somewhat towards cooling her.

They were waiting to ambush a Gruxhoon war party that had been raiding in this region, and had been fighting in this manner for the past eight weeks. Eight weeks since she had slept in a bed or eaten a kitchen-cooked meal. Rumour was that they would return to resupply in Enddaian once fresh troops arrived to relieve them. *Soon*. General Erdai's plan required regular rotation of troops and resupply to maintain strength and vigilance in their defence.

Stationed in the Plezai Valley that ran all the way to the coast, they had been involved in heavy fighting. Generals Erdai and Bransso had divined (quite accurately, it appeared) that the Gruxhoon would utilise two main entries into Pandi—the first by crossing from Cinnae, and the second by landing on the west coast, on the border between Cinnae and Pandial, and then funnelling through the large north-western valley towards central Pandi and the rest of Cinnae.

A combined force of Pandial and Cinnaen troops had been sent to the main border crossings between the two nations whilst the most experienced guerrilla fighters had been deployed in the Plezai Valley. Despite heavy losses, the cast net seemed to be catching the detritus washing up on their shores and entering Pandial territory.

The primary objective was to maintain a strong base to avoid Pandi being invaded; the secondary objective: to slowly push into Cinnae and reclaim the strongest of the southern strongholds. Eventually, the military councils hoped to push the Gruxhoon out, past the northern and western shores of Cinnae, all the while maintaining the integrity of Pandial territory.

At that very moment, Ata was in the north-western valley, Kai on the northern Cinnaen-Pandial border, and everyone else in Enddaian. Well, not everyone... General Svensso had departed on the same day as she did, but to the north-eastern Uurgonna Mountains to try and broker an alliance with the Vürgøn tribes that lived there. She still cringed at their parting words upon their departure from Enddaian Keep.

"Lady Ata," he intoned colourlessly, clearly unwilling to engage in conversation with her. She had been utterly mysti-fied and slightly hurt, if she were honest, when he began to completely ignore her presence or person in the days subse-quent to the Pandial and Cinnaen 'competition'. Where before he had seemed to unbend slightly, even showing hesitant camaraderie after his difficult bout with Kai, he now treated her as though she were part of the furniture. He did it to such an extent that even Mindaia noticed and asked Ata the reason in private, to which question she could not provide a satisfactory answer. Ata's confusion and hurt soon blazed into

anger, and she then made a point of avoiding and ignoring the general's presence in return.

Unfortunately, they had been caught up in a collective leave-taking that morning at the stables as multiple parties waited on their horses. Kai, also present and readying for deployment, had orchestrated a conversation with the Cinnaen general, forcing Ata to play nice or risk a comment from her best friend. The idiot.

"General Svensso," she responded, equally cold and stoic. Upon first noting his purposeful disregard of her she had suspected he harboured a grudge due to the Cinnaens' loss, but that did not seem to correspond with his character as she had come to know it.

"Here we go! Looks like mine will be the first company to leave," Kai enthused, clasping General Svensso's arm in farewell, then saluting Ata with a grin as he walked off. "See you when I see you!" The silence between them following Kai's departure was excruciatingly awkward.

"Ah—I see we are leaving as well," the general volunteered as his party received their mounts, his dismissive tone rubbing her up the wrong way. "Farewell, Lady Ata."

"Best of luck with the Vürgøn, General. Let's hope you have more success with them than the Gruxhoon," she had snapped at his retreating back. Pausing, he swung back to her, indecision flashing across his face followed by an angry frown. It felt good to give vent to her caged emotions.

She continued: "I am told they respond to earnestness and transparency in their dealings... Some of your less developed characteristics, based on your reputation and my own experience." This seemed to break the final seal on his self-imposed reticence; striding back to her, he stopped much too close.

"Perhaps you'd best keep your advice for yourself, Lady Ata, regarding reputations and transparency. There can be too little of the former and too much of the latter, which makes you vulnerable to exploitation. Especially in your precarious position!" he had not raised his voice, but his tone and manner conveyed his fervid stance on the subject.

Ata was nonplussed——what was he talking about? Her confusion must have shown, because his aggression appeared to subside and he continued, somewhat more controlled: "I saw you and Lieutenant Kaimam in the alcove that night during the storm. It is the height of impropriety to carry on an affair in such a public place, where those who would spread the tale far and wide could witness it..."

Oh! That's why he had acted so strangely. He was angry with her for trysting with Kai where anyone could see them. Where he had obviously seen them——or at least <u>thought</u> he'd seen them.

She was going to <u>kill</u> Kai and Min. It would take just one person who knew better, or had a better view, to get to the truth of the matter. Thank goodness she and her cousin resembled each other, or it would have been a lot worse. They should have known better! And now she had to suffer the general's poor opinion for <u>their</u> injudicious carryings-on; an opinion she couldn't disabuse him of without betraying them.

"So... that's why you've been so rude these past few days?

Because you saw... us... in the recess?" she asked. He bristled in his emotionally repressed way.

"I have never been <u>rude</u> to anyone," but he didn't sound particularly convincing.

"Why would my personal relationship with someone give such offense?" she asked.

"In and of itself, it doesn't, I assure you. But to publicly act in such a... an indiscreet way would give offense to many Cinnaens. Perhaps not most Pandial, from what I've learnt, but still: it damages your reputation and could result in potential problems in the future." He sighed, having been hailed by his group who awaited him.

"Far be it from me to judge anyone else's behaviour, but I've found that anything a politician or courtier could use to sling mud at their opponent should be avoided as much as possible. Behaving circumspectly is the best way to ensure this." He seemed embarrassed by his loquaciousness, bowed abruptly, and was gone.

Ata had much to consider, not the least of which how she'd thump Kai soundly when she saw him again. Also: the audacity of the Cinnaen general in judging her perceived exhibitionism... Clearly the conservative Cinnaen mindset at work!

Yet a niggling sense of fairness undermined her internal tirade. He had provided a valid reason for his change in behaviour; perhaps he had been too severe in his conduct, however, this possibly indicated how strongly he felt about the subject. She found herself more and more confused by her *own thoughts on the matter, and eventually set them aside to focus fully on her mission.*

Adjusting her position amongst the bushes, Ata gingerly rolled her shoulder. She was stiff and her arm itched so deeply it ached; a Gruxhoon had managed to scour her with its filth-ridden claws the week before. She glanced up and down the road they were staking out, then furtively looked to her battle buddy (a soldier named Brezder with a wicked sense of humour and a foul mouth) who crouched a few feet to her right.

Upon spying no ostensible change in the emptiness of the road, as well as the fact that her partner was ultra-focused in the direction from whence the raiding party would come, she promptly dropped into herself. Having become highly adept at impromptu workings, most specifically related to her body and health, it didn't take more than thirty seconds to ease the most pressing of her physical issues through Commanding.

The angry, red-tinged putrefaction of the funnels in her flesh she had doctored and bandaged as best she could on the march, but now they required the most of her in terms of energy and attention. Of secondary importance were her aching muscles and exhaustion, so she focused on the first till none of the subcutaneous rot remained and only glossed over the others. It was imperative she retained as much vim as possible for the fight ahead. *And the possible wounds thereafter.*

Miraculously, Ata had seemed to stumble across the

ability to Command healing—a heretofore impossible act of the science, according to all conventional wisdom and the accompanying texts. She had made the discovery on her trek back to Enddaian after escaping the Cinnaen military camp, it merely being an extension of the impromptu mental scripts she had dabbled in during her mission in Hårbørgen palace. More importantly, though her initial experiments were all self-administered, her ability was not limited to her own body.

A first attempt at healing another had happened quite accidentally. Ata didn't know why she had constructed the simple casting as she stood clasping General Svensso's arm for the first and only time, but for some reason she had been hyper-attuned to the exhaustion radiating from his body and the build-up of some kind of fluid in his muscles that she inherently sensed would result in pain and stiffness later.

So she had cast a script then and there, feeling the thrill of energy run from her to his flesh, sensing the suppression of the acidic liquid, and knowing he was no longer suffering the building ache from before. Of course, the ungrateful sod hadn't deserved any such intercession on her part, unknowing though he was of her altruistic largesse.

She had cursed herself afterwards when she needed to sleep almost 12 hours due to the extensive draining effect healing another had had on her own body. But the seal had been broken, and she now knew the heretofore impossible *was* possible. In the days that followed, she became fixated on continuing her experiments (cautiously and conscientiously) to ease minor physical issues in others.

A persistent itch from flea bites on one of the hunting hounds, a pinched nerve in Svensecond's hock that might have resulted in lameness for the old hack, and even alleviating the pain of a stable cat during the birth of her four kittens. Of course, she avoided using this windfall to frivolously interfere in other people's health till she had been faced with an untenable situation.

They had been fighting for two weeks, trekking across the valley with all swiftness possible. As usual, discomfort and filth quickly became the norm and hardly noticeable, but every engagement with the Gruxhoon resulted in horrific wounds for the soldiers involved. This was a normal, if heart-breaking consequence of combat, however during one violent fight, a young Pandial had interceded just as Ata would have been cut down from the side whilst engaged with another Gruxhoon. The result was the boy's lower arm savaged beyond recognition, his screeches echoing through their makeshift camp that night as their woefully overwhelmed medics amputated the shredded and splintered limb.

In the deepest watch of the following night, after

another patrol during the day, Ata had crept to the designated area where the wounded were cared for in their camp. She found the young soldier in a bad way. Fever ravaged his sweat-soaked body, his twitching limbs and pitiful whimpers compounding the unwarranted guilt she felt for his condition.

"His health has worsened consistently. He will die within the next day," the medic had surprised Ata by appearing beside her. The woman was middle-aged and motherly despite her matter-of-fact tone. "If the fever doesn't break soon, anyway." A sorrowful look settled over her coarse features, then she moved away to check on another wounded soldier.

Ata's guilt and sympathy soared, and in that moment, without considering the moral implications of gaining his consent, she placed her hand on his bare shoulder. Despite the marked difference between settling into her own body during her previous experimental forays and finding her way into another's, she immediately sensed the epicentre of his ailment. Manifesting almost like a red-black oil slick in his stump, some of the creature's vile grime had remained in the wound and was causing the corruption that was killing him.

So she had repeated a simple script of purification, imitating what his body was attempting in fighting the infection, but which was draining his own strength and feeding the febricity that scorched through his reserves.

Essentially, she merely enhanced what his body was already doing and providing the power to feed the process.

By the time the shadowy greys of morning crept over the edges of the surrounding valley, Ata's energy was completely sapped, but none of the filth or fever remained in the soldier. A mere three days later, he was well enough to ride back to Enddaian to be decommissioned and redistributed in the war effort, none the wiser as to the ground-breaking shift that had enabled this.

Since then, Ata had not been able to remain uninvolved in the plight of the wounded. Despite the hardships faced by all soldiers, she had somehow been blessed with an ability that she couldn't explain and the consequences of which she couldn't begin to fathom. Inasmuch as she was able, she alleviated the pain and suffering of the wounded, apportioning her finite energy based on the seriousness of their need.

As time passed, she noticed a conspicuous increase in her capacity to heal, the limits of which she was still trying to ascertain. Most importantly, due to her recent brush with the Gruxhoon's claws and the very real possibility of her own death in this conflict, Ata had taken to documenting her discovery and its applications as succinctly and simply possible. She had promised herself she'd pass on the information to Lord Danai once she had completed a version she felt was accurate and useful (which was not yet the case).

"Gruxhoon sighted. Approximately a hundred and twenty paces out," Brez grunted softly to her, and she immediately signed that information to the rest of their company along the road. The war party was moving swiftly, the Gruxhoon's lanky, seven-foot height rendering their stride gargantuan. Seeing them in the daylight still disturbed Ata, as most of their clashes had been nocturnal; their grey-black hides were leathery like bat wings whilst their muzzled faces were reminiscent of grotesquely misshapen wolves.

Beastly in every sense of the word, their bloodlust was only outpaced by their physical capacity to ravage. They were creatures of destruction, crafted to inflict indescribable damage to a human body. The fact that she had heard them use Bithian added an additional dimension of intellect and adaptability to their already formidable arsenal.

"We wait until they are at the marker," Ata reminded the troops via signing; they acknowledged succinctly. Then, as all the times before, Ata Commanded a veil of sensory concealment over the soldiers lying in wait for the beasts. They wouldn't be able to anticipate the attack until it was too late...

"You cut off all your hair!" Min cried in poorly concealed dismay. Ata shrugged in irritation but couldn't keep from ruffling her short hair and fringe—a habit she had picked up in the field to dislodge dust and sundry particles, as well as unstick the ends from her sweaty scalp.

"It was necessary. It kept getting in the way," Ata had always been strangely attached to her locks, but practicality had won out in the end. She was still a bit heartbroken about it and simultaneously annoyed with herself for such trumpery. It could and would grow back eventually; she just had to accept it. It wasn't as though short styles were completely unheard of; most of the poorer, working women kept their hair short. It was just that such a style was not worn by the upper echelons (debatable though her station in those lofty straits were).

"Well... Let me look at the rest of you!" Min exclaimed more enthusiastically, running her hands over Ata's arms and shoulders like a mother checking her clumsy child for injuries.

"I'm fine—all my limbs still accounted for," Ata grumped, suppressing a pleased smile at her cousin's fussing. She had barely arrived and washed ten weeks of grime from her body before the princess's summons had been delivered. They were in her private parlour, a light meal laid out for them. Ata eyed the simple but ample food hungrily.

"You're all skin and bones, Ata! Weren't you properly

provisioned?" Min asked sharply, ushering Ata into her chair and serving her in apparent haste to make up for her perceived nutrient deficit. Ata tucked in without further ado, excruciatingly aware that the mirror bore out what her cousin had stated: she had lost a significant amount of weight and looked drawn and gangly.

"We had provisions, but you know how things are on campaign... orders take precedence over mealtimes," she said through a mouthful of egg and olives. She had slathered an ungodly amount of butter onto the slice of bread on her plate and didn't even finish chewing before adding that to the medley of flavours in her mouth.

"Slow down or you'll choke," Min admonished and partook of her own more modest portions with ladylike delicacy. After a pleasant lull filled with chewing and the clink of cutlery and crockery, Min proceeded to inform Ata of all that had transpired since she had left Enddaian Keep.

"I really like Princess Lenna and the young princes; they're all sweethearts... The princess seems a bit forlorn and aimless, though."

"Perhaps she's bored, though the heavens know how one can be bored when there are a thousand things to be done during these times," Ata mumbled through her munching. She was very short on sympathy at that moment.

"I know, but consider: the Cinnaen role assigned to royals, and women in particular, is quite... limited. And limiting. I believe Princess Lenna would be happier if she were more involved, or at least contributing in a more active way to the war effort.

"As it stands, she is expected to fulfil her usual role—a largely ornamental one—while everyone else is very committed in the process and therefore the outcome of the war. She just wants to matter, I think," Min had finished eating and was leaning back in her seat, pondering deeply.

"Well, we've all got our crosses to bear, I suppose. How terrible for her that she has been coddled and cozened all the livelong day... How awful she must feel," Ata responded archly, earning a reproving look from Min.

"You could be kinder in how you view her plight; we all suffer in our own ways. What might seem insignificant to *you* may be a heavy burden to her. Being caged by traditions and expectations can be just as inhibiting as a *de facto* prison." Ata felt mildly chastised, but not enough to cede the argument. She just shrugged and continued to decimate the steak strips in front of her.

"I find her brother, the crown prince, very similar to her, except he has the sense of purpose from his highly invested role in governing his people, and so he has the quiet fortitude and commitment she lacks but has the capacity for," Min continued to hypothesize; Ata enjoyed the calm familiarity of discussing other members of the court with her cousin. It had been one of the activities that had made her feel as though they were truly family when she was young.

"I must say, I'm pleasantly surprised by the Hårbørgen heirs, considering the queen, their mother." Min stated delicately, cutting a sideways glance at Ata. Oh good, the *real* gossip was about to start...

"You mean the *warm, loving, kind* woman that gave birth to them and subsequently left them to the mercies of their caretakers, except on those few occasions she had need of them to validate her status?" Ata intoned dryly. "If there are any '*gods*', they certainly have an odd sense of humour allowing that woman to have so many children..."

Ata knew she was picking a fight here, because Min was quite devout in her practice of what was considered the 'main' religion in Áitarbith—Myriadism. Multiple, benevolent gods who only meant well and blessed both the sinful and virtuous alike, as long as they were abject worshippers and followers of the "true" faith (naturally, their faith and not the others). Ata couldn't remember a time when she actually *believed*, as opposed to just followed along with the rituals, readings, and practices to appease others. Not even as a gullible child had she felt the faintest stirrings of religious wonder and zeal.

However, like any aspect of society, extensive knowledge of this and the lesser religions allowed her to navigate her sometimes-role of spy, so she walked the line of outright antagonist and reluctant follower. All the paraphernalia, the prayer beads and tomes of the Holy Sacrament of the Benevolent Order of the Gods? As far as Ata was concerned, they were tools to manipulate and mislead—whether by her or by religious leaders.

"I mean, your apostate heckling *aside*, one would think that, even given she didn't have an active hand in raising them, the mere fact they share her blood would result in much... nastier dispositions in her offspring. That, and having no strong anchor in their lives would have brought about siblings with less familial loyalty and affection."

Min was on a roll; she always liked to puzzle over the characters of people and what made them the way they were. Human nature fascinated her, thoughtful person that she was. Ata experienced another swell of affection for her cousin who had always felt like a sister in truth, despite the disparity in their statuses.

"But they did have a parental figure, or 'anchor' as you call it, who probably imposed an unshakeable sense of superiority and loyalty to the Hårbørgen name, and therefore each other," Ata said, half-admiringly, half-derisively. At Min's curious expression, she supplied: "General Svensso." Enlightenment dawned; Ata became distracted with trying to mop up the last of the sauce on her plate with some leftover bread.

"Yes, the illegitimate eldest half-brother. Another interesting character, and one you seem to have taken a telling dislike to..." as Min's meaningful tone registered with Ata, she could only huff and puff with a stuffed mouth. One couldn't convey genuine affront or surprise when eating! Min didn't fight fair, but Ata could turn the tables once she'd forced down this last mouthful.

"You've always had such a sullenly combative nature, Ata, especially towards those you have affection for... Why, after Lord Danai approached father to request the position of being your tutor, you were as prickly as anything towards the man for more than a year... Full of nasty looks and sarcastic comments, despite all his efforts and commitment to teaching you. The poor old man must have been at his wit's end with such a little porcupine." Lord Danai had approached the king to request teaching her? And her uncle had actually cared about such a task?

"I noticed your strop with General Svensso before you were deployed—I hope you haven't gone and taken offense over something trivial just because your defenses are up with the man?" Min chided.

"Well, my 'combativeness' aside, the main reason I'm currently in a 'strop' with General Svensso is because the moralizing boor had the audacity to lecture me on *my* and Kai's illicit tryst in the alcove off the main dining hall the night of the Cinnaen-Pandial drilling competition..." she watched Min process the information, then added with venom, "Ringing any bells, Cousin-mine?" Min grasped the implication, her embarrassment infusing her entire face with a reddish hue.

"Mhmm. Let's just say, it was very difficult to hold my tongue when he was being high-handed and priggish about the whole thing. How could you be so *careless*? Imagine someone else had seen!"

What followed were profuse apologies from Min and a promise to be much more circumspect in future, plus (the bonus), they swiftly moved on from the topic of General Svensso and Ata's apparent "prickly affection" for him.

ATA HAD BEEN BACK at Enddaian Keep a mere two days when, at noon on a perfectly warm and pleasant day, the watchers on the walls sighted an unexpected company of approximately a hundred men. The excitement this caused was palpable, with Ata deciding to involve herself in the party that rode out to meet them and ascertain their purpose. She had been a bit low—Kai was still away, and Lord Danai had hied off on some mission or other, so she was at loose ends until her next deployment, all said.

Min was good company, when she could be found alone, and so were Princess Lenna and the young princes, but Ata had also noticed Prince Tensso formed part and parcel of keeping company with the other royal siblings. Unfortunate, considering his shy but marked admiration for her made her uncomfortable.

Though he never pressed her for anything nor propositioned her, his eyes followed her all over the room and he was noticeably overeager to speak with her at every opportunity. Famenke would purse her lips in silent judgment and even Lenna pulled a few wry faces at Ata behind her brother's adoring back; Ata felt as though she would physically cringe from the uneasiness situation.

What might have been a sweet crush easily dealt with in any other context with a few kind but firm words now became a matter of potentially disastrous proportions, for she couldn't offend the future monarch of a great nation (even an exiled one).

Worse still, she avoided his presence outside the privacy of his sister's rooms, for there were eyes and ears that noticed all and would exploit it for their own advantage, possibly to the detriment of others. An outing that would remove her from the prince's vicinity for the day, at least, seemed like a worthwhile endeavour.

Luckily, the captain on duty liked Ata—she and his wife had always gotten along really well when they were cadets together—and so he agreed to include her in the meeting party. Brez was also amongst the number and she smiled at her battle buddy good-naturedly. He had spent the past two days in his overcrowded family home with his (very pregnant) wife and six children and was probably keen to get away for an easy jaunt and some peace.

"I love the fu—... tykes, gods bless 'em, but I just need to not *be* with them for a moment, right," he said and winked at Ata. "For ten weeks, all I longed for was to be home. But within ten fuckin' hours I was hankering for a bit of godsdamned peace and quiet." Ata didn't know exactly what he meant, but she could imagine.

Once out the gates and trotting jauntily downhill, the fresh wind wafting over her, Ata felt as though all was right with the world. Even Svensecond, the curmudgeonly nag, seemed to have a bit of pep in his step. Life was good. Until they neared the approaching company enough to see who rode at their forefront. *Oh gods.* Could she never escape the man!

"Hail, General Svensso, Colonel Breddenai!" the captain saluted them, which they returned with enthusiasm. "Who do you ride with?" For they were clearly many more than the original party of ten that had set out as many weeks before.

The majority of the men and women accompanying them were clearly Vürgøn, with their pale hair, skin, and eyes. They wore leathers and furs, as well as having paint or ink emblazoned all over their fair skin. They were big-boned and strapping, their stocky, shaggy ponies dwarfed beneath their bulks.

"These are the troops and representatives of the collective tribes of the Vürgøn," General Svensso explained, introducing a few of their ostensible leaders —Ata hesitated to assign the title 'officer' to these hostilely primitive-looking people, in the same way she would call them 'warriors' rather than 'soldiers'. No salutes were forthcoming, only some minor form of acknowledgment, or perhaps indication of whom was being named, all differing from each other.

"Welcome to Enddaian," the captain intoned, "It would be best, I believe, if you are housed in the Pandial barracks rather than the refugee settlement. Enough spaces are open to accommodate your number." And thus they set off on their return journey, Ata uncomfortably aware of General Svensso slightly behind her and to the right in the haphazard column.

"Are you well, Lady Ata?" she heard him ask and nearly fell off her horse in surprise at him initiating a conversation with her, especially considering their hostile parting. She turned slightly to find his pleasantly blank expression awaiting a response. Gone was the impassioned man who had flung judgment at her before.

"Yes, thank you, General. I'm well. And you?" she didn't want to give him the idea she had forgiven his previous rudeness, but she also didn't want to sour this interaction either.

"As you see: still here and hopefully doing something useful," the wryness of his tone caught her off guard. Was he being self-deprecating? *How unexpected.*

"I'm sure whatever agreement you've brokered would be better than no agreement at all..." at his noncommittal shrug, she continued, "Did you encounter any Gruxhoon on the way?"

"Not to the Uurgonna Mountains, but on the way back. A pack of about thirty, although with present company it was a very one-sided engagement that ended quickly." He looked her up and down speculatively, "And you? You've not been sent back to recover from an injury, have you?"

"Why? Do I look injured? Don't let the gauntness fool you—it's just the pace and lack of regular meals when marching.... I'm back temporarily according to the regular cycle of ten-week swop-outs. You know, the higher-ups' strategy of trying to keep the troops fresh." His mouth had quirked up at her light-hearted teasing and she noticed Brez had drifted closer.

"This is Brezder; we were deployed and served together in the Plezai Valley these last weeks. Forgive his salty nature and foul language—apparently he was born with those deficits..." Both men smirked at her introduction and nodded affably. What followed was a bit of back-and-forth, good-natured and superficially engaging.

"My next big effort, besides convincing my dearest wife that her harridan mother can very well sod off and go live with her sister, is to convince Ata to get rid of this poor excuse of a horse," Brez piped up at one point. Ata tensed. *He wouldn't.* But of course, he did. "Svensecond! A stupid name for the most stubborn, stupid animal. It's probably more fuckin' mule than horse!"

After brief confusion, a light of understanding dawned in the general's eye, quickly turning martial. Before he could answer, however, a shout rose up at the front of the column.

"Smoke! Fire! Enddaian and Cinnaen Landing are being attacked!" and sure enough, black columns of smoke billowed into the sky as screams wafted towards them from the other side of the vale, at the foot of the mountain.

16

THE BEST-LAID PLANS

BUT MOUSIE, THOU ART NO THY-LANE,
IN PROVING FORESIGHT MAY BE VAIN:
THE BEST LAID SCHEMES O' MICE AN' MEN
GANG AFT AGLEY,
AN' LEA'E US NOUGHT BUT GRIEF AN' PAIN,
FOR PROMIS'D JOY!

STILL, THOU ART BLEST, COMPAR'D WI' ME!
THE PRESENT ONLY TOUCHETH THEE:
BUT OCH! I BACKWARD CAST MY E'E,
ON PROSPECTS DREAR!
AN' FORWARD THO' I CANNA SEE,
I GUESS AN' FEAR!

ROBERT BURNS

C*omplete shambles*! One left them to their own devices for a few weeks, and the entire place fell apart—literally! Well, not so much 'fell' as 'was ripped apart' by invading Gruxhoon, but really: it was essentially the same thing. Danai shook his head in disgust as he fastidiously picked over the remains of a Gruxhoon lying in the middle of the Enddaian street, trying to find *something* salvageable.

The wailing of women and children hadn't yet abated, much to his annoyance. How did that racket contribute in any practical way to their plight? It didn't. But one couldn't reason with the unreasoning, and he supposed they *did* have reason to be in a passion. The death and destruction they had survived over the past few hours was not insignificant, one could argue.

Sniffing in annoyance, he came to the conclusion that the Gruxhoon's carcass wouldn't do. It had essentially been obliterated by whatever dolts had defended the town—hacked to pieces and then set on fire for good measure. *The cretins.*

He didn't want to seem ungrateful, but would it be *too* much to ask to find one corpse fit for purpose? He needed a healthy Gruxhoon in its physical prime to dissect and analyse, to better understand the enemy they had thus far only seen through a very one-dimensional viewing-glass. Was he asking for the unattainable? No, he was settling for a dead Gruxhoon as opposed to the live one he'd prefer; he had compromised on that 'unrealistic' expectation, much to his own disgust.

But such was the situation, and he was a realist if nothing else. *Much more than my sentimental sibling.* Whom he had stashed safely in his private rooms in the keep. Hopefully the emotion-driven numpty remained there and didn't risk discovery in his eagerness to seek out young Ata.

The rampant suspicion towards the former Cinnaen spymaster was rife amongst a majority of the influential Cinnaens, most of whom had now taken up temporary residence in and around Enddaian Keep. If anything pointed to the idiocy of not only the ruling classes, but humanity in general, then the Cinnaen court's suspicion of Ians did. A life lived in service to the House of Hårbørgen and without hesitation he was suspected of colluding with the Gruxhoon!

Said distrust was a regrettable result of the spymaster's immediate departure after the initial attacks, though a necessary sacrifice, all considered—despite also leaving Ata to fend for herself and find her way back to Enddaian without Ians's expected aid. Luckily, she was highly self-sufficient and competent, if untenably stubborn.

Thinking of the girl, Danai methodically scanned the sooty (some bloodied and bruised) faces of the Pandial soldiers offering aid to various injured and traumatised inhabitants of the town. The damage to most homes and buildings was great, but not impossible to fix with good planning and time.

King Addai would immediately deal with it, once he returned from the deployment of troops in the north. General Erdai and the Cinnaen general, Bransso, would remain there, in charge of the northern offensive whilst King Addai was custodian of the southern defenses. Unfortunately, this specific attack to his stronghold would make a decidedly negative impression, even taking into consideration the sheer size of the Gruxhoon force they had repelled.

Danai didn't notice Ata amongst the soldiers on the street and felt an uncharacteristic pang of worry which he immediately and ruthlessly suppressed (as he did all irrational fears and feelings verging on the superstitious). Ians would never shut up about it if he ever knew his "cold, stony automaton of a brother" had experienced anything so human as a fleeting emotion.

Upon rounding the umpteenth corner, he finally spotted Ata in a deserted little alleyway. From what he could tell, she was kneeling beside a small figure in rags, but the surrounding darkness of the smoky tunnel blocked his view. As he neared, he noticed she had placed her hands on the exposed shoulders and chest of a beggar child who, judging by the shredded clothing and exposed entrails of her belly, was either dead or would be very soon.

Typical of the girl to let her bleeding heart get her overly involved, compounding her own suffering... He purposefully made his way forward, nudging aside debris blocking his passage to snap some sense into Ata. Then he looked closer, and everything changed.

It was *her*. *She* was the one! He felt a momentary triumph flare in him, incandescent at being proven right, then quickly chased by the plummeting realisation of what that meant moving forward. For them all. He briefly indulged in wishing he had been wrong before snapping himself back to observe her progress and technique. Only sentimental fools wallowed in 'if onlys'.

So this was what it had meant, all those dry documents and esoterically abstract divinations: the manifestation of her power was to Command healing. Even having been exposed to the many arcane secrets housed in the academic institutions of Áitarbith (the collective knowledge of humanity, as it were), he still felt fascination thrill through him at the awe-inspiring nature of this discovery and skill. *Healing*. An impossibly precious commodity—nay necessity—to all living, breathing beings. And Ata had found a way.

Her eyes were shut, her face wearing an almost pained expression of concentration while she moved her one hand to press upon the girl's exenterated stomach. The child's chest was heaving up and down much too fast, eyes wide and staring as though she could see the beyond closing in on her. Suffering from shock, most likely, and not long for this world. Danai doubted Ata would have the capability to save this life, even with all the will in the world. But he would let her try, at least, and observe.

As he watched, she slowly pushed the exposed entrails back into their torn cavity; he sensed a massive build-up of energy and its flow from one point to another nearby. He himself was Abled to a limited degree and could sense the tendrils of pure energy being manipulated. Without a script of preparation! *Fascinating.*

He knew, of course, that ancient texts purported this to be a highly effective mode, but no scholars nor practitioners over the past half millennium had believed them, never mind *tried* it. With the huge amounts of energy being transferred, Ata's face became more drawn, sweat glistening and dripping from her forehead while the colour seemed to leech out of her entirely.

Danai realised his mistake in allowing her to continue to this point; Ata would exhaust herself for a lost cause, even harm herself by draining all her energy.

But his notice of the wound put paid to the intercession he was about to launch—now merely raw, angry gouge marks. Deep, yes, but not perforating the innermost skin of the girl's stomach. *Salvageable.* When Ata keeled over next to the beggar girl, Danai leapt into action. Still conscious, Ata smiled as he knelt down beside her and propped her up.

"Lady Atiyah," he greeted stiffly. "You seem to have overexerted yourself." Drily.

"I knew it was you, Lord Danai. I couldn't see you, but I sensed you..." her rather languid speech worried him but her eyes were open and sharp as always; she wasn't mindless, just exhausted. They looked toward the injured girl who was still panting frantically and whose colour was corpse-like, her eyes now shut.

"She needs the... stuff, the essence that is flooding her system and causing her heart to race and her system to shut down... She needs it dissipated, or it'll kill her. Even with the wound so much better. But I don't have the energy..." Ata closed her eyes and pulled a pained face.

"The adrenaline you mean? Yes. It will kill her," Danai offered matter-of-factly, but Ata's distraught expression made him continue, "If you explain to me what to do, I will dispel the adrenaline from her blood."

Danai offered his aid as much for altruistic purposes as to understand her method and application, wanting this healing to be a success both for Ata's sake and to further their understanding of Command healing. With this kind of historic breakthrough, the face of their entire society would be changed. The face of this war. *Changer...*

They remained beside the little girl for the next

hour, Ata quietly guiding Danai through the numerous steps as best she could, the end-result being the girl improving to such a degree as to eventually be moved by soldiers to the makeshift field hospital at the town green.

Exhaustion and fascination vied for supremacy in Danai. *The ingenuity of Ata's discoveries!* She explained her incremental unearthing of said methods as they returned to the keep, both staggering under the weight of their healing-induced exhaustion.

Following a detour to Ata's room to collect her records, they proceeded to Danai's chambers to collate and document the history and methods the process entailed. There would be widespread awe and attention once this information was shared with the academics, politicians, and leaders of Áitarbith. In his excitement and haste, Danai had made an error of calculation—very unusual for him; he had forgotten about Iansso's presence in his rooms.

"Ata, my girl!" Ians exclaimed upon their entry, joy suffusing his lined face. Danai halted, inwardly berating himself for his ill-timed lapse in memory, exhilaration over recent developments clearly having muddled his usually stellar instincts. Now they would be exposed to endless emoting. *Bother.* Ata's immense surprise was writ clear across her face, followed quickly by pleasure.

"Ians!" she rushed forward to hug the man of the hour. Since when did she use such informal modes of address? Danai felt strangely annoyed by this clear sign of closeness between the two of them. *Ridiculous.* Of course they would be familiar with each other after working so closely in Cinnae for those many weeks.

"What are you doing here now? Where have you been? Everyone's been so worried about you! Why, Princess Lenna—"

"I can only answer some of your questions, lass," Ians chuckled avuncularly, apparently incapable of keeping from tapping her cheek like a doting grandfather. They sank into Danai's chairs, Ata's dirt and soot-ridden self causing Danai to shudder, but he held back his usual exhortations about such impolite behaviour as guests sullying furniture.

"Shall I ring for some wine?" Danai interrupted their gushing reunion stiffly, still miffed but uncertain as to the reason. All considered, it was actually ideal that Ians was here so the two of them could share some home truths with Ata. It was time, it seemed, and a long time coming.

The girl deserved to know (*some of it, at least*). But all this garrulous prattling was getting on Danai's nerves. "... and I'm sorry to have left Princess Lenna—I will be sure to apologise to Her Highness at the earliest moment possible," Ians twinkled at her, holding her soiled hand between his and affectionately patting it.

"Might I interrupt this happy reunion with some much-needed business talk?" Danai finally put in once the wine had arrived and been poured for all three. As per usual, he had asked the servant to take a small sip directly from the bottle upon delivery, watched them for a space of time, and then permitted them to leave; he reasoned that any interference would most likely take place whilst the bottle was in the care of the servant, and any unsanitary considerations were superseded by ones of survival and the avoidance of poisoning. One could never be too careful.

"Of course, Lord Danai. Please—we are all ears," the know-all offered magnanimously, still holding Ata's hand. She seemed very comfortable sitting close to the man who, for all intents and purposes, she had known a mere few weeks altogether. She should be more suspicious and careful of passing acquaintances, Danai reflected. He would address this point with her *very* soon indeed. Levelling a stern look at his brother, he knew that his news would land like a blow.

"Today, I found Ata using Command to heal an injured girl in the town after the attack... Successfully." He let that information sink in, not taking his eyes from Ians's face, watching him digest it. He seemed extensively puzzled and merely mildly interested, clearly not making the connections yet.

"But... that's... that's not possible? It's never been done, despite multiple theories as to its feasibility..." he frowned, turning to inspect Ata more closely. "The energy required! You shouldn't be conscious, hypothetically speaking…"

"I helped somewhat at the end, but it seems Ata has been experimenting and expanding her abilities over the past few months—to an astounding degree. I can assure you: Command healing is very much possible. The victim survived what should have been fatal wounds inflicted by the Gruxhoon to her abdomen. Those wounds are now merely deep scratches. Not life-threatening in the least. It was… one of the most miraculous, scientifically sophisticated events I have ever witnessed."

Danai felt himself succumb somewhat to the awe that had been pressing in on him all day. He had been witness to history being made; the kind of history that only came along once in a millennium.

"But… what— how… how will this… What does this m—" Ians's voice cut off abruptly as a terrible comprehension dawned, bereavement following shortly on its heels. He veered to Ata with desperation before swinging his eyes back to Danai. "*No.*" Head shaking, a hollowness to his denial.

"I am sorry, Ians." A long silence followed, the Cinnaen spymaster clearly struggling to make sense of this new information.

"Are you, though?" bitter recrimination seeped from his words.

"You know I am… despite our differences, I also

hoped it would be a different outcome, but that is not the reality. The facts don't bend to our wishes," Danai tried for patience in dealing with Ians's devastation. Despite the inevitability of the path they now knew they must take, he could still sympathise with his brother's plight. He also loved Ata, after all, and had known her personally for much longer—had watched her grow up. His connection to her was not insignificant either.

"Well, that would be the first time you haven't crowed over being right, I must say," Ians challenged, a combative glint in his overbright eyes that Danai recognised from decades of dealing with his emotional reactions. The lines on his brother's face seemed to have deepened startlingly in the last few seconds, his pallor verging on grey.

"Do you wish to argue ineffectually against what has been preordained or do you wish to proceed in a manner that will benefit Ata?" Danai snapped impatiently. *Really!* Did he *always* have to be the voice of reason?

The confrontational spark in his brother's eyes brightened briefly before flickering out, quenched by the hopeless inevitability. Squeezing his eyes shut, he sighed and smiled ruefully upon reopening them.

"Yes, Dan. Let's address the practicalities... Our feet have been upon this path a long time. Turning back is impossible, so let us proceed," he turned to Ata, who had been silently observing the exchange. Smiling tiredly, he lightly chafed her hand between his.

"Are you going to explain all these cryptic hints to me now?" she asked, eyes darting back and forth between them, seeming to size them up. Typical Ata, assessing and trying to make sense of everything.

"Some, Ata. A lot, but not all, unfortunately. There are certain things that are not necessary for you to know, nor helpful. Though we'll tell you what you do need to know, most importantly, I want you to understand that you are not alone in this: Danai and I are here to support you throughout..." Danai wanted to roll his eyes; trust Ians to overcomplicate things by taking the emotional route.

Now the girl would be even more worried—unnecessarily so. Unpleasantness was best dealt with swiftly: a boil lanced, a bandage ripped off. The softly-softly approach would only confuse matters, so he would speedily get them back on track. He cleared his throat.

"Yes, well. What we need to explain is that, based on this newest development, we have been provided with the last piece of a very convoluted puzzle we've been collecting pieces to and building over the past twenty years..." Danai started, trying to be as succinct and factual possible, but using an analogy to help her better understand the complexity of their years-long mission.

"My Commanding healing, you mean?" Ata asked,

puckered brow showing her intense concentration on the topic at hand.

"Yes... I do not think you grasp the magnitude of your discovery, Ata. It is the discovery of a generation; of a thousand years, even. It will change our societies, our lives—the very way we perceive our lives. Death and disease will become combatable in a way heretofore impossible and unheard of! In the most basic terms, you have changed the trajectory of our continent and world," Danai stopped, letting her digest this.

She seemed slightly nonplussed by these facts, but was doing her best to work through the repercussions. "You are what is historically known as a 'Changer'—*the* Changer of our generation." Her frown deepened, her unwillingness to claim this title clear. A title of which she neither understood the full scope nor its implications.

"What is a Changer? Besides the obvious, of course," Ata pushed.

"It is a figure of great influence on their era, the bringer of a change in the *status quo* that redefines the future of all," Ians explained, his tone reluctantly helpful.

"And I'm our time's 'Changer'? Because I stumbled across a technique that allowed for something that hadn't been done yet?" the dismissiveness with which she referred to her contribution annoyed Danai, but he understood her personality, and this was exactly how she was.

"Yes. It is an extraordinary feat; a once-in-*many*-lifetimes achievement," he snapped, patience with her lack of respect at an end. *The irreverence of youth!*

"But *anyone* could have hit on it! It says nothing about my skills or talents. It was just a fluke." she shrugged, unimpressed. "Anyway... what difference does it make? Of course, many people will now be able to be saved and healed, and it will definitely have impact on the war. But I don't see why you both were speaking so ominously, full of doom-and-gloom earlier."

"Well, it was portentous that it *was* you... And, it's more complicated than what you've just described. You see..." Ians couldn't seem to bring himself to explain further; Danai stepped in.

"You are part of a larger plan—a prediction—that was made many years ago, over an extended period of time—"

"You mean a *prophecy*?" Ata snorted. "Religious mumbo-jumbo at best." Danai's temper teetered, about to be lost. Her lack of faith or commitment to religion were one thing, but to completely disregard *methodically* Commanded forecasts was beyond the pale. *The arrogance of youth!*

"I mean a blueprint of what lies ahead during these dark times. And make no mistake, Ata, these will be the darkest times our peoples and the continent of Áitarbith have ever faced. If the signs are to be believed and stock put in that 'mumbo-jumbo' you so disdain, humanity stands at the edge of an abyss, one small push away from extinction."

He glared at her, somewhat mollified by her rueful nod. "Seeing as both Lord Iansso and I have dedicated two decades of our lives to finding and unravelling these predictions, you should at least have the civility to listen without preconceptions and prejudice." Ata's mouth flattened in an embarrassed grimace she used to make even as a little girl when she felt ashamed.

Danai felt his chest squeeze as he remembered her at that difficult age when she had become his student, all awkward angles and repressed angst. The woman in front of him was very different, yet the same girl in so many ways. He would spare her this truth, if he could, but... *she deserved to know.*

"Six hundred years ago, over a period of fifty years, an Abled scholar—a priest of some renown—made multiple predictions of the 'Time of Great Darkness' when 'the beasts of myth would arise and wash over Áitarbith from shore to shore'. I translate roughly, of course, for the man wrote in Old Bithian. Anyhow, on different occasions, and throughout his travels across the continent, he made Commanding-induced predictions of these times.

"Lord Iansso and I have made it our mission to collect all of these documents in the hopes of understanding the progression of the 'Time of Great Darkness'. What we found were references to a 'Changer' who would be the key to humanity's survival..." Danai watched Ata for any reaction, but excepting a look of concentration, no other clear emotions showed.

"After many years of translation and organisation, Lord Iansso and I were able to isolate the sections that pertained to this 'Changer' and how she, or he, might change humanity's fate, as it were."

"'He'? So it might not even be me? The oracle didn't state whether it was a male or female Changer," her hopeful tone surprised him. He had not yet explained the intricacies nor consequences of being the Changer, so perhaps Ata sensed the potential danger of that role on some level. "Could you tell me the exact prophecy?" she asked, her usual tenacity asserting itself. Danai looked queryingly at Ians; they both knew they couldn't give her everything at once, but perhaps enough to convey the importance of her role would suffice for the time being.

"I shall read it to you, but nothing more. The very fact of our research is a closely guarded secret... Only Ians and I know of this—and now you." Ata nodded in understanding. Her training in espionage meant this secretive approach did not surprise her.

"Very well: '*The heir who*—' Oh! Just remember: our translation doesn't convey the lyrical nature of the original texts, unfortunately... Old Bithian had different pronunciation and emphasis, so it's not perfect, and some of the words had to be reinterpreted due to changes in meaning..." upon which clarification Ata smiled fondly and nodded encouragingly. Danai felt slightly annoyed at her obviously coddling manner toward him, a grown man, but continued.

"The heir who sets Áitarbith free,
Three parts of four the child will be,
assayed in gold and onyx,
Wrought in shade and light,
borne in secret to the Changer,
the heir will turn the Fight."

That was as much as he felt she needed to know at that point. Ata listened carefully, nodding slowly, then requested he repeat it again twice. Danai noted Ians's shoulders sagging more every time, the metaphorical weight with each rendition increasing.

"I mean, it's a bit confusing, but... if I'm the 'Changer' in this scenario—hypothetically—then, the 'heir' referred to is my child? Or future child, correct?" she puzzled over the contents. "That's what 'borne in secret to the Changer' means, right?" she glanced up and smiled brightly. "I can guarantee I haven't had a child in secret, rest assured!" But her witticism fell flat, so she continued after a short pause.

"I recognize the 'assayed in gold and onyx' bit...

That's your code phrase to guarantee trustworthiness of an agent."

Danai and Ians nodded, allowing her the leeway she clearly needed to work through the parts they had shared with her. The rest would come at a later date once she had accepted the main premise of these lines.

"Everything seems quite straightforward, except the second and third lines 'Three parts of four the child will be, assayed in onyx and gold'. What do they mean?" Then her eyebrows rose.

"'Three parts of four'—it's the child's heritage! I'm half-and-half, so if I were to have a child with a Pandial, the child would be three-quarters Pandial, one-quarter Cinnaen?" her excitement lasted mere seconds before her eyebrows snapped down. "I don't know if I approve of such a blatant manner of reference to someone's ethnicity. It seems quite... dehumanising and callous."

"Considering how unforgiving and blatant people are about your parentage, it shouldn't surprise you that centuries ago they were even more blunt..." Danai shrugged.

"So then, the 'onyx and gold' could just be referring to physical traits of Pandial and Cinnaens, like their hair?" her face screwed up in puzzlement.

"Possibly... probably. That was the conclusion we came to as well, although there might be some development unrelated to physical appearance that relates to that prediction... It will perhaps be easier to understand in hindsight, though," Ians grunted, scratching his head negligently.

"Well, I don't really believe I'm the 'Changer' referred to, nor am I planning on having any children any time soon," Ata piped up, pretending flippancy. "But even if I were, and I do, I don't understand the sense of doom you both projected earlier." Danai and Ians shared a considering glance, the latter deciding to answer this question.

"That is not the prediction in its entirety. There is more, but we both feel it would be more beneficial to tell you later, once you've gotten used to the implications of this part..." Ata pondered this, then nodded in acceptance.

"Fair enough; I don't find it particularly compelling or disconcerting, but I accept your reasoning. Though, why were you so annoyed with Lord Danai, Ians? You almost... *blamed* him for my possibly being the Changer? Why? How is he in any way responsible?"

"Danai and I had different perspectives on who the Changer could be. He was convinced it would be you, but I thought not... *hoped* not," Ians explained, some bitterness creeping into his voice towards the end.

"Who did you think was the Changer?" Ata seemed overly-interested, then: "Perhaps it *is* actually that person... It could be an important general or war hero rather than me!" the fact that Ata seemed committed to *not* being the Changer showed more clearly than her lukewarm words that she had grasped the enormity of assuming such a pivotal role. Ians pulled a rueful face, then shook his head.

"I believed it to be Kaimam ben-Emli Delbadai," he muttered. Ata looked taken aback.

"Why? What made the two of us candidates when neither of us has achieved anything particularly spectacular to date?"

"There were apocryphal writings related to the Changer. These described the star sign and year range under which the Changer would be born, as well as some weather phenomena. Lastly, the Changer would come from 'two disparate bloodlines of north and south', thus, half-Pandial and half-Cinnaen. The only children born under those circumstances in all of Áitarbith were you two and one other, however that child died in a drowning accident when he was a teenager. Thus, it was between the two of you." As Ata made to ask a question, he continued.

"Believe me, we were *extremely* thorough in checking the records. Now, though, with your manifesting Command healing, we have our answer." Ians being quietly accepting of this fact spoke to the irrevocable undeniability of their knowledge. Despite this, Ata still seemed unconvinced and mostly unconcerned.

"Well, thank you both for your honesty. You have given me a lot to think about... But please—let me know when you believe I'm ready for the rest of the proph—

the predictions? If nothing else, I'm always keen on a mystery or riddle that needs solving," and she smiled at them brightly despite her drooping frame and heavy eyelids.

"We will go on as we have before, until more of this invasion has unfolded..." Danai intoned, hoping some more clarity would come their way soon. Today's revelations were a positive step in the right direction, at least in as far as he felt less uncertain, which was a boon. Ata rose and they escorted her to the door.

"Will I see you tomorrow at breakfast, Ians?" she asked eagerly, clinging to his arm which he had offered to her as though she were some duchess instead of the little baggage who had kept her healing skills from Danai for *ages*. The gods only knew the reason for her obfuscation.

"I'm keeping a low profile, as I am not yet ready to disabuse the Cinnaen court of their suspicions regarding my loyalties," the old rogue winked at her playfully. "Best to keep those popinjays on their toes for a bit longer." The girl snickered and finally took her leave.

"It's just as well you kept the information from her regarding how we'd been prepared to actively meddle in their love lives," Danai commented drily as Ians lowered himself back into the chair, groaning and creaking.

"Well, that would have put her back up properly, wouldn't it. And I wanted to stay in her good books, if you hadn't noticed," Ians playfully lifted and lowered his eyebrows.

"Mmm, you had better hope she doesn't discover this duplicity by omission at a later date, for then you will no longer be in charity with our Ata. And she has a long memory, that one. Does not forgive easily, and *never* forgets."

"Well, at least we know she and her half-blood friend, Kaimam, have no interest in each other romantically. That would have been *unpleasant* to break up for the sake of the prediction. Luckily your Pandial princess is and has been his childhood sweetheart all these years. Sadly, my bet on them and that the heir would be 'three parts of four' Pandial has fallen by the wayside. Especially if what I've observed between Svens and Ata is any indication..."

"Possibly... I've also noted a marked interest by the Cinnaen crown prince, which would make more sense considering the term 'heir' in the predictions—"

"No. You don't understand; 'heir' could be purely metaphorical, but the connection I witnessed between Ata and Svens was profound, I tell you. That is the relationship we need to facilitate. Trust me. I just *know* it."

"You think so? Very well... We must try and think of a way to... *encourage* the match." Danai's mind began to construct various scenarios and machinations, then he glanced at his brother who had stretched himself out, feet resting on a footstool. "Don't you feel guilty manipulating your own flesh and blood into a match she might not want?" Ians opened one eye and glared balefully.

"No, Brother-mine. I don't. As you so helpfully—and regularly—point out: superfluous emotions do not negate the necessity for action to be taken. Though many have failed Ata from the earliest point of her life, including me and my wastrel son, I will not fail her now. Perhaps it is not the ideal choice for her emotional state, but for her future safety and the path she must navigate, I will equip her with the best possible protection, irrespective of feelings. And that, Dan, is Svensso Olefson as a partner."

17

PAWNS AND PRINCES

As Mars met Venus in a temple,
    And being both in the presence of Mercury,
    Mars devised a game of Chess such as yet unseen
    taking Reason for King without pre-eminence;
    And Will for a Queen of great power;
    Choosing Thoughts as Bishops and
    As Knights the praises of sweet eloquence,
    The Castles are Desires that inflame memory
    and the Pawns are Services that fight for
Victory,
    And the King, as befits a story of love,
    Was Honor, his life ever in danger;
    For faithful Pawns he took courtesy

ALL ARMED AND ADORNED WITH OSTENTATION.

— FRANCESC DE CASTELLVI, BERNAT
FENOLLAR, NARCÍS VINYOLES
(TRANSLATED: GOVERT WESTERVELD)

The list of things that still needed doing in his mind never shortened all through the long morning of performing official duties. It was now nearing lunchtime, and Addai could feel a pressing need to relieve himself before finally assuaging his growing hunger. But first, he had to sign the last of the documents arrayed in front of him as well as tolerate two private audiences. Only then could he see to his own body's needs.

Such was his lot in life; almost unlimited social and military power, yet not even ultimate say-so over when he pissed. *Give, give, give.* Keeping the bare minimum for himself, the privilege and curse he had been born to. And yet he would not exchange it for anything, despite the enormous pressure he had recently been experiencing with the second Great Áitarbithian War. A once-a-millennium, potential extermination event, and he was, currently, the most senior political figure at the helm of humanity's last defense. An overwhelming task that was slowly draining the life from him.

Clarification of certain points in the documents took some time, the signing, stamping and sanding less so.

His ministers slowly departed, passing his next appointment by the entrance.

"Lord Bendai," he intoned as the last of the pages were whisked away by the ever-efficient Lord Uldai. Indicating the seat across from his desk took some significant willpower on his part when he would have preferred the man stand awkwardly and uncomfortably before him. However, years of rigid self-denial and control meant he could be warmly welcoming to those he disliked most; a fortunate skill, for he couldn't stand the sight of his cousin, though he prided himself that no-one, not even his closest adviser, was cognisant of this fact.

Even Min was only aware of his slight annoyance with the man, nothing more. Addai had always played his cards close to his chest, even with his loved ones, never giving away the hand he held or the strategy he employed.

"Your Majesty," Bendai thumped his chest then sat down smartly in the chair indicated. Addai watched him with a blandly polite look of attentiveness—the sooner he finished this and the next conversation, the sooner he could attend to his needs.

Internally calculating the distance and route to the privy, he waited for the man who was third in line to the Pandial throne to state his reason for requesting a private audience. Despite Bendai's generally overweening confidence, he seemed somewhat ill at ease at that moment. Addai secretly enjoyed watching him squirm and wasn't going to alleviate the tension.

"I have requested an audience with you, Your Majesty, to discuss a... somewhat sensitive matter," Lord Bendai cleared his throat. "Far be it from me to advise you on the delicate balance in our dealings with the Cinnaens, for I am sure you and your other advisors have considered the possibility, but I wanted to... suggest an element that might be helpful to our current and future prospects," once he'd started, his natural overconfidence came to the fore.

"Being on the Pandial council, our discussions surrounding the possibility of a marriage connection to solidify our treaty with the Cinnaens have been relatively superficial and fruitless, to my mind. More decisive action is needed, and during these troubling times such apparently peripheral issues tend to fall by the wayside..."

Addai felt annoyance at the man's garrulousness, yet ruthlessly suppressed anything but a vaguely interested expression on his face. If he gave the duke enough rope, perhaps he'd hang himself soon, and he could move on to the next audience with Lord Danai.

"Has... Your Majesty considered whom a marriage alliance would involve? I do not wish to impose my own views, but various aspects must be taken into consideration, and I have a suggestion to that end... The marriage cannot be between the two heirs, naturally; they will inherit the respective thrones of their kingdoms. However, one or both of the heirs could marry a noble of royal blood. I would be willing to volunteer either or both of my offspring for a marriage alliance with one of the Cinnaen royals... Perhaps Her Highness, Princess Lenna would be a good match for my son, Lord Fordai?" Addai contemplated his devious family member. He never underestimated his cousin's greed nor audacity.

"What of your daughter? Whom did you have in mind for her potential marriage? Not one of the youngest princes, I presume," Addai waited. Surely the man wouldn't have the gall to suggest his daughter for the role of future queen of Cinnae? But he knew the potential match the Pandial duke had in mind would not be for the eldest, illegitimate Hårbørgen.

"No, naturally not... As to that, I was hoping you would support my proposition for a match with the crown prince?" the avaricious expression could not be completely suppressed. Addai decided to spin this out a bit before bringing down the axe. He frowned in apparent consideration.

"Would it not make more sense for your daughter to make a match with General Svensso? I can predict the Cinnaen queen would not support a match between Lady Kenttai and her favourite son, however, a general —perhaps *the* future general of Cinnae—would be a fine match for your daughter, no?" He enjoyed watching Lord Bendai struggle to contain his temper and trying not to show his absolute disgust with the suggestion. It would not do to openly disdain his monarch's proposal.

"Well... no. My daughter, though I love her dearly, does not have the wherewithal to be a general's wife. She is such a lighthearted creature, despite her obligatory military training, and does not boast the strategic mindset necessary to navigate such a role—especially in a foreign court..."

"But you believe her equal to the task of being the future Cinnaen queen? Surely she would need the strategic mindset you describe in spades? For all Pandial's disparagement of the Cinnaen approach and government, the current Cinnaen queen is no mere figurehead. Thus, should you believe your daughter unequal to the task of being a general's wife, queen of Cinnae would be out of the question, I fear." Realising he had been outmanoeuvred in this part of the discussion, Lord Bendai ceded the point with a respectful nod. Addai decided to toy with him a bit more.

"But perhaps a Cinnaen general would be a welcome addition to my own family... Princess Mindaia would be wed to, essentially, the eldest son of a king who has formidable power and influence, but no *official* claim to the Cinnaen throne." The fleeting sourness on Lord Bendai's face clearly expressed his thoughts on this suggestion.

"Does Your Majesty believe General Svensso's sway to be so extensive? The queen of Cinnae despises the man, which limits the scope of his influence… And his illegitimacy, to my mind, is more a mark against the man than in his favour."

"I do not only speak of his military role or official capacity. What you say is true: Queen Nelni cannot stand her husband's son, but she will not remain queen nor regent forever. Make no mistake: the general's royal siblings hold him in high esteem and awe—particularly the crown prince. When he is king, that connection is the one we would be able to utilise. General Svensso is a principled man who takes his duties seriously; he would honour the ties of marriage as well as the blood ties to his siblings." Bendai's doubtful look remained, when an idea seemed to occur to him.

"I have an alternative suggestion, with Your Majesty's permission?" his palpable excitement piqued Addai's interest, but also stirred feelings of unease. The last time Bendai had been this invested in something, it had been an additional and extortionate tax of his dependent tenants that almost resulted in a large-scale riot. He motioned for the man to continue.

"Princess Mindaia is the future monarch of our nation—perhaps hers should be a more… illustrious marriage? If one wanted a … an equivalent pairing for General Svensso's status and familial standing, a match with… *Lady* Ata seems logical," Addai noted the way assigning a title to Ata's name galled this elitist. Despite his efforts over the years to mask his absolute loathing of Addai's niece, the king was more than aware that her being was anathema to Bendai. The duke had never been one to forget a trespass or a slight, and Ata's very existence was that. To be rejected by a princess whom he had adored and then suffer the insult of her giving birth to an unnamed Cinnaen's bastard had been the ultimate insult to the prideful man. *What a mess Annaia had left behind!*

"I will definitely consider your suggestions, Your Grace, and I thank you for making the time and effort to impart them," Addai made sure to use a tone of finality, the dismissal clear. Despite obviously wanting to remain and discuss the terms further, his cousin rose and saluted, departing stiff-backed and with a less-than-satisfied air. Addai did not need to wait long for the seat to be filled by Lord Danai—*the belligerent old goat.*

"Was a formal audience truly necessary, Lord Danai? Would our usual mode of communication not have sufficed?" he let the annoyance he felt colour his tone strongly. Give this man an inch, and he would walk all over you—and arrange all your personal affairs to his preferences as he did so. They would inevitably be well-organised, but you would forever struggle to maintain agency in your own life thereafter. It was just a part of his nature.

Lord Danai, as per usual, did not quake in his boots as others might at this show of temper from Addai; he had been around since Addai was in leading strings and therefore felt no compunction to cater to his ego, monarch or no.

"It is good to maintain some level of public interaction, I should think. Not all matters to be discussed are of a clandestine nature, particularly not this one," the old man's dry tone irked Addai but this was not out of the ordinary; their relationship had always been one of mild animosity and combativeness. However, the man was the best spymaster bar none, plus Addai knew him to be loyal to a fault despite his coldly calculating nature.

"By all means, proceed with whatever it is you wish to petition for," Addai responded in an exact imitation of Lord Danai's tone. The dark eyes sharpened perceptibly but no other indication of his notice of the implicit mockery could be seen.

"I would like to, officially, suggest a marital alliance between the Pandial and Cinnaen royal families," Lord Danai stated bluntly. Addai couldn't stifle his huff of surprised humour at the odds; his never-voiced suspicion that the old man had some kind of extrasensory knowledge of others' minds arose again.

"Unbelievably, you are the second person to broach this subject with me today... I wonder which two persons *you* wish to match, for I have heard some rather odd suggestions thus far." The spymaster narrowed his eyes.

"Lord Bendai has put forward one of his offspring

for a dynastic marriage? No—knowing the man, he undoubtedly wanted to obliterate the odds and probably offered to sacrifice both..." The fact that Danai knew whose appointment preceded his was not surprising, but his immediate grasp of the points discussed was. Addai's efforts not to give anything away were obviously wasted, for Lord Danai read the answer on his face.

"I am not surprised. Let me make a further guess: he suggested his daughter be matched with the Cinnaen crown prince? And his son with Princess Lenna, no? The man makes up in unadulterated ambition what he lacks in subtlety, it seems. I should be pleased he chose to make these suggestions in a private audience rather than a joint Cinnaen-Pandial council meeting!" the fact that Lord Danai was so clearly incensed by Lord Bendai's petition amused Addai and apparently elicited uncharacteristic garrulousness in the man who was usually so tightlipped.

Lord Danai had always despised Addai's ducal cousin, but true to his nature, that disgust only manifested in a coldly silent condemnation; Addai was convinced the man would have quietly poisoned the aristocrat if he thought Addai would allow him to get away with it. Which he wouldn't, much as he disliked his cousin and saw him for the rogue he was.

"Well, my petition is not nearly as audacious as the duke's. I believe a marital agreement between Lady

Atiyah and General Svensso would be highly successful in various ways." Danai continued seriously, almost challengingly: "This is ideal for continued goodwill between our nations; something we should consider for when this Gruxhoon invasion is routed. Afterwards, we *must* maintain a deep connection with the Cinnaens... This opportunity cannot be squandered."

"I fail to see the benefits of this match specifically. Please, elucidate further," Addai said, his sarcasm noted and duly ignored as Lord Danai continued.

"They are both of royal heritage and influential figures in their own right, however, their statuses are such that their marriage would not cause dissatisfaction amongst the more... traditionally-minded Cinnaens and Pandial. It is an ideal match, for you risk nothing—not Princess Mindaia's future rule, nor the possibility of insulting the current Cinnaen regents...

"The Cinnaen queen could potentially be a formidable opponent should she feel slighted in a marriage agreement brokered between one of her offspring and someone she considers unworthy. Thus, with this alliance, you have two important, yet not too-important, semi-royal representatives matched; their loyalty to their respective kingdoms is unquestionable, so there will not be an imbalance of loyalty to one or the other once they are wed." Lord Danai delivered this analysis as he did all his reports: factual, yet nuanced.

Addai felt oddly torn... When Lord Bendai had

suggested the various couplings, he had thought of it as a mere hypothetical exercise. Lord Danai's petition was much more concrete and therefore a probability rather than a possibility, which Addai inherently shied away from. Squaring his shoulders and purposely pushing through his reluctance, Addai refused to acknowledge the reason (even to himself).

"What made you think of this pairing in particular?"

Lord Danai's response was prompt. "The two have interacted on various occasions since Lady Atiyah was sent to the Cinnaen court. The idea of their marriage occurred to me only recently, when I considered the diverse players in the upper echelons and who would be the 'safest bet' for an alliance, as it were. From there, it was merely an exercise in logic."

Ah, the old man and his 'exercises in logic'... Addai could not fault his reasoning except for the one element he was avoiding—the one that would expose the true source of all his misgivings. He tried to word it ambiguously.

"Will such a match be... successful?" The spymaster frowned in annoyed confusion.

"I have explained the reasons for its success, I thought—"

"No, I mean... will the marriage be... happy? Could it be? Do General Svensso and Ata have anything in common besides all the external elements you have so *efficiently* listed?" Understanding dawned on Lord

Danai's face; Addai found he didn't like the knowing look—never had.

"Is happiness in marriage a prerequisite for a dynastic match? I would have thought it was of negligible importance myself," Addai wanted to strangle the old pedant for making him verbalise what he tried to avoid in general. His temper asserted itself.

"We both know you are being facetious, Lord Danai! Of course arranged marriages do not require the participants to be in love, or even to like each other. But I do feel some sense of responsibility to the daughter of Princess Annaia—"

"To your niece, you mean," and Addai smashed his fist onto his desk. Hard. The silence that followed was heavy, but the cursed man did not seem in the least cowed by Addai's unusual show of temper. "Based on my observations, and conversations with both parties, I believe they will deal well with each other in such a marriage." Lord Danai relented, paused, then added meaningfully, "I would not have proposed it if I did not."

"I will definitely consider your suggestions, Lord Danai, and I thank you for making the time and effort to impart them," Addai finally intoned, wanting time to consider the implications of the decision now resting on his shoulders. Lord Danai, uncowed, rose and saluted, but as he reached the door, Addai felt the need to discompose him just a bit.

"You will, no doubt, be surprised to learn that your

petition for a match between General Svensso and Lady Ata was the second of today, as you were preceded in that by Lord Bendai," a flicker of surprise in the spymaster's eyes was the only satisfaction Addai was given. "Good day, Lord Danai."

"Your Majesty." Then the man was gone, finally leaving Addai to his much-anticipated ablutions.

OVER THE NEXT FEW DAYS, despite being dragged in different directions by his unending responsibilities, Addai was unduly consumed by thoughts of orchestrating a marriage between General Svensso and Ata. He finally acknowledged to himself that his trepidation in authorising the match lay not only in his worries for Ata's wellbeing in such an arrangement, but also the consequences for the Pandial royal family.

It had always been a closely guarded secret how much he cared for his niece, largely to protect her from unsavoury elements at court. Even more secret, though, was his deep-seated humiliation, for despite all his love and affection for her and for her mother, Addai was ashamed of Ata's existence.

He had adored his younger sister and had placed her on a pedestal; her ignominious tumble from that plinth could be traced directly to Ata's conception, and in the deepest recesses of his heart where he hid all his most shameful shortcomings, he resented Ata. Even worse: he suspected she would come to the same kind of ruinous fall from grace as her mother and embroil them all in an irrevocable scandal.

Thus far she had not exhibited any great capacity for chaos, merely dabbling in the same mischief all young people did, but then she had only recently celebrated her twentieth year, a mere six months older than his Min. There was still plenty of time for potential disaster...

Also, as far as he was aware, Ata's childhood sweetheart, Kaimam ben-Emli Delbadai, was still and had been her lover for more than four years. Knowing Ata as he did, the blow of an arranged marriage would be a cruel one. Min had joined Ata and Kai's merry duo when they were still children and they had come to form a kind of triad that had lasted through the years.

Though this childhood alliance had become less conspicuous in recent years, for the purposes of protecting the two half-Cinnaen friends from the barbs of the court, Addai was under no illusions regarding their connection—it remained as strong as it had been during their childhood and adolescence. Thus, when Min noted Addai's distraction and commented on it during one of their private breakfasts, he chose to share his worries.

"Lord *Danai* put forward this proposition?" Min clarified, apparently just as surprised as Addai had been upon receiving the spymaster's suggestion.

"Yes. He was quite insistent, even for him, that it would be the ideal arrangement for all involved... But... I am hesitant, despite the manifold positive aspects." Sighing, Addai rubbed his eyes pensively.

"What causes you to hesitate? Something relating to General Svensso's character?" Min queried, appearing slightly alarmed by the thought he had unearthed something sordid about the general.

"No, nothing like that. Further investigation has merely confirmed what we had surmised before: he is an upstanding man who is loyal to his family and kingdom. Strict, as would be expected with his military background, but surprisingly compassionate as well. No, my hesitation doesn't stem from *him*, but rather on Ata's side of the equation," Addai said. Min immediately looked incensed.

"How would Ata be deficient in such a match?"

"Not in any way. I just worry that her... longstanding romance with Lieutenant Kaimam would mean she'd oppose the marriage, and consequently be made miserable with the consequences thereof..." Addai trailed off, frustrated that such an ideal situation—and he was convinced it *was* an ideal way to strengthen the bonds between the Cinnaen and Pandial houses—should be scuppered by a run-of-the-mill amorous liaison.

But he couldn't bring himself to force the issue; if he

had been more conscientious arranging a match a score of years before, then perhaps Annai— but no, these thoughts were not helpful. Suffice it to say: he would not make the same mistakes with Ata that he had with his sister. Looking oddly discomfited by his statement, Min fell into a brown study.

"Is Ata's... relationship with Lieutenant Kaimam the only stumbling block to your agreement of this mutually beneficial marriage?" Min finally piped up, eyes intense. Addai nodded.

"Then... you shouldn't worry. At least, not about *that*. Though her and Kai's relationship is... complicated... she will not resent the match on the grounds of her amour with him. They are not particularly committed to that side of the relationship at all," and Min blushed hotly, looking away. *Curious.* But then, Min would never express such a decisive opinion unless she were completely sure. What did Addai know about things? Perhaps that was how their understanding worked, then. Which was quite a relief.

"You believe she will be amenable to a marriage arranged with General Svensso, then? You think it is a good idea?" he pushed, for he trusted Min's judgment in most things, but especially with regard to her cousin. She seemed to ponder for a few seconds; her response did not disappoint. She would be a thoughtful and conscientious ruler one day.

"I... I believe that Ata has a kind of fascination with

the general. She behaves with that peculiar antipathy she initially develops when she cares for someone... You know what I mean? The same as when she first met Kai, and then Lord Danai, and sometimes even with me and you. I imagine she will vehemently oppose the match in the beginning—it is her way. But, all considered, it would be the safest kind of outcome for her under the circumstances. She is in the unenviable position of being royal but not, with powerful enemies even within our own court.

"We cannot predict the outcome of this invasion—how long it will last, who will perish—and I think a guardian with some kind of power and status outside of Pandial would be ideal. It's more complex than merely considering such a fleeting thing as happiness, or even love... At least she'll have protection and we would have a stronger alliance with Cinnae." Min looked slightly sickened by her pitilessly objective outline, yet still committed.

"Very well... I shall inform the Pandial council of our decision, and then make the proposal to the Cinnaen one," Addai concluded, comforted by Min's reasoning and the lightness that came with having made the decision. He was not worried about the arrangements; with enough authority, one could bring about anything one set one's mind to, especially if one was a king.

STRANGELY ENOUGH, Queen Nelni had been the most enthusiastic supporter of the proposed marriage. Based on Lord Danai's recommendation (a wise one at that), Addai had met with a skeleton council of the Cinnaens within a week of the initial suggestions of the marriage. Though it felt underhanded not having General Svensso present during the preliminary negotiations, the arrangements could not wait until his return from deployment with the Vürgøn company on the north-western border where they had recently been stationed.

The Cinnaen queen's wholehearted support of the match mystified Addai, until Lord Danai drily noted in an aside that she feared the Cinnaen heir's growing infatuation with Ata, whom she considered far beneath his touch.

"She worries the boy will take Ata as a mistress and that she would thereby exert undue influence over him as well as over the youngest princes. She has said as much to her ladies-in-waiting," Lord Danai had muttered into Addai's ear. Addai tempered his surprised expression. It seemed Ata had somehow inextricably inserted herself into the Cinnaen royal family. Danai continued: "This is the ideal answer to her prayers, for the young prince respects his older half-brother too much to take his wife to mistress. Say what you will of her rages, but the Cinnaen queen understands how the wind blows..."

"Perhaps we should have suggested a match between

Ata and the crown prince? He would have been over-joyed," Addai mocked quietly; he more sensed the spymaster's amusement than saw evidence of it. All said, the negotiations were concluded speedily and success-fully. The only one to nominally veto the contract was Lord Haaviso, the late Cinnaen monarch's cousin.

"Would it not be more prudent to defer this marriage till a more suitably stable time? This arrange-ment seems slightly precipitous, and neither party is actually here to discuss the agreement..." his monotonous dissent fell on deaf ears; he was immedi-ately overruled by the Cinnaen queen in conjunction with Addai. Now that they had committed to this path, he felt an intense edginess to accomplish General Svensso's and Ata's joining as soon as possible.

"To a stronger bond between our houses!" one of the Cinnaen ministers raised his voice and glass upon the conclusion of the contract, its terms neatly noted, and signed. It only awaited the signatures of the two people to be joined in matrimony. Though no date had yet been agreed upon, the general consensus was that it should be soon—as soon as both the necessary individuals were present at Enddaian Keep.

Lord Bendai had also been in attendance, yet did not seem particularly pleased that the only arrangement had been between the illegitimate offspring of the two houses and none besides. Addai felt no compunction to address him, however, a vague concession had been made regarding potential future marriage contracts. Nothing concrete, just a general goodwill and accord to consider future matches at some point.

Finally, after the long-winded negotiations, Addai readied himself for bed once back in his chambers. It had been an exhausting two weeks, mostly due to the constant presence of Ata in his mind. Her marriage. Her happiness. Her future. It was therefore not surprising that he dreamed of her entry into this world.

"Your Majesty—it is time! You requested I inform you when Her Highness's time was upon her, no matter the hour!" his valet's features blurred in the flickering candlelight. His wife, Allaia, muttered and sat up.

"Stay! I will go to my sister," Addai urged his wife, loathe to bother her with this family problem; she was herself a few months along and not particularly well. Nodding and smiling at him, she squeezed his hand in support. She knew the furor and fallout his sister's unplanned and unsanctioned pregnancy had caused in his court. What it had cost him.

Upon arriving at Princess Annaia's chambers, he was kept waiting in her private lounge. The sounds of distress from the bedchamber scraped along his nerve endings. When he finally snapped and stormed towards the doors, intent on bursting through them and forcing his way to his baby sister's side, they opened without fanfare and a diminutive figure blocked his path.

"Her Highness... she's— ... she has not fared well in the delivery, Your Majesty," the man trembled. Addai had not

wasted breath on the creature, but brushed past him to get to the bed. Annaia's figure looked unnaturally shrunken, her usually golden countenance greyish-white. Death hung over the canopied bed—Addai had too much experience with its spectre in battle not to recognize the inevitability of its presence there.

"Sister!" he grasped her cool, lank hand tightly, feeling breathless and overwhelmed. Her eyes were shut, mouth slightly open while her breath was barely a whisper. She clung to life by a wispy thread. She could not leave him alone now. Not so shortly after their parents had departed this world too!

"Annaia! Ann! Listen to me! You cannot go... You must stay with me!" but his words did not cross over to wherever she had departed. Then a loud squeal rang through the chamber. The child's lusty wails. Ann's eyes flew open, staring unseeingly upward and her anguish clearly written across her face that had been so passive before.

"Ata!" she gasped, her hand softly squeezing his. Then she closed her eyes and was no more.

The meaning of her last words escaped him. The meaning of everything escaped him.

Addai had been inconsolable. Remembering the birth of his sister and her childhood had compounded his pain to the point where he could not face anyone. Slowly, over the following days, the requirements of the kingdom superseded his own grief, which he then buried deeper and deeper within himself. The child, whose entry into the world had stolen his sister from him, was set aside—he neither cared nor enquired where. It must have been his wife, Queen Allaia, who arranged for nurses and care.

And thus it continued for months. As far as Addai was concerned, the spawn of his sister's mystery lover did not exist. Until the gods lay him low for the final time: his own beloved wife died in child bed as his sister had, leaving him a daughter. And it was when he went to see his daughter in the royal nursery that he discovered the baby who had ceased to be in his mind. His new-born lay in her crib, sleeping, when he noticed a servant moving back and forth across the floor.

"Your Majesty?" the young wet nurse saluted, then continued to sway back and forth, another baby held against her body. His interest must have shown, for she promptly handed the infant to him. The child looked like any other he had seen, with lots of dark hair. Perhaps a bit paler than usual, but negligibly so, and large, unusually blue-green eyes.

"What... what do you call her?" he asked gruffly, an odd tenderness taking a hold of him, despite his unwillingness for it to do so.

"Nothing. She has no name, so we don't call her anything," the girl responded offhandedly, then, noticing his look of displeasure, flushed and scurried off. But Addai had not been frowning in anger at the nurses; he had been overwhelmed by a feeling of guilt. His beloved sister's only child, his most direct blood relative besides his own daughter a few feet away, had been left for months to the mercies of others. Had not even been given a name.

"Ata," he said loudly, startling the child in his arms, who was watching him wonderingly.

"Your Majesty?" the same girl sidled closer. He cleared his throat.

"Her name is 'Ata'," he stated emphatically, ignoring her look of surprise. "Her mother named her before she passed."

And so was born his relationship with his niece. Even when she did not know of or disagreed with his protection, he gave it to the best of his abilities, irrespective of the ultimate cost to himself or their kinship. Notwithstanding his deeply held fears that she would somehow shame them all; despite his illogical anger for his sister's demise—he loved her more than those things.

Upon waking, Addai lay for many minutes and considered his latest move to unassailably secure Ata's future protection.

18

SPELL BINDING

BE TO HER, PERSEPHONE,

ALL THE THINGS I MIGHT NOT BE;

TAKE HER HEAD UPON YOUR KNEE.

SHE THAT WAS SO PROUD AND WILD,

FLIPPANT, ARROGANT AND FREE,

SHE THAT HAD NO NEED OF ME,

IS A LITTLE LONELY CHILD

LOST IN HELL,—PERSEPHONE,

TAKE HER HEAD UPON YOUR KNEE;

SAY TO HER, "MY DEAR, MY DEAR,

IT IS NOT SO DREADFUL HERE."

EDNA ST. VINCENT MILLAY

There was a saying: 'ill news spreads apace'. Sadly, this was not completely true based on Svens's experience—or at least, not to the degree he would have preferred when he returned to Enddaian Keep. He would have expected, as per this age-old adage, that immediately upon his arrival the news of his impending nuptials would have been shared with him. As it happened, he had already been ensconced in his chambers adjacent to his siblings', along with Rans, availing themselves of the stocked liquor when his valet, Perkki, tentatively broke the news.

"What did you say, Perkki?" Svens had jovially enquired, all ease and good humour upon finally arriving back at the Pandial stronghold after riding for many days. The seasons were shifting, rain being their constant travel companion more often than not, and within the next month, winter would be fully upon them. Though milder in Pandi than Cinnae, a military campaign would be highly constrained by the practical difficulties resulting from the weather. Hard months lay ahead and their campaign's status was currently undefinable.

Svens had had the immense good luck of meeting up with Rans and members of his company on the way back to Enddaian and was making the most of the indeterminate amount of time they had to socialise before returning to their divergent duties.

"Just... I—I heard some rather... concerning news these few minutes past," Perkki reluctantly volunteered. Svens was sure even the most dour of tidings couldn't dampen his current good spirits. There was a blazing fire in the grate, he had washed away the mud and grime of their travels earlier, and Perkki had just brought their hot dinner. Life was incorruptibly good at this moment.

"Well... What gossip has your Pandial sweetheart whispered in your ear *this* time?" Rans teased, knowing Svens's man became quite flustered when accused of being a lothario or a gossip. Puzzlingly, this time his teasing had no effect on the man's notably nervous disposition.

"For goodness' sake, Perkki. It must be something very dire indeed to have you this rattled. You are worrying me—out with it!" Svens said, to which the usually unflappable valet responded by opening and shutting his mouth like a gasping goldfish. Finally, after gulping loudly, he appeared to steel himself.

"I had it from... well, it doesn't really matter, but a very reliable source of information. The Cinnaen and Pandial councils—those that remained once most of the others had been deployed throughout Pandial and into Cinnae for the war..." his courage seemed to fail him momentarily before he pushed forward. "Well, that is, apparently they've signed an official contract... of marriage. A marital alliance. Last week, they did. But it's very hush-hush." Rans made a sound of keen interest, which Svens mirrored. Of course, it was an inevitability that they would tie one of his siblings into a noose of their arranging, but he had not expected them to do it so swiftly.

"It was only a matter of time; discussions have been underway for a while, but no clear ideas committed to. They will probably discuss it officially at tomorrow's meeting, of which I was informed when I arrived... Does your 'source' know which of the Cinnaen and Pandial aristocrats or royals have been contracted?" Svens asked seriously, his mind jumping to the person he had considered the most probable from the moment the topic of such a marriage agreement had been broached in council meetings. *Lenna.*

He would do all in his power to try and deflect such a commitment on her behalf, for she was too young to be bartered. At least, not *yet*, the more cynically realistic part of his mind interjected. Such was the nature of royal and aristocratic families: they married for alliance and mutual benefit, thereby strengthening their standing and providing security for their future offspring. Perkki looked about ready to faint at this point, but he managed to expel what he knew in a rush.

"You and the Lady Ata, my lord!" A jarring silence followed. Svens was temporarily flummoxed—he clearly hadn't heard correctly. It must be a manifestation of his own annoying obsession with seeing the exasperating woman again, hearing her name now.

"What? Who did you say? Only, I thought yo— you said..." Svens stammered.

"The two people they contracted to each other are *you*, my lord, and the Lady Ata," Perkki seemed to take Svens's continued lack of reaction as a sign to continue. "At least, that's what my... friend told me." Rans swore loudly.

"They can't do that, can they? Make such an agreement on your behalf without even informing you? It's not possible to have a marriage contract without the parties' signatures, is it?" Rans hissed, clearly incensed by the entire thing. "Tell me there's a way for you to veto this deal, Svens? The audacity to sign away your future without a 'by your leave'..." and he continued to rage while Svens wrestled with this new state of affairs.

"I..." Svens tried to organise his thoughts, but everything was in a fluttering chaos, even his stomach. *Nauseated*. He felt nauseated. "You... *How* could that be? It makes no earthly sense to match two—the two of *us*!" his initial stupor was giving way to ire, but he clamped down on it. Rans's anger (so unusual for his best friend) was enough to be getting on with.

Needless to say, with Svens's reticence and Rans's roiling fury on his behalf, the night's dinner and socialising were concluded rather abruptly. Later, Svens lay in his bed, mind racing from one thing to the next, one option to the other. It was only when the gray light of morning and the tentative birdsong heralding the sunrise washed into his chambers that he nodded off.

SVENS FELT HUNGOVER; he had a thumping head on him and a dry-cotton feeling in his mouth. 'Foul' did not begin to describe his mood as he stalked into the dining hall of Enddaian Keep, only to be brought up short by the sight of his nemesis and apparently future bride. She was seated in her usual place, smiling happily and conversing with her lover, the merry Pandial lieutenant. Svens inevitably bristled. Well, if they were to be married, that would be the first law he'd lay down: no more Lieutenant Kaimam.

"How are you taking 'the great betrayal' as Rans has labeled your marriage contract?" Blÿns muttered when Svens chose to sit down beside him and across from Rans at one of the lower tables. "Not overdramatic *at all*," he added sarcastically, upon which Rans chucked a piece of bread at his head.

"But seriously, Svens, I'm so sorry for your predicament... *Imagine* the gall of those old fogies to marry you off to such a hideous hag, whom you would be expected to bed, and father children with... What a hardship that will be, I'm sure." Svens responded by subtly elbowing the buffoon in the stomach, enjoying the low "oof!" it elicited. Strangely, his mockery conveyed his solidarity and significantly lightened Svens's spirits.

"On the brighter side—if you don't get along, you could just have the stereotypical court marriage: she lives her life and you live yours. No harm, no foul. And doubly easy because you're from different countries!" Blÿns smirked. "But we're getting ahead of ourselves... We shouldn't believe every bit of gossip at court; perhaps it's all just a misunderstanding. You haven't actually been told anything concrete, have you?"

"I'll probably be informed officially during our joint council meeting this afternoon," Svens murmured as he buttered his bread.

"What will you do till then? A training session?" Rans asked hopefully, but Svens shook his head.

"I... I feel I should try and speak with... *her*. It seems unfair that I know what is afoot, but that she's clueless as to her fate. It would only be fair to forewarn her," Svens said unwillingly. Rans pulled a face but nodded in understanding. It was the decent thing to do, after all, and had *absolutely* nothing to do with him wanting to see and speak with her after all these weeks of absence. They proceeded to finish their breakfast, Svens constantly suppressing the need to turn around and look at his unknowing intended.

"Oh! Your bride-to-be is about to depart with her current paramour—maybe you should try and catch up with them now," Blÿns cackled beside him; he gave the man a coolly disdainful look before making to leave.

"Perhaps you can convince them to substitute your name in the marriage contract with mine, eh? I'd be more than happy to fall on that sword for you. Anything for a friend!" the last part was almost shouted as Svens departed, trying to ignore the stares of other diners and seriously considering finding some new friends.

Unfortunately, he was not successful in tracking down his quarry, yet his catch was much more significant than expected. As he hurried along a corridor, still in pursuit of Ata, he was grabbed by the arm and dragged into a tiny passageway off the main ones he usually frequented. Before he could defend himself, he noted the familiarity of the stranger's scent and stance. Upon glaring accusingly at his assailant, his confusion left him gormlessly staring with mouth agape.

"*Ians!*" he cried, only to be shushed patronisingly by the object of his indignation. "What are you *doing* here? *Where have you been!*" he whisper-shouted. Ians just shook his snowy head repressively, holding his hand to his mouth in a silencing gesture, and then proceeded to hurry away from Svens down the winding corridor.

Naturally, Svens followed. He needed—was *owed*—answers by his oldest friend. After winding through other obscure passages, they finally entered a modest room. Ians immediately went to the fireplace, turning his backside to the lit fire and groaning as he rubbed his nether regions and warmed them.

"Old age is murder on the joints, I tell you, my boy. I ache in this cold stone box!" Ians volunteered, then smiled at Svens. "Please, Son, take a seat! We have much to discuss, I think." Trust him to sound perfectly reasonable; no reference to the fact that he had disappeared without a word or trace during one of the worst situations in Cinnaen history. And yet, Svens couldn't bring himself to be difficult—huffing and then plopping down into one of the shabby chairs arranged in Ians's usual array around the hearth.

"Where have you been, Ians?" Svens immediately began quarrelsomely.

"Ah... I knew this would be your first question, and I am very sorry, that is, to tell you that I *cannot* tell you. At least not yet... Perhaps not ever, though, so I won't make any commitments to that effect," Ians said as he also sat down in a chair. "Would you like some refreshment? A drink?" the consummate host offered, but Svens was not interested.

"No, thank you. So, what *can* you tell me, then?" he eyed his mentor suspiciously, "Can you tell me how long you've been here, hiding from the Cinnaen court?" the disdain in his voice not subtle at all, although he knew his face was in its habitually passive mask. It had taken him years of childhood distress to perfect it, and now he was inevitably stuck with it as his default expression.

"I have not been here more than a week and my presence is temporary. Thus, I do not see the point in 'presenting' myself and going through the tedious process of clearing my name only to leave shortly thereafter. Next question," Ians responded lightly, purposely ignoring Svens's prior rudeness. Apparently, he was not prepared to sink to Svens's level and give him the argument he was so clearly spoiling for. Consequently, Svens tried to temper his annoyance.

"I suppose you cannot tell me why or when you will leave again?" Ians just knowingly tapped his nose with his finger in response. So *'no'*. "Am I sworn to secrecy on you being here, then?" Svens enquired fractiously and Ians shrugged good-naturedly.

"Naturally, should you choose to disclose my presence here, it would cause some fuss and annoyance, but nothing I cannot manage. I would, however, hope that our longstanding friendship would prohibit you from descending to such levels of juvenile spite." His pleasant tone had not varied one whit. *The manipulative old scalliwag.*

Ians watched him, head cocked askew and eyes too knowing. "You seem slightly... unsettled, my young friend. Is there anything bothering you—besides my miraculous return, of course," spreading his arms like a showy performer, Ians's eyes twinkled merrily. It was impossible to stay angry with him, which he well knew. Svens exhaled huffily in capitulation.

"I have a joint meeting with the Cinnaen and Pandial Councils this afternoon..." Ians looked vaguely interested, "... where, I have reliably been informed, my engagement to Lady Ata will be announced. An arranged match that I had no notion was in the works, only to arrive here yesterday and hear the servant gossip declare it's been all but settled." Svens couldn't keep the bitterness from his voice.

"Ah! So, they've hit on a couple to act as their nations' representatives in a political alliance, yes?" Ians looked pensive but not particularly surprised.

"Did you know about this? Only, you don't seem as shocked as I was when I first heard the news..." Svens tried not to sound accusatory.

"I *swear* to you: I had no idea that a contract had been agreed upon between the two councils. To be frank, a marital alliance was to be expected at some point, but I would have bet my last gold piece that Princess Lenna would have been the sacrificial lamb tied to some horrible, high-ranking Pandial." Guileless, as always, yet skipping to the most salient point. Svens sensed, despite Ians's 'obvious' ignorance, that he was choosing his words carefully and navigating the truth masterfully.

"Yes... I thought the same and was completely prepared to intercede on her behalf should that have been the case. Now, I find I am the one that needs an intercession," the irony was galling, really.

"Technically, your presence in the contract instead of Princess Lenna's could be viewed as you sparing her that sacrifice..." Ians was staring off abstractedly, almost unaware he was voicing his thoughts. But voice them he did, and Svens found they made a huge difference to his point of view; a titanic shift in his stance.

"I hadn't considered it in that light, Ians, but you're correct: if it weren't me and Lady Ata, then it definitely would have been Len and whichever Pandial they selected."

"Yes, well... sometimes the 'bigger picture' eludes us and it is beneficial to have others help us contextualise. Young Ata, for example..." Svens knew the old man wanted him to ask, and he knew the old man knew that he knew; and yet he couldn't keep from asking.

"What about her?" his feigned nonchalance was thin and fooled no-one.

"She's made the most momentous discovery of the past... I cannot even say! Of the past century? Five centuries? Of all times? She has cracked the long-held yet unproven hypothesis that one could Command healing!" Ians's usual enthusiasm had reached fever pitch, and Svens had to admit that such an achievement was enormously impressive. Naturally, his mind immediately sprang to how it could aid in the war efforts.

"I can already see your one-track mind make its dash, so I will put you out of your misery. Yes, Lord Danai has already taken all arrangements in hand to a) record all the techniques involved, and b) to train up as many Abled healers as possible... This discovery will essentially change the very nature of much of our lives and society. It's quite something!" And the two of them fell to detailing the possible outcomes of the amazing new avenue open to humanity.

The rest of their conversation progressed well, their easy camaraderie never having left their interactions despite months of separation. Svens felt slightly comforted by the insights Ians had shared; he no longer felt the driving need to oppose the marriage contract, but saw it in a new light: a way to protect Len from being exploited in a dynastic match, for the time being.

Thus, when he entered the council meeting chamber later that day, Svens was more than prepared to be reasonable and sign the agreement despite still experiencing a distracting sensation in his belly like fizzing bubbles or butterfly wings, when he considered the magnitude of the next step. *Marriage.* A lifelong commitment to a woman he barely knew and, at best, had inconsistent feelings towards. Luckily, as he knew what to expect, they could hammer out the details of the union during the meeting, which made him feel more at ease.

What he was *not* expecting was to find Lady Ata stood beside the King of Pandi, wearing a simple forest green dress and a bewildered scowl. Though plain, it made her eyes look even greener, he thought before metaphorically shaking himself. His confusion at her presence was compounded when it was announced without much fanfare that he and Lady Ata would marry then and there, with the council members as witnesses. A wedding ceremony without much ceremony, as it were.

Upon reflection afterward, Svens had to commend the architects of the union for their ingenuity. Had Ata been forewarned, he doubted she would have been wrangled into it. As it happened, she'd been so shocked by the entire affair (not least of all the king's wholehearted and forceful endorsement) that the vows had been spoken and the contract signed within the space of fifteen minutes. Thus, they were man and wife.

They only began to truly understand what had transpired when the meeting came to an end, the members dispersed, and the two of them remained, shellshocked, with only King Addai and his trusty clerk (Svens did not know the paragon of efficiency's name).

"I would once again like to offer my congratulations to you both, as well as to thank you for your commitment to this politically necessary bridge between our nations. I realise it must have been... *unexpected*, but you are both very capable individuals who, I am certain, will make the best of this alliance." He was very self-contained, this king—very much in opposition to the character he had portrayed when acting as Tens's guide into Pandial. He seemed to be focused almost exclusively on Lady Ata, in his restrained way, but she was unusually unresponsive. The king cleared his throat when his well wishes were met with stony silence from his niece.

"Apart from Lady Ata's stated dowry in the marriage contract, I have added an additional gift of a small estate on the Cinnaen border... It is not particularly ostentatious and is situated in a very rural Irie community, but has good annual yields and would make a fine home, should you choose to take up residence there after this war."

It was generous—exceedingly so. But no thanks came from the bride, so Svens made all the right noises and saluted the king, who suddenly seemed eager to be gone. Still, he paused and studied her minutely before finally departing.

They were now alone, standing beside each other yet feeling worlds apart.

"Did... did I just hallucinate all of that?" she finally whispered hoarsely, unbending enough to glance at him with huge eyes. Though Svens felt equally discombobulated, her obvious distress grounded him and made him feel unusually protective of her.

"Yes, it did," he tried to sound sympathetic, yet irritation flared in her eyes.

"Your tendency towards succinctness is not particularly helpful right now!" she snapped, surprising him with her venom. He tried to maintain a calm mien.

"I apologise if you expect more information, but I know as much as you do about this."

"I find that hard to believe, you being on the Cinnaen Council who negotiated this 'alliance'," she retorted hotly.

"Well, it was as much of a surprise to me, for your information... The councils negotiated it while I was away with the Vürgøn delegation and decided not to include me in the decision process at all! I thought this meeting would merely be the announcement of the engagement, not the actual we—"

"Why would you expect the announcement of an engagement if you had no notion of the entire arrangement?" she shot back; Svens suddenly felt on the spot.

"It's not... I *did* hear some gossip about a possible match between us via my valet last night, but nothing concrete. I was planning on dealing with the details today," he supplied unwillingly, knowing it sounded like a weak qualification.

"So, you've known since last night that something was afoot and didn't think to at least warn me?" she was now facing him squarely, anger radiating from her expression and stance.

"I tried to catch you after breakfast, but you and Lieutenant Kaimam slunk off somewhere together— "

"We did not 'slink off' anywhere!"

"Fine! You both happened to depart at the same time and in the same direction! Happy?"

"NO! I'm not 'happy' at all; not with this entire situation and definitely not with *you*!"

Svens experienced the distinct urge to strangle her for going on like a petulant child, but viciously suppressed it. He seldom lost his temper. Except with her, apparently... Breathing deeply, he attempted to de-escalate the situation.

"Irrespective of how either of us feels about our... marriage, it's done now. We simply need to make the best of it." Her mutinous expression said she thought otherwise. Svens felt his patience fraying at the edges; this woman managed to get his back up every time. "Perhaps the best thing now would be to discuss our living arrangements while here in Enddaian Keep and—"

"I'm not moving anywhere! I'll be keeping my rooms, and you yours, of course. I don't see why anything in our current lives should change... We can be married on paper, but that would be the extent of it. No muss, no fuss," she interrupted flippantly. They were not going to get anywhere helpful with her in this untenable mood.

"I see yo— *we* are both too off-kilter to consider the entire affair in an objective light... Maybe we should take some time for ourselves to think over the potential implications of this. We could meet again this evening, after dinner, and discuss our path ahead? Or would you prefer to sleep on it?" Personally, Svens thought more time would be beneficial to them both. Ata eyed him with a hostility, clearly not in the mood to be reasonable.

"Fine. I don't see how all the time in the world will make this entire fiasco make more sense, but let's meet tomorrow morning, if you're available," the woman conceded. Hence, they agreed on a time and place to discuss their marital implications and consequent arrangements.

Unfortunately for Svens and Ata, their ordeal for the day was not at an end. Without much pomp—very similar to their wedding, really—King Addai stood up during dinner that evening and announced their marriage to all and sundry.

Naturally, his matter-of-fact announcement, with additional phrases like "a Cinnaen-Pandial alliance of influence" and "to the mutual benefit of our two great nations", was met with categorical silence, followed immediately by a wave of discussion in the dining hall.

Svens, who had been sitting at the royal table once more, found himself the object of all eyes, while Ata managed to avoid widespread gawking for a short while but was soon also being studied and discussed openly. Some of the soldiers seated at her table began to congratulate her enthusiastically. In an effort to avoid the invasive looks and constant attention, Svens busied himself with his meal, like a coward.

He scrupulously avoided looking in Tens's direction, knowing his half-brother would feel hurt and betrayed by this recent development, whether because of his crush on Lady Ata or the fact that Svens had refrained from telling him. Sensing Lenna's attention fixed on him as well, he assiduously focused on his dinner.

Allowing his eyes to wander over the tables before the royal table, he noted the meaningful looks from Rans and Blÿns, both clearly wanting to meet up after dinner to discuss this newest development. But for once, he wasn't in the mood for a dissection of his current predicament; he just wanted to steal away and lick his wounds after a harrowing day that saw his entire life upended.

As soon as he was able to do so politely, Svens took his leave from the royal table, somehow managing to exit the dining hall beside Princess Mindaia.

"May I congratulate you on your marriage to Lady Ata, General," said the woman who bore an uncanny resemblance to his new wife. "I wish you both every happiness." Her smile was kind, but a twist to her mouth implied reservations. She had a highly expressive face, to his mind—just like Ata.

"Thank you, Your Highness. It was... surprising, in terms of its suddenness, but I'm sure we will make the best of it," Svens supplied, trying for honesty and diplomacy simultaneously. *A difficult balance.*

"I'm sure you'll find a way to get along; you have a lot in common, after all," Princess Mindaia responded. Svens immediately homed in on her expression, looking for any signs she meant something disparaging about their illegitimacy. When she noticed his scrutiny, Princess Mindaia must have reconsidered her words, for she blushed and hurried to add: "I didn't mean... I only meant you are both very loyal and kind people who are self-sacrificing and committed to your kingdoms." Svens merely nodded in acknowledgment.

The princess's entire demeanour, quite surprisingly, was one of support for the marriage. Svens would have thought, considering her closeness with her bastard cousin, that she would be incensed by this ill-conceived match. The wind would definitely be taken out of his bride's sails when she realised her cousin was not unequivocally on her side in this.

THE FOLLOWING days and weeks were marked (or rather 'marred') by Svens's and Ata's newly-married state. Despite meeting the morning after their hasty wedding, Ata could not be made to see reason when it came to their marriage and had taken to insisting on petitioning the Pandial king for an annulment.

Svens tried to reason with her, but was completely ignored and finally left her to march off in a highly charged emotional state. The fact that all her belongings had been moved to his apartments a mere two hours after her exit bespoke the Pandial king's commitment to the continuation of their union. From then on, Svens and Ata were two unwilling roommates.

Having clearly been thwarted in her appeals to the king, she must have approached her remaining family and friends for support; as Svens had predicted, there had likely been a falling out between Ata and her royal cousin, for she returned to their apartments in a high dudgeon but refused to speak to him about what had caused it. From muttered epithets and vengeful monologues, he gathered Princess Mindaia had not been sympathetic to Ata's efforts to nullify the contract, nor, it seemed, were any of the other major players in her life.

The consequence of this was that she removed herself from their spheres as much as she was able, her expression generally stony and sullen. She even stopped sitting with her boon companion during meals—the bane of Svens's existence, Lieutenant Kaimam (though this development didn't trouble Svens overmuch).

Having been taken off of active military duty, she assisted her former tutor, Lord Danai, in the large-scale scheme of training up healers as well as documenting and distributing the amazing discovery of Commanding healing. Her role was an important one, and she was therefore accorded every form of support she could possibly need in this regard. However, her apparent withdrawal from her loved ones included Lord Danai, whose presence she appeared to merely tolerate under sufferance as they worked. Towards Svens, her behaviour was initially coldly angry.

"You'd better not be expecting a consummation of this farce of a marriage!" she'd snapped at him the first night of their enforced living proximity.

"Don't worry—I have never aspired to such relations with you, nor will I ever," Svens had lied blithely, more concerned with getting one up on her than being honest with the little brat. This response seemed to rob her of fuel for the fire of her anger.

"Good, then," she huffed and proceeded to roll around to an annoying degree in the bed. The first night, Svens had tried to be considerate and accepted the settee as his designated sleeping spot, however, a few days of constantly being on the receiving end of her acidic temper saw him challenge her wholesale occupation of the bed.

"It's more than large enough for both of us; I cede you the right side and I'll occupy the left. We can even place this blanket down the middle as a border, if you feel it necessary," he belligerently asserted, taking up residence on 'his' side of the subdivision. She had tried to argue, but as it was already a *fait accompli*, she mutteringly settled into this agreement.

Eventually, her openly stroppy attitude towards him eased, the woman having realised with the passing of time that he had been just as caught in a trap not of his making. Being a (relatively) reasonable individual, she appeared to accept him as a fellow-sufferer and comrade opposing those who had colluded against them. Being loathe to return to their chilly relationship from before, Svens privately foreswore disabusing her of this notion.

Nevertheless, a reprieve came three weeks into their "wedded bliss"—he would relieve their fighters on the north-western border of Pandial along with a company of fresh troops. Though it had only been a few weeks since he'd last been there, the oppressive situation at Enddaian Keep as well as a feeling of uselessness meant Svens was as excited to return as it was possible to be.

"Don't worry, my friend," Blÿns looked up at him as he mounted his horse in preparation for their departure. "I'll be *sure* to look after the welfare of your lovely new bride while you're away. She will be in *able* hands," ironic, really, when the aspiring cicisbeo's one arm was in a sling. But before Svens could respond appropriately, Rans smacked the baggage's noggin from behind.

"Ouch!" Blÿns rubbed his head and eyed their other mounted friend who would be the secondary Cinnaen officer in the group, "I was being *genuinely* helpful..." turning back: "Who knows, Svens. Maybe absence will make the heart grow fonder? Even a *bit* of fondness would be an improvement at this point, eh?"

Svens had made the mistake of discussing the dire state of his fledgling marriage with them and was now paying the price for it by constantly having to stomach his jokester friend's sly innuendos. *Served him right for oversharing.* He noted one of the other officers—a Pandial named Fordai, he remembered vaguely—shamelessly listening in on the ribbing he was getting from his so-called "friend".

It was only a day later that Svens had cause to remember their conversation regarding his potential absence and its positive effects on Ata, for his company was ambushed by a Gruxhoon party and almost completely decimated except for the four officers, who were then dragged to the creatures' den for some ungodly reason. It seemed a permanent absence was inevitable. *Ata would undoubtedly be pleased.*

19

___

TIED IN KNOTS

How fickle my heart and how woozy my eyes

    I struggle to find any truth in your lies

    And now my heart stumbles on things I don't know

    My weakness I feel I must finally show

Lend me your hand and we'll conquer them all

    But lend me your heart and I'll just let you fall

    Lend me your eyes I can change what you see

    But your soul you must keep, totally free

Mumford & Sons

It was ironic that tying the knot, in Ata's case, meant the severing of all her other meaningful ties—or at least the fraying of them. Following her lightning-fast wedding ceremony, she had been completely overwhelmed by the magnitude of this life event, but after sleeping on it (where very little actual restful sleep had taken place), she realised that their union could still be set aside. She just had to petition the most powerful person she knew... Unfortunately, that had also been the person who had orchestrated the entire farce: King Addai.

What she should have done was approach him with humility and well-structured arguments as to why her arranged marriage was not viable long-term, but due to the kerfuffle with her "husband" that morning, she'd thrown caution to the wind and imposed on the king in a highly emotional state. Needless to say, the audience did not go to plan.

Her uncle had been firm and unbending in the face of her admittedly haphazardly scrambled reasons to annul the contract, eventually losing his own temper with her stubborn refusals to commit to the union and enforcing the clause that required them to 'dwell in a single domicile as and when practicable', per their marriage contract. Thus, far from finding herself freed from her marital ties to the most annoying man in Áitar-bith, she was now caged in close proximity to him. Her hormones and eyes were well-pleased, her ego decidedly not.

Additionally, her fallings out with all the people she considered her nearest and dearest—Min, Lord Danai, and even Kai—isolated her to an alarming degree, with only her "spouse" having even an inkling of or sympathy for what she was going through. She still shuddered at her interaction with Min on the day after her wedding.

"Min! I need to talk to you urgently," Ata had interrupted the discussion her cousin was having with a minor noble who bristled at the unprecedented rudeness.

"I... very well; my apologies, Lady Vrennai. We shall continue our discussion at a later date, if that is acceptable to you?" Min tried to cover the awkwardness of the interaction, but Ata was beyond caring. Having just stormed from King Addai's presence after being summarily dismissed, she was desperate.

"What is it, Ata? Is it about your marriage?" Min asked with a subtle tone of dread, guiding Ata away from the cluster of ladies wandering around the meeting room and into a quiet alcove.

"Yes!" Ata hissed, helpless rage having made her less circumspect in her behaviour; she shuddered to think how far she forgot herself with the Pandial King earlier. But if she could get Min on side, then she could help smooth any feathers Ata might have ruffled.

"I went to your father and begged him for an annulment, but he absolutely and categorically refused... Isn't there some-

thing you could say to him? Something you could do to help convince him?" She clung to the hope that Min would try her best on her behalf. The thought that her cousin wouldn't wholeheartedly support her in this hadn't even occurred to Ata.

"I... I'm truly sorry, Ata. But even if I could convince the king to consider an annulment, I wouldn't," Min replied hesitantly, confounding Ata completely before rushing on in a whisper, "I understand this is a huge change for you, but it isn't as though you would have escaped an arranged match, being who you are... And General Svensso is the best option —you could deal very well together. You could even be happy, if you'd put all your efforts into trying to make it work!"

Clutching Ata's hand desperately, Min tracked her facial expressions minutely. The betrayal Ata felt at her cousin's words could not be described; she felt as though an indefatigable truth she had held throughout her life had been proven a fallacy. Clearly, she could not trust nor rely on this person whom she'd loved all her life the way she thought she could.

What followed had been a painfully personal argument in which Ata had told Min some home truths, including a few related to her covering for Min in her secret relationship with Kai. By the end of her whispered tirade, Min was pale but remained resolute in her stance on Ata's marriage. Ata had stormed off and henceforth ceased speaking to her cousin except in a formal capacity when interaction was required by the presence of others.

Though Ata missed her cousin and her staid council desperately, she couldn't forgive her her monumental betrayal. Despite the regular earnest looks Min directed at her, she blithely looked the other way and maintained her stoic adherence to silence.

It didn't help that Ata had proceeded from her argument with Min to seek out Lord Danai, whom she hoped would at least provide emotional support in the face of her blood relations' renunciation of her side on the subject of her marriage. This had not been the case.

"Lady Atiyah, too much is riding on your union for you to cry off. It would result in King Addai's leadership being questioned and undermined. And frankly: your personal concerns are of little consequence in the greater scheme of dynastic affairs. An arranged marriage is par for the course for someone of your status and familial connections, and your obstructive behaviour thus far is juvenile and counterproductive."

Lord Danai's habitually repressive tone was like hot coals on Ata's head, fanning her already formidable temper into an inferno. She did not dignify his words with an answer, summarily taking her leave of his presence.

The last of her great disappointments on this subject was Kai, whom she sat beside that evening at dinner. As with everything, he'd tried to joke and mock the situation, but when pushed had been relatively dismissive of her concerns. Ata quickly realised from his noncommittal evasions that he and Min had already discussed the entire debacle and her best friend was not willing to support her at the cost of supporting his sweetheart.

"It's actually good that I see where I stand in the hierarchy of your esteem," she said before leaving the table, Kai trying to call her back. She ignored him and returned to her and her husband's quarters.

Now, she was stuck working closely with Lord Danai, maintaining a politely distant relationship, and actively ignoring Min and King Addai. Kai had been redeployed, so their rift had not been patched up prior to his departure. She'd been surprised when a small parcel from him had been delivered to her the day after his departure. Inside were two charms for Enstroi chains (she assumed for hers and for Svens's, even though—being a Cinnaen—he did not have one), two halves of a gold coin.

The accompanying note had been brief:

Don't hold a grudge, Woman. It makes your face all pruned and ugly. At least I found a good use for one of the two you won for me in that bet.

She hadn't attached a charm representing this marriage to her Enstroi chain; she wouldn't ever, if she had anything to do with the final outcome.

Yet the gift left Ata feeling somewhat guilty and very alone, especially when Svens also departed for the northern border. Though she was by no means more amenable to their union, she had come to the realisation that he and she were in the same boat, and if anything, he knew to some extent how she felt. This provided a level of solidarity between them, as well as the fact that he'd been surprisingly patient and long-suffering in the face of her admittedly childish behaviour towards him.

She was very surprised, therefore, at being summoned with all due haste to speak with King Addai shortly after Svens's departure—she had been under the impression she was currently a *persona non grata* in the king's eyes. Upon arriving, she was further taken aback by the presence of Min, a Cinnaen officer, and Lord Bendai of all people. For once, the horrid man didn't go out of his way to subtly belittle her; he wore an expression of pained concentration, face pale and drawn. A feeling of foreboding immediately took hold of her.

"Thank you for coming so soon, Lady Ata. We have received news that our troops who departed two days ago under the leadership of General Svensso, Lieutenant Colonel Ransso, Captain Fordai, and Sergeant Nedam were attacked by Gruxhoon approximately eighty miles from Enddaian. Almost all the soldiers were killed except fourteen, who were severely injured and survived long enough to receive healing. They informed us that the Gruxhoon had taken the officers with them, all of them wounded to some degree..." the

Cinnaen officer rapped out in short order, emotions completely absent from his rendition.

"We wanted to inform the families of the officers separately from the families of the soldiers, as their absence is an ongoing concern... Particularly as it relates to the security of our military plans. If the Gruxhoon are as advanced as has been purported—even being able to communicate in Bithian—then it is highly probable they will be attempting to extract useful information from their captives," King Addai continued, face serious.

"So... what is being done to retrieve the officers?" Ata asked, ignoring Min's presence beside the king. She could *feel* her cousin's eyes boring into her.

"As we are unsure where they have been taken, and the wounded soldiers are unclear in terms of specifics—"

"You haven't done anything to retrieve them yet, have you?" Ata's disbelief and censure were apparent. Before anyone could respond, the door flew open and Prince Tensso marched in accompanied by Lord Haaviso.

"Good day all. What is the reason for this meeting? The messenger provided no additional information besides the summons," he rushed to ask, clearly sensing the mood in the room.

"General Svensso and other Pandial and Cinnaen officers have been taken hostage by the Gruxhoon when their troops were attacked; nothing has been done thus far to even *plan* a retrieval operation," Ata snapped, clearly surprising the prince with her vehemence.

"Your Majesty, I do not say this often, but I am in agreement with... Lady Ata. We must dispatch troops immediately to find our officers—the more, the better. A show of force is necessary to rout the animals and save our officers!" Lord Bendai finally piped up, even his distress at his son's situation not diminishing the arrogance with which he barked his orders.

"Respectfully, I disagree, Lord Bendai," Ata returned, seeing the flash of rage in the man's eyes at being gainsaid in the presence of their monarch, being 'undermined' as he perceived it. "We should send as small a group as we are able; they can travel fast and light and, most importantly, without forewarning to the Gruxhoon of their approach.

"If an Abled were to accompany them to cloak their approach and help track the men, then it would be like a lightning-fast stab with a spear-tip rather than a clumsy bashing with an unwieldy club. Even better: if the Abled is versed in the recent science of healing," Ata stated.

"I agree with Lady Ata," Prince Tensso supplied, Lord Haaviso nodding emphatically beside him. "And the more expedient, the better. We can have as many of our best men as needed ready to ride within the hour; we would only require an Abled person with the skills described," Prince Tensso continued. King Addai nodded.

"Thank you, Prince Tensso. We will offer ten of our own men, including scouts who are familiar with that region, if you would be willing to offer ten of your own," he responded; as he drew breath to continue, Ata interjected.

"I volunteer to accompany the retrieval party as their Abled guide and healer," she stated forcefully, forestalling the king by adding, "I am the best-versed Abled healer, and I am a soldier too... It only makes sense for me to go along, as our entire military plan is potentially at stake the longer those officers remain in the Gruxhoon's power." After a momentary pause, the king nodded in agreement. As they all moved to leave, Min cornered Ata in the corridor.

Grabbing Ata's arm when she tried to brush past her, Min hissed: "Why are you insisting on going? You've been trying to nullify your marriage since its advent." Ata paused in shock at her words.

"Whyever *wouldn't* I volunteer because of that?" Min eyed her guardedly.

"Because your marriage end goal would be much better served should those men never return—the exact opposite of what your aim would be in rescuing them," she responded, phrasing it almost like a question. Ata felt another ache grow in her chest.

"So, you believe I'd leave them to their fate with the Gruxhoon? That I wouldn't try my best to bring them back? Regardless of my own situation, I would never wish any harm to befall another merely for my own convenience or benefit... And in this case in particular, the potential extraction of our military plans and secrets from the officers by far supersedes any personal gripes I might have," Ata's disgust seemed to shame Min.

"I'm sorry, Ata... I didn't mean—"

"Yes, you did. But it's fine—I don't care what you think of me, frankly. Clearly my thoughts and needs don't carry much weight with you, and the very *fact* you think I would capitalise on this situation shows how *little* you understand me," then she walked off without a backward glance.

As she hastily threw some clothing into a rucksack in their rooms, Kai's gift box with its contents caught her eye. Without exactly understanding why, she took the charms and fastened them to her chain—*temporarily*—for safekeeping.

THEY HAD RIDDEN as though hellish hounds were snapping at their heels, Ata taking the lead and constantly coordinating with the two other guides and trackers in the group. Having built up such a vast capacity and reserve of energy through practicing healing over the preceding weeks, Ata was able to power a tracking script for hours at a time, while the traditional trackers took over leading the group during her periods of rest. Thus, they found the Gruxhoon hideout within a day and a half.

When they were within a few miles of their quarry, Ata insisted on stopping. She cast a script of clarification and modeling in a secluded glen, providing a clear layout within her mind of the abandoned mining tunnels the Gruxhoon had co-opted as their den. She carefully studied and memorised the intricate passages, drawing a map in the dirt with a stick so they could plan an offensive with minimal potential loss or injury.

Ata insisted it would be best if she maintained her mental connection to the script whilst they were inside the mines; that way, she would know specifically where the prisoners were as well as the movements of the Gruxhoon and be able to guide the group accordingly. Although, that would also mean she would be distracted by the internally projected information and therefore needed someone to protect her at all times as she piloted them through the tunnels.

"I don't know how you feel comfortable with this whole fuckin' situation," Brez muttered, having volunteered to accompany her as her standing battle buddy. Ata didn't know herself how she was going to manage being so sensorily deprived and vulnerable—completely reliant on the protection of others due to the debilitating nature of not being able to see anything besides the projection.

"It's the best plan with the highest likelihood of

success; I just need to push through the personal discomfort," she shrugged, feigning good-natured acceptance while her belly roiled with tension.

"I'm trusting you won't run off and leave me blinded and vulnerable in the tunnels," she quipped. He snorted derisively.

"I'm going to leave aside your lack of godsdamned trust in my personal loyalty and point out we're as dependent on your hocus pocus to get us out alive as you are on me... Even if I have to bloody carry your arse out of there, you're coming back with us." It was quite sweet and comforting of him to say. *Despite the profanity.*

Their small group approached a side entrance to the mines, the main one being heavily guarded by eight Gruxhoon. She held tightly onto Brez's arm, staring blindly at her projection but hearing their real-world surroundings. It was very disorienting. They waited for the sign... When the ten nominated soldiers began noisily moving through the woods, acting as decoy and drawing the Gruxhoon from the entrance, their remaining incursive group of eleven entered through the side hatch.

It was cramped but manageable to crawl along, Brez dragging her and holding his sword in his other hand. Once inside, she scanned ahead and manipulated the projection within her mind's eye.

"There are four Gruxhoon in the larger tunnel off to our left; we should take the narrow tunnel second from the right," she whispered, following Brez's guiding hand and continuously scanning through countless tunnels and pathways in the rendering to find a route through the maze. The four captives were being held in a small cell-like room in the bowels of the earth.

At one point, she told three of their number to run interference down a side-tunnel so the main rescue party could proceed unhindered in the direction of the captives. A little further on, another two soldiers needed to distract Gruxhoon guards and lead them in the opposite direction.

They were down to five soldiers besides herself, and though she couldn't quite make out the state of the prisoners in the 'vision' provided by her script, their passive, outstretched body positions suggested injury and (potentially) the inability to move by themselves. So, they definitely needed at least four soldiers besides herself and Brez, as he had to act as her guide if they were to use the same procedure to leave. Luckily they were close now.

"They're in the next room, but there are two Gruxhoon inside with them, guarding them," she whispered. "We need to take them out quietly or we'll have the reserves sleeping three corridors over upon us—which we will *not* survive," she warned.

There was no collective response, though Brez murmured an affirmative in her ear. Her heart beat wildly as she heard the muffled sounds of what she assumed were the soldiers overpowering the Gruxhoon, followed by the shuffling of dragging feet. The smell of unwashed bodies, sweat, and old blood hit her. *The prisoners had joined them.*

"Are they all here? Ready to go?" she whispered urgently, trying to manipulate the rendering to find the best route out but simultaneously burning to know if *he* was alright.

"We're here. Ready when you are," a hoarse but familiar voice quietly offered. He was there and able to talk calmly enough.

Buoyed by relief, she whispered: "Okay, let's go," taking the lead with Brez—the two oddly guiding each other like a pair of drunken sots winding their way home after a night out. Though Ata desperately made an effort to view and anticipate all the moving parts in her projected maze, inevitably, a fish slipped through the net.

She smelled the beast at the same time its roars filled the narrow stone corridor they were in, and the immediate sounds of a fight—men's shouts, the ring of metal blades glancing off rock—echoed all around her. She tried to maintain her focus and the flow of energy to the projection, tried to find a path to the outside as well as to the other fighters that had separated from them.

"We need to go now!" she yelled at Brez, no longer aiming for subtlety, "An entire group of at least twenty is in the tunnel behind us and heading our way!" he gripped her arm uncomfortably tightly and urged her forward, shouting for the others to follow.

As they rushed through the winding passages, Ata guiding them almost hysterically, they were joined by four of the five soldiers they had shed earlier. Two of them appeared injured in their movements and were being propped up by their compatriots.

"We're almost there!" Ata gasped, her energy starting to wane due to the past days of almost constant Commanding. But she needed to hold some back for the inevitable healing once they left this underground prison... She was tempted to drop her internal projection when she smelled the fresh air, but fought against the urge: she still needed to 'see' where the Gruxhoon were all around the mines too.

"We're out!" Brez cried, yanking her unceremoniously through the narrow aperture and propping her up while the others followed.

"Move south-south-west quickly; the Gruxhoon in the tunnels can't follow us through this narrow shaft, but they're making for the main entrance. We need to hurry to avoid them and meet up with the decoy group!" Ata instructed.

"You heard her! Look lively!" Brez encouraged as they began to jog, Ata stumblingly while Brez tried to guide her into the woods. Branches and leaves snapped against her face and arms, the surrounding foliage dragging at her hair. Nickering and stomping told her they had reached their comrades who awaited them, steeds at the ready for a hasty escape.

She was promptly hauled onto horseback, Brez taking a seat behind her, grabbing the reigns and securing her with one arm. With a disconcerting jolt when the animal leapt into motion, the jarring movement of its strides caused her to feel precariously unmoored. Finally, after riding for a significant amount of time without Gruxhoon being visible, even at the edges of the layout projection, Ata wearily let it drop and could once again see her immediate surroundings.

They continued for a short while more, the commanding officer of the rescue operation finally calling a halt so they could see to the rescued men. Ata rushed over to where they were propped against some tree trunks; Svens, though tired and pale, held her gaze steadily.

"You should check the young Pandial officer, Fordai, first. The rest of us will keep, I think," he stated, his gaze turning toward the man furthest from him. When Ata hurriedly knelt beside Lord Fordai, the bane of her childhood and teenage existence, she immediately realised he was already dead. *No!*

Putting both her hands against his forehead and neck, she constructed a basic script of diagnosis. But there was nothing to diagnose. Just empty flesh remained. The man's vitality had fully dissipated, leaving only an empty husk behind. Ata plucked her hands away, shying from the all-encompassing emptiness she sensed through her ability. She looked inquiringly at the soldier standing over them—the one who had carried Fordai out of the tunnels.

"He was in a bad way when I grabbed him from the cave... I... I think he passed when we were climbing through the last, small tunnel," though he was young and hesitant, there was a hardened resignation to his words. He'd seen plenty of death before and would no doubt see plenty more. Ata felt chilled by this reality.

She avoided thinking on it too much by moving on to the other prisoners. The worst one, besides Fordai, was Lieutenant Ransso, the other Cinnaen officer. If she remembered correctly, he and the general were quite close friends.

"Thank you," the man rattled as she Commanded the healing of his punctured lung; the rib had still been poking into it, somewhat blocking the flow of blood that would otherwise have filled the organ and drowned him. From what Svens explained, the Gruxhoon had just finished 'interrogating' Lieutenant Ransso for the time being when they had been rescued.

"Then our timing was good, at least in your case. You would've died with this wound within a few hours," Ata tiredly blurted. She had been trying to ration her energy, only healing the most dire, life-threatening wounds. Yet, as she finished a script on a Pandial's masticated thigh, she heard a ringing sound increase in volume and white light permeated her vision. A strange lightness struck her mind while her limbs felt weighted down by sand... and then everything cut out at once.

"YOU'RE YOUR OWN WORST ENEMY!" Svens snapped, Ata staring ahead of her and doing her best to ignore the man as they rode back to Enddaian. They were going slower on their return than the breakneck pace they'd set before. "Are you listening to me, stubborn woman?" he griped.

"No." She didn't even look at him. After she'd been brought back around by Brez unceremoniously chucking water in her face, Svens had been yammering nonstop for the past few hours, muttering about her overextending herself as she proceeded to marginally heal him. He then continued to grumble about it once they mounted for the return journey. Her response now seemed to surprise him, for she hadn't deigned to answer him thus far.

"Well, you should. At least *sometimes*," he said in a disgruntled tone, then, eyeing her slyly added, "I am your lord and master, after all." Without thinking, she stepped into his trap by swinging to him with a scathing retort on her tongue, only to see he was watching her with fond amusement on his usually stoic face. In a moment of pique, she defaulted to her usual way of needling him: she pulled a ridiculous face, surprising a laugh out of him.

"I knew I'd get a rise out of you sooner or later... You're not the 'suffer in silence' type."

"Neither are you," was all she could think to respond with.

"Why on earth are you always pulling faces at me? Do you do that to everyone you antagonise?" he groused, but she wasn't fooled—her faces amused him now. The initial shock of her tactic had worn off. *Shame.*

"Because you always seemed so incensed by my lack of decorum. And it's fun." Although she had tried to hide it, she felt oddly saddened by Fordai's death, which was confusing to her because of their fraught relationship in life. The man had been nothing but execrable to her since she could remember, but she had not wished him dead. She shuddered to think of how Lord Bendai would react to the news of his beloved only son's death.

"What is it?" Svens asked, suddenly solicitous. The man watched her much too carefully. *Not as carefully as you watch him, though.* She sighed, ignoring her internal voice.

"I was thinking of Lord Fordai..." she said; when he didn't respond except to wait patiently for more, she continued. "I... He and I never got on... He was a complete arsehole, all told." A smirk spread over Svens's face, the black and blue bruises decorating it stark against his current pallor.

"I wasn't particularly fond of the man either... Even when we'd been captured he tended to lord it over us. *Even* while we were in a shithole and being tortured," Svens said, his smile turning bitterly cynical. "But all men bleed the same, irrespective of birth or rank, I find." Ata frowned at him curiously.

"You don't think me... callous? For remembering how unpleasant he was when he so clearly died in a horrible manner?" she asked tentatively.

"No. I don't. It's clear you mourn the loss of his life, as any decent person should. But that doesn't mean that you should sing praises for him that are undeserved. Death doesn't automatically sanctify the life of the one who has passed... It is just a passing—the end of life— and a rite of passage we will all eventually endure."

Ata felt somewhat awed by his calm response, the way it cut to the heart of her struggle. There was a depth of understanding to General Svensso Olefson (despite his innumerable annoying habits) that she had not permitted herself to appreciate before. She smiled and nodded in quiet gratitude for his words. They rode in companionable silence for the rest of the afternoon.

When the sun set, their company were still a significant distance from Enddaian, but had been able to beg the hospitality of a small village on their way. After a warm meal at the communal public house and an excess of wine, Ata felt in charity with all the world and the edges of her strange sadness over Lord Fordai's death were pleasantly blurred.

Making her way to the back room assigned to her in a local widow's home, she traversed an empty cow paddock and became distracted by the bright swathes of stars above. Head tipped back, she found the guiding star of Hancin among the sea of its brethren; a breeze whispered through the grass and caressed her face. For the first time, she thought of Hans and was comforted.

"What are you looking at?" a familiar voice asked, but Ata did not feel startled. Without looking at her husband-in-name, she answered.

"The guiding star." Silence. Then closer.

"Hancin? Like the charm Jans told me about?" A perceptible interest. She looked at him, his face wearing its usual, apparently-impassive expression. But a growing familiarity with him meant she could discern his underlying emotions despite this.

"Yes. Like the charm," which reminded her, "I have something for you. Kai gave it to us, and I didn't know if you'd want it. But..." though she noted his subtle withdrawal at the mention of her friend's name, she found her Enstroi chain beneath her shirt and proceeded to remove one of the half-coin charms. Holding it out to him, he finally closed the remaining distance between them.

"Is it a charm? For a... the chain Pandial wear?" he asked, curiously examining it.

"An Enstroi charm for an Enstroi chain, yes."

"It's half a gold coin..." he looked at her enquiringly, and she shrugged with a wry smile.

"Kai is trying to be funny. His father's a silversmith, so he knows some of the tricks of the smithing trade, at least as far as basic trinkets go... It's half of one of the coins he won when he bet on my shooting."

Svens, apparently having completed his inspection, tried to hand it back to her, but she shook her head. "No—that one's yours. I have my own, see," and she lifted her shirt and grasped her half-coin charm where it hung from the life chain around her waist.

His gaze sharpened and he crowded her, taking a hold of her marriage charm, warm fingers brushing hers. She felt breathless with him so close to her, her heart beating a rapid tattoo.

"Two halves of a whole." His voice was low, like he was speaking to himself, but she heard him. She could smell the wine on his breath, the same as her own. Then, without warning, he leaned in and kissed her—the stars, the breeze, and grass their only witnesses.

20

TIES THAT BIND

I ENVY YOU THE QUICK, CLEAN CUT,
THE CLEANSING, CRIMSON TIDE,
AND THE SHORT-LIVED BURN OF HOPE
    DASHED QUICKLY TO THE GROUND.

NO STICKY SAD GOODBYES,
GLANCING BACKWARDS TO AND FRO,
AND HEARTSTRINGS STRETCHING ENDLESSLY
    WITH EYES REFUSING REST.

SO PICK THE FLOWERS FAST,
PRESS THEM PERFECT BETWEEN PAPER,
AND LEAVE LOVE'S SWEET AROMA TO SCENT
    THE LONGINGS OF YOUR DREAMS.

BRONWYN EGAN

Ata had learned from her earliest experiences that awkwardness was the overvaluing of one's own ego; that when a situation had you cringing by just thinking of it, it was merely an overweeningly central designation of your own status relative to others in said scenario.

As such, she had tried to train herself through logic and analysis to eschew feeling shame over most incidents. Unfortunately, she could not sufficiently separate her emotions from her most recent blunder to facilitate such clear thinking.

She could have (falsely) claimed impaired judgment due to her consumption of alcohol, but her sense of justice and honesty wouldn't permit such a travesty. At the very least, they had been equally intoxicated, and for her part, the motivations had definitely not been wine-induced.

Her almost rampant attraction to the man over the months they had dealt with each other would have been enough in and of itself, but add elements like her epistemic crisis, the starlight, and their shared warmth, and what happened was essentially a foregone conclusion...

Waking up next to General Svensso Olefson—the man whose discovery of her in Hårbørgen Palace all those months ago had terrified her beyond description, whose aloofness and condescension had grated on her subsequently, and whose surprise allocation to the role of 'husband' had enraged her—was quite the experience. An experience in shock, awkwardness, and, much to her self-directed chagrin, pleasure.

Every time she thought back on the previous night, she blushed *horribly*. And she *never* blushed (due to almost never being embarrassed). Except when this particular man was involved, apparently. *Oh, joy.* Her newfound shyness seemed to amuse him once he woke to find her hurriedly dressing and mumbling about finding some breakfast before rushing out of the hospitable widow's guest room. Her temporary peace of mind at the breakfast table in the public house was interrupted when he joined her uninvited.

"You should try the eggs. They're very good," he suggested casually, giving his full attention to the plate before him. His circumspection in dealing with her obvious gaucheness after their night together annoyed her unduly. *How dare he be so understanding and obliging!* Luckily, before she could retort with what would undoubtedly be a childishly petulant riposte, the bench shuddered beneath her as Lieutenant Ransso sat down.

"Good morning. I hope you both slept well," she eyed the lieutenant askance, looking for any hint in his expression that he was aware of their tryst and therefore baiting them. The man seemed wholly preoccupied with his meal. "Good eggs, these!" he muttered through a huge mouthful. *Could they not shut up about the bloody eggs?*

When she glanced back at her 'husband'—she almost blanched when she realised that it was now both in word *and* deed—he was watching her closely. Though his face wore its customary placid expression, she sensed his amusement at her hypersensitivity and narrowed her eyes. Whether in warning or ill-humour, she wasn't sure herself. He ignored it.

"How did you sleep, Rans?" Svens asked.

"The best night I've spent in as long as I can remember, that's for sure!" *Rans*, as Svens addressed him, supplied.

"Same," Svens answered lightly, fastidiously buttering his bread. Ata gulped and began to choke loudly on her first mouthful of food for the day. Once Rans had helpfully slapped her back multiple times and she had drawn the entire room's attention with her scene, she managed to regain control of her body. Red-faced and wheezing, Svens's politely professed sympathy grated on her.

By the time they'd finished eating, the two men chatting easily while she stewed in her newly-enhanced tumultuous emotions, she was more than ready for some quiet time in the saddle to allow for introspection. Unfortunately, her ever-conscientious husband stood beside her horse, ready to help her mount. Pointedly ignoring his outstretched hand, she pulled herself into the saddle. *She wasn't falling for that ploy again—the last time she let him touch her hand she had proceeded to let him touch a whole lot more!* Good-naturedly ignoring her rudeness, he proceeded to mount his own horse beside hers. Said horse fell in step with hers, predicting a lack of privacy for her to arrange her thoughts on the last leg of their homeward journey.

Thus proceeded her entire day: constant attempts at interaction on his part with her rebuffing them without exception. Worse: the man didn't lose his temper even *once* with her stiff-necked bellicosity toward him. He just remained patient and smiled slightly, continuing on his way without commenting on her insolence. He seemed *genuinely* happy. *Of course he would be.*

By the time they arrived on the outskirts of Enddaian, Ata had worked herself up into quite the impotent rage. Long gone was the sense of peace and contentment she had basked in the night before under the stars. And all because of *him...*

She assiduously avoided thinking about her own enthusiastic participation in their night together—of how happy she had been during and directly after. She knew better: all happiness was paid for in the end with equivalent or even more pain. It was an inescapable fact of life. *This* was just another complication added to her interminable list of loyalties and unwanted commitments. Another unsolicited charm on the chain weighing her down.

"Welcome back!" the guard at the gate of Enddaian Keep enthused, but upon noting the covered body on the pack horse, a grimness descended over his countenance and he waved them through.

When they entered the courtyard and began to dismount, multiple figures came from the castle to receive them, the one at the front in sweeping robes hurrying toward them with undue haste. *Lord Bendai.* Ata experienced an unpleasant dip in her stomach when she noted the frantic way his eyes jumped from one face to the next, searching... Tallying their number.

Once he'd rushed through them all, he paused and frowningly did it again, more slowly. A female figure joined him, dressed in opulent fashion—Lady Kenttai, the duke's daughter and Lord Fordai's sister. Finally, his gaze found the wrapped body. The usually dignified duke scrambled forward and before anyone could intervene, reached his heir's body and tore the makeshift shroud away.

Ata cringed at the wailing shriek that escaped him; it was impossible to miss the piercing anguish that it voiced. She had despised this man and his offspring since her earliest memory, but could not remain indifferent in the face of their agony. Lady Kenttai's muffled sobs joined her father's cries.

"My son! My child!" Lord Bendai cried, clasping the cloth as though he could wring a change of circumstance from it. Ata looked away and busied herself with dismounting, however, once she was on her own two feet, the situation became worse.

"You did this!" he screeched madly, "You little *conniving*, whoring bitch!" his grief instantly turning to rage, with Ata as its main target. He had stalked towards her with clawed hands outstretched, apparently unaware of the presence of Princess Mindaia, who had joined the welcoming party along with a few Cinnaen and Pandial ministers. Before any of them could intercede, and as Ata readied herself for the physical assault the crazed father was undoubtedly about to unleash on her, she was thrust unceremoniously back against her horse. A wide back covered in a dusty Cinnaen uniform filled her vision.

"Lord Bendai! I understand you're mourning, truly. But *do not* take out your anger and grief on my wife," Svens enunciated clearly and calmly. "She has pushed herself beyond the bounds of reasonable expectations to the brink of exhaustion trying to save us. *All* of us. Your son passed as we exited the tunnels we had been held in —only navigable because Lady Ata guided us at great personal cost."

"Don't give me that horse shit, Cinnaen! That bastard slut has always hated Ford! He's dead because of her and I insist— " Svens's body shifted slightly in front of Ata; what Lord Bendai was about to insist on would remain a mystery as a sudden silence blanketed the courtyard.

"General Svensso! Release Lord Bendai immediately, if you please!" Min's almost panicked tones arose. "I suspect we are all under immense strain and cannot be held accountable for our words or actions at this time." Her conciliatory voice was apparently followed by compliance from Svens. Scrabbling and an immediate increase in conversation echoed through the courtyard as everyone proceeded to dismount and unload.

Ata's arm was gripped and she was swept along into the castle; glancing up, her guide turned out to be her inescapable spouse who was speaking politely to Min as she accompanied them to the meeting room for a debriefing. Luckily, Lord Bendai didn't join them in King Addai's presence for the rescue operation's post-mortem.

Ata spoke minimally, only affirming the rendition provided by the two officers in charge. Svens, Rans, and the remaining Pandial officer also described their imprisonment, which included beatings and torture to try and extract military secrets.

Information of a very limited nature had been shared, all captives having agreed to this to ensure their survival for longer—an ingenious strategy, all said, as well as the fact that they had conspired to obfuscate Svens's elevated rank and consequent knowledge of army movements.

Once they'd returned to their quarters, Ata had wrestled her demons into submission, compartmentalising the most recent scenes until she was mentally and emotionally able to unpack and deal with them.

However, as they both washed and dressed, her simmering irritation with Svens flared up and became impossible to suppress.

"Why did you intervene like that earlier?" she asked pointedly, trying not to gawk at him where he stood at the basin. It was very difficult to avoid looking at his tall broad frame stood at the window, but she did her best.

As she had noted the night before, even with the single candle burning in the room, his torso was bruised and scratched all to hell. She'd specifically (and conscientiously, to her mind) asked if it wasn't too painful for him to continue, but he'd laughed off her concerns dismissively and proceeded without any apparent deficits. Purposely avoiding going down that particular memory lane, Ata now made a mental note to heal him later in the evening, once she'd had some food and rest. For now, she didn't want to pity him.

"What?" he asked absently, evidently not paying attention. *How annoying.*

"Why did you intervene earlier, with Lord Bendai?" Ata repeated.

"Should I not have?" guileless, he turned to her as he dried his ears with a towel, hair sticking up in all directions. It had grown ridiculously long since she had first met him, before fleeing Cinnae, when he'd sported close-cropped bristles.

He had also stopped shaving completely since returning with the Vürgøn delegation—probably inspired by their own style of growing full beards. Thus, he looked quite scruffy by Cinnaens' 'immaculate' standards... Ata didn't think it detracted from his looks at all. *More's the pity. If he'd been less attractive, perhaps she wouldn't be subject to this mindless infatuation.*

"I can stand up for myself." Ata yanked a brush through her hair.

"I know you can." *Well.*

"I don't need you to undermine me like that. It makes me look weak—a *Pandial* would understand that," she had added the last jab to remind him how different they were, and for the first time since the previous night, annoyance flashed across his face.

"Fine. In future, I won't intercede on your behalf if you feel so strongly about it," he continued to get dressed, maintaining a strained and chilly silence toward her until they went to bed that night.

She had spent the entire dinner pondering how to dissuade his conjugal attentions once they returned to their rooms. *Dissuade her own eagerness to his proven dexterity, more like.* She needn't have worried. Once in bed, he promptly turned his back to her after a terse "good night". That suited her just fine. *Really.*

Once his breathing had deepened to a soft snore, Ata had braved reaching across their mid-mattress border line, gently placed a finger against his skin so as to avoid waking him and alerting him to her touch. She tried not to let her hand linger once the healing was complete, then rolled over and fell into a deeply restful slumber.

"WELL, well... if it isn't the woman of the hour!" Ians welcomed Ata into the rooms he had been using since arriving at Enddaian Keep. Ata had made her way from breakfast to the main library where she was training groups of Abled to Command healing, and just before they ended the training session for lunch, a page brought her a note requesting her presence in a certain set of rooms. No signature. There were only two options as to who could have sent it, and she already knew all Lord Danai's hidey holes.

Upon her arrival, the white-haired gallant had swept her inside and plied her with compliments and effusive praise for her most recent rescue of the kidnapped officers.

"You are becoming quite the heroine to the Hårbørgen family, my girl!" the manipulative rogue twinkled, but she only glared at him suspiciously.

"Don't try to charm me into a better mood, Ians... I *know* you somehow knew about my 'marriage' before it took place," at his exaggerated look of offended innocence, she continued, "Either you did know and are pretending otherwise, or you are much worse at your job than you'd like to have me believe. Which is it?"

After a beat he sighed deeply as though being unfairly maligned.

"You have an acid tongue today, dear Ata. What could have put your nose so out of joint?" his demeanor became playfully sly, "Could it be that your new husband has somehow gotten under that thick skin of yours?"

She stared at him stonily, not willing to give away how close he'd hit to the truth. She had been panicking about their most recent intimacies, for it muddied the waters of her planned separation from him. Seeing she wasn't going to indulge his teasing, Ians pulled a wry face and sat back in his chair. "Well, be that as it may, I have decided to impart the rest of the predictions regarding the Heir and the Changer to you." All playfulness had dropped away.

"Shouldn't Lord Danai be present too?" Ata frowned.

"No. He would not be... *completely* in agreement with your being told the entirety of your fate, but I happen to differ from my brother on many topics, not the least of which is this. In most of the other decisions, he has gotten his way, but in this, I have decided to thwart his cold-hearted logic." Ata felt as though the earth had lurched beneath her, despite sitting securely in an armchair in front of the fire. *His brother!*

"Your—... your *brother*?" she choked; Ians's amusement returned temporarily.

"Why, yes... I thought you had connected those dots

when you saw us together previously." At her blankly confused look, he snorted. "No? Well, I grant you: we don't resemble each other in any obvious way. But nevertheless, we are twins, if you can believe it." He gave a short laugh at her pronounced disbelief.

"But... But how did one of you end up in the Cinnaen court and the other in the Pandial? Which one of the two are you both really?" Ata's mind couldn't seem to catch up with this newest revelation.

"We are as you have known us; I am Cinnaen, and Dan is Pandial," he cocked his head, then continued as she opened her mouth to rebut. "In the strictest sense, you would call Dan a half-blood Pandial, as our mother was Cinnaen. My father was her husband and Cinnaen, while Dan's father was Pandi—"

"But—"

"But we're twins? Well, extraordinarily, it is biologically possible for twins to have been fathered by different men. It is highly improbable—anomalous, even—but possible, nevertheless." Ata wrestled with the facts, wanting to pry further yet unsure how to broach such a personal subject delicately. As usual, Ians preemptively knew her conundrum.

"Ah, I see you are wondering how to ask whether our mother had had an affair with Dan's father? Unfortunately, as much as I have shared thus far, that is not something I feel I can impart. That is Dan's heritage and identity to disclose or not. I will, however, say that our mother was completely blameless in the entire affair, for I don't wish you to think poorly of the dear woman, the gods rest her soul."

And that was that. Ata was sure she would never be able to extract the information of Lord Danai's origins from the man himself. He was as forthcoming as a rock.

"But let's rather look to the future than the past, hmm?" Ians prompted. At Ata's nod, he smiled.

"Well, as you know from what we told you before, there was an Abled scholar-turned-oracle some six centuries ago, who predicted this continent-wide siege of Áitarbith. Now—the man also wrote, in the vaguest of terms, about a group of Abled scholars who... *dabbled*... in magics they oughtn't have. And I use 'magics' very specifically here instead of Commanding, for what they practiced was in no way scientific nor moral. It was the darkest of esoteric practices that required the sacrifice of living beings for their life force—their energy—to power their abominations.

This group of 'scholars' had formed over six hundred years prior to our oracle's own existence; a secret society of practitioners he referred to as the 'Witchlings of Hoondær', Hoondær being an isolated region in the Uurgonna Mountains." Ians broke off and sipped some water before continuing.

"In his writings, our scholar accuses these 'Witchlings of Hoondær' of creating the Gruxhoon. He purports they produced the beasts using their unholy magics, slaughtering many hundreds of men to achieve their goal of creating a 'super being'. Thus, the bane of our ancestors was born and eventually expelled to the Debrion wastelands just under a millennium ago." Ians dusted off his hands theatrically to punctuate his words.

"*But!* Our ancestors had not dealt with the originators of this blight—the 'Witchlings of Hoondær', *of whom they had not been aware*. Enter our brave little oracle, four centuries later, whose visions inspired further research and reading on his part, following which he discovered the truth of the matter.

"He then proceeded to write his predictions and the history in various scrolls, hiding the information so that, should the 'Witchlings' come to learn of his discovery, they would not be able to remove all of his clues for future searchers. *Us*." He patted his knees in glee and despite her growing dread, Ata smiled indulgently.

"So... you and Lord Danai discovered this? His predictions and history?" she prompted. "Do these 'Witchlings' still exist, do you think?"

"Undoubtedly, for our nameless, diabolically clever oracle tells us so. He has predicted this incursion of the Gruxhoon, and he insists the 'Witchlings of Hoondær' are behind it. Furthermore, he tells us how to defeat them!" his voice was hushed but full of fervour. Ata felt a chill.

"The prophecy about the Changer?" she unwillingly supplied.

"The prediction of the Changer and the Heir," he confirmed solemnly.

"What else does the prophecy say?" He hesitated, then spoke.

"We gave you the first part to get you used to the idea of it; the scale of it—the momentous nature of it... But the entire prediction would have been too much to work through at once. Now, I believe it would benefit you to 'chew over' its words, so to speak. So, here it is; listen carefully:

> *The heir who sets Áitarbith free,*
> *Three parts of four the child will be,*
> *assayed in gold and onyx,*
> *wrought in shade and light,*
> *borne in secret to the Changer,*
> *the heir will turn the Fight.*
> *Beware betrayal by blood of kin,*
> *Death from enemies will come from within.*

> *Heir's Breath will Command all before them,*
> *Heir's presence give succour in lees,*
> *the blood of the child will call to the earth,*
> *call to the rocks, and call to the trees.*
> *And all will answer, all will bend,*
> *Ere Changer's child them all defend.*

> *Wait on the child.*

Await the heir,
Saviour of Nowhere."

At that moment, a key scraped in the door, and it promptly swung open—Lord Danai entering without any preamble. Eyes pinging between them, his passive demeanour remained unchanged, yet the temperature in the room seemed to drop by a few degrees. One could sense his disfavour.

"So, Ians. You've decided to circumvent our agreement?" when Ians made to answer, Lord Danai lifted his hand in a gesture for silence. "Nevermind. You and I will *discuss* this later. Seeing as the horse has apparently bolted, all that remains for me to do is to join the conversation and ensure it is conducted *thoroughly* and *factually*." Not looking chagrined in the least at being caught out, Ians turned back to Ata with a wide grin.

"Questions?"

"Could you repeat it again a few times? Then we can discuss specific lines?" He nodded and did so, only to be interrupted by Lord Danai in the second half.

"It could also be:

Heir's Breath will Command all before them,
Heir's presence give succour in lees,
the blood of the child will <u>cover</u> the earth,
<u>cover</u> the rocks, and <u>cover</u> the trees.
And all will answer, all will bend,

Ere Changer's child them all defend.

The Old Bithian word for 'cover' also means 'call to' in certain contexts. In this case, I suspect it means 'cover', but Ians in his unrealistic idealism 'just knows' it means 'call to'... Similar to how you 'just knew' it was not Ata who was the Changer?" Lord Danai plainly had an axe to grind with his twin brother, but Ians ignored him. Ata was appalled when she put the meanings together, though.

"The heir's blood will 'cover' everything—to protect everyone? Like a sacrifice?" her wide eyed horror must have been blatantly obvious, for even Lord Danai paused in his own grousing.

"Not necessarily. These writings are very old, their manner of expression very symbolic... We—*both* Dan and I—don't for a second believe the child will *literally* be sacrificed to save Áitarbith," Ians rushed to explain, trying to soothe her obvious distress.

"But it *might* mean that? There's no way of actually knowing till it happens?" she persisted, unwilling to be pacified with half-truths. Their silence spoke volumes.

"I told you we should have waited to tell her," Lord Danai muttered wrathfully at Ians, and if Ata wasn't feeling so sickened she would have laughed at the comical aside.

"You both would risk my future child as a potential sacrifice? For this prophecy?" she asked.

"NO!" both of them shouted, visibly appalled by the prospect.

"The very ambiguous nature of the wording and translation means it *could* mean 'covers' or 'call to', and even if he *did* mean 'covers', then even that would have been in a metaphorical sense," Ians emphatically stated. Ata was not completely convinced, however.

"I think... I think I need some time. To digest all that I've learnt," Ata frowned, looking pointedly at the corner of the room and not at the two men who had, essentially, turned her entire existence on its head with their talk of prophecies and saviours.

"Of course... There is still plenty of time to discuss the minutiae of the predictions, when you are ready," Ians soothed, Lord Danai making no comment. When Ata left Ians's rooms shortly afterwards, she knew one thing for certain: she would *not* be having any children, ever. The prophecy, the oracle, the spy twins—they could all go hang! And the best way to completely thwart this potential life path was to dismantle her unwanted marriage once and for all. She *had* to engineer an annulment. *Somehow.*

WHAT FOLLOWED over the next few days was an unceasing campaign by Ata to alienate her husband. She utilised every weapon in her arsenal—nagging, bullying, childish tantrums, and jealous rages. The latter had not taken much effort, for she'd noticed before how Svens drew the eye of many women in and around the keep, however, her main irritant was Lady Kenttai, daughter of Lord Bendai.

The woman had already shown a marked interest in the general as far back as the Cinnaen court's arrival in Pandi, and Ata had had to ruthlessly suppress her jealousy whenever she saw the woman shamelessly flirting with him. Now that they were married, the spiteful woman had increased her inappropriately coquettish behaviour towards him tenfold.

Even in public, it appeared she was all but propositioning him. To be fair to Svens, he always tried to maintain an appropriate physical distance and regularly asked Lady Kenttai to respect his personal space. Her eyelash-fluttering and huskily whispered innuendos were met with his characteristic stoicism, yet Ata's green-eyed monster saw all and she exacted revenge for her own unwanted preoccupation with him by picking apart every interaction in the privacy of their chambers, accusing him of everything from encouraging flirtations to outright infidelity.

"You're... ugh! You're driving me insane!" he finally ground out, pushed beyond all bounds of self-control and storming from their rooms. Ata knew she should feel a sense of victory, but all she felt was churning self-loathing. Her hopes that she had finally driven him too far were dashed

when she was awoken some time later by Svens crawling into bed beside her.

"What—I thought I drove you 'insane'? Have you not decided to petition for an annulment from your crazy wife?" she muttered peevishly. He snorted good naturedly, his usual, unflappable equilibrium clearly returned.

"Unfortunately for you, wife, we no longer qualify for an annulment, strictly speaking... I hold quite strong views on lying on official documents," and he tried to clasp her to him as he had done multiple times on previous evenings. It had taken her a moment to realise his meaning, at which point she swore heartily and pushed him off, dragging their blanket-border between them while he chuckled at her ill humour. Trust him to refer to the technicality that a consummated marriage couldn't be annulled. Back to using jealous barbs to try and push the man away...

Her one comfort, in a twisted, warped sense, was the fact that she wasn't the only one plagued by possessiveness. Shortly after their return from the rescue mission, Svens had made a throwaway comment at dinner, where they had taken to sitting together at the 'lesser' tables, but higher in the ranks than where she used to sit with Kai.

"I miss my old seat... It was easier to see everyone from the back and discuss them all with Kai. Here, I'm the one being seen and discussed," she had grumped, expecting his customary chuff of repressed amusement. Instead, she got some meaningful eye contact.

"Well, you won't be sitting nor 'discussing' anything with Lieutenant Kaimam in the future, so you might as well put it from your mind." It was so unlike the Svens she had come to know to be so chauvinistically prescriptive that Ata had laughed outright in his face, ignoring his darkening expression.

"Don't be ridiculous! I've been best friends with Kai since I was seven years old... I'll continue to sit with and talk to him as and when I please." That dismissive remark, along with her obstinate refusal to give in to Svens's ultimatum that she cut all personal ties with Kai, had resulted in a monumental fight that night. Behind closed doors, naturally, for even Ata did not relish public interest or notoriety.

Another instance where she'd definitely wounded him had been after an apparent throw-away question he had asked unexpectedly one evening.

"Why don't you pull funny faces at me anymore?" Svens had asked, out of the blue, when they had been preparing for bed. She was in a bitchy mood because she'd missed dinner in the dining hall due to healing lessons running overtime, only to find he had been joined by Kenttai in her absence. Annoyance was <u>not</u> a sign of possessiveness, she reminded herself.

She shrugged: "I just don't feel like it anymore." Blasé.

"But why? What's changed? Do my reactions not amuse you anymore?" he pressed, seeming genuinely nonplussed.

"I told you: I used to do it when I didn't really know you, to get a reaction... They say 'familiarity breeds contempt', so maybe that's why I'm not that fussed, because now I know

you and it's not as exciting tweaking your nose." She was being a malicious harpy, but he had not reacted in any immediately discernible way. They had just silently finished their ablutions and gone to bed, and he didn't mention her pulling faces again.

Despite all of her exaggerated (and woefully unsuccessful) attempts at pushing him too far by personifying the worst kind of wife, the final nail in the coffin of their relationship came when she had casually mentioned having known about Ians's presence in the keep and purposely keeping it from Svens. He'd been incensed.

"You're Cinnaen, and I'm Pandial... You cannot expect my loyalty to *you* and this sham of a marriage to ever supersede my loyalty to my kingdom? To my *real family*?" Ata had flippantly (cruelly) quipped. Shocked hurt had shown on his face for a second before an icy disdain had replaced it.

"I knew what you were—have always known—but had somehow convinced myself I'd been mistaken. That I could find something salvageable in you," he said, shaking his head in disgust. His words hurt, but she decided to twist the knife further. After all, she was holding onto the blade too, inflicting equivalent wounds to herself as she did so to him.

"And what am I, exactly, that is so reprehensible?"

"You're a lovely serpent. Beautiful to look at, but unpredictably treacherous and deadly... I don't know how you have managed to insert yourself so thoroughly into my family, into my h—"

"You've always disliked me and judged me; you've been prejudiced against me since Ians told you I was... an agent—"

"A *spy*. Let's not mince our pretty words," he interrupted, "a conniving, underhanded liar who was sent to Cinnae to facilitate our destruction, thereby making us more vulnerable and hence tractable to treat with Pandial... You were there to watch us burn and to take notes!"

"But I didn't, did I? Your lack of preparedness, your *serious* misjudgement of the entire situation would have led to your little brothers' deaths if I hadn't been there to intercede! Thank the gods I don't ever need to rely on *your* protection, for—based on the showing you have given so far—I'd end up a corpse in a ditch!"

The dead silence that followed unnerved her; she knew she had gone too far, pressed him beyond what was tenable. Somehow, all the engineered marital torture she had perpetrated over the past weeks was no match for a simple untruth uttered in anger—that she didn't think she could rely on him. *Patently untrue.*

She was on the verge of apologising when he stated icily: "Well, it seems we now understand each other's perspectives fully. I will grant your dearest wish and petition for an annulment of our marriage. I wouldn't want you to suffer my *inept* protection any longer." With that, he took his coat and his rucksack, and left their room. Ata watched the door shut, her legs suddenly giving out beneath her. She slumped into a kneeling position on the floor.

She had done it! She had *finally* managed to drive him far enough to agree to a formal separation. She had succeeded.

Then she curled up into a ball like when was a little girl, and cried.

21

THE OTHER HALF

I SPEAK NOT FROM MY MOUTH
BUT THROUGH MY HEART.
CAN YOU HEAR ME SCREAMING,
BEGGING FOR YOUR OPEN EYES?
I WANT YOU TO SEE ME,
BARE AND OPEN FROM THE INSIDE.

STEFANIE FONTKER

The winter frost had finally arrived at Enddaian Keep, mirroring how Ata was feeling; the stone edifice to security dissipated any flicker of heat that might be coaxed by hopeful hands within its confines. Since she had been a child, the keep had been her safe place, irrespective of regular bullying, the uncertainty of human kindness and affection, or its sometimes-questionable creature comforts.

The place had been a fortress of the familiar; imperfect in many ways, but nonetheless a beloved home to a young Ata. Now, for the first time, it felt more like a prison than a safe haven, with Ata noting more and more troubling commonalities between *it* and her. Cold, with long-held secrets and lacking any guarantees of a true welcome.

After Svens had left her, he had also left the keep altogether. "Off to coordinate with the military leadership in the north" was the reason provided by his madcap friend, Captain Blÿnsso, when she healed the last of the torn ligaments (which had not been able to heal naturally) in his arm. She did this as part of a demonstration for her newest group of Abled healing students.

"Do you know when he'll be back?" she had enquired carefully as he'd been taking his leave; yet he seemed to see through her nonchalance.

"You know how it goes—nothing's certain except death and taxes... And in our current situation, I think even the taxes aren't a given... One needs a kingdom and government to have those, right?" His morbid humour made no impression on her; he left without providing any more information than Svens himself imparted in the letter she'd received after he had left.

"I was not able to speak with King Addai to petition for

the annulment before my most recent orders came through. I will do so once I have returned."

His handwriting was bold and without any signs of hesitation. To say the tone was coldly peremptory was to be generous. *She deserved it.*

To Ata's dismay, the sadness and deepening depression that descended after her 'victory' and Svens's departure didn't dissipate over the weeks that followed. She did not feel 'free' as she had expected to; she felt rudderless. It seemed impossible that the destruction of such a fledgling thing, a thing she had despised from its very inception and had tirelessly campaigned against, could somehow bring her so much anguish.

The reason as to why came to her one night when she was rolling around and unable to sleep (on her side of the bed as usual). Ata was aware she was obtuse in many ways and that she tended to be self-sabotaging, per Min's numerous lectures during their adolescence as well as Lord Danai's. Hence, when a moment of blinding clarity had descended upon her—that she had somehow developed strong feelings for Svens—she was both shocked yet unsurprised.

Once the thought had been planted, it had taken root and sprouted, its growth so exponentially extreme that by the following day Ata had reached a complete acceptance of her feelings. To be fair: plenty of information had been shared with her prior to her epiphany, buffeting her initially intractable stance on the inherent fallibility of their marriage.

"Didn't you know? Svens never knew his mother... He was passed from pillar to post as a toddler—out of sight, out of mind—and then very quickly sent to the military academy once Queen Nelni came on the scene," Ians had explained when Ata had purposely thrown a baited lure out.

The only reason she was able to get away with it without his piercing eyes (and mind) seeing right through her was because they were poring over indescribably boring documentation on then-hypothetical healing lore. Also: he had drunk almost the entire bottle of wine by himself and was therefore in a nostalgically reminiscent mood.

"But King Olefso acknowledged him... He vigorously promoted him throughout his career. Unduly so, some would say. He clearly loved and cared for his illegitimate son," she argued, then bitterly added, *"His family openly, publicly, adore him."*

"Ah, but <u>did</u> the king care, though? No, dear girl, I like to think I understand the context and background, as well as the characters of the people involved in this situation, better than you do, if you'll forgive me saying so. No, no. Svens was and is to this day, a means to an end for the House of Hårbørgen... It is his role: to protect and serve the crown till his dying day," he sniffed, tone heavy with irony.

"But isn't that all of our fates? To serve our kingdoms?"

"Yes, that is true. But, ideally, one should not be taught as a child, as Svens was, that your <u>only</u> value lies in the service

you can provide. A king largely thinks thus of his subjects, fair enough. But a father, a parent, should not." Ians became distracted by some arcane formula, so Ata brought him back to the issue at hand.

"I've had a similar upbringing and don't feel particularly 'hard done by'..." she hedged and for the first time ever, Ians appeared to lose patience with her.

"Use your head, Child! Can you honestly say you have not been loved for your own sake? Since childhood? Naturally, your cousin and uncle have been careful in not publicly expressing their love in an effort to protect you. But make no mistake: you have been cherished merely for being you.

"Your use as a kind of 'political tool' only came later when my sainted brother decided to stick his nose in. Not that I judge him for it—training and tutoring you was his way of preparing you for the life you would inevitably lead. Also an act of love, I might add, though the heavens know he struggles to articulate any kind of feelings in a constructive way, that one." Ata felt slightly ashamed when she considered his words. He continued more kindly.

"For General Svensso, his inherent value—his reason for existing—is to protect the Hårbørgens, their rule, and by extension, the Cinnaen kingdom as a whole... This has been drilled into him since birth: that his only value lies in how well he meets that brief.

"The first and only warmth and love he has garnered in his life was through his own initiation—the friends he made in the military academy, the half-siblings he insisted on

knowing and caring for. Insisted on being part of their lives. That boy has suffered from a lack of unconditional affection his entire life, and despite that, he has become a good person who, once he trusts someone, gives his regard freely and without limitation."

Ata sensed personal criticism that was probably not meant; unlike her, Svens had been willing to find a shared affection in the almost untenable situation of their marriage. Of the two of them, she was the one that 'benefited' the most, having had an infatuation with him for ages, while he most definitely had not felt any attraction toward her based on his long-suffering demeanour during their interactions over the preceding months.

"He seems to be a very good man, I grant you," she placated, truly believing her own words.

"He is a good man, but flawed like any other... No-one is a paragon of virtue, not even I," he winked at her playfully. "As he has been my friend and pupil—similar to your relation-ship with Dan, I'd say—I think I know his failings, few though they are, quite well...

His greatest flaw, in my humble opinion, is that he equates his success or failures in protecting anyone and everyone in his life to his very being. The sheer span of his self-inflicted circle of protection means that he can never fully succeed in this goal he has set himself and will therefore always feel like a failure. He is setting himself up to fail, but is unable to see it," Ians shook his head sadly, slipping into a brown study.

"And his other faults?" Ata prompted.

"I would have thought, as his wife, you'd manage to sniff out his faults very quickly?" the old man teased. "Well... not to influence you unduly, of course, but you might have noticed how reticent he is? He does not show his feelings easily, which could lead to... people believing that he held no affection for them, or worse, actively disliked them. That is not necessarily the case," he looked at Ata meaningfully, so she assumed he meant her and responded by watching him in overt anticipation.

"The last failing of our Svens is that he absolutely abhors deception and consequently espionage. I have tried and tried to cure him of his suspicious and judgmental nature when it comes to spies and agents, but alas! He tends to be quite unrepentantly high-and-mighty in his dealings with anyone he thinks is an agent. Which, all considered, means his and my friendship is quite the miracle!" And with that, Ians emptied the last of the wine into his glass.

"ATA! ATA!" Elsso crowed in excitement as she joined her little brothers-in-law on their daily walk. The bracing weather had lured her out of the stuffy library (overheated to provide comfort in the usually freezing room for her healing courses) and stumbling across their cheery little party of wayfaring wanderers had immediately lifted her depressed spirits. It had been three weeks since Svens's departure.

With no word, either from him or from the powers that be, she assumed 'no news was good news', but that didn't alleviate the ache in her chest that just seemed to increase with his absence. She hated the feeling which she had accurately identified as a growing dependence on his presence for her continued happiness. But there it was. Additionally, she had no idea how to fix what she had broken and now desperately needed to cure, or suffer this feeling of absence for the interminable future.

"We didn't see you yesterday!" Jans cried as he ran up to her, taking her hand in his gloved one. He looked comically chubby, wrapped in layer upon layer of woolens to stave off the cold air. His face was pink and eyes shining beneath the knitted cap he wore to keep his ears warm.

"I'm sorry, Your Highness. I was quite busy with all my teaching—"

"No you weren't! You usually come and see us after, and yesterday your classes ended the same time as always," the little baggage quipped. Els had grabbed her other hand and was swinging it vigorously back and forth. Princess Lenna and Mistress Famenke walked along behind them, a party to all that was discussed. *Great.*

"Fine! You caught me, Your Highness. I have this

amazing book that I'm reading and I skipped having snacks with you two ingrates so I could read it. Happy?" she lied blithely. She had avoided the two princes because, despite the fact that she loved them as though they were her own brothers, she couldn't face their familial cheeriness when she was feeling so low. She had locked herself in her dark chambers and crawled into bed, lying there for hours without being able to sleep. Jans peered at her suspiciously, then shook his head furiously.

"Nope. You're lying. I know when you're lying—your eyes change colour. They get bluer," Ata knew this was categorically untrue. At least, she sincerely hoped she didn't have such a tell. "Why don't you want to tell us where you were and what you were doing?" *He'd always been a suspicious little pest, and nosy beyond belief!*

"She misses Svens, *stoopid!*" Els piped up matter-of-factly beside her. He had recently discovered a multitude of insults that he could safely hurl at his brother in the name of boisterousness. Jans seemed surprised at his little brother's emotional acuity.

"Is that true, Ata? Do you miss Svens?" he pushed. She sighed deeply at this interrogation. *Was a bit of peace too much to ask for?*

"Yes, you pushy boy! I miss Svens. There—are you happy? I didn't feel like looking at multiple little copies of him last night," she kept her tone playful while sharing this truth. Famenke snorted in amusement behind her and Els giggled uproariously in response to their nursemaid's show of humour.

Ata turned and frowned in mock-annoyance. "Oh, wonderful! Now everyone is laughing at my heartbreak. I like that! You're all cruel, heartless creatures!" her exaggerated play-acting caused hilarity amongst the small group.

"What are you all laughing at?" a male voice asked. Prince Tensso had appeared, followed at a distance by two personal guards. Ata smiled at him in welcome; he had been present on quite a few occasions during her visits over the past weeks and had become less tongue-tied in her presence.

"These horrid children have been making fun of my heartsickness, Your Highness! They seem to think it's *funny*," she grabbed Els at that point and poked and tickled him wherever she could, the boy wriggling and shrieking in glee, "that I am a tragic wreck, waiting on the return of my beloved husband after he has abandoned me to languish alone!"

Despite the facetious monologue, it was quite cathartic to use words she hadn't heretofore even allowed herself to think. Jans had jumped on her back to 'save' his little brother from her attack and their play quickly evolved into a snowball fight amongst the group. Even Famenke joined in, somehow managing to avoid being hit altogether, but doling out multiple punishing shots to them all. *The woman was diabolically accurate!*

"If you ever reconsider your employment as a royal servant, I believe you'd make an amazing archer, or—barring that—you could train with a leather sling and pebbles. You are *painfully* accurate," Ata gasped as they made their way back up the hill towards the keep; she rubbed vigorously at her shoulder where she was sure a bruise was already forming. The woman just chuckled evilly. Apparently, even after all this time, she held a grudge against the erstwhile 'Anita'.

Shortly after, they were all gathered around the fireplace in Princess Lenna's rooms, drying and warming their snow-drenched limbs.

"Ata, explain to Len and Tens about an Enstroi chain," Jans imperiously ordered. "They keep trying to stop me from getting one, after I've been asking for *forever*." She cocked her eyebrow at the little terror, but proceeded to explain the premise of their Pandial practice of wearing a 'life chain'.

"It's a tally of all our earthly achievements and experiences... The important ones anyway," she supplied.

"Show 'em yours!" Jans enthusiastically demanded. At Ata's hesitant expression, Princess Lenna quickly interceded.

"Jans, perhaps it's impolite to ask someone to show you a record of their private life history—"

"No, it's not—Ata showed me hers before!" he bit back defensively.

"You're right, I did... And I don't mind showing you

and your siblings, because we're family and you're interested. But just so you do know: most Pandial would consider you asking to see their Enstroi chain quite rude and entitled," Ata offered politely, unclipping her chain from her waist. It was passed between Princess Lenna, Prince Tensso, and Mistress Famenke with all due respect shown.

"Do you mind if we ask about some of the charms?" the princess asked hesitantly.

"Of course not. Although, I might only provide the sanitised version of the event," Ata smiled. It felt good to open up to her siblings-in-law; their genuine interest in and fascination with this Pandial cultural practice warmed her to them. What followed was an afternoon of personal discovery.

"My favourite's the Hancin star," Jans said, his serious face on.

"Mine too!" Els added his two cents.

"I really like the charm for your birth—the jade teardrop," the princess volunteered.

"It's actually quite unusual, because a tear charm is traditionally worn by the mother, the shape representing the pain endured and the joy experienced in bearing the child. A birth charm is usually a fruit or a flower, symbols of nourishment and beauty, while the colour and material can be chosen based on any number of things... My uncle gifted me that charm first. Because my mother died in childbirth, he chose the teardrop shape. The jade is for the colour of my eyes," Ata explained. Princess Lenna listened raptly.

"And the half-coin?" the prince asked.

"That's for my marriage. Svens was gifted one too… My friend, Kai, made them for us. 'Two halves of a whole'. Your brother insisted I take the right half, because I always have to be right," Ata chuckled (Svens had flung that quip at her during one of her many orchestrated arguments). The crown prince and princess laughed outright.

"And this black one?" Famenke asked sombrely. The woman had a knack for finding people's soft spots.

"Black charms are quite common, but this one, specifically, is onyx. And that stone is used exclusively to represent death on an Enstroi chain. The shape of mine is a Liata flower and represents my mother's death," Ata pointed at it and tried to keep her tone factual, but all the faces seemed stricken by this turn of the conversation.

"The Liata flower?" Prince Tens seemed startled. "The poisonous one?" Ata was impressed by his knowledge.

"Yes and no… It *can* be poisonous, but if used correctly, it can be very useful."

"So, your birth charm is shaped to indicate a mother's pain, while your mother's death charm is represented as your birth charm should have been? And that shape is of a sometimes-poisonous flower?" the servant said sharply, slicing to the heart of the complex symbolism Ata carried with her always. Lenna, who seemed to become more and more agitated by this turn of the conversation, decided to intercede.

"Let's choose more favourites! What's your favourite, Menke?" she asked in an upbeat voice. The servant pondered, having become used to the more informal inclusion of herself in activities of the royal siblings.

"It's not my favourite, but I suspect it has... *signifi-cance*. The cross-shaped knife." Ata should have known *she* would remark on it. It was, after all, a miniature of the real thing she'd seen Ata wield throughout their 'Night of Terror' together.

"That's quite a painful memory. The charm was made for me by my friend's father, who is a silversmith, and represents my first weapon, though he didn't know it's deeper significance... A gift from my— from the king. Jans and Els know it well," she smiled as they nodded eagerly, despite the negative connotation of its use in their escape so many months ago. "That partic-ular charm represents the first time I ever took a person's life." At the silence, Ata stared into the fire.

"How old were you when you got it?" Jans asked, clearly intrigued by the shock everyone else had displayed.

"Quite young, but the details are too ugly to explain here. Maybe when we all know each other better," Ata suggested lightly. Under none but the most extreme circumstances would she recount *that* tale of her eleven-year-old self.

Luckily, the evening moved beyond discussing her Enstroi chain. They played parlour games with exuberance and glee, and when they learnt of her artistic abilities from Famenke (*would the irascible woman never leave her be?*), she found they were all easily pleased with quick, comical portrait sketches. Spending time with them, unfettered by pomp and ceremony, loosened a lot of Ata's self-imposed restraints and allowed her to be light-hearted and happy.

Other than drawing Ata closer into the family circle, these visits with the Cinnaen heirs showed Ata that openness with others was rewarded with reciprocal candidness on their part. The more she showed them of herself, the more willing they were to show her who they were.

Thus, as time passed, she became a true confidante of Len, whose greatest fear was to be a useless ornament, and Ata fell into an easy camaraderie with Tens, although he still displayed signs of a harmless infatuation.

She even managed to convey to Famenke how much she liked and admired her no-nonsense personality, which the woman accepted with all the recalcitrance Ata would have expected. However, despite the many subtle overtures Ata had made over the months since the Cinnaen court's arrival at Enddaian to discuss

Famenke's assault by the Gruxhoon, her former supervisor had categorically rebuffed any and all such heart-to-hearts. Ata had come to accept Famenke's choice, though she worried over her mental well-being beneath her ever-capable façade.

The two youngest princes, as always, gave wholeheartedly to their relationship with Ata, and she loved them unconditionally in return.

Most importantly, though, she was provided with an idea of how to convince her angry and disillusioned husband, once he returned, that she was committed to their union despite all her previous efforts to subvert it. Ata had finally faced the fact that she wanted to remain married to Svensso Olefson and be a part of his family. Hopefully, he would be open to forgiving her childish reign of terror that drove him away.

"Good day, Lady Ata. My apologies for interrupting, but would you happen to know where General Svensso is?" Min graciously interposed; Ata had been speaking with two overeager students she'd been training in Commanding healing. When they saluted and scurried off, she turned to Min in perplexity.

"Meeting with the other generals in the north... He's been gone for over four weeks—I'm surprised you didn't know," she and Min hadn't mended fences yet, having fallen into a strange, disconnected state. Ata looked at her cousin properly for the first time since their falling out (she usually just let her eyes glide over the Pandial princess during any forced interactions) and worry immediately took over.

"Are you alright, Min? Have you been ill?" To say her royal cousin looked under the weather was an understatement. She was pale and quite thin, dark circles under her eyes and a listless air about her.

"I'm fine—just some bad food and an upset stomach," she briskly waved off any concern, "General Svensso and quite a large company of soldiers returned early this morning. I thought you knew."

"He's back?" the physical blow the joy that notion caused was in itself a clear sign of her affections. She must not have concealed it well, because Min's reserved mask slipped, her face softening in commiseration.

"Yes. He was apparently kind enough to bring me a letter from Kai as well, but I haven't been able to track him down to get it," her eagerness bled through her usually controlled bearing, stirring Ata's sympathies.

"All reports from the northern front are lauding our Lieutenant Kai as a legendary war hero... I feel both proud and worried, but mostly annoyed that such a twit could be on the receiving end of such accolades. There will be no living with him, his head will be so big when he returns!" she tried to keep it light to alleviate the tension that still lay between them.

"True. I strongly suspect I will read all about his exploits in vivid detail... once I get my letter. It's really lifted my spirits, knowing he's sent it," Min's face was noticeably pale, so Ata decided not to keep her talking much longer.

"So, it is a *very* good day, then," she smiled happily, still nervous at seeing Svens again.

"That it is," Min confirmed.

It turned out not to be a very good day, though. For, try as she might, Ata could not seem to track down the Cinnaen general. He also didn't appear in the communal dining hall for dinner, nor did he come to their chambers afterwards.

Eventually Ata went to bed, spirits the lowest they had been up until that point. Unfortunately, as she discovered in the days that followed, her spirits could sink even lower. It appeared that Svens had decided not to interact with her at all, her efforts to find and speak to him constantly thwarted by everyone and everything.

Finally, she managed to corner him in the stables as he was choosing a mount with which to execute some mêlée manoeuvres on the training grounds. Ignoring the almost debilitating buzz in her belly at finally being in his presence, she noticed his hair was even longer and he'd taken to tying it back in a short queue. She found it inordinately attractive. *He* was inordinately attractive... She shook her head. *She needed to focus!* Upon spying her, he stiffened perceptibly, his face an impassive mask as he gave a minute bow.

"Lady Ata." Silence. *So, he hated her, then.*

"I am so pleased you're back safely!" she blurted gauchely, his slight frown showing his shock at her eager welcome. "I was hoping to be able to talk to you... about— about the annulment, because—"

"I've scheduled an audience with King Addai for tomorrow morning and aim to discharge that responsibility as soon as possible," he interrupted brusquely, and her heart quailed at his apparent dismissive attitude.

"I don't— I don't want an annulment anymore... I don't want a formal separation, rea—"

"You don't seem to know what you want, or if you do, previous experience indicates you'll turn around the next day and completely commit to undoing your prior actions. Forgive me if I'm not eager to experience another Ata about-face," he stated coldly and turned back to the horse he had begun saddling. It seemed she would have to execute her haphazard plan after all. A last chance, for Svens seemed unwilling to give her another.

"Please! I'm— I'm begging you. Just give me an hour of your time. This evening, for a proper conversation... If after that, you still want to be shot of me and our marriage, I will accept your choice," Ata rushed, pushing and praying to the gods in whom she wasn't sure she believed. He appeared unmoved, his gaze skating past her face and focusing behind her head.

"I don't see the point—"

"Please. Just an hour of your time. *One hour*," she pleaded, all pride forgotten in the face of this immense potential loss. Heaving a long-suffering sigh, he nodded curtly.

"I will meet you at the dining hall at seven," and with that, he turned back to the horse and dismissed her completely.

"WHERE ARE WE GOING?" Svens's deadpan expression didn't distract from the irritation in his voice as Ata lead him through the winding passages of the keep.

"We'll be there in a second," she assured him, doggedly continuing. Her palms were sweaty and her heart thumped loudly enough to drown out most other sounds. She was about to completely lay herself bare to this man. He was a good man, and she was in love with him, but that in no way guaranteed that he would accept her in all her awkward, honest brokenness. Yet she had to try, even it meant intense humiliation and rejection. The only way forward was through.

When they reached the small, unremarkable door that was her destination, she fumbled with the lock and key in her nervousness. Taking the key from her with a wry look, he neatly unlocked and opened the door, waving her in ahead of him.

"Where are we?" he peered around the small interior as Ata lit a lone candle. At least she wouldn't be exposing herself to the harsh light of day. *Small mercies.*

"This is my room," at his look of confusion, she added, "This is the room I've had since I can remember. I grew up in this room." Understanding crept over his countenance, and he looked around with more interest. He wandered over to the wall across from her narrow bed; it was covered from floor to ceiling in her sketches. Over the years, she had replaced most of the juvenile ones with more advanced versions, but she had kept some of the key childhood portraits for nostalgia's sake.

"It's impressive, your talent. You somehow manage to capture the essence of the person or the place with your charcoal and paper. Remarkable, really... I've never seen its equal," then he seemed to shake himself from his admiration. "Why are we here? Couldn't we have had this discussion in more comfortable, and frankly, warmer rooms?" His manner was as cold as the walls that currently surrounded them.

"I thought it might help..." at his sceptical look, she continued: "Please, take a seat." He sat down on the bed after assessing the three-legged stool—the only other furniture on offer—and finding it inadequate for his bulk. *Wise man.* Her nerves returned in full force when he trained his eyes on her in polite but distant enquiry. Her moment had come. *Just do it.*

Ata kept her eyes fixed on his face as she methodically began to remove her clothing. At first, he looked vaguely surprised, which then quickly escalated to strongly voiced alarm.

"What are you doing? You don't think we're going to... *here*? *Now*?" clearly, he was so disconcerted by her actions that he didn't think to get up or interrupt her by actively intervening.

Sooner than she thought possible, she had stripped down to only her skin and Enstroi chain. *Of course she'd choose the coldest time of year to make this particular grand gesture.* Luckily, the extreme physical discomfort distracted her from cringing with embarrassment at her blatant nudity, standing before him in the altogether.

To be fair to him, he was trying his damndest to limit his regard to the 'safest' areas of her body, finally settling with exaggerated self-possession on her face, though his cheeks were ruddy.

"What— why are you doing this? What's the point you're trying to make?" he asked, a note of frigid condescension in his voice. Choosing her words carefully was essential; she had now secured his undivided attention and had shocked him enough to give close consideration to what she said. She needed to make it count.

"You said before—and I understand why—that your previous experience with me showed that I could change my mind completely, without much justification... And I know you— you... *despise* the fact that I was a spy. That the secrecy of it, of *me*, is off-putting to you. Anathema to who you are because you don't know if you can trust me. So, I've decided to lay myself bare to you," he had been listening carefully, but shook his head now.

"I know what you look like without clothes, Ata—"

"Yes, I know. You managed that the first night we met and without meaning to... But I don't just mean *physically* bare. I want you to know me. All of me. And I needed to show you with more than empty 'pretty words' that I would 'undo' later... So, for example..." Ata lifted her arm, feeling gooseflesh break out all over her skin, and pointed at the jagged scar tissue across her bicep, "... I was clawed by a Gruxhoon during the first weeks of my one and only deployment in this war.

"And here..." she turned slightly so he could see her back and the perfectly linear silver lines that spread across it, "...here I received a lashing from my superior 'officer' when we were on survival manoeuvres. None other than the inimitable Lord Fordai, who had overstepped, as usual, when put in charge of others. I was sixteen."

He was silent, his eyes tracing the marks that peppered her body; no signs of disinterest. "Here—" she lifted her leg so he could see the oddly twisted scar on top of her foot, "Kai and I were messing about in his father's workshop and a coal from the furnace fell onto my foot—burnt straight through my shoe and blistered my skin badly. I was seven."

"What are you hoping to achieve with this, Ata?" Svens suddenly interrupted; he looked tired and was rubbing furiously at his scar and nose. "Why are you showing me all of this... telling me all of this?"

"I want you to *see* me. All of me. To know me like no-one else does. Because if you know me like that, with all my warped and twisted parts, then you can decide whether you want to keep me. Because, from what I've come to know about you, I want to keep you. Unequivo-cally." At his frown, she hurried to add: "I would want to know all of *you* too, of course." He kept his hand over his eyes, hunched forward.

"And you just decided you want to 'keep' me? Just like that?" he asked. He didn't sound particularly convinced.

"One of my greatest flaws, as my family often like to remind me, is that I... I try to push away those I like. Those I love. I don't know why—well, maybe I do, deep down. But, in practical terms, it means that I alienate those I want with me the most. So, after much soul searching, and amidst the very real pain I experienced of missing you, I realised that I've come to love you, somehow, despite my own best efforts not to. And I can't seem to be happy without you. I don't *want* to be without you."

The silence after her statement was deafening. *And*

she was freezing. But she waited for the final verdict. His hand dropped from his face and he looked back at her, assessing.

"You know it will take a lot of work, right? Any relationship would, but as you point out: we are both complicated people with our flaws. So we would *both* need to be prepared to work on ourselves as well as work together, despite them. Despite external pressures, of which there will be *many*."

"I know that, and I'm prepared to work at it. I might be... difficult sometimes, and reticent, but I want this." *Just say it already, you coward.* "I love you, Svens." That moment was when she had her answer, because— though his expression was ever-neutral—she saw the minute shift to joy there.

"Well, that's good. Because I love you too, Ata, and have for quite a while," she smiled so widely her cheeks hurt. "Now please! Just take this blanket and cover up while you enumerate your various childhood accidents to me," he added drily, holding the bedspread he had snagged from the cot out towards her.

He caught her eyeing his scar and correctly surmised she was going to ask him to tell her about it. Rolling his eyes in exasperation, he pushed the blanket into her hands. "We have all the time we need to share all the stories of our war wounds, but only if you don't freeze first..."

22

DESCENT INTO DARKNESS

In a dark time, the eye begins to see,
I meet my shadow in the deepening shade;
I hear my echo in the echoing wood—
A lord of nature weeping to a tree.
I live between the heron and the wren,
Beasts of the hill and serpents of the den.

What's madness but nobility of soul
At odds with circumstance? The day's on fire!
I know the purity of pure despair,
My shadow pinned against a sweating wall.
That place among the rocks—is it a cave,
Or winding path? The edge is what I have.

THEODORE ROETHKE

Contrary to its inherent significance in terms of hope and rebirth, spring brought only the looming destruction of Áitarbith. Wave after wave of Gruxhoon had landed on the entire western coastline, north to south, and had utterly annihilated the Pandial and Cinnaen troops like a tsunami obliterating inadequate wooden fences on the shores.

Further inland, their momentum was barely checked by the thousands of Áitarbithian soldiers already fighting the first barrage of invading Gruxhoon. There were indiscriminate massacres of civilian communities caught between the two sides, as well as the gratuitous torture and destruction visited on far-flung towns and villages. Neither the aged nor children were spared in the Gruxhoon's obvious aim of completely subjugating the peoples of the continent.

The city-state of Karppen had been overwhelmed and consequently, its citizens had sought succour in Pandi in general, and Enddaian in particular. The influx of refugees who literally only managed to flee with the clothes on their backs meant resources became more strained for their Pandial 'hosts'. However, the Karppenians who were able joined what had become the Áitarbithian Alliance Armies, thereby contributing to the war effort, as well as many Vürgøn. The latter came down from the mountains in smaller fighting units, no official alliance having been agreed upon by their collective tribes' leaders, but the freedom permitted warriors meaning they could join the war, or not, as they preferred.

The initial, grimly proud determination of all Pandial and Cinnaen forces, as well as the civilian refugees, at the outset of the conflict had been replaced by a hollow-eyed desperation. Now, more than ever, young and old, rich and poor, women and men realised that their survival was inextricably tied to their fight against these beasts.

Len herself had buckled down and committed as much of her time and energy as she could to supporting the cause; this collective cause of survival, irrespective of personal and national loyalties. She also became used to the inevitable isolation from those she generally looked to for authority and support.

Svens had been gone almost constantly since his short return at the beginning of winter. She still caught sight of him every now and then, but these sightings were few and far between, showcasing, in sharp relief, the changes in his appearance and demeanour.

"He's looking positively barbaric these days!" Lord Iansso had joked. Lenna had discovered his presence in the castle with great joy and was sworn to secrecy— though the heavens knew why. If *she* could stumble across him in the library, then surely anyone else could too?

"With the general's long hair and bushy beard, he

resembles the Vürgøn more than the cultivated prim-ness of the Cinnaen military," the secretive, possible-spy had sniffed.

Not that the Cinnaen military entity had retained its pristine appearance in these times of devastating defeat. Everyone looked shabby and overwhelmed, the best they could achieve with dwindling resources and being under constant attack being cleanliness. Widespread rationing was being imposed, even at the tables of Enddaian Keep, and all able bodies were being drawn into the war effort, with fewer and fewer servants committed to waiting on the courtiers due to being redistributed to industries that needed their labour more.

The desperate need for more soldiers was not being met, resulting in the age-limits on joining the armed forces being relaxed, sixteen years being the youngest, and people into their fifties being called up. Women and men alike joined, although the Cinnaen and Karp-penian women were, in Len's own impassioned words to Ata "less than useless due to being treated by their respective societies like spun glass. Now we will all shatter for our lack of usefulness."

Once the age-limit changes were decreed by the war council, Tens had left shortly after his and Len's seven-teenth birthday to join Svens—despite heavy censure from Queen Nelni, Lord Haaviso, and what remained of the Cinnaen council.

"With all due respect, Your Highness, Your Grace, and my lords: I have three heirs who are going to remain safely here, should I fall in battle. I cannot—*will not*—cower behind these walls while our host nation sends boys and girls my age and younger to fight our common enemy!" were his exact words, according to Menke, who had managed to be present (serving) in the council chambers during that show down.

Len had been indescribably proud of her twin. *And unconscionably jealous of his self-determination.* After his departure, the compromise having been made that he was to remain with General Svensso *at all times*, Len saw him more often during his company's short sojourns at the Keep than she did their eldest half-brother.

"He's spending every second he can with Ata," Tens had remarked drily when Len had commented on his absence from their private dinner the night before they were due to leave again. "I'm sure they have better things to do than make polite conversation over the dinner table." This last had been said in a light-hearted manner, but Len had picked up on the underlying bitterness.

"Are you jealous?" she asked before thinking better of it.

"Of whom?" he bit back, faux playfully.

"Of him, or her. Of them? I don't know—whichever!" he pulled a face, dropping his lighthearted mien.

"Yes, I'm jealous, alright. A little because... *you*

know..." yes, Len did know—and so did everyone else—about his boyish crush on their sister-in-law, "but mostly, I envy how they have each other and are supportive and content with their marriage. Even under these awful circumstance, and even though it was an arranged match. I really admire them for making the effort to make it work." Len agreed.

"I know. Though they don't flaunt it in a public or obvious way, they're quietly committed to each other... It's like this inner strength that they both have and share with each other. As if they know the other completely, and always know where they stand. I hope I can have that one day," she whispered, oddly fervent. Tens snorted.

"Fat chance!" At her querying look, he smiled, "With our luck, we'll each end up with some stuffy elitist with no notion of self-sacrifice and no redeeming qualities. Worse: no sense of humour."

She laughed at his joke, noting that despite the dire circumstances they were all facing, he looked happier than she had ever seen him. Clearly, being actively involved in the defense of their people was helping to build his sense of self-worth. He also couldn't stop talking about the camaraderie he experienced amongst the rank and file—the barbarically blunt Vürgøn warriors, who made up the majority of the troops under Svens's command by this point and who had saved Tens's skin multiple times.

"I really want for us all, the different peoples of Áitarbith, to form closer bonds and to retain them once we've driven the Gruxhoon out... We should encourage ties between all of our nations," he had enthused on multiple occasions. "When I'm king, that will be my main aim; to bring people together."

To Len's mind, despite all the hardship and horror they were faced with, the war seemed to be bringing out the best in many—including her once-morally-indolent brother.

It was shortly after this conversation and the departure of her brothers' company that the Cinnaen council made the decision to send the other Hårbørgen offspring into hiding in the Uurgonna Mountains.

Over the two preceding weeks, with all remaining soldiers thinly dispersed throughout Pandial territory, Enddaian Keep had been on high alert due to the constant threat of attack by Gruxhoon bands closing in from numerous directions, based on scouts' reports.

The council therefore concluded that, due to the keep's status as the headquarters of the Áitarbithian Alliance's war efforts, its likelihood of falling under long-term siege negated its defensive capabilities and made it a less-than-ideal haven for the remaining heirs. Also, the Vürgøn had recently offered succour in their virtually impregnable mountain dwellings to those civilians who would make use of their wartime protection and hospitality.

Hence, the Cinnaen council elected to send their remaining heirs to safety, along with large numbers of Cinnaen women and children. Many of the Karppenian civilians would do the same, including their royal family.

When called before the collective Pandial and Cinnaen council to receive this information, Lenna had unequivocally refused to go and was both surprised and heartened when Ata had unstintingly supported her in her rebellion.

"Respectfully, Crown Prince Tensso, who is of an age with Princess Lenna, is at the front, fighting and risking his life. If Her Highness wishes to stay close to the warfront to provide support, then she is owed the same independence of choice and agency given her brother."

Ata had regularly been attending the combined council meetings on behalf Princess Mindaia over the past three months, speaking with her royal cousin's authority. Though no reasons had been provided for this substitution, and there had probably been plenty of opposition from various camps within the two governments, the mindset of 'all hands on deck' had carried the day. Interestingly, Lady Ata's Pandial detractors had all been redistributed or deployed in the scramble to protect their kingdom.

Though the Cinnaen council would have preferred to make these decisions amongst themselves, they would need Pandial support and cooperation to accompany the group of refugees into the Uurgonna Mountains. Thus, Lady Ata's input carried significant official weight these days—especially during meetings like this one, where King Addai was not present—much to the chagrin of Queen Nelni. As Princess Mindaia's proxy, Ata had the highest standing amongst the Pandial members.

"You have no authority to make decisions on behalf of Cinnaen subjects!" the Cinnaen queen had raged. Ata just smiled politely.

"That is true. However, under *Cinnaen* law, and during wartime occupation specifically, the standard laws regarding minors and their independence of movement are curtailed—the war effort taking precedence over familial considerations. In this instance, for example, Princess Lenna is perfectly within her rights to remain if it is in practical support of the war." Lenna had not even been aware of such legal precedents, but the ancient legal scribe who advised the Cinnaen council confirmed its veracity.

Accordingly, Lenna had been permitted to stay behind. This was both a blessing and a burden, for she had to relinquish the care of her younger brothers to Famenke, who would accompany them to the mountains and remain with them.

Despite the heart-wrenching goodbyes and constant worries as to the wisdom of allowing themselves to be separated, Len logically knew that splitting up their little family increased the probability of at least one of them surviving this historically momentous time of uncertainty. For the sake of their Hårbørgen legacy and their future responsibility to govern the Cinnaen people, it was necessary.

"I'll be sure to communicate regularly via Lord Danai or Lord Iansso," Ata said as she readied to depart with the large group of women and children. The council had agreed to add Pandial women and children who were unable to contribute to the war effort to the group of assembled refugees making for the mountains. Ata and half of the remaining soldiers in Enddaian would accompany the group into the mountains, protecting them from the potential attacks of raiding bands of Gruxhoon prowling the countryside largely unchecked.

At Len's obvious look of worry, she smiled encouragingly. "Be sure to keep practicing your archery, and use the techniques I showed you last time. I expect you to give me a run for my money when I return." Len couldn't find it in her to smile in response, but nodded nonetheless.

Her sister-in-law was something of a hero in her eyes; disregarding all her awe-inspiring battle and rescue feats, she was one of the most advanced Abled in existence. No-one had actually verbalised this outright, but Len had surmised as much from the hints dropped by Lord Danai and Lord Iansso, as well as the fact that

Ata had been the one to discover healing through Commanding and had then proceeded to teach as many Abled as possible.

Setting aside all of these accomplishments, Ata was Len's personal idol because she had seen her almost manic need to be useful and skilled, and in response had taken Len under her wing, training her in basic hand-to-hand combat and archery whenever she could. To Len's mind, Ata was the perfect partner for her ever-competent, larger-than-life half-brother, because she herself was a metaphorical giant of aptitude and loyalty.

"Don't worry! I'll be back soon enough, and besides: you are the captain of your own ship and have all the tools you need to carry you," her inspiring friend said, thumping her chest in a farewell salute and quickly mounting. Trotting out the gates without a backward glance, she joined the mass exodus down the streets of the town.

Len slowly lifted her fist and pressed it to her heart. She had not missed the significance of that specific salute being used for her—she who had never officially served in the armed forces. It was a message. *They were sisters in arms.*

The 30th day of the 1st cycle, Year 1071 pera Áitarbith

AS THE FIRST *spring after the Gruxhoon invasion ages, the tidings we receive from assorted fronts are inconsistent. All of our northern troops have suffered immense losses, relinquishing ground to the invading tides of Darkness.*

The creatures we are fighting are bestial in every sense of the word, killing all who cross their path. They spare neither the suckling nor the ancient, they decimate all before them— man, woman, child, elder. They do not distinguish between soldier and non-combatant, mowing down every human and most animals they encounter.

From the northernmost coasts in Cinnae, the western coasts of Cinnae, right through the inland territories and up to the Uurgonna Mountain Range, the Gruxhoon are engaging in a collective act of annihilation. They will leave nothing of us should they triumph over our continent.

However, there is hope; small points of light in this overwhelming shadow of death that haunts us. One such light is the Pandial commander, Kaimam ben-Emli Delbadai, the only son of a Pandial silversmith and his Cinnaen wife, whose feats of bravery have become legendary over the past months of unimaginable losses. He and his ragtag band of guerilla fighters have snatched victory from the jaws of defeat on multiple occasions, bringing hope to those of us who fight for our very future existence.

The one northern company that holds the line originally assigned is his; their loyal and unwavering hearts pushing them beyond the bounds of normal human endeavour. Their unfailing rescues of innumerable displaced and terrorised people numbers in the hundreds, their heroism becoming lionised.

Similarly, King Addai of the Pandi Kingdom has not shirked his unenviable duty of carrying the lion's share of this war on his shoulders, his people suffering endlessly under the attacks of the Gruxhoon.

Yet, still they provide a refuge for all the displaced Cinnaens fleeing from the north, and even though they were the first of the Áitarbithian nations to welcome the Cinnaens who fled the unexpected incursion and massacre—the beginning of which is known as the 'Night of Terror', and which this author witnessed personally and survived by a narrow margin.

Len carefully transferred the pen to her other hand and straightened out her stiff, clawed fingers, the candle burning low. When ink dripped onto the scroll from the nib, she swore and quickly blotted it with another piece of paper.

She'd been at this for hours; the documenting of events as they unfolded seemed like an important act that was being overlooked by all. Sadly, the reason she felt so compelled to write down all their experiences, all their fear and horror, was because she suspected very few of them would survive this war.

Yet *someone* had to bear witness for future generations, even if that someone wasn't a particularly accomplished writer and had imperfect penmanship. Even if it was just her. There needed to be a record, a *true* record, created by someone who was there, at the center of it all, before they were all gone and events passed from mind and memory of the ones who *did* survive.

She had taken to writing long descriptions of what was happening and who was involved. During her days, she tirelessly fetched and carried, doing tasks usually reserved for working women, but nevertheless contributing as and when she could.

Then, in the evenings, she committed events to paper so they would not be forgotten. She told no-one of her documentation of the war, but carefully rolled up scrolls and folded parchment—sometimes multiple copies of the same text—then proceeded to hide them in as many different places as she could find. Within the keep, in the town, and even further afield in the woods nearby. In books in the library, behind bricks in the kitchens, and in the legs of furniture.

She seeded her environment as thoroughly as she could with her words, with the heroic deeds of others, and with the facts of their potential annihilation. Whether they would one day find a fertile mind to populate? She had no assurances, but she lived in hope.

The flame dancing feverishly on the barest remnant of a wick guttered and fizzled out, leaving her in cold and empty darkness. She couldn't see her hand in front of her face, the pitch black engulfing everything completely. *Like the Gruxhoon have engulfed Áitarbith*, she thought bitterly. But as they said: 'it was darkest before the dawn', and she clung to that adage to get her through the days of watching and waiting. Waiting on news about the war, waiting on news of her loved ones, and waiting to somehow make a tangible difference. Watching for the little pinpricks of light to keep their hope alive.

LEN HAD NEVER BEEN OVERLY virtuous, though many thought she was 'holier than thou' and a 'goodie two shoes'. This was a misinterpretation of her disposition, taking her quiet, well-spoken reticence as signs of an elevated moral character. She just didn't share all her deviousness with the world at large. Her brothers, however, knew her shrewd mind and consequently trod carefully whenever she was involved in a scheme.

"You have everyone fooled with that 'butter wouldn't melt' manner you have," Tens had grumped at her when they were thirteen and he'd been punished for something she had done—not because she'd lied and blamed him, but because their tutor had simply *refused* to believe them both when they said she had been the one to glue all the pages of his geography primer together.

"It's a gift," she had shrugged. She tried to make it up to him by giving him her entire dessert that night.

"It's diabolical," he retorted, but polished off both

desserts, so her offering had been accepted, and by default, her apology.

Consequently, when faced with the opportunity to eavesdrop on a conversation she would normally never have been privy to, Lenna would usually have had no qualms about remaining and listening carefully. That was not, however, the case when she was surprised mid-climb up a towering bookcase in the smaller, (customarily unused) librarian's office off the main castle library. She had been hiding her most recent document which lauded the heroic efforts of their fighters, when she was unceremoniously interrupted.

Upon hearing hurried footsteps, she realised she would be horribly embarrassed, being caught half-hanging from the shelves like a primate, irrespective of who the footsteps belonged to. Thus, she did the only thing she could: hauled herself up to the top and lay down flat, avoiding thinking about how high up she was. Or that the castle staff had not dusted up there in well over a year, judging from the layer she was resting in.

"What do you mean you're pregnant?" a husky female voice demanded in a whisper. Usually, a whisper was not easily identifiable, but in this case, Len immediately recognised it as Ata's. *Oh no!* She could tell this was not a conversation she wanted to overhear, if only because she respected Ata immensely and felt this was a kind of betrayal, however inadvertent. She should just announce her presence, apologise, and climb down from her perch. Then hightail it out of there. No harm, no foul, no betrayal. However, as she was about to do just that, the other person answered tearfully.

"Exactly what I'm *saying*, Ata!" Oh no. This voice was not lowered enough to make identification impossible, and the speaker and her revelation meant extracting herself now was *impossible*. She crossed her fingers and fervently hoped she'd been mistaken.

"How could that be, Min?" *Well, that dashed those hopes.*

"What do you mean? You know that Kai and I have—"

"I meant 'how could you let that happen?', not 'how does one become pregnant?', *Mindaia!*" to be fair, Ata was maintaining a whispered tone despite her obvious emotional distress. A gulping sound floated up to Len. "I'm sorry! I'm sorry! *Please* don't cry, Min!" Ata's desperation was obvious. "I didn't mean to upset you—"

"It's not *you*, though, is it. You're right: this is *all my fault*," it was difficult to believe that the ever-serene Pandial princess could sound so frazzled and hysterical, hiccupping like a child. But then Len remembered: she was not much older than Len herself, a mere two years separating them.

"I think Kai also bears some responsibility in this, Min," Ata said drily, "Don't even pretend as though he's blameless! As I said: I know how one becomes pregnant, and more specifically: I know how *you* became pregnant.

Because he's a self-involved, pleasure-chasing, uncontrolled, impatient—"

"All the adjectives in the world aren't going to solve this problem, though, are they," Min said hopelessly.

"No, but tell me it wasn't because Kai was being Kai that you missed drinking the *ditan* tea at the correct time?" censure dripped from Ata's words. A beat of silence. "*Exactly.*" More quiet and a few muffled sobs. "What does he say about it?" This was business-like Ata, ready to solve a problem. A muffled mumble answered, but Len couldn't make it out. The princess must have been blowing her nose.

"What do you mean *he doesn't know!*" Ata cried, Min shushing her desperately; Ata lowered her voice to repeat: "Like, he doesn't know *at all*? Why *didn't you tell him*?"

"I— I didn't know for sure at first, then, when I *did* know, everything was so ghastly with the war... and, he's been away almost five months now, Ata. When was I supposed to impart this *highly sensitive* information?"

Some fire had returned to the princess's tone. All Len knew was that the dust was causing a tickling sensation in her nose, and she had completely overstayed the limit of time when she could safely extricate herself from this situation—it was completely impossible for her to graciously leave now. *She had to remain hidden.*

"Wait! If Kai's been gone five months, which he must be, though I haven't been counting... How far along are you?" the dismay in Ata's whisper carried all the way to the top of the bookcase.

"I think... I suspect I'm at almost seven months. Just over two cycles." A long silence.

"Oh, gods!" More silence and the scrape of chairs as they sat down (at least, Lenna *surmised* they sat down). She was doing her utmost to rub away the effects of the dust in her nose, as well as being highly invested in this shocking revelation. "How have you managed to conceal it from everyone? You don't look much different to me, even now..."

"The high-waisted fashions have been a boon, but also: it isn't particularly obvious except when I'm in my underwear or naked. Dreka says—"

"So, she does know? I'd been wondering..."

"Of course she knows. I'd never be able to conceal something like that from her; she's with me constantly," the princess sounded nonplussed.

"And you trust her to keep it to herself?" Dubiously.

"Don't be ridiculous—I'd trust her with my *life*. She raised me and is completely loyal to me!" now the princess sounded incensed.

"Alright, alright, I apologise for asking! It's only because I worry..." Ata placated, "What did your nurse-maid say about your pregnancy not showing?"

"She said my mother carried me to full term with very little change to her figure, just a slight belly. The physicians had apparently worried over it incessantly, but I was born completely healthy without any problems, so they thought it was just a quirk of her body. One I seem to have inherited."

"Well, how *fortunate*, under the circumstances," Ata's sarcasm didn't disguise the hopeless note. "What's the plan, Min?"

"I—I don't really have one. The only plan thus far was to conceal it from everyone until we could come up with a better one. I haven't yet... That's why I'm asking you."

"Yes, I feel so honoured. Very well done, by the way... We don't talk for months and you decide to break the stalemate with your own personal crisis that will have a massive impact on the kingdom," sourly.

"Our estrangement was your doing, Ata, so I won't be lectured by you about it. Also: what was I supposed to do? I trusted you and thought you'd value our entire lifetime over our recent falling out, but apparently—"

"Okay, Min. I won't bring it up again... I'm being stupid. It's not helpful, and you're right: *I'm* guilty of most of the issues that caused it. Let's talk about how to deal with this situation now, moving forward," Ata's apology seemed to calm the princess.

"I think..." Ata began, then petered off.

"Yes?"

"I think you should tell Kai as soon as possible. It's only right that he knows he's going to be a father..."

"I can't. I *won't*— no, listen: Kai needs to focus on

fighting the Gruxhoon—surviving the Gruxhoon. He's at the forefront of it and clinging on. This would completely overwhelm him and put him in danger. He needs to focus only on making it through these battles now. He can deal with the question of fatherhood later." The audible sigh indicated Ata disagreed, but she left off arguing.

"Well, then I think you need to tell your fath—"

"No! He would be *livid*. I cannot even describe to you how angry he could be... Especially after..." an awkward hush followed.

"After my mother's 'mistake', you mean?" Ata prompted, not sounding put out.

"Yes. I'm sorry, I didn't want to insult you. But yes, he still smarts from the shame of his sister's fall from grace all those years ago and the consequent political mess he'd been left to deal with. I can't even *imagine* his reaction to mine," the anguish that bled through Mindaia's voice was tangible.

"I hate to break it to you, Min, but he's going to notice when you go into labour and suddenly have a baby... There's no getting around this: the king needs to be told. The sooner, the better, because then he can plan and execute damage control," a reasonable take, Len thought.

"Ata, the problem is: yes, it sounds like a logical argument, but once the information is shared, it can never be taken back—we will be at the mercy of my father. No, the mercy of King Addai of Pandi, for he won't think of this as my father, but as the monarch whose daughter has shamed his entire line," the princess no longer sounded like a lost waif, but like a seasoned debater.

"What do you propose, then? Because I'm out of ideas," Ata sounded tired. A long silence followed where Len tried to ignore the ache in her hip, as well as ruthlessly repressing the instinctive urge to move; the bookcase would undoubtedly creak and give her away.

"I don't know. The fear of what comes next chokes me and I can't think straight," Mindaia's voice was small with this admission.

"How about... what if I spoke with Lord Danai?" Ata suggested, her tone brightening with excitement.

Princess Mindaia sounded vastly unimpressed. "Why would I want the *Pandial spymaster* to know this immense, life-changing secret?"

"Well, because, even though he is loyal to your father, his primary loyalty is to the crown in the abstract... He is coldly logical in all his calculations. He doesn't let emotions interfere, and at the very least he would give us sound, well-reasoned advice on what to do next. He'd outline the different scenarios and all their potential consequences. It's perfect!" the longer she explained, the more enthusiastic Ata became.

"You're sure he won't just run to my father with the information?" Mindaia seemed to be considering it.

"If he did, he would give us fair warning, especially if I pinned him down on it. He's deceitful, in his own way, hence his success as spymaster. But I know all his tells and tricks, and so would be able to suss out his next play —if it should threaten the secrecy, anyway."

Len couldn't see what was happening below, but assumed an agreement had been reached because the chairs were moved, the door unlocked, and the sound of two sets of footsteps receded in the distance.

After waiting what felt like an interminably long time, Len carefully shimmied to the edge of the bookcase and cautiously picked her way down the shelves until she stood on firm ground once again. She was absolutely covered in dust and stiff from lying still with her muscles contracted for so long. Keeping her mind carefully blank, she slowly made her way back to her rooms and requested hot water be brought for a bath. She didn't usually indulge in nor overburden the servants with those kinds of requests (especially over the past few months) but this time she decided it was necessary.

Stripping out of her soiled garments, she sank into the hot water to soak away the accumulated sweat and grime from her eavesdropping foray. At that point, she untethered all her thoughts and reactions to the information she had just been exposed to, an overwhelming barrage of questions and exclamations running rampant through her mind.

Her sympathy for the princess was paramount, but she also worried over the long-term consequences of this situation. What could she do to help? She had this burning need to be useful. *Somehow.*

The one fact that could not be denied: this was going to change things in a *significant* way.

23

REVENANT REVELATIONS

WE MAKE OURSELVES A PLACE APART

    BEHIND LIGHT WORDS THAT TEASE AND FLOUT,

    BUT OH, THE AGITATED HEART

    TILL SOMEONE FIND US REALLY OUT.

'TIS PITY IF THE CASE REQUIRE

    (OR SO WE SAY) THAT IN THE END

    WE SPEAK THE LITERAL TO INSPIRE

    THE UNDERSTANDING OF A FRIEND.

BUT SO WITH ALL, FROM BABES THAT PLAY

    AT HIDE-AND-SEEK TO GOD AFAR,

    SO ALL WHO HIDE TOO WELL AWAY

    MUST SPEAK AND TELL US WHERE THEY ARE.

ROBERT FROST

Tumultuous times, unsettling news—secrets that needed to be dealt with carefully. Ata's head spun with the complexity of what she now needed to juggle: a royal secret beyond anything she could have expected, as well as its potential impact on the future of the entire continent. As she rushed down the abandoned corridors of Enddaian Keep towards Lord Danai's rooms, she tried to calm her pattering heartbeat, to breathe deeply and order her thoughts.

It was of paramount importance that she approach with caution the revelation she was about to make to one of the most manipulative men in Áitarbith. It was well after midnight, and though Ata was exhausted from her weeks-long dash to the Uurgonna Mountains (from whence she had only returned that morning), her nerves and adrenaline completely negated her tiredness. She'd pay for it dearly later, though.

Knocking quietly on the door, she noted the flickering golden light underneath. After a few moments' silence, Lord Danai's voice enquired evenly who it was.

"It's Ata," she murmured, taking a final calming breath before entering.

"It is unusually late, Lady Atiyah..." Lord Danai remarked, implying, in his usual, roundabout way, that something momentous must be afoot.

"It is, but I wouldn't be here if it weren't necessary. I

need to share some information with you, and I need your counsel quite desperately," Ata dispensed with the social niceties and sat down, eyeing her mentor expectantly. With a slight frown, he took the other seat, across from her, at his small dining table.

"I suspect from your demeanour that it is related to the predictions of the Changer?" he hazarded. She nodded and rubbed her eyes tiredly.

"I went by Ians's rooms, looking for you both, but they were completely empty—abandoned," his non-reaction told her all she needed to know. "Has Ians left the keep, Lord Danai?" He shifted his attention to the carafe of wine and attentively proceeded to pour two glasses.

"He was needed further afield." His tone unmistakably conveyed that no further discussion on this topic would be entertained. Ata shrugged inwardly, too focused on the huge news she had to impart to dwell on it. She would consider Ians's absence more carefully once she'd discharged her duty to Min by asking Lord Danai's advice on their conundrum.

"Anyway—the reason I've come to speak with you..." he sat perfectly still, patiently awaiting the words that were choking her. "I just— I need you to promise me that it will remain between us? What I know has larger implications than the ones immediately apparent..." she continued to babble as his frown deepened incrementally.

"For heavens' sake, Ata! I did *not* train you to be such an utterly dissembling shambles when reporting," he snapped, the end of his patience officially reached. It was the verbal slap that she needed, so she just blurted.

"Min's pregnant." She never thought she would see such surprise on his countenance. Still, even when faced with the unexpected, he proceeded with a methodical approach, exhaustively questioning from the outset.

"Who is the father?" *Ah! Of course he'd ask that first.*

"It's Kai... He and Min have— they've been in a relationship for years now. I covered for them by pretending to be in a romantic entanglement with him, but—"

"But it was only in service of this poorly thought-through affair," Lord Danai interrupted, "I have known for quite a while that that was the case. I just did not foresee this..."

"Well, after the initial shock and all the questions about what to do and whom to tell, and in what order, my mind reverted to the prophecy... Do you know what Kai is being called, after his amazing victories on the northern border?" Lord Danai merely looked at her in his customarily closed-off, enquiring manner.

"They call him 'The warrior who will change the tides'... Someone who exerts great influence and brings about phenomenal change, like *the Changer*." Ata was leaning forward, earnestly trying to convey her point. "And now: Min is pregnant with Kai's child. A child—an heir, in all senses of the word—being born to a future queen. Born to a changer."

Lord Danai's face looked to be carved of stone though she knew that behind his impassive façade his exemplary mind was working nineteen to a dozen. However, her impatience wouldn't allow the newly discovered truth to remain unspoken.

"Don't you understand? It was never me! I wasn't the Changer—*Kai* was. And his and Min's child will be 'three parts of four'. It all makes so much sense!" Lord Danai sighed and drank deeply from his goblet.

"Ians is going to be absolutely *impossible* to live with after this!" he stated flatly.

"What do you mean?"

"He was convinced, once he had learnt of the clandestine affair between your half-blood friend and the princess, that they would produce the Heir. Don't ask me *how* he could have predicted it, for all logical reasoning would have pointed to their relationship not bringing forth a valid heir due to its inevitable end, the couple being who they are socially. But I stand corrected, it seems..." Lord Danai shook his head in apparent disgust at the irrational nature of human beings. "When is the child due?"

"Soon. Within less than a cycle; about two and a half months..." Ata experienced a sense of relief at being able to speak to someone who would know what to do;

she felt ill-equipped to deal with this current predicament.

"So the princess was able to conceal her pregnancy well. That is very good."

"But the main question is: what should we do now? Whom should we tell? How should we go about managing this crisis?" she prodded, needing his assurances and a plan on how to proceed.

"No-one else should be told. This pregnancy and the birth should be concealed from everyone. The child must be concealed from all, for its own survival." Completely stunned by his uncompromisingly factual tone, Ata spluttered.

"What— But... that's *impossible*! Conceal a royal child? How would we conceal the birth? *Why* would we?" she had risen from her chair, looming angrily over Lord Danai who just watched her dispassionately. "Because it's a *half-breed bastard*, is that it?" she snarled.

"You forget, I myself am a 'half-breed bastard', as you so eloquently put it," his freezing tones halted her building rage, dousing its fire in one fell swoop, and she dropped leadenly back into the chair.

"I apologise, Lord Danai. I'm not thinking clearly and am exhausted from days of constant travel without proper sleep. Please explain to me your reason for wanting to hide Min and Kai's baby." Despite his usual piercing look, she noted a slight softening in his manner.

"I refer you to the part of the prophecy only very recently shared with you. Once again, my brother's intuition in pushing forward with informing you despite my protestations has proven to have been the wisest course of action. Insufferable, I tell you."

Lord Danai explained: "The line '*Beware betrayal by blood of kin; Death from enemies will come from within*'. I put it to you: the child born to the Changer *will not survive its first year of life*—the Witchlings of Hoondær will not allow it. And, like all insidious groups, they have their tentacles everywhere. There are spies amongst our own ranks, even...

"How do you think they have managed to undermine our positions? How are our troops constantly on the back foot? And, based on this prediction, it will be the very family of the child who will betray it." Such horrifying rhetoric in Lord Danai's dispassionately rational voice was awful to hear. Awful to believe, but believe it she did.

"But, if it's a foregone conclusion, what can we do? How can we subvert what's been predicted?" she asked, feeling both hopeless and enraged by the cage imposed by both the prophecy and the reality of their current situation.

"Just what I said: we conceal the child. We pretend as though it never existed."

"How would that even work, though? We can't hide a child—hide their birth—in a castle filled with people,"

Ata argued, annoyed that he wasn't being more forth-coming as well as the fact that he kept referring to the baby as 'it'.

"You are absolutely correct. The only solution to that problem would be to spirit the princess away, have her bear the babe in secret somewhere, and then raise the child there. Unbeknownst to the courts, and most importantly, unbeknownst to their family. Besides you and Her Highness, of course..." he set out.

"There has to be a better way! I know Min as well as I know myself, and I can say, for a fact, that she'd *never* relinquish her child to anyone else. She would never give over the raising of her child, of Kai's child, to some obscure stranger. It's an impossibility." Annoyance flashed over Lord Danai's face.

"Then we must find a situation that she can live with, but there is no question about it: the child cannot be raised here, at the centre of the kingdom and the courts. It would be as good as signing the babe's death warrant. Her Highness would need to choose which is the lesser of the two evils!" In the silence that followed, the crackling of the fire echoed in the room.

"I don't know what to do," Ata finally broke the stalemate hoarsely, rubbing her face. "I promised Min speaking to you would provide answers and options, but instead it provides... it only offers her the loss of her child, either through predicted death or through alienation. It's a very bitter thing and I don't know if I can do that to her..." she trailed off, tears gathering in her eyes.

"What if I spoke with her and explained the situation? You should be present, of course, but I would be the one to lay out the options and the reasoning behind them," Lord Danai offered.

"Would you? It would help a lot, because I'm not sure how much of the prophecy mumbo-jumbo I should include, yet it needs to be mentioned." Her erstwhile tutor nodded grimly.

"I think you should rest now. You are exhausted and this will result in a lack of control over your emotions and behaviour. You and I shall speak to Princess Mindaia tomorrow first thing, for we need to make arrangements as soon as possible once she has made a final decision." And with that, the worst conversation Ata had ever had in her life was deferred to the next day.

"I cannot do that! You can't make me do that!" Min wailed, clutching at Ata's clothing as Ata tried to prop up her cousin's prostrate form from where she was seated on a chair beside the Pandial princess. To say their discussion with her cousin was not going particularly well was an understatement. Though initially collected and open to options, the princess had devolved into an emotional wreck when a sanitised version of the prophecy had been shared with her. Upon being told the horrifying truth that unknown spies were waiting in the wings to kill her baby, naturally, Min became quite distraught.

"Your Highness, I know this is painful to hear, but you need to keep your head. If for no-one else, then for the babe you carry!" Lord Danai had to shout to be heard over her protests.

"Min—just listen... *Calm down*, and *really* listen," Ata soothingly hugged her kneeling cousin and swayed side-to-side, waiting until Min's cries had diminished to hiccups. She had always suffered from hiccups after a bout of crying, even as a little girl. "I understand that all the options sound bad, but you need to choose the least horrible one... Something that you can live with more than the others."

"But is there no other way? Are you *sure* about your intelligence regarding the agents and lack of safety?" Min whispered desperately.

"I have been the spymaster to Pandial for over thirty years, and I would risk my entire reputation—my life— in backing what we have told you: the powers that have driven the Gruxhoon to invade will, without hesitation, make the death of your and Lieutenant Kaimam's child their main aim. And they have the eyes, ears, and hands within these very walls to make it so.

"The only action with even a modicum of potential success in allowing your child to grow until it can defend itself is to birth and raise the babe in complete secrecy and isolation. Far from this or any other court." Oddly, Lord Danai's clinical manner and dry tone were comforting; they held authority in this fraught situation. Min's eyes clung to him frantically.

"How do you suggest we do that? Where?" she asked.

"The 'where' is immaterial, really; anywhere rural and cut off from the main trade routes would be ideal. The child would need to be raised in expectation of their eventual status, but we can get to that later on. The first step, over which there can be no question: you must be taken to a place in secret and birth the babe. I am certain Ata would be more than willing to accompany you and protect you and the child. She is uniquely qualified for such a mission, I would say, with her healing and defensive skills... She is also one fewer person that would need to be included in the scheme.

"Following this, you would have two paths open to you, each with its negatives. The first: you and Ata return to court, to the centre of our conflict, the child remaining with a protector—one I will arrange and has unimpeachable loyalties to the Pandial crown." At this point, Min had started shaking her head, but Lord Danai continued.

"The second option is that you remain with your child and raise it in isolation. But before you choose this option, consider! You will not be able to remain in contact with *anyone* from this world until your child has reached its majority and can safely return..." A pause followed his dire warning.

"I would be willing—happy, in fact—to take the second option you mention. But why can't I communicate with my father, or with Ata? With *Kai*? That's impossible! We're a family and *they* are definitely not spies. That much I know." Now it was Lord Danai who shook his head emphatically.

"Think, Your Highness. A betrayal is not necessarily a purposeful act; it can be an unconscious disclosure, a message that goes astray and is seen by the wrong person. There is plenty of historic precedent showing that keeping a high-priority secret is impossible if too many people, no matter how loving or loyal, are privy to it.

"Let me ask you this: if one hypothetical scenario meant complete and utter certainty of your child's safety, and the other scenario, more comfortable to your preferences, allows, with the narrowest of margins, a chance your offspring might be harmed—which would you choose?

Min had begun to cry again, but this time they were silent tears that streamed down her face. Shudderingly, she replied.

"I wouldn't risk my child's life in any way, not even by the 'narrowest of margins'."

"That is what I suspected... And so, your two choices are clearly outlined: you either surrender the raising of your child to a third party until it reaches its majority and returns to court and to you; *or*, you remain and raise your babe, but then you must completely cut ties with everything and everyone from your current life. Without exception. These are your two choices."

"Could I have some time to decide?" Min murmured, taking a deep, convulsive breath.

"You cannot delay this decision, for I need to make the arrangements pursuant to your choice. I would need your answer within a week, Your Highness. Two weeks at the most. And, naturally, your commitment to not spreading the news of your pregnancy or this plan beyond the three of us... Not even to your ever-loyal nursemaid, Dreka, though she knows of your condition, I take it. But regarding the plan for the birth and the child's future: *not a word*." Lord Danai's manner became even more remote and foreboding.

"I would never endanger the life of my unborn child... and I trust your intelligence as to the seriousness of the threat to it. I won't say a word," some of Min's strength of purpose shone through. Thus, their audience was over, their futures completely uncertain and dependent on a choice that would be made within the next few days.

That night, Ata lay in deep contemplation of the entire situation they faced. There were quite a few elements that disturbed her about how they were going about things. The main aspect she took issue with was the rank travesty of not informing either her uncle or Kai about the child. She couldn't even confide in Svens, had he been there, for secrecy was of the utmost importance. It was just as well, then, she surmised, that he was absent. Finally, she drifted off only to dream vividly of her mother.

OVER THE NEXT TEN DAYS, a massive offensive from all sides was launched by the Gruxhoon forces. Even Kai's 'undefeatable' company was driven back relentlessly. Cinnae was completely out of reach at this point, the initial plans at the beginning of the war to re-take the territory almost laughable in their current situation with news of immense battles and skirmishes taking place from the north all the way to the south, and also from the west.

The forces of darkness were pushing them inward, and it was clear that a major battle was on the horizon. In between collating all the information pouring in from across the continent in drips and drabs, Ata began to panic over Min's final decision. Under these circumstances, their disappearance and plan seemed ludicrous. They might be alive in two weeks to make the journey, but how were they to travel in such dangerous surroundings?

Her answer was provided in thunderous tones by

Lord Danai when she had the temerity to voice her doubts one evening.

"This 'scheme' you refer to as though it were some side project is the *only* path to our *only* salvation! This child will save our entire nation, and whether we will be here to witness it is immaterial—the child must be protected at all costs. But I say this to you today, Ata, and do not forget it: though things seem dire, any light, no matter how small, can diminish and thus dispel the deepest darkness. Do not be distracted by the chaos that currently surrounds us, block out the buzz of a thousand voices and needs, and focus only on your role in the most important act that will result in our eventual victory. No other battle plans, no other commitments matter now besides this one. Do you understand me?" She had nodded, wide-eyed in the face of his atypical anger.

Finally, Min communicated her choice. Ata was not surprised; her cousin had chosen to eschew her current life so she could raise her child in secret, protected from all potential harm for the foreseeable future.

"I'll miss you, Ata," Min had whispered when they ate a quiet dinner together in her rooms. Rationing meant the meals were unvaried and sparse, however, they still made the most of the sustenance.

"I know, Min. But I'll wait for you here, ready to welcome you and your son or daughter back when the time is right," Ata smiled sadly.

"You *will* be there for the birth, though, before you leave me and come back here... So at least my baby will be known to one of their family members besides their mother," her cousin said with forced cheerfulness, clearly trying to raise her own spirits.

The dire situation surrounding them as well as the imminent battle in the hazily obscure near-future hampered their planning. Lord Danai had at least arranged a little cottage that was far-removed from the fighting and armies, however, the fact it was remote meant a significant distance had to be crossed to reach it. He had decided the small estate King Addai had gifted to Ata and Svens for their wedding was the perfect place to 'hide in plain sight' as he put it. It was on the northern border of Pandi, but also at the foot of the Uurgonna Mountains in the north-east between the Smul River and Smelln Tower, so the Gruxhoon would hopefully continue to avoid it as they had done thus far.

Just when Min and Ata were about to sneak away on some concocted mission for which Lord Danai would provide cover for them, the collective Áitarbithian Alliance armies as well as the Gruxhoon descended upon them, congregating on a large open stretch of land nearby in their thousands.

Massive clashes and offensives were launched, with the Gruxhoon clearly trying to break through to Enddaian Keep to besiege it. Consequently, Ata and Min were stuck, for no clandestine mission could justify their leaving the keep at this fraught time. Even the king would notice, though his attention was wholly focused on holding the tenuous line drawn around his shrunken territory, increasing the immense strain he was under daily. If the line broke, they would be overrun, and all would be lost.

"What should we do? My time is about four weeks away, but anything can happen in the meantime! We need to leave before we're completely caged in from the east as well," Min desperately whispered to Ata when she came to the princess's rooms to inform her they needed to wait some more.

Their bags had been packed for days and they had been on tenterhooks, waiting for the right moment to sneak from the keep. Min was becoming more and more frazzled by the day, which in turn was not good for the baby. Worse: Lord Danai had been dispatched to the battlefield to assist their command there and could not advise them. He had imparted all the relevant information to them so they could reach the safehouse he'd arranged. All that was left—completely up to them, it seemed—was to find the right moment to depart. An impossibility at this point.

"Let me think; I'll come up with something, I swear," Ata promised before hastening off to meet with the last of the Cinnaen council for some final arrangements. A massive battle was expected on the following day, which Ata had begun to think of as the ideal opportunity to run east and then north after a few days. The battlefield was to the west of the keep and almost every able-bodied fighter would be there.

She decided that she and Min could dress in their battle leathers with their bags, pretend to be going to the battle, and then sneak off when no-one was paying attention. That still left the 'minor' problem of search parties and questions afterwards, for if the battle went well and their people regrouped as Ata truly believed they would, then they would very quickly notice the absence of their princess and the wife of a general. She would need to think of a way to divert the attention from their non-appearance subsequent to the battle...

After the meeting, which was essentially just many practicalities including the act of hiding the few remaining non-combatant women, children, elderly, and infirm, Ata made a last-minute decision and sought out King Addai before he departed for the battlefield.

It was still early evening, but a storm had been raging for two days, darkening the sky prematurely—horrible conditions for a battle and for travel, but unavoidable. She found him in his private study hastily packing some scrolls and maps, assisted by a clerk who, upon seeing her entrance, made himself scarce.

"Ata!" he was clearly surprised and shaken enough at her presence to fall to such an informal mode of address.

"I need to speak with you about something very urgent—"

"Can it not wait till later? I don't know if you noticed, but there's a battle raging just outside this castle..." his dry tone was dismissive, his face drawn and his skin displaying an almost greyish tinge. His hair had greyed significantly at his temples and he had also lost a notable amount of weight. Clearly, their current precarious state was affecting his health. Even this bastion of dependability seemed to be hanging on by a thread, causing Ata a momentary pang of guilt for heaping more worries on his shoulders.

"It really cannot wait, Your Majesty. Believe me, I would not bother you now if it could," he gestured impatiently for her to speak as he kept searching for something in the drawers of his desk.

She was about to break her tacit agreement with both Lord Danai and Min, but it was a necessary evil. One she secretly felt was only right. Despite the king's long-held resentments over her own conception and birth, she was certain his coolheaded logic and stoic dependability would win the day. Taking a deep breath, she plunged in, for there was no time to be wasted.

"Min is pregnant and needs to be taken somewhere safe to give birth. I cannot tell you all the details now, for as you rightly say, our kingdom is in a dire position that requires your full attention. What we need from you is a guarantee that we won't be followed or searched for after the battle, once our absence is noted."

Ata quaked at speaking so authoritatively to a man who had always intimidated her and whom she had looked up to as her only parental figure throughout her life. He had frozen at her words, face completely unmoving.

"My daughter is pregnant?" the king's voice was quiet but the tone terrible. Ata began to suspect she had made a mistake. "Pray, who is the father?" His sharp dark eyes pierced Ata. She could not lie or pretend ignorance; she had always been honest with her uncle. *Except about Min's and Kai's relationship.*

"Lieutenant Kaimam," at his incredulous look, she rushed to explain: "They have been romantically involved for years..." again, she realised her mistake too late.

"And you knew about this relationship? For all this time? I thought you and the silversmith's son were sweethearts—" at her guilty grimace, understanding dawned. "Ah! I see... You *covered* for them; pretended to be his lover, when in fact, it was my daughter. How fiendishly clever of you three," but it was definitely not meant as a compliment. Ata now *knew* she had made a grave error in speaking with the king. She put up her hands in a placating gesture and tried to salvage the situation.

"I am sorry for the deception, but that's not what is most relevant now. What's pertinent is—"

"I should have *known*... I should have listened to my councillors when they advised me to rid my house of your presence after my sister's death. But did I listen? No, I didn't," his eyes were like onyx blades, his features sharp and raptorlike. He had clearly closed his ears to all reasoning. Ata tried to block out the words that were gouging her heart, but they kept falling like axes. "And now you have proven what they had tried to show me even then: that you would be a snake in our bosom. That you would betray me and mine. Why not? Your very existence was a betrayal by my sister."

"Please, Uncle—"

"I will not listen to your poisonous words, Woman! Like mother, like daughter. Although, you must be commended for surpassing even my devious sister in the scale of your deceit and the destruction you have wrought upon my trust!" Ata felt the blood drain from her face as his words landed like blows.

"I'm sorry, I know this was a shock, just please listen —" but he had turned dismissively from her, ignoring her words as he continued.

"You may tell my faithless, stupid daughter that she will be going nowhere to try and escape the shame she has brought on us in this time of trials. You and she will remain here, and she will bear the lieutenant's get. She will face the consequences of her actions. Our family is used to raising bastards, after all," he finished cruelly.

Then he shouted for his clerk who eventually returned, grabbed the bags of papers and touted them out the door. The king turned to her, his cold fury battering at her as though it were a physical thing.

"I do not want to see you, Ata Denada. Not tomorrow, nor the day after. You will not come before me, nor will you be welcome anywhere within my sight until I tell you otherwise. In fact, though I won't enshrine it in law, you are banished from my presence for good. Do not test me on this." Then he stalked out, slamming the door behind him.

Ata was in shock. She had not moved an inch from where she had stood when her uncle—no, *the king*—had unleashed his vitriol upon her. Feeling as though she had been beaten black and blue, her mind couldn't seem to engage with what had just been said.

When she finally managed to slot the words and their meanings into her frame of reference, she carefully locked down her emotional response to what had just occurred. *That* could be dealt with at a later date. For now, she needed to be logical, she needed to be strong, and she needed a plan. For Min's sake, and for the sake of the baby's prophesied future. She also swore to herself then and there that she wouldn't breathe a word to Min about King Addai's hateful words; Ata would find a way, after her return, to fix this so Min would be received with open arms and no ill-feeling upon her eventual homecoming.

Luckily, Lord Danai had unquestionably trained her to be devious (whether the king appreciated it or not, she thought wryly) and an idea had already taken root on how they could escape without eliciting pursuit afterwards.

Her discussion with King Addai had had the exact opposite result to what she expected, adding another layer of complexity. They could not merely disappear for any 'run of the mill' reason—it needed to be fool proof to deceive the king too, or he would undoubtedly hunt them down. Her plan, should it succeed, would be quite cruel to their loved ones, but unfortunately that was unavoidable under the circumstances. All considered, the ends justified the means; at least Ata would eventually return and correct the misunderstanding in her case.

She went to the house of Verana, the ancient local midwife in Enddaian Town. Having known the woman all her life and through her dealings with Lord Danai, in his capacity as spymaster, she would be able to utilise the midwife's assistance to attain what she needed for her planned deception. When she finally returned a few hours later, it was well past midnight and the storm still raged on. What she did *not* expect was for there to be a light burning in her rooms. Immediately on guard, she drew her knife from its scabbard, only to be met with the most welcome of sights.

"Svens!" he grabbed her, disregarding the blade which she quickly dropped, then clung to him as he kissed her enthusiastically. "What are you doing here?" she enquired breathlessly when he finally gave her some space. He wasn't paying particular attention to what she was saying, starting to pull his boots off as he tried to keep kissing her.

"We were told to get a good night's sleep; I was told —nay, *instructed*—by Lord Bransso to come and kiss my pretty wife, because it might be a last goodbye. But I plan on doing a whole lot more than kissing... If it's goodbye, then we should make it count, eh?"

It was so odd to see her usually prim and proper husband so effusive and playful. But then, every moment they'd been able to spend together since that fateful night where they had fully committed to their marriage had been filled with stolen hours of joy.

Even though the world was crashing down around them, and in spite of their complete immersion in and dedication to the cause, they had found love and respect together. Despite doing nothing worthwhile or deserving, to her mind, Ata had managed to marry a man who was stoically kind, awkwardly gentle, and unabashedly loving—to say nothing of his loyalty and strength of purpose. Even his humour appealed to her, dry and subtle as it was.

She'd never been happier within herself, but sadly his words were true: they might not have much time left together. No guarantee existed beyond that moment.

Smiling brightly into his now-beloved face, with its shaggy, pale golden beard and white-blond hair, her eyes traced his scar that had become, if not imperceptible, then a part of him to such an extent that she no longer noticed it as a separate aspect of his face. His pale blue eyes were warm, despite her always thinking them so cold when they had first met, and they seemed to be eagerly cataloguing her every feature too. So they stood, breathing in each other's breath and staring besottedly into each other's eyes.

"If we want to do more than kissing, then I suppose we need to at least move, no?" Ata finally teased, grabbing her shirt and pulling it over her head. Svens displayed an extreme level of enthusiasm and efficacy in undressing, then "gallantly" assisted her to do the same.

Some time later, with the storm finally subsiding to a light patter, Ata lay next to Svens while he played idly with her Enstroi chain. Its slight movements around her waist tickled, and she snickered as she slapped at his hand.

"If you are so fascinated with it, get your own!" she griped, but he caught her flapping hand and held on, tangling his fingers with hers.

"I'm only fascinated with *your* Enstroi chain, Ata. Only yours. I don't want my own because I'd rather be most of the charms yours," and he kissed her fingers gently.

"When are you going to tell me what all these charms represent?" he asked, "I don't see why my siblings get all those stories and I don't..." he hedged playfully. Ata rolled her eyes.

"You got the scar anecdote series and will just have to wait for my Enstroi stories. They say patience is a virtue..." she smirked, and he snorted in disbelief.

"This coming from you, the least patient person I know?" she gasped in mock outrage and sat up.

"I take issue with that statement, General. There is no way in the hells that I am more impatient than your friend, Captain Blÿnsso!"

Svens gave her a pained look: "Can we not talk about my friends at this moment?" and looked meaningfully at her uncovered torso. She snickered and lay back down, at which point Svens hugged her closer to him and sighed contentedly.

"Fine, I admit you're not the *most* impatient person I know, but nor are you particularly patient. Definitely the most stubborn, though."

"I prefer 'unwaveringly committed'," she teased, but was surprised by his suddenly serious response.

"Yes. It's one of the many things I admire about you."

Ata's heart did a strange, off-kilter gallop that ached, her throat feeling as though it were completely obstructed. She needed to tell him... he needed to know.

But the last time she trusted someone enough to entrust them with this huge secret, it had backfired badly. She opened her mouth, but changed her mind at the last minute—substituting another as-yet-unshared truth in its stead.

"I love you, Svens. So much," when he squeezed her fingers again, she added, "Every part of my life belongs to you. My Enstroi chain and all its charms. They're only yours."

"I love you too, Ata," he responded, kissing her ardently. Ata took issue, naturally.

"Why is it that *I'm* always the one to tell you I love you first?" she griped, trying to pull away from his questing hands and mouth. He was having none of it.

"Next time, I promise I'll say it first," he murmured, snagging her and dragging her to him.

When a knock at the door woke them some time later, Svens hurriedly dressed and told Ata to rest a bit more before coming to the battlefield with the last recruits still staying in the town.

"Sleep for a short while longer. I have a debriefing and some tasks that can't wait," he whispered as he leant over her, saying goodbye. Abruptly making one of the ugliest, most comical faces she could, she had the pleasure of seeing him pull back suddenly in complete shock, followed almost immediately by spontaneous laughter. He drew her to him and hugged her tightly.

"We'll see each other again soon, Wife," he

promised, all lightness and mirth gone from his manner, then kissed her goodbye.

Once he'd left, Ata rushed to dress in her battle leathers, strapped on her various blades, and grabbed her bow and arrows. She hurried to Min's rooms, finding her dressed and ready to leave, though looking quite pale and fragile. Dreka, for as anciently frail as she was, was in a huff.

"It is not seemly that Her Highness go to the battle-field in *her condition*," she said, clearly aware that Ata knew too.

"I am her bodyguard, Mistress Dreka. She will not be participating in the battle, but the king has insisted she be present to support the people," Ata lied smoothly. The old woman grumbled some more, but allowed them to depart. Min managed to keep her farewell to her nursemaid light, as though she expected to see her again soon. She had always been a master prevaricator, Ata thought.

Then, they walked through the corridors of their lifelong home for what would be the last time for the foreseeable future, and made their way to the midwife's house in town.

24

TO BREAK A SPELL

Let me not to the marriage of true
minds
Admit impediments. Love is not love
Which alters when it alteration
finds,
Or bends with the remover to remove.
O no! it is an ever-fixed mark
That looks on tempests and is never
shaken;
It is the star to every wand'ring bark,
Whose worth's unknown, although his
height be taken.
Love's not Time's fool, though rosy
lips and cheeks
Within his bending sickle's compass
come;

LOVE ALTERS NOT WITH HIS BRIEF HOURS
AND WEEKS,
BUT BEARS IT OUT EVEN TO THE EDGE OF
DOOM.
IF THIS BE ERROR AND UPON ME PROV'D,
I NEVER WRIT, NOR NO MAN EVER LOV'D.

WILLIAM SHAKESPEARE

The endless rain had caused the ground to become waterlogged, the battlefield comparable to a bog due to the knee-deep mud everywhere. The same could be said of the army encampments—little tents perched precariously on the sludge, stretching as far as the eye could see.

Approximately twenty-thousand troops stood in defence of the last true bastion of Áitarbith, Enddaian Keep and environs, in resistance to the Gruxhoon. Casually rubbing the charm on his Enstroi chain, Kai looked at the sky calculatingly and tried to gauge from its pale monochrome shades whether more rain was to be expected on this day. The day that, potentially, could mean the fall of humanity in Áitarbith.

He'd spent the night preparing for his and his troops' functions in the battle, having been promoted to the rank of captain a few weeks prior. His two hundred soldiers had received instructions to encircle an extended outer perimeter of the field, employing the guerrilla tactics they had perfected over the past six months of intense fighting on the border.

In this way, they would harry the Gruxhoon at the back of their massive formation, as well as stop similar attempts from Gruxhoon guerrilla bands. It was dangerous—deadly dangerous—but then so was every fighting role on this day, whether on the actual battlefield or in smaller missions on the periphery. All risked their lives today. With the very real threat of not seeing the next day, Kai had been thinking constantly of Min.

Their contact had been sporadic at best over the past half-year, their only means of communication the heavily encoded phrases sent between Abled communication officers at the front and the Abled within the military council in Enddaian Keep. A letter passed on by friends here and there? They were like crumbs to the starving, but somehow sustained him. Despite their separation and their inability to speak, Kai knew she remained as steadfast as ever.

She was, without a doubt, the greatest grounding force in his life; a safe harbour to return to. For that very reason he had made her Enstroi charm on his chain a lode stone roughly in the shape of an anchor.

Despite their disparate statuses, he'd begun to consider their ill-conceived love as less hopeless than before. Their world and its structures were collapsing around them in the face of this monumental aggression, and despite his mourning the unimaginable harm it had caused, he could not but be hopeful that their relationship would be viewed more favourably in the new world that was on Áitarbith's horizon—the new world that would inevitably be born from the ashes of the old one. If they survived and made it so.

Though he'd been within sight of the castle for the past few days, he had been unable to leave the army because of his constant involvement in skirmishes. Per fluke, he saw his father at the encampment, assisting several other smiths in arming soldiers. It had been a good reunion, if brief; since Kai's mother's death a decade before, he and his father had developed an understanding and camaraderie seated in brevity. It worked well for them, and Kai had appreciated the chance to speak with him at this juncture.

Unfortunately, he hadn't had the opportunity to speak with Min the night before, when the ever-proper General Svensso had managed to slip away to see Ata. Though he envied the man, he didn't begrudge Svensso and his lifelong best friend their time together—perhaps their last time together. They all needed to take what moments they could while they were able.

The next best thing he had done through the long vigil he kept that night was to write Min a letter. Having suppressed his natural tendency to make a joke of everything, he had penned an ode to her and their love. It was probably just as well he had avoided his easy-going humour in the missive, for he found that his jovial persona sat uncomfortably upon his shoulders in recent months. Like a skin that no longer fit and was being shed in painful shreds, though he didn't dwell on it overmuch and tended to focus on the job at hand, or Min.

His letter to her in no way managed to convey the fulness of his regard, but it was better than nothing, he reasoned. How he would get it to her was still uncertain, but he would try to grab one of the ubiquitous message runners soon, if he could.

'My Beloved,

I am not a poet, nor am I a serious man. In fact, I often use humour to relate to people and situations. You know this and have known this all our lives, yet you never dismissed me as a buffoon. You are the resolute and well-read one, the stable heart in our relationship, the believer in the gods. The voice of reason. I have not heard your voice in longer than I care to think, but its steady and even tone are always present in my mind—when I sleep and throughout my every waking moment. For those are the times when I think of you.

I remember the first time I ever met you; we were just children, and you were a quiet, serious little thing with big eyes in a small face. Eyes that judged my clownish behaviour and a mouth that never once smiled at my outlandishly stupid japes. Yet I knew from that very moment that, as different as we were, you and I would always be the best of friends. I did not know then that you would come to mean everything to me, that you would come to be my entire reason for being.

Did I ever tell you these things in the early, infatuated days when my teenage self thought he would die for love (and lust) of you? Did I tell you these things when I said 'goodbye' to you for the last time those many months ago, marching off to war, but not glory? If I did not tell you these vitally essential things, then I do so now: I love you more than my own life; you are the best part of me. I long to see and hold you again, in this life or the next, and I would wait for you always.'

Kai left his company at the furthest exit of the camp, to the north-east. They were finalising preparations for their part in the day's fighting, prepping the last of their gear and saying goodbye to their loved ones, for there were those whose family members were also in the camp. Kai's duty meant he had to attend one final meeting at the command tent. Upon reaching it, he bumped into the very Cinnaen general whom he had envied.

"General Svensso," Kai thumped his chest, the other man nodding in greeting.

"Captain Kaimam," his usual non-expression gave away none of his thoughts. "Are you ready for your mission today?" They entered the tent together.

"Yes, General. Ready as we'll ever be for our jaunt in the woods. We all like a good hike, eh," though he tried for light-hearted, the less said, the better. Talking too much about feelings with your fellow soldiers prior to military action could have the opposite effect of bolstering courage. He did need to ask, nonetheless.

"How did you find them up at the keep? Running around like headless chickens?" Of course he wanted to know about Ata, but he was hoping more for some reference to Min. Though the general looked somewhat suspicious at his line of questioning, he readily answered.

"All was well. The few remaining people seemed to have plenty to do, though there was a definite spirit of anxiety that pervaded the place. Lady Ata will be joining the healers in the medic units in a short while. Pray to the gods their energy lasts throughout the battle."

Kai nodded in wholehearted agreement while trying to think of a way to ask after Min without tipping the general off. At that moment, the meeting began, almost all the commanders being present. Generals Bransso and Erdai took the lead, the Pandial king respectfully standing by and giving them his fullest attention. The toll of this war was written harshly across the man's entire appearance, especially obvious to Kai, who hadn't seen him in months. *Min must be so worried about her father looking so worn out.*

The Cinnaen crown prince was also present, along with Lord Haaviso, who had joined this battle just like almost every other able-bodied person had. All their faces were grave as they discussed what could be, potentially, the final battle in the war for Áitarbith.

"Where is Her Highness, Princess Mindaia?" Kai murmured insouciantly to Ata's husband. "One would think she'd be here, sending the troops off to their glorious demise." He found, these days, every time he tried for 'comical' or to poke fun, he ended up making bitter pronouncements with a sarcastic edge.

"I don't know... She's been absent from quite a few official meetings over the past months. I only know because Ata mentioned having to stand in for her on multiple occasions," Kai had to repress an immediate need to insist on more information. *Was Min ill? For months?* He prayed that subtlety would win the day and merely pulled a puzzled face. The Cinnaen general took the bait.

"Ata appeared completely fine with acting as her proxy and didn't seem particularly worried about the princess, so I must assume it's just due to practical considerations and nothing serious or problematic."

Kai immediately felt his tension ebb with these assurances. He suspected that if Min were to come to the battlefield, she would be kept well back from the fighting; though she had done the requisite basic military training required of all Pandial in their youth, she hadn't excelled as he and Ata had. As the Pandial heir, she would be kept safe, he had no doubt. A boon, really. He was even relieved Ata wouldn't be directly involved in the fighting, although the medic units would still be in active combat areas.

He mentally shook himself, then rubbed the talisman on his Enstroi chain once more. He needed to focus on the task at hand, on his mission. Everything else was superfluous to his survival on this particular day. *Ground your emotions*. He always heard good, solid advice within his mind in Min's voice. The voice of reason in all things.

"... courage today, soldiers. May the gods grant us victory this day!" Lord Bransso finished. General Erdai never bothered with any flowery pronouncements and did not do so now. He was more of a 'doer' than a 'talker'. They all swiftly dispersed. When Kai and Svensso parted ways outside the tent, Kai was surprised the general offered his hand. He clasped the man's arm as he had been taught by Ata so many months ago on the training fields.

"May you be successful today, Captain. I hope to see you on the other side," the Cinnaen said stiffly, but Kai could see through to his decency, considering he thought Kai and his wife had been lovers before and still acted honourably. Kai suppressed the usual feeling of guilt bubbling up at the deception. He wouldn't be so sanguine with any of Min's ex-lovers, if she'd had any.

"And you, General. Ata will be absolutely impossible to live with if you go and get yourself killed," he poked at the man, though it was only met by a wry smile. Then they went their separate ways.

'YOU HAVE TAUGHT *me so much over the years, my love. Patience, kindness, fortitude. The magic you have wrought is incalculable, the spell you have cast over me ineffable. Though my parents were good people, I lay my moral upbringing completely at your feet, where I would also gladly lie given half the chance. At, by, under; it matters not, as long as I am near you.*

Though we are separated by all that matters in this world—blood, rank, virtue—and were never meant for each other, I cannot come to regret our years together, for the lightness and goodness you have shown me have shaped me into a person I am proud to be. Should you be taken from me, though my heart would break and my soul cry out in anguish, I could never be made to regret us. In life, in death, you would always be a part of me and never regretted.'

"Put that damn thing out of its misery before we have another band of them upon us!" Kai snapped at two soldiers from his company who stood over the body of a mortally wounded Gruxhoon whose keening was building in volume. Both of the soldiers were young and relatively inexperienced, eyeing the bloody mass that twitched at their feet with equal parts fear and revulsion.

Kai swore colourfully and stalked over to them, heaved his battle-axe high and brought it down with a sickening crunch on what was left of the creature's neck. The sounds immediately cut off and the quaking stopped.

"When I give you an order, you *immediately* carry it out! Am I understood?" he hissed, trying to keep the volume down but still maintain the fierceness such instructions required. They thumped their chests immediately, the girl's wounded arm jostling and making her groan.

"My orders are there for a reason. Though these creatures have no compassion for us, *we* are human and humane, and will not leave them to suffer before they die. But most importantly: we do not want their FUCKING compatriots to be drawn to us by the sounds of their pain! Do you understand me?" At this point, the entire squad closest to him was listening and responded by saluting. Good.

"Now, as you were briefed: put all Gruxhoon bodies together. If there are any human fatalities, whether soldiers or civilians, make sure to place them together and note their position on our maps. When the fighting is over, we can direct others to retrieve their corpses for proper identification and burial." Honestly, his promotion was an honour, but having to take charge of such a large number of green recruits was a hassle.

His own, battle-hardened squads had had to be

redistributed amongst a majority of teenagers with no battle experience, which meant a lot of 'babysitting' despite the intense skirmishes they were involved in. He watched as a young boy vomited forcefully behind a tree. The loss of their innocence was tragic, but just as with everyone else: anything and everything could be required as a sacrifice on the altar of survival. Innocence, integrity, and humanity, though he tried not to think too much on that. He reverently touched his Enstroi talisman again.

"Let's move out!" he instructed once the two groups of dead had been arranged; the human bodies were significantly fewer than the Gruxhoon, with only one soldier among them. So they continued from tree to tree, clearing to clearing, and overtook bands of raiding Gruxhoon. At one point, Kai and his second-in-command, Lieutenant Brezder, decided to split their forces into two main groups with Kai's doubling back in the direction of the keep while Brez would continue in the initially planned 'surrounding move' to come up behind the Gruxhoon forces on the battlefield.

"We'll come back and follow your trail once we've cleared the Gruxhoon bands towards the north and east for a few miles," Kai explained to Ata's former battle buddy. He and Brez got along like a house on fire, and the latter's service in Kai's company on the northern border had been exemplary. He was good people; a solid man to have at your side or at your back.

"Aye, Captain. We'll see you in a few, then," thumping his chest in farewell, he added: "Try to keep most of these little fuckers alive, yeah!" He grinned and hustled out of there with his troops. Kai and the remainder of his company, most of whom were young-sters barely into puberty, made their way to the more open areas north-east of Enddaian Keep—farmland. Within a few hours, amidst the loud sounds of fighting that floated to their ears from the battlefield a few miles away, they had already routed two large bands of Gruxhoon.

With over a hundred Gruxhoon already killed that day from what Kai had been counting, it seemed that there were shockingly large numbers still randomly roaming the area. This was worrying; they had inter-rupted one of the bands as they were terrorising the few remaining farming communities whose inhabitants hadn't fled to the mountains. The fifteen-odd Gruxhoon had tallied up a shocking fifty kills, the butcher's bill including women and children. As Kai helped place the bodies together and respectfully covered them with whatever cloth was handy, he noticed many of his soldiers crying in earnest as they continued to work.

"I know this is difficult and you feel as though things cannot get worse," he said loudly to the group as they continued to work. "But if we don't do it, who will? If we don't remain strong, don't do this soul-destroying, heart wrenching work, *who will*?" they listened in silence. He noticed a few shoulders more squared, a few backs straighter and heads higher.

"We're not here for glory or for fame. We are here to do *one thing only*. To serve. We have to serve in every sense, now. We serve when we fight, we serve when we build, and we serve when we give the dead some small measure of dignity, even at the cost of our own comfort and mental well-being. It's not pretty, but it needs to be done."

Though he knew the truth of it himself, he also felt the hollowing-out of his soul with every corpse he carried, with every empty gaze he met, with every ending he faced. Hopefully they would have souls left after their service.

"Let's move out!" he repeated. Again, and again. It was already after dark and they had come across the remains of another village left thus by the Gruxhoon they'd killed earlier. More bodies. And then the *treiks* echoed all the way from the battlefield, many miles away, the rhythm and notes familiarly welcome. *Victory!* The battle had been won! All the soldiers, despite their grisly surroundings and audience, cried out in relief and joy, some hugging each other and laughing hysterically.

"Alright!" Kai shouted, halting their effusive celebrations. "We're all grateful for this great victory for Áitarbith, but look around you. These people have not won. They do not share in our victory. The best that can be said for them is that they are free from the pain that was inflicted on them before their passing." The silence was deafening. "Continue with your task; we will set up camp and begin to bury these locals. Also, remember: the Gruxhoon who survived the battle will have fled in all directions, including *ours*. Sentries—be vigilant. Wounded creatures are the most dangerous."

After that, Kai felt more relaxed, although they were still technically on high alert and in territory the enemy roamed freely. They set up a command centre in one of the small cottages with Kai assigning one of their elderly combatants, a fifty-two-year-old lawyer from Enddaian Town, to oversee the documentation of the bodies and where they were buried.

They didn't have access to any registers of the village's inhabitants but would somehow use the physical descriptions and Enstroi chains (where present) as means of identification, then try to go from there once things had settled enough for the administrators to get involved.

Kai was not a bureaucrat, but he deduced the scale and chaos of death during this war would cause years of administrative bedlam afterward. He also sent a messenger to try and find Brez so he could check in with their progress and then decide how to proceed over the next few days. Once a sentry rota was cobbled together, Kai sat down for the first time that day.

Staring into the distance, he idly fiddled with his Enstroi chain that he usually wore wound around his forearm. He studied the charm he was forever touching, its originally jagged edges worn smooth from years of religious rubbing. An anchor. He held it, as he always did before sleep, and proceeded to catch one of his 'naps' with his eyes half-open.

'I THINK *about our future a lot these days; a lot more than I used to, for before it seemed an impossibility to even imagine one together. Now, as much as I dwell on our childhood and teenage friendship, our adolescent love affair, and our years of secret assignations, I also anticipate a future with you. A future with an engagement, a wedding, a marriage. A future with <u>many</u> children, for we have both lamented being only children. A future of growing old and annoyed with each other, surrounded by our progeny.*

Though I do not know if I will be here from one day to the next, this envisioned future remains in my mind, clear as day. For irrespective whether we <u>actually</u> live it, the mere dream of it has sustained me through the worst of what this life has to offer. My eyes had seen things none should see, my hands have done things none should do, and the only thing that has helped me retain my sanity has been the promise of that future with you.'

"Captain! Captain!" he had still been sitting upright in sleep, arms crossed, but his eyes sprang open and he jumped up at the shout. A Cinnaen girl, probably about sixteen or seventeen, stood wide-eyed in front of him, clearly shocked by his speedy response. At his frown, she quickly thumped her chest.

"What is it?" he urged, his initial panic that they were being attacked somewhat mitigated by the fact she was not hysterical, but rather uncertain.

"We found two more bodies and—"

"So, record their features and give them a proper burial beside the other villagers," he enunciated, rubbing his eyes in frustration.

"But they're not villagers... At least, we don't *think* they are," she rushed on, blushing at his pointed stare. *Great.* Another girl with a crush. He was getting sick and tired of the adoring looks—clearly he needed to make them clean the privy more often.

"Who's 'we'?" if it was just her and a little friend playing at detective, he would lose his calm completely. Though he'd always enjoyed a joke and banter with youths, he found herding them through a war less amusing; babysitting a company of teenagers whilst trying to keep them alive in an active war zone had wiped most of the laughter from his day-to-day life. Not that there wasn't plenty to provide amusement in their ineptitude and petty squabbles, but after a while their minder no longer found it fun; *nothing* knocked the humour out of you like burying their not-yet-fully-grown corpses when you failed them as a commander.

"Master Fridner," the girl replied promptly, naming

the lawyer he had left in charge. This put her estimation in a completely different light, for he had faith in the older man's judgment, and if he thought these bodies were not local then Kai trusted the assessment. He absent-mindedly rubbed the now-smooth charm where it dangled from his arm.

"What leads you to say they're not villagers?" he asked as they made the short walk to the barn that had been designated an interim morgue. As far as they'd been able to ascertain, no-one from the village had survived the scourge of the Gruxhoon band.

"We found them quite far away from the village, in the forest proper, and—"

"What were you doing that far out?" he asked sharply.

"Patrolling," she answered hastily, but her heated blush implied she and whoever else was out there were up to no good. He'd deal with that later. Unsanctioned walkabouts were a good way to get yourself killed.

"And what else, besides the isolation of the place the bodies were found?"

"They're dressed well—expensively compared to the villagers' homespun. Velvets on the one woman, full military leathers on the other. It looks like a high-born lady and her bodyguard, although, identifying them will be tricky..." for some reason, the description of the two bodies caused a feeling of anxiety in Kai's belly, and he walked faster.

"Why would it be tricky?" he asked intently. The girl looked slightly ill as she answered.

"Because most of their faces... their *heads*, really, are missing. A few limbs as well. Their bellies also seem to have been... eaten." The Cinnaen teenager hurriedly put her hand over her mouth and closed her eyes tightly. "Sorry," she mumbled. "I feel sick just thinking about it. I don't think I can go in there with you."

They had just reached the barn, the girl resolutely taking up a position at the entrance. Kai didn't insist she go in with him. Inside, the long-suffering Master Fridner sat on a high stool with a ledger and quill, scratching away in the dim light of two small candles while the dead were all spread out on the floor like some macabre installation, all in rows and columns.

"Ah! Captain. Young Edna found you, I see. Good!" the neat little man scurried along to the furthest wall of the barn carrying one of the candles and carefully avoiding stepping on any of the corpses. Though Kai wasn't particularly superstitious, the darkness and passive presence of so many dead ordered so specifically caused a chill to run down his spine. The combination of such clinical organisation with such brutally barbaric deaths, although helpful to them at that moment, was completely jarring.

"These are the two bodies, both female. The one wore a golden Enstroi chain around her neck, but I didn't see one on the bodyguard's body..." Kai slowly picked his way to where the little lawyer hunched over. "The woman wearing the chain is definitely an aristocrat, I would say. Her clothes are heavy, brocade velvets, and the fact she wore a golden chain with almost all golden charms also supports my theory. Plus: the other woman was clearly a warrior and her bodyguard, wearing leathers as she does, and carrying a bow and arrows. Perhaps they're stragglers, fallen behind from the large group that fled to the mountains?"

The vague feeling in Kai's stomach had increased to become a clawing fear, visceral and overwhelming. *He was imagining it.* He was imagining a catastrophe that was *impossible*. He *must* be imagining it.

Upon finally reaching the corpses in question, he immediately saw what the Cinnaen soldier had said was true: the Gruxhoon had clearly feasted on these corpses, essentially obliterating any identifiable physical features.

It felt as though he were looking through a long, narrow tunnel. He recognised the dress. It was one of Min's favourites. With a whooshing sound pulsing in his ears, he looked toward the other body. *Those leathers!* He knew them too. He didn't even notice that he had dropped to his knees beside them. *No, no, no!*

"Uh, Captain?" the lawyer was an insignificant gnat in the maelstrom of his mind.

"The— the chain. Give it to me," Kai choked out, sure that this unique piece of evidence would disprove his suspicions, would dissipate this nightmare. It *had* to. He felt the cold metal links pressed into his hand and looked down.

For a moment, his mind refused to register what his eyes saw. Refused to acknowledge that it recognised the life chain of his beloved. The chain he had seen on her neck, with the distinctive charms that represented every milestone of her precious life. And there, amongst all the gold and gem-encrusted charms was a single, simple silver charm. A love knot. One he had painstakingly crafted with his own hands for her to represent their relationship. All gone now.

As he struggled to contain the grief that spilled from every crack within him, a further horrifying thought pushed its way through the excruciating agony. Without hesitation, he grasped the bodyguard's torso, scrabbling around in the mess that used to be a stomach.

He didn't even notice the other man's exclamations of horror or his calls for assistance from the guard outside the door. Finally grasping what he was looking for, deeply embedded in the corpse's spine, he snapped the chain as he pulled it close to his face. Again, he was battered by a hammer of pain as he recognised Ata's Enstroi chain, complete with her life's charms. He recognised the half gold coin through the muck and blood that covered it. *His wedding gift to her.*

Here, before him, lay the only two women he loved. Gone forever. He let the dark tide of anguish overwhelm him as he clutched the lifelines of his only love and his best friend. Gone! All gone! The letter burning a hole in his pocket didn't matter. Nothing else mattered, no reality beyond this. He was anchorless. Untethered.

'AND SO, *after waxing poetic (even though I'm a poor poet, as a I mentioned before), I will end this love note to you. I could go on... and on... and on. But the birds are awakening and herald the first light, the camp guards are changing, and the messengers are beginning to enforce the wake-up calls. This day will change everything. For our people, for our continent, but most importantly: for me and you.*

Think on the future I have painted for us—though, again, I am a poor artist—and dream with me. Soon, that future will be within our grasp; all we must do is prevail as we have done until now. With my stubbornness, my service, and my commitment to you, and your strength, your fortitude, and your indomitable spirit, nothing but death will part us. Even if that be the case: what is death but a short stay until we are reunited with our loved ones? I will wait, in perpetuity if need be, for our future together.

Yours forever,

Kai'

25

BIRTH AND REBIRTH

If I should die,
And you should live,
And time should gurgle on,
And morn should beam,
And noon should burn,
As it has usual done;
If birds should build as early,
And bees as bustling go,—
One might depart at option
From enterprise below!
'T is sweet to know that stocks will
    stand
When we with daisies lie,
That commerce will continue,
And trades as briskly fly.
It makes the parting tranquil

AND KEEPS THE SOUL SERENE,
THAT GENTLEMEN SO SPRIGHTLY
CONDUCT THE PLEASING SCENE!

EMILY DICKINSON

For all intents and purposes, Min was dead. It was difficult to contemplate such a thing, especially considering she was feeling distinctly uncomfortable, both physically, and emotionally, the latter regarding her official death and the former because Life abounded within her body. *The baby wouldn't stop kicking.*

Ata, who was as dead as Min, told her to stop over-thinking their current state of being—both dead and alive simultaneously—but she just couldn't. Especially considering the effect their deaths would have on their loved ones.

"Do you think I don't feel bad enough about that, Min? Do you think I enjoy the thought of Svens, and Kai, and Jans, and Els, and Len, and Tens, and Dreka, and Famenke, and Brez, and *everybody else* mourning our deaths? Suffering because of it?" Ata's mood had been distinctly foul over the past two days. The rain had come back with a vengeance, and they were on foot because Ata didn't want to draw attention with horses.

"A donkey might've been nice," Min muttered, only to be met with a stink eye from Ata.

"No four-legged pack animals… Stop listing various beasts of burden besides horses as being viable options!" she snarled. Min had been intermittently, perhaps spitefully, commenting about which animals might have benefited their trek.

She wasn't being purposely bitchy, but her feet were ridiculously swollen and painful. She only felt it fair to regularly remind Ata of her gaffe in planning this 'escape'. In all other aspects, she had delivered a stellar performance: she'd arranged for two corpses similar enough to them and that had, shockingly, been extensively chewed on by Gruxhoon.

Min had been horrified and at least a *bit* sceptical that such perfect substitutes had been found at such short notice, meeting their needs exactly. The midwife who had facilitated the acquisition had then pointed out that there were many such corpses to be found everywhere in Cinnae and Pandial. That had shut Min up good and proper.

"You didn't say my father…" Min pointed out, surprised at Ata's oversight, and even more: impressed with herself for having noted it. Her mind had been very spotty lately, with long periods of forgetfulness and vagueness. Dreka had told her this was normal during pregnancy, but she found it highly frustrating and bothersome. When she noticed Ata's fixed avoidance of eye contact, she latched on. "Why didn't you add King Addai to the list of people who would mourn us?" her voice had risen significantly. Ata, predictably, had shushed her imperiously.

"I just forgot," her cousin deflected, completely forgetting that Min knew her, and knew when she was lying—as well as lying by omission.

"No, you didn't, and what's more: it was very deliberate... I know you, Ata bent-Annaia Delnada, and you look like *that* when you're playing with words and meanings. Why do you think my father wouldn't mourn our deaths, hmmm?" Min was like a dog with a bone, and much pushier than usual. It must be the pregnancy too.

"You're really rude these days, you know," Ata grumped.

"Don't change the subject!"

"Fine! I only left him off because I didn't think he'd really mourn *me*. You? Of course. Me? Maybe not. But I'll add him to the list if that will make you stop interrogating me," the last part she added sourly. They were both in an abysmal mood and had been snapping at each other all the way. Though she sensed Ata was still concealing something, she decided to let it go for the time being. In an abrupt about-face, Min felt bad—and teary.

"I'm sorry! I didn't mean to nag at you... And after you've sacrificed so much to help me!" Min sniffled. She thought she heard Ata groan.

"No, Min. *I'm* sorry... I shouldn't take my anger and

annoyance out on you. Forgive me," she haphazardly hugged Min. They were both wearing sturdy peasant garb: tunics, leggings, and warm cloaks. Ata had kept her knife but had left her favourite bow and arrows behind. She had another, less impressive bow with her now, and had used it to hunt their food.

That had been another huge argument, the leaving behind of certain "key pieces of evidence to identify us" as Ata had called it. Min had been livid about not only leaving her favourite dress on a corpse, but also having to tear it to shreds where the body had been mauled. However, her anger over that did not hold a candle to her fury upon being told to leave her Enstroi chain.

She'd refused point-blank, until Ata had raged at her and said that *she too* was sacrificing her custom-made leather armour, her favourite bow, and her own Enstroi chain, all for her cousin's secret baby that needed protecting. Min had shut up and handed over her most treasured possession. She could tell that Ata was also profoundly affected by leaving her life chain—any Pandial, whether religious or not, would be. But she also noticed that Ata had kept a half-coin charm.

When Min pointed out that people would be suspicious if a charm was missing, Ata explained that she had taken her husband's charm from their room the morning of their escape (Kai had apparently made a matching pair for them).

"I took the left one, because I've left," Ata had whispered, not making any sense to Min, but she clearly ascribed a lot of value to it, as she wore it on a string around her neck (a makeshift, temporary Enstroi chain, it seemed). "Besides," Ata had perked up, "once I return in a few weeks, after the birth, I can reclaim my chain and I'll find a way to send you yours." Min thought this a bit naïve but didn't puncture that particular fantasy bubble of her cousin's. She had so few.

The real problems started almost three days into their journey toward the north-east of Pandi. The entire journey would take between two and three weeks, depending on their pace, but that was based on the assumption that they travelled via the most direct route. However, they had been taking a more 'weaving' approach due to circumstances.

Ata's Commanding ability was impressive to behold, for she could construct scripts at the drop of a hat and produce castings tailor-made to their every need. Yet, for some reason, she wasn't able to utilise these abilities to ferret out the presence that was following them. For they were, most definitely, being followed.

"Argh! That *thing* is using some kind of cloaking script!" Ata quietly raged as they huddled together in the musty barn of an abandoned farm. "I just can't seem to find its edges to get around it. Ideally, I should be able to construct a script to unravel the one it is using, but it must have a built in script to counteract that kind of tinkering. It's so *frustrating*!"

Instead of having them exhaust themselves with sentry duty in the evenings as they slept, Ata had taken to casting a script that warned of anyone coming within a hundred-yard radius of them, though it drew a lot of her energy. Min had thought this ingenious. Apparently, Ata could even sense a disturbance within that space if the untraceable entity that was following them entered it, meaning their follower was remaining close but far enough for them to feel physically safe.

"Well, there's one positive thing..." Min supplied helpfully.

"What's that?" Ata retorted.

"If the script being used is so advanced, then whoever is using it is probably not Gruxhoon... they must be human."

"You'd think so, wouldn't you," came the tart reply, "but you fail to consider it might be a nice little custom script created by the Gruxhoon's Abled puppet-masters to facilitate them in tracking us down." And with that cheery bit of news, Ata promptly fell asleep and left Min to wakefully catastrophise for the rest of the evening.

In the days that followed, Ata kept trying and failing to infiltrate their stalker's casting. When Min suggested they simply double back and confront the person or thing, Ata had categorically refused.

"You're heavily pregnant, despite not really looking it, and vulnerable. I'm not taking you there and serving you up on a platter to them! Use your head, Min!" When

Min alternatively suggested Ata go by herself, Ata had rebutted by saying that leaving Min alone would give potential partners of the follower the opportunity to snatch her. Caught between a rock and a hard place, they maintained the stalemate by continuing as they had thus far, following a zig-zag path to their destination.

"Well, you always envied me my 'adventures' and missions—welcome! Par for the course: everything's decidedly uncomfortable, and just one shitty thing after another," Ata had gritted out when the heavens opened and caught them in the middle of nowhere, with no shelter in sight and a significant way still to go before dark.

"Huh. I feel short-changed. You always made them sound so exciting and fun… I'd like a refund on this one, I think," Min teased, seeing a slight smile on her cousin's face. Ata turned and focused intently on Min.

"You know there was nothing to envy in my going, right? I wasn't off gallivanting and having a grand old time while you were stuck at home… At least, I hope you didn't feel like that." Min smiled self-consciously.

"Of course that's what I thought and felt, but as you say, reality is much less glamorous. Yet, despite there always being 'one shitty thing after the other', I *still* feel pleased to be doing this with you…" they smiled at each other, then lightning struck a tree not fifty feet from where they were on the road, sending them scurrying off. It really was one shitty thing after the other.

More bad news abounded, for when they managed to find a travellers' inn still open and functioning at a major crossroads, the innkeeper and his wife warned them of gangs of bandits roaming the surrounding areas.

"With all the kingdoms a mess because of the Grux-hoon invasions, lawlessness amongst *humans* has become worse!" the inn keeper had complained loudly, clearly incensed at the perfidy of these low lives. "And they've taken to gratuitously maiming their victims in 'clever' ways as a kind of 'calling card'. It's absolutely sickening! Gangs of thieves, rapists, murderers..."

He kept a well-sharpened battle-axe behind his counter while his wife had a meat cleaver stuck prominently in the band of her apron. They were very welcoming, but definitely not to be trifled with. Despite the much-needed respite their hospitality in the form of a warm bed and hot stew offered, their news added a further potential threat to Min and Ata's ever-growing list of dangers.

"We'll just be extra vigilant and careful as we go; there's nothing else for it," Ata had said tiredly as she lay down beside Min. They always slept together now, even when given the option of an additional room; Ata wouldn't hear of being parted from Min for even a second. It initially made for very awkward ablutions, but they had become so used to the status quo that they barely noticed it now.

"Ouch!" Min twitched, grabbing her ever-so-slightly distended belly.

"What! What is it? Is it time?" the panic in her body-guard's voice was comical.

"No, the baby's just moving... I think he's turning around... Oof! But it feels *really* strange!" she had flipped up her tunic and rolled down her leggings to see her pale belly undulating freakishly. Ata's eyes were huge as she watched the show.

"It tickles, but doesn't. I can't even describe the sensation," Min said.

"It looks very weird! I've seen pregnant women before, and their bellies, but this seems... *different*, some-how," her cousin said, strangely fascinated.

"It's because it's closer. It's *us*, you know?" Min supplied, and Ata smiled in acknowledgment.

"Can I... can I touch it? Your belly?" Ata asked tenta-tively, seeming half-intrigued and half-horrified by the notion.

"Of course!" and Min had seized Ata's hand, placing it on the oddly distended shape poking out and clearly visible through the skin. That night, they were wonder-fully distracted from their cares by the fascinating acro-batics of her tiny miracle.

～

AFTER TEN DAYS of hard traveling, Ata proclaimed them slightly more than halfway there; a relief, but Min's increasing discomfort spelled problems over the next few days, for she couldn't keep walking at the pace they had set before. Though Ata tried her best, she was becoming frustrated with what she perceived as Min's lack of effort, but Min simply couldn't make her body do what was expected.

Upon finally stopping for the evening (Ata tight-lipped and testy), Min felt ready to cry. She actually did start to tear up when she removed her boots and saw the size of her feet. They were hugely swollen, imprinted with the inside template of her boots where the puffy flesh had been squeezed.

"Oh gods! That looks awful!" Ata exclaimed upon returning with fresh water from a nearby creek. "No wonder you can't walk as fast anymore! I'm so sorry, Min. Let's see if I can Command some healing..." This approach seemed to help; with a concerted effort on Ata's part, the swelling and pain subsided and thus they proceeded to utilise this method regularly as they continued to travel.

The frequent stops ate into the distance travelled, but Min managed much more than she would have been able to without. Ata even carried her piggy-back for parts of the way, for she was quite a bit taller than Min and much stronger. But it took too much of a toll on her, to Min's mind, and she insisted that they minimize these 'lifts'.

"Remember when you, Kai, and I used to trade piggy-back rides for various things? Almost like curren-cy," Min whispered into Ata's ear during one of the times she had mulishly *insisted* on carrying Min. Ata snorted.

"Yes! And you were such a scrooge! You accumulated rides owed and wouldn't cash them in. For weeks! And then you had finally saved enough and tried to make Kai carry you around nonstop for days like some ancient queen!" Min felt her cousin's laughter vibrate through her body. She joined in exuberantly.

"How else was I supposed to get close to him? Do you know how much willpower it takes to save for so long; to barter for so long? I was infatuated, even at eight, and he was at a stage where he wouldn't give me the time of day!" she laughed more. "Do you remember you told him to tip me into the stream, when I clung to his back and refused to get off?"

"Ha! Yes. He didn't know what to do, the princess of the realm having decided to keep him as her personal donkey... Not that I blame you, he's always been an ass," Ata preened at her pun.

"I was so worried he'd do it, seeing as he'd inevitably get into trouble because of who I was... And then also, because it would've broken my little heart if he'd been coldblooded enough to throw me away," Min intoned in a mock-serious voice.

"Huh. But lucky for you, he showed mercy and

suffered the monkey on his back for the rest of the day, against my advice." Later, when she had disembarked the good ship Ata and they were drinking water, her cousin piped up:

"If Kai had dumped you in the stream, you say it would have broken your heart?" at Min's perplexed nod, Ata continued with a twisted grin, "So, if he'd just listened to me back then, we wouldn't be in this situation today!" she winked conspiratorially and Min smacked her on the shoulder. Despite all the pain and suffering, despite their constant stress, she and Ata hadn't spent such carefree, childlike time together in many years. Min suddenly stepped forward and embraced her cousin. When had she last done that? After a short pause, Ata hugged her back.

"You know you're more than my cousin, right? You are my sister and my best friend." It felt critically important to tell her this now. "I love you, Ata."

"Me too, Min. Me too." And then they continued on their way, reminiscing about their various shenanigans growing up. Upon being unable to find a building to shelter in that evening, Ata suggested climbing a tree. Min was dubious but acquiesced when Ata explained *how* she had become so familiar with the efficacy of trees as shelters. It took quite a bit of heave-ho-ing from Ata beneath her, but finally, Min was perched comfortably on a thick branch and tied to the trunk with some rope. It was then that Ata revealed her true reason for this tree-climbing lark: she would double back and expose their unfailing follower.

"This way, I won't be worrying about someone grabbing or attacking you while I'm away," Ata supplied eagerly, annoying Min more.

"But what about *me* worrying about *you*? What if someone grabs or attacks you and I'm stuck up a tree waiting for someone who never returns?" Ata tried to placate Min, but after almost an hour of not succeeding, she summarily marched off amidst dire warnings and threats from the stranded Min.

Sat stewing in her frustration and anger with her cousin, it took Min quite a while to realise she was no longer alone in her neck of the woods. Hence, when she heard a branch snap immediately beneath her and looked down, right into a face staring hard at her not three feet below, she shrieked *loudly*.

The fact that the face immediately disappeared as the person fell from the tree indicated that *they* had been just as startled as Min had been. A muffled groan came from the ground below where the person must have fallen; Min tried to loosen the ropes enough to be able to look down and see. Crashing bushes meant someone was rushing nearer and nearer, and just as she became fearful the somebody on the ground had a violent accomplice, the shuddering bushes shouted.

"Min! Min! Are you okay—tell me you're okay!" *Ata.* Ata was coming.

When she burst through the bushes a second later, panic clearly etched on her face, Min couldn't hold back.

"I *told* you this was a bad idea!"

"What happened?" she saw Ata approach her tree carefully, eyes scanning in every direction for a potential threat.

"Someone climbed my tree, but they fell ou—" Another loud moan, now clearly definable as female, came from the foot of the tree. Ata sprang forward, knife at the ready, just out of Min's line of sight.

"Len! What in the *hells* are you doing here!" Ata exclaimed.

"You're not coming with us!" Ata persisted. It was two days later, and they were sheltering in some very dark and creepy woods, to Min's mind. Ata had hunted, built a fire while it was still light, and then doused the flames after they'd eaten to avoid drawing attention after dark. They were preparing to climb another tree and Min was not looking forward to it. In theory, sleeping tied to a tree for security's sake sounded brilliant; in reality, it was the worst. *The absolute worst.*

"Why not? I know I'm not in the 'secret circle' as far as all this is concerned and that I don't know exactly what's going on, but I told you I accidentally heard some things; I know *enough*. And I want to help!" Even Min didn't know where she stood anymore in this argument, for she'd heard the same points repeated over and over, *ad nauseam*, by both parties and was honestly so tired of it she was ready to capitulate. She just wasn't sure to whom.

"Let's get climbing," Ata cut Len off, also clearly beyond tired of the same argument. Plus (and Min hadn't pointed it out because she was quite sure Ata already knew this): they couldn't send Princess Lenna back on her own, as she would be in danger from Gruxhoon and human bandits. Also, what would Princess Lenna tell everyone once back—that Princess Mindaia and Lady Ata were not dead, just on a jaunt through the war-torn countryside?

They had to face facts; Princess Lenna had to stay with them till they could come up with a better plan. Lastly, Lenna had succeeded quite well in avoiding the detection of a powerful Abled in Ata by utilising a ring that had been in the Cinnaen royal treasury for many generations and allowed the wearer to 'block' any Commanding or scripts. Ata had never heard of artifacts with such abilities and had taken careful note of it (no doubt to discuss thoroughly with Lord Danai at a later date). A stroke of brilliance on the princess's part to protect herself from Abled charlatans who might try to harm her on her journey. The Cinnaen princess was a lot more astute than Ata gave her credit for, it seemed, and could be a definite asset on their mission.

"Watch your arm, Len... I'll help you," Ata offered, referring to Princess Lenna's newly healed arm that she broke when falling out of Min's tree. It had drained Ata significantly to fuse the bone, so she'd left the tendons as they were to heal naturally. She still had dark circles under her eyes and hadn't managed to restore the vitality she lost in that gambit.

"Okay... Maybe you should help Princess Mindaia first, and then—" But at that moment, an arrow felled Lenna. Ata instantly snagged an arrow, nocked it, and drew the bow fully as she swung in the direction the attack had come from. She loosed in the same, split-second motion, a cry resounding through the woods.

"Min! Up the tree!" she commanded. Despite her worries for Len, Min recognised an inflexible order from her prior military training, reacting without further thought. She scrambled up the trunk, pure adrenaline driving her.

Without pausing to check on Min or Len, Ata drew again and let fly... and again, but by then, the bandits were upon them, so she unsheathed her long knife and short dagger. As she engaged with the first two men who crashed into her, her mouth had started moving with quick silent words. *She was Commanding.*

From her precarious perch quite high up, Min looked down at Len, frantically trying to see if she was breathing. She lay as she had fallen, the arrow sticking out of her chest, and it made for an oddly grotesque tableau viewed from above. Then Min saw the arrow fletching shudder slowly and rhythmically with Len's breaths.

"Len's alive, Ata!" she cried, hoping to help by letting Ata know all wasn't lost. She had dispatched the first three attackers but was being completely overrun by almost ten others. They were filthy, bearded, and poorly armed, but they had strength in numbers and a lot of enthusiasm.

As she watched, Min felt a very unpleasant tugging sensation in her lower belly. A *strong* tugging, squeezing sensation. *Oh gods, no! Not now!* Trying to ignore her body's intermittent cramping, Min watched Ata suddenly raise her empty hands.

"I surrender! I'm unarmed!" she shouted, but the two bandits closest to her still pounced and beat her unceasingly. Min cried out in distress, drawing the attention of some of the other bandits.

"We've got a little bird in the tree!" one chortled.

"Come down, pretty bird, or we'll pluck your little friends *bare!*" another baited. She saw that two had grabbed Lenna, callously dragging her to where they had dumped a badly beaten Ata. She didn't look conscious and her face was already swollen, black and blue. *Heal yourself!*

Lenna, however, seemed to have awoken and was

moaning as their rough treatment jostled the arrow sticking from her chest. When they'd dragged her, they had clearly rebroken her newly-healed arm, for it stood out at an awkward angle.

"Look at them!" the largest bandit chortled gleefully as he carefully inspected the two women at his feet, then turned his gaze to Min. "Just *look* at the pretty songbirds we've caught, men!" He grinned with blackened teeth up at her, all animalistic greed and violence. "Don't you want to fly down here, pretty bird? It would be a shame if we had to break one of your friends' wings because you chose to be disobedient..." Min felt the same tugging sensation in her belly, sweat breaking out over her brow. She felt ill and light-headed. Maybe she *should* climb down...

"Oi! This pretty lark's got some treasure," another piped up, followed closely by a muffled shriek and some kind of kerfuffle—a few of them huddling around Ata. Min surmised, from the howling of one of their number, that he had tried to take Ata's wedding charm from her neck, and she had damaged him in some way.

"Now, now, lark... gougin' ol' Dern's eye was foolish... And you must be punished. No scratching in future, I think!" the hulking leader had bent down over Ata, but his voice carried. Min couldn't really see what was happening, her cramps distracting her and the huddle of bodies blocking her view. A protracted, muffled shriek from Ata almost saw Min lose her grip on the branch. After what felt like an eternity, the leader stood back up, grinning evilly; when he noticed Min's rapt attention, he lifted his bloody hand to show her his prize.

Two, thin pale stumps. For a moment, Min's mind couldn't process what she was seeing. *Fingers.* He had cut off Ata's fingers! Min's gorge rose and her heart thundered painfully at the swell of horror. *No, no, no, no, no, no...*

"Perhaps our little dove in the tree will finally fly down?" he crooned, playfully throwing Ata's fingers in the air and catching them, laughing uproariously. His fellow miscreants joined in, when suddenly, he heaved his arm back and threw the fingers far out of sight, somewhere among the trees. "It's cruel to mock the less fortunate with what they can't have," he intoned sagely, but a huge evil grin remained on his face. "That's the little lark put in her cage, and Dern can have the first turn on her... Can't say fairer than that!" To which the others loudly agreed. Ata just lay there; eyes closed, pale and beaten.

"Now, birdie—are you coming down, or should I trim some more of this lovely lark's feathers?" he taunted Min.

"Don't listen to them, Min!" Len screeched suddenly. The same one—clearly the most depraved of them all— was immediately upon her, lifting her roughly so her feet dangled above the ground. She was a petite woman, and he was a behemoth.

"A few feathers from one wasn't enough, it seems, to shut the little bitches up. And our tiny sparrow already has a broken wing..." he turned so Min could see how Len dangled from his grip, her right ulna and radius clearly snapped judging from her forearm's unnatural bend. The bandit grabbed the wrist of her broken arm, pushing it backwards, and she cried out in pain. The others, forming a half-circle around to enjoy the torture spectacle, chuckled with glee.

"Shall I keep pushing till we see the bone? It won't take much for it to *pop* right through her pretty pale skin!" Min felt nausea roiling in her gut (the same gut that was clenching sharply), completely out of her control. And she could feel something running down her inner thighs, dripping down her legs. Her water had broken. She glanced down quickly but wasn't able to catch sight of her feet from where she precariously hung off a branch.

"Don't come down, Mi— AAAGGHH!" Len shrieked as the miscreant forced her arm back, and to Min's horror, she saw the pale, pointed bone appear amidst a spurt of blood near Len's elbow.

At that precise moment, multiple snapping sounds began to echo through the clearing, the bandits dropping like marionettes whose strings were being cut. One by one in quick succession, until only the leader was left, still clutching Len's bleeding arm and looking around in confusion. Then, just as his gaze fell on Ata's prone form, a sharp snap sounded, and his head moved absurdly to the side on a now awkwardly angled neck. After a split-second delay, he collapsed to the ground, dragging Len, shrieking, with him.

Min looked at Ata in confusion; she saw her cousin wasn't passed out—she was slowly sitting up despite clearly suffering from serious internal injuries, her bloody hand clamped tightly to her body. Len had wriggled out from under the body of the leader; she was lying, whimperingly clutching her arm and appearing as though she was trying to push herself into the very soil to escape the pain. The arrow that stuck out of her body jammed cumbersomely into the ground due to its angle of extrusion.

Ata slowly and methodically dragged herself over to Len, making soothing shushing noises as she took her arm in her uninjured hand and then closed her eyes. Len's whimpering immediately stopped and she half lifted her head, an awed expression on her face, to watch what Ata did. Though the cramping pains in her belly kept seizing her body one after the other, Min gritted her teeth.

Using her still-bloody, grotesquely maimed hand, Ata slowly pushed the protruding shard of bone back into Len's arm, then continued to quietly mouth words, eyes closed. She proceeded to carefully work the arrow out of the girl's chest, muttering more and more loudly as she did, finally pulling the entire thing out. Len's ashen face regained much of its colour, and when Ata finally let go of her arm, it looked normal, if badly bruised and scraped. Ata looked like a worse wreck than before.

"Min! You need to come down!" Ata called hoarsely, looking up at Min.

"What if they wake up?" she responded, eyeing the men lying all around. Ata snorted in disgust.

"There's no waking up for any of them. I broke all their necks... Can you climb down by yourself, or should I help you?" her tone supremely dismissive of the amazing feat of multiple deaths she had just enacted with apparently minimal effort. She walked to Min's tree slowly, carefully—as though she were in pain.

"I don't think I can climb down by myself, but neither can you, from the looks of you!" she tried to tease, then suppressed a grunt as another contraction struck. It was taking a long time, and though Ata was speaking, Min couldn't seem to focus on or hear what she was saying.

"... can you hear me?" Ata's face had come back into focus below, a worried expression just discernible among the swelling and discolouration.

"You have to heal yourself first; I can't climb down, but you're not in any shape to climb up!" Min repeated.

"I've healed myself enough to stave off any immediate threat," Ata dodged. Min shook her head.

"What about your hand, Ata? Can you... find your fingers? And reattach them?"

"I'll do that later; I need to be sure all of our life-threatening injuries are taken care of... You look very pale, so let's get you down so I can check you. After that, we'll try and fix my hand." Min wasn't falling for her calmly reasonable tone, though.

"You need more healing! I can see you clutching at your ribs! I'm not letting you drop me on my arse when you're supposed to be rescuing me," then another cramp struck, and she wasn't aware of her surroundings for a while. By the time she came to, Ata had almost reached her, clearly having healed herself up a bit more. Min was impressed she had managed to cling to the branch during her 'blackout'.

"Let's go, Your Highness."

"You look truly terrible," Min tried to divert, then groaned. "I didn't want to cause any more trouble than you were already dealing with, but I think I'm in labour." The complete and utter panic that washed over Ata's face was hilarious to see, had Min not felt so ill. "I really need to get down from here or my baby's going to be born dropping out of a tree."

It took quite a bit of manoeuvring, for as strong as Ata was, she and Min were in very poor shape, making it difficult to shift back and forth. Len was waiting below to help once they reached the ground, and they quickly guided Min into a sitting position, propped up against the tree that had saved her. From the strength of the contractions, Min had been convinced her baby would be born in short order, however, what followed was hours of contractions and useless pushing. The baby wasn't coming.

"The baby was moving into the birth canal, but now it's stopped... There's something wrong—an obstruction, maybe—and I don't know what or how to fix it!" Ata yelled, her hands trembling as she Commanded more strength and healing into Min. She'd been doing that periodically over the past few hours, but she was clearly reaching the end of even her impressive energy reserves. Her right hand looked oddly misshapen where it rested on Min's arm, the pointer and middle fingers missing.

A calm had settled over Min; an almost otherworldly serenity. As Ata and Len scrambled for answers, for more water, for a blanket, Min knew what to do. She just needed to convince Ata. Putting out her hand, she grasped Ata's trembling wrist firmly, drawing frantic eyes to hers.

"Cousin. You need to cut him out," at Ata's ostensible lack of comprehension, she repeated, "If the baby stays where he is, he'll suffocate and die—and I'll die too, regardless. If you do nothing, we'll both die. The only thing to do is to cut him out so he'll live."

"No... No. We should wait a bit more. To cut him out is too dangerous; if we wait, maybe—"

"Nothing will change, except my baby will die faster. Please, Ata? Save my baby," Min looked calmly into Ata's red-rimmed eyes.

"Min... If I do this... I can't guarantee I have enough power left to Command your healing. It's a massive risk; I can't promise you'll survive," Ata started crying.

"I know... I know. As it stands, there's no guarantee I'll make it through either way. Just do what you can, but please save my baby." Min placed her filthy hand on Ata's bowed head as she sobbed; Len was kneeling on her other side, wringing her hands and crying silently. "Hurry!"

As Ata moved away, Min caught her arm with urgency. "You must take care of my baby," Min's voice had lost all its command, but she knew Ata listened and would heed. "Swear it to me, Cousin. Swear you'll raise my child." She felt a touch on her hand, as though from afar.

"I swear it, Min."

Then, without much fanfare, Ata took the knife Min's father had gifted to her so long ago, doused it in some alcohol she carried in a flask, and sliced into Min without preamble, no awkwardness despite her injured hand. Ata must have used a script to dull her pain, because she didn't feel anything except the strangely awkward movements, the snagging of the blade on her belly, and then inside it.

After the first cut it was difficult to follow what was happening, because Min was drifting in and out of consciousness. Maybe it was all the blood she felt running out of her and into the soil? She was watering the tree with her lifeblood, she thought lightheadedly, then laughed at the absurdity of it.

Feeling what seemed to be a large part of her own flesh pulled out of her body, Min's eyes wouldn't focus beyond vague shapes and shadows no matter how hard she stared. All detail was lost from her sight and the light began to brighten and dim like the last flickering before a flame died. Min still needed to keep the light on for one more thing. Something she *needed* to say.

"I hope the birth of your baby will go better than mine, Cousin." She vaguely sensed scurrying, frantic motions beyond her sphere of clear perception.

"He's not breathing!" Ata's urgent cry and Lenna's panicked questions rang out.

"So, heal him," Min urged, not sure her wispy voice carried.

"He's still not breathing! What do I do?" the voice was hysterical, yet Min struggled to remain connected.

"Just— just give him everything you've got! If you pass out, I'll keep going!" *Lenna.*

Then she heard it; a loud, cacophonous wail. A baby's cry. Hers. The sound of relieved laughter mingled with the cry. Her flickering light became unimaginably bright. The pain was gone. And then there was just light, an overwhelming lightness, and freedom...

IF YOU ENJOYED THIS BOOK, please remember to leave a review (especially on <u>Amazon</u> and/or <u>Goodreads</u>).

Also, for early access to writing and publishing announcements, as well as additional scenes and promotional material, subscribe to my author newsletter at **https://k-i-s-inc.com/subscribe**

GLOSSARY*

Abled—those who have the ability to Command (what was historically known as doing magic).

Áitarbith—the continental setting of these tales, divided into two large kingdoms, Cinnae and Pandi, and multiple smaller city-states, Karppen, Çetiz, and Veron.

Aixa—a relatively mysterious monotheistic religion practiced almost exclusively by the Irie.

Bitheism—a pun on Bithian, this is a minority religion that adheres to the belief of a dichotomous reality and that the balance of all things is required for an ideal world, or utopia. Thus, the aim of this particular religion is to achieve that balance (mostly through peaceful means, although there are peripheral practitioners who accept that violent means might be required).

Bithian—the standard language of Áitarbith and the native tongue of most Pandial and Cinnaens. Other, minority languages still exist on the continent but have largely been displaced by Standard Bithian. Old Bithian (spoken more than 500 years ago) is relatively similar to current Bithian in its written form, though it is hypothesised the pronunciation was quite far removed, based on what is observed in the rhyming sounds in Old Bithian poetry. ALSO: an alternative to 'Áitarbithian' for an inhabitant of Áitarbith.

Canø—Cinnaen capital city, a stone's throw from Hårbørgen Palace.

Çetiz—a city-state run entirely by a council of elderly women, it gained the nickname 'City of Witches' (though citizens resent the moniker) and is constantly at odds with Veron over the rights to the fresh water contained in the northern lakes. Due to the somewhat secluded geographic position of both these city-states, their involvement in larger Bithian affairs is limited.

Cinns—the indigenous people of what is now the Cinnaen kingdom (and the ancestors of the current inhabitants); described as the first of the Áitarbithians to practice agriculture, these people lived in large family groups and were generally described as being red-haired and of stocky build. The Irie are some of the only remaining Cinns, though they were originally only a smaller, insular group of families amongst Cinns who managed to retain their culture and ethnicity subsequent to the Vürgøn's descent from the mountains.

Cinnae—the northern Áitarbithian kingdom (one of the two largest kingdoms on the continent), the name derived from the original inhabitants of this largely agricultural region, the Cinns. Considered highly sophisticated, the Cinnaen kingdom is thought to be at the forefront of arts and culture on the continent. Citizens almost exclusively prescribe to the religion of Myriadism, though (like all other states in Áitarbith besides Veron) the religious and governmental structures of the kingdom are distinctly separate. The Cinnaen people are descendants of the original inhabitants, the Cinns, and the Vürgøn who descended from their mountain strongholds over a thousand years ago.

Command—to perform the working of a script (what was historically known as casting spells or doing magic).

Debrion—a large continental wasteland south of Áitarbith, across the Debrion Strait. The full continent has not yet been mapped and all parts explored thus far indicate a never-ending desert where no water can be found. Gruxhoon were expelled to these wastelands subsequent to the Great Áitarbithian War.

Enddaian—the Pandial capital city, it developed around Enddaian Keep due to its stellar qualities as a secure stronghold.

Enexha—the Gruxhoon practice of committing suicide rather than allowing themselves to be taken prisoner.

Enstroi—the Pandial practice of always wearing a 'life chain', a metal chain that represents the wearer's life. Charms on the chain represent the most important events and people in the wearer's life. Initially a religious practice, it has become more cultural in recent years. A remnant of the religious requirements, Enstroi chains are *always* buried with wearers (because they are required as a record of the mortal lives they represent upon arrival in the afterlife for entrance to the heavens).

Gruxhoon—large, beastly creatures that have threatened the lives of Bithians since their appearance more than a millennium ago. Subsequent to their defeat in the Áitarbithian Continental War, all Gruxhoon were expelled to the Debrion wastelands, where they were thought to have perished. Though clearly intelligent enough to organise mass military actions as well as communicate with each other, not much is known about their cultural or religious practices. Known to be extremely violent and bloodthirsty.

Hancin—the guiding star of Áitarbith.

Hårbørgen—the dynastic name of the ruling family of Cinnae.

Irie—a cultural group descended from the original Cinns who populated the northern lowlands, their historical homeland fell between the Smul River, Smelln Tower, and Pansø, but had been assimilated into either Pandi or Cinnae (the border of which this region straddles). Many Irie left the region, crossed the Uurgonna Mountains and resettled in eastern Áitarbith. Those that remained staunchly hold fast to their religious and cultural practices, being a minority group, and are quite an insular community. Unlike the Myriadism followed almost exclusively in Cinnae and to the greatest extent in Pandi, Irie adhere to an older, monotheistic religious practice known as Aixa.

Isles of Eile—islands off the south-east coast of Áitarbith, only the main island of Ra'aen is inhabited by a few hundred mainlanders who sailed over 300 hundred years prior. The island is known for its rich crops of Dren, a wheat staple consumed on the mainland.

Karppen—a minor coastal principality north of the Plezai Valley and nestled between the Cinnaen and Pandial territories. A wealthy city-state with a royal family that rules in name only—their strong aristocratic class exerts almost exclusive power in the form of a high council.

Knowledgeable—those who, though not Abled, know the lore and can construct a script that is then cast by an Abled practitioner of Commanding.

Myriadism—the main religion of most of the continent; it supports the belief in and worship of a collection of deities according to the doctrines of the faith expounded upon in the tomes of the Holy Sacrament of the Benevolent Order of the Gods.

Pandi—the southern Áitarbithian kingdom (one of the two largest kingdoms on the continent), the origin of the kingdom's name is unknown. With a warmer, more arid climate (especially the further south one goes), the people are distinct from their Cinnaen counterparts in that they have darker features—black hair, dark eyes, and a range of darker skin tones (depending on which regions within Pandi people hail from). This kingdom, in particular, is known for its rigid military competence. The majority of citizens follow the Myriadist religion, although a growing segment are converting to Bitheism. As with all other states in Áitarbith besides Veron, the religious and governmental structures of the kingdom are distinctly separate.

Pansø—a town near the Cinnaen-Pandial border.

Treik—a trumpet-like brass instrument with a distinct sound that is ideal for playing a finite number of notes, and of which the sound has a surprising travel range in terms of distance. Though both Cinnaens and Pandial claim the invention of it, the true origin of the instrument cannot be determined.

Uurgonna Mountains—the only and largest mountain range on the Áitarbithian continent; home to the Vürgøn.

Veron—a city-state run by the religious order of Veronda, highly conservative adherents to Myriadism. Constantly at odds with its 'neighbour' across the strait, Çetiz, due to the disputed water rights of the northern lakes. The never-ceasing hostilities have come to be known as the 'Water Wars'. Due to the somewhat secluded geographic position of both these city-states, their involvement in larger Bithian affairs is limited.

Vürgøn—nomadic mountain tribes who adhere to a simple lifestyle, known to the lowlanders as violently barbaric yet displaying equivalent bravery and battle prowess. Very fair, with pale hair, eyes, and skin, the Vürgøn and Cinnaens share heritage—the Cinnaens' ancestors were Vürgøn who came down from the mountains and settled in the valleys of Cinnae, intermingling with the redheaded

Cinns who were the original agricultural inhabitants. Not much is known about Vürgøn religious practices; they are notoriously tight-lipped about their spiritual beliefs.

Witchlings of Hoondær—an obscure group of Abled practitioners who, historically, possibly utilised 'black magic' to create the Gruxhoon. Though most are unaware of their existence altogether, those that are are mostly convinced the group no longer exists.

Cinnaen and Pandial naming conventions

Pandial naming practice usually indicates noble birth by '-ai' as the final syllable in a male name, and '-aia' in a female name (though there are exceptions to this, like with Ata's name).

The family names acknowledge both the mother and father, the former with a 'ben-' hyphenated prefix for a son and 'bent-' for a daughter, followed by the latter with a 'Del' prefix compounded to form the patronymic, e.g., Kai's full name is Kaimam ben-Emli Delbadai—he is *not* noble (hence no '-ai' ending to his name), but his father was the youngest son of an impoverished lord and there-fore has the name 'Badai'. Kai's Cinnaen mother's name is 'Emli'). King Addai's full name, for example, is King Addai ben-Feraia Delannai, so he is of high birth and the son of Queen Feraia and King Annai.

Illegitimacy makes no difference to Pandial naming practice, except if the father of the individual is unknown. In those cases, the 'Del-' prefix is followed by the term '-nada', originating from an ancient Pandial language and believed to mean 'of none' or 'of nowhere'. Thus, Ata's full name is Ata bent-Annaia Delnada.

Cinnaen names, also, indicate nobility in the case of male individuals with a '-so' final syllable; females have no nobility-indicating naming practice. Similarly, Cinnaen family names do not acknowledge the maternal input; surnames consist of the father's name with a suffix '-son' for a male offspring and '-dor' for female offspring. Thus, Svensso Olefson is the noble son of King Olefso, while Lenna Olefsdor is the daughter of King Olefson.

***Please note: some of the terms defined in this glossary are not mentioned in the text of this novel, however, they are connected to the Map of Áitarbith and will feature more in future books.**

AFTERWORD

This book started, like the majority of the many, many, many projects I've begun over the years, with an excess of enthusiasm on my part and a lack of practical considerations. You see, I have always been full of ideas, plotlines, and characters, but sadly deficient in follow-through. Enter: the (newly rediscovered) trend of serialised fiction! I thought: *This is my chance—I can eat this elephant one bite at a time!* And I was right; I was able to plan the plot and sectioning of a story I had been playing around with in my head for a long time. Once I had reached 10 episodes without any signs of losing steam, I decided to publish the first of those online.

Surprise, surprise! The highly reputable platform I had been planning to utilise did not offer that specific publishing service to anyone living outside the US. *No problem*, I thought, *I'll publish on one of the various other platforms available. We live in the age of technology, after all!*

Again, easier said than done. After publishing almost 10 episodes on one such platform, I had had a mere 23 views altogether—all my own, it turned out, once I checked the stats. Apparently, I was required to read and engage with other authors on the platform to gain any kind of 'promotion' and 'searchability'. *Right*, I thought, rolling up my metaphorical sleeves and rubbing my hands in glee—*reading is my grande forte in life, after all.*

I *genuinely* tried but, with all due respect, even the highest rated publications on the platform for genres that I adore were permeated with grammatical errors and factual inaccuracies (we're talking MAJOR historical anachronisms). I just couldn't wade through even one, though I tried multiple times—not even for the sake of promoting my own story. I gave up, deleted my profile, and moved on.

By that point, I'd written more than three-quarters of the episodes planned without finding a place to distribute them properly and I was faced with the question: should I still keep writing to publish in serial episodes online, when clearly, my lack of practical considerations had caused this disconnect? I decided to push through and rather make it a full novel. 'In for a penny, in for a pound', as they say (not that I have either a penny or a pound).

Thus, I continued to write for my expansive readership of two—my lifelong best friends and fellow fantasy enthusiasts, my sisters—and their eager reception encouraged me beyond words.

Regular requests for the next episode/chapter and annoyance when one ended on a (semi) cliff-hanger inspired me to persevere until, FINALLY, I had completed my first full-length fantasy novel. Some additional scenes and paragraphs were added, flow was adjusted to suit the revised novel structure (as opposed to the original serials), and so was born the first of the Áitarbith trilogy, *The Assays of Ata*.

The second and third novels, which I plotted and planned (I sound like a villainous hag) at the same time as *The Assays of Ata*, are preliminarily called *The Trials of Ata* and *The Dispersion of Ata*, respectively. They are already being written and shared with my two biggest fans (and harshest critics) as you read this. Hopefully their assiduous quality control will stand the test of time.

ACKNOWLEDGMENTS

While I'm monopolising your attention with all this 'me, me, me' text, I would like to squeeze in a few 'thank yous' (it's only polite, I suppose).

To my family (my mother, father, and sisters—Greta and Liesl): you loved me and raised me to be who I am (flaws and all), and I owe everything I achieve to you.

To my brothers-in-law... Roy: thanks for always pouring the wine when needed; and J, for your infinite patience while your wife was reading drafts instead of spending time with you: your forbearance is much appreciated. To my niece, Charlie: you keep us on our toes and never let us forget who's boss—you. You're the best, Boss!

To all my favourite authors (too many to mention individually by name!): why did you not clearly state how hard it is to write a whole book? Please, in future, include how much existential suffering it entails in your author's note. That is all from me; in all other senses, you are awesome and awe-inspiring (plus I'm still waiting to devour your next books, so put your noses to the grindstones and pens to paper)!

Then also, to you, the reader: thank you for taking a chance on this book. I hope it entertained and transported you to another world for a while and that you found Ata's tale worth the hours/days you committed to it (time being the most finite of resources, after all).

Lastly, to my God, to whom I owe my very existence: *Liewe Vader, als waartoe ek in staat is, is deur U genade. Amen.*

K.I.S. 2024

Procrastinator.
Putterer.
Escapist.

Despite growing up in sunny South Africa within walking distance of the wide, sandy beach, K.I.S. was forever carrying a book around and hiding out of sight somewhere, getting lost in the drama on the page. To this day, her idea of perfection is a cup of tea, a comfortable armchair, and a good book (not breaking the bookish, nerdy stereotype at all). To complete this cosy picture, she is also an avid knitter and crocheter, with a definite penchant for cats.

Her first, full-length story was about two ducks that go on a farmyard adventure, bashed out on her mother's dated typewriter at the ripe old age of seven. An English teacher by trade, K.I.S. always envisioned herself as a writer but never got around to actually completing a story after her epic poultry escapade... Until now.

Her greatest ambition, like Jo March, is to move

beyond the (admittedly ever-supportive) readership of her sisters and family, and share her tales with others.

X x.com/sara_skulks
instagram.com/master_of_noniin
amazon.com/author/k-i-s
youtube.com/@shooterznednol

ALSO BY K. I. S.

The Separation of Briin

Freak.

Brother.

Apprentice.

All these labels ascribed to Briin he had never taken issue
with. The truth, no matter how unpalatable, was a necessity.
And above all else, Briin was a truth-teller.

Until now.

Carer.

Eldest.

Diplomat.

Despite his many responsibilities, Hiirn was finally able to
realise his dream and travel on the wings of ambition to far
off climes, leaving the chains of familial obligation
temporarily behind him.

Follow the struggles of these two brothers as they face
secrecy, dark threats, and prophecy whilst traversing the
shifting political and religious landscapes of a much less
settled Áitarbith. In dealing with the hardships of uncovering

a hidden enemy's insidious plot, they must redefine their own relationship through the interaction of self and truth.

This is a prequel novella to *The Chronicles of Áitarbith*.

The Trials of Ata

Mother.

Peasant.

Healer.

Ata had assumed these identities wholeheartedly, but her true self never ceased to be:

Wife.

Royal.

Fugitive.

Their inevitable truth clawed at her carefully constructed life of lies... But all truths are eventually revealed, even her own painfully buried past.

For the greater good.

Continue following Ata's adventures fifteen years on through family crises, besiegement, and long-held loyalties as she battles beside kith and kin for the very existence of Áitarbith. She rediscovers old relationships and establishes new ones in her hard-won conflicts against the evil that has permeated the land, potentially reigniting love as she does so.

Facing bestial puppets whose masters pull the strings from the shadows, as well as the potential of betrayal by those closest to her, the eventual outcome will inevitably change their entire world forever.

This is Book 2 of the trilogy *The Chronicles of Áitarbith*.

Chronicles of Áitarbith

The continent of Áitarbith has faced many historic clashes; the wars and battles raging throughout its long history birthing the greatest of heroes.

Its diverse peoples and kingdoms have many stories to tell, from the cold northern coasts to the sunny southern beaches. From the high, frozen climes of the Uurgonna Mountains to the Isles of Eile, the struggles faced by Bithians make for grand stories.

These are their tales.